Jo Bartlett

Jo Bartlett has been a teacher for longer than she ever expected, which made it difficult to choose names for her children because 'challenging' students put her off so many potential choices. She now combines educational consultancy, teaching in HE and blogging as one of The Write Romantics, with writing both fiction and non-fiction, and lives so close to the South-East edge of England that she's very nearly French.

Website: www.jobartlettauthor.com

Among a Thousand Stars

They say you'd do anything for love, but what happens when you don't believe it exists?

Jo Bartlett

It's a So Vain Book

Published in Great Britain in 2015 by:
SO VAIN BOOKS Ltd
75 London Road
Oxford OX3 9BB

www.sovainbooks.co.uk
Email: info@sovainbooks.co.uk

The moral rights of the author have been asserted
A catalogue record from this book is available from the British Library

ISBN: 978-0-9930660-8-5

This book is a work of fiction. Names, characters, businesses, organizations, places and events other than those clearly in the public domain, are either the product of the author's imagination or are used fictitiously. Any resemblances to actual persons, living or dead, events or locales is entirely coincidental.

Cover Design by Marco Dusi

For my dad – the ultimate raconteur.

Ten years earlier

Ashleigh flicked through her sketchbook; turning to the life drawing from the previous week, she barely stifled a snort.

'You captured his essence-of-silver-back quality really well.' Stevie grabbed the pad and let out a low whistle. 'Did you have any pencil left?'

'He was a tad on the hirsute side, wasn't he?' She grinned. Whoever was modelling for them this time couldn't be as challenging to draw as the last burly nude; body hair was surprisingly hard to get right.

'To be honest, I thought he was wearing Velcro! This week I'm hoping for lots of folds and wrinkly bits.' Stevie winked, crossing his fingers. They'd met on the first day of college and even the history of art classes weren't too bad with Stevie next to her. They'd only known each other for a couple of months, but she couldn't imagine life without him.

'Welcome class, welcome!' Lissy Bainbridge, their life-drawing tutor, swept into the room with her usual flourish. Her long purple skirt was decorated with tiny mirrors and tassels on the hem that brushed across the floor as she walked. When she spoke she waved her arms around her, so that the thirty or so bangles she wore on each wrist banged and crashed against one another. 'I have a treat for you this afternoon, the female form… in all its glory!'

Lissy insisted that the life models were initially positioned behind screens, so that their outline could be seen first and the screens drawn back slowly, as though they were stars on stage on the opening night of a play. 'Looks a bit too skinny to have the sort of folds and lumpy bits I was after.' Stevie sounded disappointed. 'Still, I suppose it means we can get out of here a bit quicker. Might even catch the start of Countdown.'

She wasn't sure if she could stomach spending two hours staring at another hairy trucker; this was more like it. Glancing down at her sketchbook, just as Lissy began to draw the screens back, Ashleigh breathed a sigh of relief. Looking up again, she could see the back view of a woman draped on her side along a chaise longue, with pale red freckles dotted across her shoulders. Her hair was red too – almost certainly with the help of a bottle, but red all the same – a sort of natural henna dye, that looked as though it had come straight from the earth.

The first uncomfortable tug of familiarity took hold at the sight of the woman's leg. Something about the shape of it, and the slightly weathered look of the hand that rested halfway down the thigh, made Ashleigh's stomach flip.

It couldn't be. Gulping, she shook her head, as though that might help dislodge the unwanted thought that had settled there.

'Now my darlings,' Lissy clapped her hands together and smiled broadly, 'when our model turns around, that's the view I want you to capture. The female nude is, after all, an artist's purest muse.'

'Do you think she's actually bonkers?' Stevie muttered

under his breath. 'I'm not sure I'm ready for this. I might need counselling to get over what we're about to see.'

Ashleigh wanted to scream, or run and hide and never come back. But she couldn't say anything, couldn't move. All she could do was to wait frozen as the woman turned over.

'Jeez!' Stevie appeared to lose the ability to whisper. 'It's an education if nothing else, but she hasn't got a bad body for a woman of her age. What do you think?'

'What do I think?' The heat of a blush crept across Ashleigh's skin. The woman lying on the chaise longue was now waving at her; it was too late to even try to deny it. 'I think, once again, I have proof that what I've known since I was thirteen is true – I officially have the most embarrassing mother in the world.'

'That's, that's your...' Even Stevie, who generally didn't pause for breath, was at a loss.

'Yes. That's my mother.' Slamming her sketchbook shut with considerable force, Ashleigh stood up. 'So, sadly, I'll be first in the queue for that counselling.'

Chapter One

'Do you think he looks suitably menacing for the Halloween issue, with a Chihuahua clutched to his bare chest and just those devil horns to give a hint of the theme we're going for?' Stevie raised an eyebrow and Ashleigh couldn't help laughing. Ben Finnegan, the reality TV star and subject of their shoot, was as wrapped up in himself as ever; smoothing down his six pack with one hand and clutching the pint-sized pooch he took everywhere with the other.

'What he looks like is your fantasy! Ashleigh lined up her camera to take the last few shots of the day, capturing Ben staring into Muffin's eyes with the type of passion usually reserved for looking at himself in the mirror. She had to hand it to Stevie, the devoted teenage girls, who had made Ben's reality series so successful, would be queuing up to buy their copy of *Glitz* when this issue hit the stands. 'That's a wrap then, Ben.'

'Thank God for that. Don't you know it's autumn? I'm bloody freezing!' Ben, whose alarmingly high-pitched voice suggested that steroids might have been at least partly responsible for bulking up his body, acted as though he'd spent a day down a coalmine. In truth he'd passed a few hours posing for photos in his flashy apartment and the last twenty minutes or so finishing off the shoot on his roof terrace. 'Hold Muffin a minute, I need to get myself a robe and a shot of wheatgrass before I literally fall down!' Ben clipped a glittery lead on to the Chihuahua's diamante collar and thrust her into Stevie's arms, before disappearing inside the flat.

'Wheatgrass my arse!' As Stevie spoke, Muffin curled her lip, protective of her owner despite her diminutive size. 'Whatever it is he's really taking has shrivelled his bits to the size of a cocktail sausage. I had to make him wear padded shorts in every shot.' At the mention of the word sausage, Muffin started to growl.

'Do you think she's hungry?' As she spoke, Ashleigh moved towards a trolley of food that had been set up earlier by an assistant from *Glitz*. It was mainly the stuff that Ben supposedly lived on to build all that muscle. Strips of chicken were just the thing to appease a snappy Chihuahua. Grabbing a few pieces of the meat, she walked back to Stevie. The dog, clearly sensing she was about to be given a treat, shot out of his arms and towards her – like a bullet out of a gun.

'Jesus Christ!' He let out a scream as the dog lurched forward and the end of her lead seemed to get caught up around his belt buckle.

'What the hell are you doing? Muffin only eats organic meat and God knows what your assistant put in that!' Ben had crossed the terrace in two strides. The sight of his precious dog squirming in Ashleigh's arms, whilst still attached to Stevie by her glittery pink lead, made his voice more high-pitched than ever.

Suddenly Stevie made a strange gasping sound. 'I know you two are more worried about the dog than anything else but, just so you know, I appear to be bleeding. Quite a lot.'

Looking down at his T-shirt, where a circle of lurid red was rapidly spreading across the white fabric, she felt her own blood rush to her head and down to her feet in a matter of seconds, before everything went black.

'Have you forgiven me yet?' Ashleigh handed Stevie a cup of something hot, which claimed to be coffee, encased in the type of polystyrene cup that only added to its synthetic taste.

'Of course, honey.' He took a sip of the offending liquid, pulled a face and handed it straight back. 'I'll be glad when they come and take this bloody thing out. How long did they say it would be? Do you think it's more serious than they're letting on?' He shifted position on the hospital trolley and lifted the sheet back a fraction, so she had to look away.

'You heard what the doctor said, it's where the belly button ring has torn into your flesh and got embedded when the lead was yanked out. It needs an experienced nurse and she's dealing with something else at the moment.' She leant forward and spoke in a low voice. 'I overheard him telling another doctor that it's a patient with a toothbrush stuck somewhere that it shouldn't be.'

'Ooh, pull back the curtains a bit, honey, so we can see what's going on out there.' Stevie perked up quite considerably. 'It's like being in our own hospital drama.'

They'd always loved people watching, it made working for *Glitz* magazine a natural choice, but it was one of the things that her ex-boyfriend had hated about her. Liam had said she was nosey. Only, as it turned out, she hadn't been nearly nosey enough. She hadn't checked his mobile phone for suspicious messages or his pockets for unexplained receipts, and they might still have been together if it hadn't been for a slip of his texting thumb. When she'd received a text with a photo of part of his anatomy carefully sandwiched between the pages of Harry Potter and the Deathly Hallows, which was as far as Liam's reading had ever progressed, she'd been surprised to say the least. The accompanying message of 'Darling Millie, can't wait to slip between the covers with you again – it's magic!' had been even more of a surprise. Millie, as it later emerged, was Liam's secret lover and a librarian of all things. Given the play on words, and pictures, the text had actually been quite well thought out. Except, of course, for the small detail of sending it to the wrong girl.

'I thought this would all be a bit low rent for you. You know that coffee is as good as it gets, don't you?' Ashleigh raised an eyebrow. She loved Stevie, he'd been her best friend for over ten years, but he had what her father had always called "champagne tastes and lemonade pockets". A freelance stylist, who barely knew where his next job was coming from, but with aspirations well above his means.

'No, I'm enjoying roughing it honey.' Stevie's trademark grin was back. 'You get a lot more drama on this floor of the hospital!'

'Okay, your wish is my command.' She pulled back the curtain of the cubicle so they could see into the corridor, where two plastic seats straddled a fixed table that was laden with dog-eared magazines and rack of leaflets about domestic abuse. Her life was all glamour, just as her old friends assumed.

'Ooh, this looks like it could be interesting!' Stevie spoke out of the side of his mouth, as a couple of world-weary looking women plonked themselves on to the plastic seats outside the cubicle.

'God, I'm worn out.' The younger of the two women sighed.

'I can't wait until your Terry picks us up, so I can get home, have a nice cup of tea and put my feet up with a magazine.'

'Me too. Terry will kill me if he sees the price, but I treated myself to a copy of *Glitz* from the hospital shop. I figured I deserved it after an eight hour shift scrubbing the Sussex Ward.' Her companion snorted with laughter. 'You can laugh, but it's three pounds fifty! Terry always moans that he can get two weeks worth of his newspaper for that price and there's not even a nipple on display in *Glitz*!'

'Oh, I don't know about that, Sandra.' The younger woman grabbed the magazine from her friend's hand. 'I'd say Zac Starr looks a right tit in that photo! For God's sake who chose those clothes? He looks like a Rod Stewart tribute act!'

'Did she just say what I think she did?' Stevie's injuries appeared to have been forgotten, as he sat bolt upright on the hospital trolley.

'Sshh, she'll hear you.' Though her own heart was sinking into her boots, Ashleigh couldn't help agreeing with Sandra's friend. 'And you must admit, Zac did look quite… *colourful* in that shoot.'

'Maybe.' Stevie stuck out his bottom lip like a sulky toddler. 'But look at the state of her. Not even Gok could make *that* look good naked!'

'I thought we weren't mentioning Gok?' Ashleigh smiled in spite of herself. Whenever one of his shows appeared on TV, Stevie would hurl a cushion at it and demand it was turned to a different channel. As far as he was concerned the TV stylist has stolen his dream job and that made it unbearable for him to watch.

'That's as maybe, honey, but he's a genius and all I'm saying is that even he couldn't play up her good points.' Stevie bristled.

'She needs a damn good bra for a start.'

'I think the old man might be right about this mag being a waste of money!' Sandra's voice drifted across the corridor as she flicked through *Glitz*. 'I mean the photos and the houses are glamorous all right, but the captions are so cheesy and who the hell cares where they chose their bleeding soft furnishings! Listen to this.' She was pointing to one of the photos from the Zac Starr article. '*Zac relaxes with fiancée Leanne on the luxury chaise longue, covered with fabric chosen on the glamorous couple's recent holiday in Marrakech!*' The two women got up as a middle-aged man approached them and Sandra stuffed the magazine into her bag before following him back down the corridor; her contraband copy of *Glitz* safely hidden away.

'Well, that was charming.' All the excitement at eavesdropping on someone else's conversation had drained out of Stevie and he slumped against the pillows. 'Rod Stewart? Bloody cheek, they should see how hard I had to work to persuade Zac not to wear that jumpsuit he had made. Maybe I should ask them if there are any jobs going spare doing cleaning instead!'

'Zac *wanted* to wear those clothes; it really isn't a big reflection on your styling and even you must admit that some of the captions are pretty cringe worthy.' She pushed a strand of dark hair behind her ear.

'It's okay, honey, I'll get over it. Anyway, it's you who should be complaining, I had the styling forced on me by Zac's appalling taste, but your photographs were bloody brilliant.' He was at his best when he smiled. He had the kind of dimples that meant he could pass for a member of the upper sixth, even though the big three O was looming large. 'Still it could be a lot worse. Just think, you could be working for Mark Harris.'

They both grimaced. Mark was an old friend from art college and he ran one of those awful make-over studios in outer London, where disillusioned women were plumped and preened to within an inch of their lives to create a soft focus portrait that only the vainest few would ever dare hang over the fireplace.

He was right, of course, but she couldn't shake off the feeling that she'd never be really happy working for *Glitz*. Sometimes she wondered how she'd ended up there. She knew there were other struggling photographers who'd sell their grandmothers to get a job like hers. She loved reportage, had always felt it told a much truer story; yet here she was photographing an ageing rock-star, draped across a chaise longue with fiancée number seven clinging on for dear life.

'There'll be no begging Mark for a job for you, honey, your career's on the up!' Stevie had called her honey ever since they'd met. There was real affection between them from that first day, a kind of instant chemistry. 'Didn't Zac say something to you about shooting his next album cover?'

'Yeah, yeah, but his six previous fiancées have learnt to their cost what he's full of.' Ashleigh shrugged. Zac was every bit as fickle as his string of broken relationships suggested. 'I don't suppose he'll even ring me.'

'Well, he won't do better.' Stevie pulled her towards him again. 'Sod Zac, we've got a big day tomorrow. Although I've got a feeling I won't get to do much.'

Angus, their jovial editor at *Glitz*, had sent them both an email outlining the expectations of Tom Rushworth, the focus of their latest assignment. He was a man who knew what he wanted and more importantly what he didn't want, and that included a makeover.

'Never mind, there's always someone in desperate need of a restyle!' Stevie grinned and it seemed he was in possession of a sixth sense. An elderly nurse, with a surprisingly bushy salt and pepper moustache, was striding determinedly towards him, wielding a large pair of tweezers like she meant business.

Chapter Two

'It's all come out, Tom. I don't know what to do.' Chloe's voice on the other end of the phone line was almost impossible to make out. She was doing that thing young children did when they were really upset, punctuating every few words with an intake of air that was half-breath, half shuddering sob.

'Have you said anything to the press?' Tom Rushworth was nothing if not calm in a crisis. Over a decade in celebrity PR had provided him with a thorough grounding in managing the drama that so frequently went hand-in-hand with his clients.

'No, but they're outside, in the bushes and everything. They keep shouting through the letter-box!' Chloe sounded more fragile than ever. 'I'm scared.'

'I'll send Shaun round with a couple of his heaviest side-kicks.' Tom suppressed an urge to laugh at the mental image that conjured up. His head of security was a genius at recruiting shaven-headed, Neanderthal-types, who could put off even the most determined journalist with threats they'd be only too happy to carry out. 'They'll make sure no-one pushes it too far.'

'Thanks, but maybe I should just let them in and get it over with. My career's in ruins anyway.' Chloe had given into crying and Tom wished he could go round there, but he was hemmed in by Susie-Anne's plans for a pantomime of a photo-shoot to celebrate their engagement. Hemming him in seemed to be an unfortunate knack of hers.

'Is your mum there, sweetheart?' He paused and strained to hear Chloe's response over the crying. What little control she'd had at the start of the call had disappeared, but he just managed to make out that Gilly was with her. 'That's good, Chloe. Listen to what she says to you and listen to me now.' Her mother being there was the next best thing to being able to get round there. 'Nothing is over. In a way this could be the making of your career, if we play it right. Which is why it's really important that you don't say anything to the press without me. Do you hear me? Not a thing.'

'But what are you going to say, how are you going to fix things after this?' Chloe sounded desperate, confirming that her speaking to the press would be an unmitigated disaster.

'I don't want you to worry about any of it, that's my job.' Tom paused and metaphorically crossed his fingers that he wasn't about to break a promise. 'All you need to know is that I will fix it and make sure you have the career that a talent like yours deserves.' It was easy for him to be sincere with Chloe; a client with genuine talent motivated him more these days than his fifteen percent cut, not that he'd ever admit that in public of course.

'Thank you, thank you! Oh, Tom, I don't know what I'd do without you.' Chloe's relief was tangible, even from twenty miles away at the other end of a phone line.

'You don't have to. Just call me if you're worried again, okay? Come in and see me tomorrow morning and we'll work out what we're going to do. It's all going to be okay. Shaun will be with you within the hour and you can leave the rest to him.'

If only all his problems were as easily solved. The thought of the photo-shoot, and everything tied up with it, consumed his thoughts; fate was taking away the one woman he loved at the same time as he was getting more and more entrenched in a relationship with another woman he could barely stand.

'You're so sweet Tom, I really wouldn't want anyone else looking after me.' Chloe was calmer already.

'Ssshh, for God's sake don't let the press hear that or it will be me who ends up being ruined.' Tom was only half-joking, his public image a persona he'd almost forgotten how to turn off. Somehow he'd become a version of his father in his professional life and now his personal life was following suit. The idea of history repeating itself hemming him in more than ever.

※

'Oh my God! How much did we have to drink last night?' Ashleigh's throat ached and her voice was so raspy that she figured she could make a good living on one of those sex-line numbers if it didn't go back to normal.

'I don't know, but I feel like crap!' Stevie stretched out and pushed her towards the edge of the futon on which they'd spent the night.

'Why don't you get a proper bed?' Hauling herself to her feet, she already knew the answer. The flat was one room with a tiny corner partitioned off for the smallest wet room she'd ever seen.

'It's the only way that I can have something to sit on and sleep in.' It was true. Stevie might well be in possession of West London's tiniest flat. 'I don't think, if I ever meet my dream man, he'd be too impressed when I brought him back here to find we're going to spend the night in bunk beds!' He got up and poured black coffee the consistency of treacle into mismatched mugs. 'Anyway, until Mr Right comes along for one of us, we get to collapse into bed without even having to move.'

'And we wonder why we're both still single!' Ashleigh grinned, it was a good job they had each other. Glancing at her watch, it was later than she'd thought. 'We'd better get a move on. I read somewhere that Rushworth sacked a member of staff for being late the day after her mum's funeral.'

'Sounds like a right charmer. Although I do quite like them mean.' Winking he squeezed past her with all the ease of an airline attendant wedging past the duty free trolley in the narrow aisle of an airbus. 'Bagsy first in the shower, there may not be enough hot water to go round!'

'Just as well neither is out to impress, then.'

'That's as maybe, honey.' Stevie dropped another casual wink. 'But I'm going to put my lucky pants on just in case.'

Dashing across London to Tom Rushworth's office on the banks of the Thames, Ashleigh and Stevie called in to grab some equipment and a bag of accessories from the *Glitz* offices. Tom Rushworth had insisted on the smallest team that *Glitz* could send. He absolutely refused to have a make-up artist present and was evidently only tolerating Stevie's attendance under duress.

With ten minutes to spare they managed to make a pit stop at *Costa* for a second injection of caffeine and a Danish and, by the time they reached their destination, Ashleigh felt almost ready for the challenge she suspected was coming.

The offices of *Rushworth Associates* were every inch the steely, modern, glass fronted environment that she'd expected them to be. Tom's reputation as head of the PR firm, which had celebrities queuing round the block to join his client list, had made him almost as famous as some of them. He had a reputation as the King of Spin and it seemed there was nothing he couldn't turn around. From the glamour model caught snorting cocaine, to the movie star caught with his pants down in a seedy Soho club, Tom Rushworth had spun them all. Somehow these celebs not only held onto their careers, but had turned the exposure, in some cases literally, to their advantage. Over the years, Zac Starr, a *Glitz* magazine favourite, had given Rushworth Associates plenty of action to spin.

'We're here to see Tom Rushworth. Ashleigh Hayes and Stevie Smith from *Glitz* magazine.'

The receptionist looked them up and down and smiled at Stevie.

'I'll ring through to Mr Rushworth's PA and let them know that you're here.' She gestured towards the plush waiting area and gave Stevie a coy smile, passing him a business card. 'My personal number is on here, just in case you need me when I'm not at the reception desk.'

'She's cheerful. I might even give her a call, we could go out on the pull together.' Stevie grinned at Ashleigh, when he was out of earshot of the reception desk, and slumped on to one of the squashy sofas, flanked by huge arrangements of very modern and somewhat lethal looking flowers.

Not trusting herself to speak, Ashleigh had that sense of foreboding that normally only accompanied a trip to the dentist or one of those appointments with a doctor that forced you to leave your dignity in the waiting room with the back issues of *Good Housekeeping* and *Gardeners World*.

A click clack of heels signalled the arrival of Tom's PA.

'*Glitz Magazine*?' Francine, who had a "balls of steel" repu-tation and was widely regarded as the super efficient backbone of *Rushworth Associates*, apparently didn't bother with names unless she was addressing someone she considered important. Not waiting for a response, she turned and walked back along the corridor with Ashleigh and Stevie having to half run to catch up. 'Tom and Susie-Anne are ready for you now, but I warn you, we've only got twenty minutes, he's got a meeting with Chloe Nicholas at eleven.'

Chloe Nicholas was the latest winner of the UK's most successful TV talent show and her squeaky clean image had just been blown apart by the revelation that she'd given a baby up for adoption at age fifteen. It had been on the front of every newspaper in *Costa*, with the headlines and speculation about the girl with the "voice of an angel" being devoured as hungrily as the chocolate muffins.

'I'd like to be a fly on the wall for that one!' Stevie spoke in a loud stage whisper and Francine shot him a look that could curdle milk.

Their editor, Angus, had regaled them with the juiciest of gossip after he blagged an invite to the *Rushworth Associates* Christmas party. He'd told them one of the secretaries, who couldn't stand Francine, had decided to spike her drink. Inhi-bitions to the wind, she'd made a blatant pass at Tom, which had gone down as one of the most embarrassing rejections in history. Ashleigh might have felt sorry for her if she wasn't so hateful.

Francine led them into Tom's office, which was dominated by a huge desk, but was also home to another group of luxurious

suede sofas and more huge futuristic flower arrangements.
The view of the Thames was spectacular and would make a
fantastic backdrop for the photos of the happy couple. *Glitz*
would make it official for all those who doubted that Tom
Rushworth really had got engaged to TV weather girl, former
Miss Texas runner up and all round Southern Belle, Susie-
Anne Summers. If he was glass and steel, she was candyfloss;
the most unlikely pairing since curry ice cream and to many
people every bit as unpalatable.

Susie-Anne burst into the room and Stevie's jaw almost hit
the floor. She was wearing a bubble gum pink mini dress, that
looked as though it had been shrink wrapped to fit, and her
white blonde hair vied against her magnificent cleavage to be
the first to catch the eye.

'Christ, it's Dolly Parton's granddaughter!' Stevie seemed
determined to rock the boat but, as luck would have it, Susie-
Anne was far too busy air kissing Ashleigh to overhear.

'I'm Ashleigh Hayes, the photographer.' She barely caught
her breath to speak in the haze of the other woman's perfume.

'I thought you'd be a man.' Susie-Anne took a step back and
regarded her with an air of disappointment. 'Quite deceptive
having a name like Ashley.'

'I'll mention it to my mother next time I see her.' The sarcasm
went over Susie-Anne's head, which was probably just as well.

'Okay, how quickly can we get this over with?' As soon
as Tom Rushworth came in to the room he dominated the
space. He was well over six feet tall and an air of no-nonsense
matched his strong features. His coal black hair was flecked
with just a dusting of grey at the temples and he had the sort
of navy blue eyes you couldn't help staring at.

'I understand you've agreed to just one publicity shot to

announce your engagement?' Ashleigh tried and failed to hold his gaze.

'That's right, just one and I'm only doing that because *Glitz* has done us a lot a favours over the years and there's a chance we might work together even more in the future. I hope they told you we're not being dressed up by some slave-to-fashion stylist to look like a couple of shop window dummies?' Tom looked horrified as Stevie removed his coat, revealing an orange sleeveless vest top and lime green skinny jeans – yet, somehow, pulled off the look. Admittedly, a similar outfit would have been ludicrous on Tom Rushworth, who looked much more at home in his Armani suit.

'That's right and no make-up either, I prefer to do my own.' Susie-Anne's slow drawl was already starting to irritate Ashleigh and the make-up she was so determined to show off looked like it had been sprayed on. The glow from her fake tan reminded Ashleigh of the first car she'd owned, a bright orange Ford Fiesta.

'Okay, well this shouldn't take long, I know you're both very busy.' Ashleigh adjusted the settings on the camera and Stevie tried to justify his existence by making some small tweaks to Susie-Anne's hair and attempting to straighten Tom's tie, before being batted away like an irritating insect. The bag of accessories he'd bought with him, hoping to dress up their outfits, sat redundantly in the corner of the room. The shoot was over within the allotted twenty minutes and might have been quicker still, had Tom managed to drag up a smile from somewhere.

'Thanks, that's great,' Ashleigh lied, packing up her equipment, keen to make a quick get away. 'Is one of the journalists interviewing you for the article?'

'We've written our own press release.' Tom ran a hand through his dark hair and didn't bother looking in Ashleigh's direction. 'I've told your Editor to use that.'

'I'm real disappointed though.' Susie-Anne lent forward to give Stevie the full benefit of her cleavage as she spoke, not realising how wasted it was on him. 'I so wanted to talk about the baby, how excited we are and how Tom can't keep his hands off me since the pregnancy has made my boobs even bigger!'

Ashleigh doubted that pregnancy hormones could do anything to Susie-Anne's breasts that silicone hadn't already taken care of.

'Why don't you just put a poster up at Piccadilly Circus?' Tom might have been teasing Susie-Anne, but his tone wasn't what you'd call affectionate. Sensing an atmosphere, and keen not to get on the wrong side of Tom Rushworth, Stevie and Ashleigh beat a hasty retreat.

'So are we still going out to lunch to celebrate?' Susie-Anne draped herself across Tom's lap, as the photographer and stylist from *Glitz* shot out of his office like two kids desperate to escape at the sound of the school bell. 'You did promise.'

'Did I?' Tom barely resisted the urge to tip her off his lap. He couldn't think when she clung to him, in fact he could barely breathe. It was like the walls were closing in on him, as if the instinct just to survive was taking over.

'Don't be mean, you know you did!' She stood up and put her hands on her hips. 'Isn't it bad enough that we're doing this engagement as though we're ashamed of it?'

'I never pretended that I was going to go in for a big show of this. I think I made that clear when I asked if you wanted to get married.' Irritation at having to go through it all again gave an edge to his voice, although she didn't seem to have noticed.

'Sugar, you made that real clear, but I never realised just how low-key you wanted to make it. Not even family in the photos?' She looked at him almost pityingly. 'I mean I know things are a bit tricky, but it wouldn't have killed your mum to come up for the shoot. My mum would have got on a plane like a shot if you'd said the word.'

'Not everyone's as fame hungry.' Tom couldn't keep the disdain out of his voice. Susie-Anne's selfishness took his breath away at times. If only she knew how instrumental his mother had been in bringing about the proposal, she might well have been more gracious to the older woman. Although, knowing Susie-Anne, possibly not. How a drunken one-night stand had led to this he'd never know. If his clients hadn't swept the board at the People's Choice awards, and he hadn't been at the hospital that morning for the devastating diagnosis, he doubted very much that they would have got together. After all, she was hardly his type. The astronomical bar bill he'd had to settle, and his raging hangover the next morning, had been the least costly consequences of that night.

'You can get photographed wherever you go, but it would have been a treat for my family.' Finally seeming to sense that she was in a losing battle, she changed tack. 'So, having denied me that, doesn't the mother of your baby at least deserve a little celebration lunch out?'

'Anywhere you want.' Something in the corner of the room caught Tom's eye and he felt like a drowning man having just spotted a life raft. His excuse to get out of there, rather than face an enforced celebration lunch at whatever celebrity hotspot Susie-Anne had her heart set on. 'Only I won't be able to join you. Something's come up.'

'Now, hang on a God damn minute!' She was about to launch into a tirade, but he took hold of her hand.

'It's business and I really need to see to it. You know how important all this is and I'm doing it for the baby's future. Don't forget your career is part of all this too.' Feeling her relax somewhat, he smiled. He was an experienced negotiator and Susie-Anne was easy to read, her motivation for almost everything came back to her quest for fame. 'I'll get Francine to book a table, anywhere you want, for you and Janey and any other friends you want to take out and celebrate with.'

'*Nobu* or *The Ivy*?' Susie-Anne was smiling as she stood up, probably imagining the celebrities she might rub shoulders with, not to mention the press. No doubt she'd be only too pleased to regale them with news of their engagement, to make up for the lack of fanfare on Tom's part.

'That's fine, wherever. I'll tell Francine to organise it on my way out, but there's something I've got to sort.' Stopping to grab what he'd spotted from the corner of the room, Tom rushed past without so much as a kiss goodbye. She was right. It hadn't been the world's most romantic engagement announcement and it wasn't the best sign when the groom-to-be took the slightest excuse to escape. It wouldn't be forever though, that was his mantra. The extensive legal advice he'd sought before the proposal had convinced him that his parental rights would be enhanced if they were married, at least until after the baby arrived. There was no need for guilt though; Susie-Anne didn't love him either, what she loved was his profile and connections. He just hoped she'd love his baby.

'God I need a fag after that.' Stevie pulled a packet of cigarettes out of his pocket as soon as they got outside the office block and leant nonchalantly against the wall, not giving a damn whether it was a designated smoking area. 'Remind me to make sure Angus puts "Clothes – couples' own" alongside the photo. I'm not having anyone thinking I put Susie-Anne's look together!'

'Do you think they're in love?' Ashleigh sighed. The whole thing had been quite depressing.

'Christ, no! I can't believe he'd be marrying her if he hadn't knocked her up.' Stevie took a deep drag on the cigarette and closed his eyes.

'It's got to be more than that! Getting married because you're stupid enough to get someone pregnant by mistake is never a good idea, whatever old fashioned sentiment might be behind it. You only have to look at my parents to see that.'

'Thanks for the relationship counselling.' The deadpan voice made Ashleigh jump. She hadn't seen Tom Rushworth approaching them. 'You forgot this!' He thrust Stevie's unused bag of accessories towards her and, without saying anything else, turned on his heel and left. For a minute the two of them just stood open-mouthed, like a couple of fish out of water.

By the time they got on the tube, Stevie was laughing about it. Never one for worrying, he was impersonating Susie-Anne and holding a couple of small spot lights up to his chest, until Ashleigh laughed too. Maybe Tom wouldn't mention it to their Editor and, even if he did, she was sure Angus would see the funny side.

Stevie's mobile rang just as they emerged from the station, still giggling. It was quite hard to pick up on the one-sided conversation but, from the look on his face, it was fairly intense.

'Well?' Her stomach knotted as his face clouded over.

'That was Angus.' Stevie paused, as though he was trying to find the best way to share what he had to say. 'Guess who just became the majority shareholder in *Glitz* magazine?'

'I don't know… Zac Starr?' Ashleigh giggled, relieved that the call from Angus hadn't been a telling-off for their faux pas.

'Bloody Tom Rushworth of all people!' Stevie's voice was suddenly high-pitched and her shoulders dropped. 'So we've been called into the office tomorrow. Make-over studio, here we come!'

Chapter Three

'I still can't understand why he came chasing out of the office to find us.' Stevie mumbled the following morning, as he pulled on a pair of pink trousers that clashed horribly with his blood shot eyes.

'He probably knew we'd be bitching about him and Susie-Anne, since they look so mad together.' Ashleigh spoke with her mouth full and shoved another handful of Maltesers in as soon as she'd finished speaking.

'You slipped out early this morning. How was the retail therapy?' The lack of any shopping bags made Stevie's question unnecessary, but she answered it anyway.

'It didn't work. I thought I'd hit the shops early since I couldn't sleep last night.' She shuddered slightly, as memories of the day before came flooding back. 'After meeting Tom's PA, I thought maybe power dressing might help me hang on to my job'.

'It'll be alright honey, we don't even work for *Glitz* and, even if Tom does give us the old heave ho, we'll make a buck freelancing somewhere else,' Stevie grinned. 'I quite fancy myself as an artist. I can even cope with the idea of starving in a garret, as long as I can still afford the odd designer label!'

'There'd be no eating out then, you know? You probably couldn't even keep yourself in Cornish pasties,' She managed a weak smile. 'But you're right, there'll probably be work elsewhere. It was me that jinxed it after all, I'd been moaning about how working for *Glitz* wasn't what I really wanted.' She just wished she could really believe it would be okay either way. As much as the work with *Glitz* sometimes frustrated her, she knew it was what paid the mortgage on the flat and kept her head above water.

'So what happened to the power suit?' Stevie pinched one of the Maltesers out of the pack she was gripping as though her life depended on it.

'I tried on my usual size and it wouldn't even do up. I was so disgusted that I just walked out of the shop, bought the paper, a shed load of chocolate and haven't stopped eating since.' She gave him a wry grin. He'd understand the total lack of logic in her actions, even though he'd never put on as much as a pound in the ten years she'd known him. She was just too curvy to ever be skinny, but she wasn't ready to move out of her size twelve comfort zone just yet.

'Best get on with it then, honey. If they're going tell us they don't want us darkening the door of *Glitz* again, I want to know in time to hit happy hour at Carly's new cocktail bar.' He grabbed her hand and squeezed it. 'Who knows, we might just bag ourselves a couple of millionaires and not have to worry about work anymore.'

It was one of those bright, crisp days that Ashleigh loved, the sort that made you feel alive. Despite the knotted feeling in her stomach, she was glad they'd left enough time to walk from Stevie's flat to the *Glitz* offices. The fresh air was doing her good and it was dry enough to ensure that straightening her hair in his tiny bathroom, which required all the skill of a contortionist, hadn't been a complete waste of time.

Normally she'd imagine photographing the homeless woman, who was pushing a shopping trolley full of other people's lost belongings past the designer stores and boutiques, for her book about London life. Dreaming about seeing her book in the window of an actual bookshop had got Ashleigh through many difficult days. Not today, though, the impending meeting with Tom Rushworth pushed everything else aside.

'You okay, honey?' Stevie squeezed her hand as they walked the last few hundred yards to the Glitz building.

'I think so.' She didn't want to speak any more than she had to and her stomach was churning. The conversation Tom overheard wasn't that bad, but his reputation suggested he didn't give second chances.

'Listen, Ash, if he's going to get rid of one of us, it'll be me.' Stevie pulled her closer. They were more or less the same height, but the contrast between his lean angled physique and her hourglass shape would have made them a slightly odd looking couple, had getting together ever been on the cards. 'You saw what his opinion of stylists was.'

'Only for himself. You've styled loads of his clients, I just don't think he's a skinny jeans kind of guy!' She smiled, somehow Stevie always made it better. 'Angus will tell him how important you are to making a photo shoot work and making his clients look good.'

'Here's where we find out honey… Come on, let's do this thing!'

As it turned out, when they got to the office, Stevie wasn't invited into the meeting and Ashleigh knew that meant one of two things. Either it was a photographer's briefing for a forthcoming shoot, which she would share with Stevie and the rest of the team later… or Tom wanted her on her own when he sacked her. Given recent events, she'd have bet her life on the latter.

'Thank you for coming in.' Tom looked up from the huge leather chair behind the Editor's desk. Poor Angus had already been relegated to one of the chairs at the side of the office, where Ashleigh joined him.

'You've heard that my company has taken over majority ownership of the magazine?' Tom didn't wait for her to answer. 'Angus tells me that you're the best at what you do.' The tone of Tom's voice hinted that he doubted the truth of such a statement, but at least he hadn't started by mentioning the events of the day before.

'Thanks Angus.' Ashleigh squeezed the Editor's knee, making him blush.

'She's really great, Stevie too.' Angus enthused, his Glaswegian accent still distinctive despite thirty years in London.

'I hope so.' Tom directed his gaze to Ashleigh again, but it was as if she'd been struck dumb and hadn't been able to do more than mumble or nod since she'd come into the room. 'I bought into *Glitz* so I could have ownership of a magazine that could present my clients in the best light, particularly in…' He paused for a minute, as if searching for the right words, 'trying circumstances.'

'One of Tom's clients has had some revelations concerning her private life all over the tabloids this week. The plan is to do a photo shoot for *Glitz* and get it into next month's issue of the magazine as a kind of damage limitation.' Angus, who was well known for his love of gossip, was barely able to contain his excitement.

'Thank you, Angus. All you need to know for now is that it's Chloe Nicholas and I'm sure you've heard the rumours?' He fixed her with a look that clearly said she wouldn't be getting any gossip from him. 'If you're happy to take the job on, my PA, Francine, will contact you with the details. The shoot will need to be done on Monday.' Tom raised an eyebrow, as if daring her to object at the short notice.

'Thank you, we'd love to. I'll brief Stevie and the rest of the team.' Ashleigh finally found her voice. Like a speeding motorist who'd been let off with a warning, rather than three points on her license or an immediate ban, she couldn't believe her luck and couldn't wait to leave, in case he changed his mind.

'Oh Ash, before you go, I meant to tell you that Zac Starr has been asking for your number, apparently he's lost your card. I can give you his details if you want to call him?' Angus beamed at her, clearly delighted that his favourite photographer had seemingly hit it off so well with the magazine's new owner.

'I don't think that's a good idea.' Tom's tone was forceful and, before she could object, he went on. 'If Ashleigh is happy for Zac to call her, she can give permission for her number to be given out if he calls back again. In the meantime, I don't want anyone working with *Glitz* to start hassling my clients.'

She wanted to scream at the unfairness, remind him that it was Zac who'd asked for her bloody number and not the other way round. She knew, though, that rocking the boat with Tom would only result in her being the one to topple overboard and end up being eaten by sharks. For now, it was time to quit while she was ahead and say nothing.

'Have you and Stevie got time to look at some samples I've been sent by that new Russian designer? You know, the one who was the talk of London Fashion week,' Angus furrowed his brow. 'I can't for the life of me remember his name, but they're outrageous and might be perfect for one of next month's shoots. It won't take long.'

'Can you make do with Stevie on his own, surely it's more of a stylist thing?' Although Tom was asking a question, it was fairly obvious he only expected one answer. 'There's something else I'd like to speak to Ashleigh about.'

'Absolutely, they're much more up Stevie's street!' With a quick wink in her direction, Angus was gone. The silence in the room, as she and Tom were left alone, was one of those awkward ones that you were just desperate to fill, no matter how inane the conversation that resulted.

'If this is about yesterday…' As soon as she'd started speaking she realised that she wasn't sure what she wanted to say. Should she apologise?

'I just wanted to make it clear that, whatever you've heard about me, I'm not in the habit of sacking people for putting their foot in it.' Was that a hint of a smile playing around Tom's mouth? Ashleigh noted the strong jaw and full lips, realising to her embarrassment that she was staring. 'Not that it's any of your business, but I'm not just making an old fashioned gesture, as you put it.'

'You're right, it's none of my business.' She blushed partly because of what he'd said, but mainly because he'd caught her staring. For as long as she could remember, she'd had an inconvenient habit of blushing at the most inopportune of times.

'No, it isn't. But like I said there's more to it than there seems and for some reason I feel the need to justify myself to you. For a start, Susie-Anne's from the States and, if we don't get married, she might end up having to go home at some point and I'd prefer it if my son or daughter didn't grow up living thousands of miles away from me.'

'I see. So not because you're madly in love then?' Ashleigh reddened again. Had she gone mad? It was like she'd developed some form of Tourettes, only without the swearing. To her surprise, Tom laughed.

'Not madly in love, no, but starting to wonder if I'm crazy to take Angus' advice when it comes to you.'

'Off so soon? That went well, don't you think?' Angus was beaming like a proud father as he passed Tom on the stairs.

'Are you sure those two are as good as you say they are?' Tom didn't know what it was he wanted to hear. Angus had already enthused about them so much that there really wasn't anything left to say. There was something about Ashleigh though, something that made him need to hear it again, to make sure that there weren't other reasons why he'd agreed to give her another shot so easily. He'd noticed her lively amber-coloured eyes the first time they'd met and he'd realised that he didn't even know the colour of Susie-Anne's without looking. He couldn't afford to let anything distract him from the right business decision, though, he only wanted to hire Ashleigh if she was really the best. The takeover at *Glitz* was bound to cost jobs and the last thing he needed was any further complications. Those who had been loyal friends to *Rushworth Associates* over the years, and were good at what they did, like Angus, would be well rewarded. Others might not be so lucky, but in the end you made your own luck and any action Tom took wouldn't keep him up at night. If he ever felt guilty about a business decision it didn't last long, he could still hear his father's voice ringing in his ears after all these years, "If you're not a man in business you're not a man at all".

'Honestly, Tom, don't worry. They're the best I've worked with.' Angus was using the kind of tone he must have used to reassure the magazine's biggest advertisers that their marketing budget was well spent. 'You won't find a stronger team than the two of them, they've been together years.'

'As a couple?' Tom felt oddly disappointed. He tried to shake the thought that it would bother him if Ashleigh and Stevie were together.

'No!' Angus roared with laughter. 'You clearly don't listen to gossip do you?'

'You should know by now that I don't.' Despite his protestations Tom smiled, for some reason knowing that Stevie and Ashleigh weren't a couple mattered. He told himself it was just about professionalism, though. There was a lot riding on the photo shoot and it could end up being the biggest celebrity story of the month either way. Although, in the world of celebrity they inhabited, the next front-page sensation was often just an indiscretion away.

Chapter Four

Carly's might not have been the most original name for their friend's new nightclub, but, with a larger than life personality like its owner, it suited the place and they wouldn't have missed the opening night for anything. Carly Harper was an ex-glamour model, engaged to premiership footballer Duane Johnson and *Glitz* had covered every aspect of her personal life for the past ten years. Duane had bought the club for Carly in an attempt to keep her out of trouble, since she'd given up modelling. It was a good opportunity to catch up with people who could put some freelance work their way and even Tom Rushworth couldn't complain if she just happened to 'bump' into Zac to discuss his album shoot.

'My darlings, I knew you'd make it.' Having no doubt air kissed a string of B list celebs and most of Duane's team-mates, Carly reserved a proper smacker for Stevie and Ashleigh, as her magnificent boobs threatened to escape from her skimpy dress.

'You look delightfully tarty as ever sweetheart.' Stevie's teasing was affectionate. They'd become friends after photographing her a few years before and the three of them had shared more than a few drunken nights out.

'Don't listen to him Carls,' Ashleigh hugged her tightly, 'We've been celebrating some good news since lunch time and I'm afraid he's in an even more indiscreet mood than usual.'

'Plenty of good looking men in tonight?' Stevie craned his neck to look past her. The nightclub was heaving with people trying to out do one another in the name of knickers-dropping stakes. 'We're both hoping to pull tonight!'

'In that dress Ash won't have any bother. I do believe it makes her tits look even better than mine!' Carly snorted as she laughed. With anyone else it would have been annoying, but because everyone loved Carly, it somehow just added to her charm. 'There's a big crowd of footballers in tonight and a game show host who is right up your street Stevie, if you know what I mean!'

'Shit, have you seen who else is here?' Stevie gestured to the other end of the bar where Jade Ivory was deep in conversation with one of Michael's team-mates.

'Did you invite her?' Ashleigh raised an eyebrow. If that wasn't surprising enough; the fact that their ex-colleague had actually turned up was even more of a shock.

'Jade was on the list before Angus sacked her and I didn't want to cause a scene by getting her chucked out now that she's here. It would just give her the ammunition she's looking for.' Carly shrugged and Ashleigh wasn't sure if she could have been as forgiving in her friends' shoes. Jade Ivory had been a journalist at *Glitz*, but had been caught-out leaking photos of Carly and Duane's engagement party to a rival magazine, alongside 'insider' gossip that owed more to the world of Jade's imagination than it did to fact.

'She's freelancing now, isn't she? Hopefully, with her talents, she'll be begging for a job in McDonalds by Christmas', Stevie, who'd never liked Jade, was already headed in her direction. 'You grab a table, honey, I'm going to have a word with Poison Ivory and tell her I've seen her future in a vision.'

Stevie's exchange with Jade must have been short because he was back within minutes, with a tray of drinks in hand. The atmosphere in the club was buzzing, which matched Ashleigh's mood. Despite the arrival of Jade, she was on a high.

Stevie caught sight of his quarry for the evening, game show host Paul Hanks and in an instant he was gone again. It was going to be one of those nights. She could see him throwing some interesting moves, as she sat down at a table in sight of the dance floor, but far enough away not to be deafened by the music. Stevie's seduction technique seemed to be having the desired effect.

'All alone? That's what you get for not returning my calls.' The voice was unmistakable, and the outfit was entirely in keeping with someone who might have been styled as a Rod Stewart look alike.

'Zac, so nice to see you.' Ashleigh stood up briefly and leant forward to kiss him on both cheeks. 'Where's the lovely Leanne?' She scanned the crowd, looking for fiancée number seven. She'd photographed all of Zac's engagements from fiancée number four onwards.

'History darlin'.' He grinned and through the cheesy rock star look he sported, Ashleigh saw a flash of what made him attractive to his millions of female fans. 'She hardly made it past the photo-shoot, and, by the time the *Glitz* issue with our engagement in it came out, I'd had enough.' Zac sat down beside her, immediately placing a hand on her thigh. It seemed he might already be on the prowl for fiancée number eight. 'Anyway, I think you'll be reading all about it in the papers tomorrow. Apparently she's doing a kiss and tell.' He took a swig of his champagne cocktail and pulled a face.

'Oh shit, that doesn't sound good.' Somehow she suspected there'd be plenty for Leanne to tell.

'No doubt you'll read about what a small cock I've got or how I like to wear her knickers to bed!' Zac took another swig of his drink and his hand started to travel up her leg.

'And do you?' She moved slightly in her chair and his hand slid off the silky material of her dress, avoiding the embarrassment of having to brush him away.

'No. Well not to bed anyway, but there is something strangely comforting about the feel of satin against your tackle.' His hand was back on her thigh again.

'And what about the tiny cock, will you sue if she says that?' Ashleigh tried to move again, but this time his hand didn't slip off and it continued to travel upwards.

'No, but it's not true and I'm happy to prove it to you anytime.' Zac leant in closer to her and she could smell his aftershave mingling with a hint of the dope that he'd obviously smoked before hitting the club.

'I'm sure there are plenty of girls here who would be only too pleased to be on the receiving end of your advances, but I'm afraid I'm not one of them.' She grabbed hold of his hand and firmly pushed him away, having finally had enough of him pawing her. She wanted the job photographing his album, but not that much.

'I'm sorry, old habits die hard and you can't blame a guy for trying.' He looked genuinely contrite and there was a note of a resignation in his voice. If she hadn't known better, she'd have thought he was lonely. 'I promise to try and behave and you've got permission to slap me if I step out of line again.'

'Don't worry, I will, and I'm sorry I didn't call about the album. Angus did tell me, but my new boss didn't think it was a good idea and wouldn't give me your number.'

'What, that old bastard Tom?' Zac grinned, perking up again. 'He probably just wants to shag you himself, bit of a ladies' man that one.'

'Coming from you, that's an interesting comment! That's the last thing he wants. Never mind the fact he's engaged, he also thinks I'm a complete idiot and I barely held on to my job this week.' The thought of what she'd said to Tom made her uncomfortably hot.

'We all know how much an engagement means, just look at me. Hey, I do believe you're blushing!' Zac snorted with laughter, nearly falling off his stool in the process.

'Maybe engagement is nothing to you, but I think he intends to make a go of it with Susie-Anne.' Ashleigh wished they could talk about something other than Tom. She needed to put the embarrassing encounters with him to the back of her mind if she was going to have a good time. She'd been forced to admit to herself that she found Tom attractive, it was the only real explanation for her behaviour, but there was no way she was going to share that with Zac. In any case, she didn't want to be a cliché, having unrequited feelings for her prickly new boss. Even if she had been on the lookout for a new man, which she absolutely wasn't after the disastrous relationship with her horrible ex, Liam, she definitely wouldn't pick someone like him – he was far too complicated. She wanted someone who never got bored listening to her problems and was always there to comfort her. A straight version of Stevie perhaps. Or maybe a dog.

'Well, ignore him anyway, I want you…' Zac fixed her with a look that he'd probably used on groupies a thousand times.

'To photograph your album cover?' She cut him off, half hopeful for a yes and half just wanting to make sure that Zac really had got the message that she wasn't interested in anything else.

'That too. Listen, call me on Monday?' He grabbed her bag, took out a lipstick that she'd grudgingly spent thirteen pounds on and reduced it to a stub by writing his number on a napkin. 'I've gotta go, darlin', I'm meeting a man about a dog.' Zac kissed her on the mouth, just a little longer than was comfortable, but at least he didn't try to stick his tongue down her throat. It was progress of a sort.

Stevie was still bumping and grinding with his game-show host on the dance floor. Having consumed four champagne cocktails, Ashleigh decided to check out the executive Ladies' room, which Carly had told her was reserved just for the privileged few. It was as plush and over the top as the rest of the restaurant, black marble floors and surfaces created a shiny, ebony cocoon. Even the toilet bowls and paper were black and only the fluffy white hand towels offered any contrast in the room.

Expecting to have to squeeze past groups of women preening and lined up two-deep at the mirror, Ashleigh was pleasantly surprised to find herself alone.

She'd barely closed the cubicle door when she heard it, the distinctive southern twang. There was no doubt; it was Susie-Anne. Ashleigh peered through the alarmingly wide crack in the door and could just about make her out, reflected in the huge mirrors in front of the basins.

'If Tom could see me now he'd freak out!' Susie-Anne was giggling with another girl. 'But I don't care. Michael Cox wants to take little old me home.' She made an attempt to sound coy, but it didn't quite come off. 'One little fling won't hurt anyone.'

'Well, I wouldn't say no!' Susie-Anne's friend let out a high-pitched giggle. 'Who knows, maybe he'll manage to get you pregnant and Tom will be none the wiser.'

'Sshhh, Janey, keep your voice down, there's someone in one of the johns.' Susie-Anne was giving every indication of being drunk. Yet, somewhere in the recesses of her brain, she must have realised that the conversation she was having wasn't for public consumption. Unfortunately, the bucket of champagne she'd obviously consumed had resulted in her protestations drowning out the relatively quiet indiscretion of her friend. 'I'm beginning to wonder if Tom is firing blanks though. I haven't taken any precautions since we met and nothing… I missed a couple of periods and I really thought I was pregnant, but, guess what, I wasn't! I spent a fortune on tests and every single one of them was negative. But he thinks there's a baby; there had to be for me to hold on to him and if nothing happens soon I could be in deep shit, sugar. Although, given the fact that he hardly touches me these days, I think it might have to be an immaculate conception!'

'Perhaps you should go to the doctor. It could be you if you've been missing periods and stuff.' Janey pulled a face. 'There's always an upside, you'd never have to worry about remembering your pill again!'

'That's just why I didn't bother going.' Susie-Anne fiddled with her hair and then repositioned her sizeable breasts in the bra that they were threatening to over-power. 'I've always been rubbish at taking the pill and I ended up having three pregnancies taken care of by the time I hit my twenties. So, sugar, I know it's not me.'

'Oh well, I hear Michael is Cox by name and cock by nature, so I bet there's no blanks there!' Janey shrieked again and, in a flurry of laughter and an overpowering cloud of hairspray, they were gone.

Ashleigh couldn't move. Why did this kind of crap have to happen to her? What the hell was she supposed to do now? Tell her new boss that his fiancée was sleeping around? Quite easy news to take, in comparison to the fact that his baby to be wasn't going to be after all.

Opening the cubicle door, she looked in the mirror, still wondering what on earth to do. Could it get any worse? And then she heard it, the click of the lock in the cubicle furthest away from her. It opened slowly, like a creaking door from a horror movie. She hadn't been alone. Ashleigh held her breath as the occupant finally emerged – Jade Ivory with the smuggest smile in the world on her horrible face.

'Jesus, honey, I was in there!' Stevie looked pissed off when she dragged him away from his game show host. He'd been trying out some Patrick Swayze style moves, which seemed to be having the desired effect, when she'd interrupted him mid flow.

'I'm sorry, I'm sorry, but I didn't know what the hell else to do.' Ashleigh was breathless, it had taken all of her strength to pull Stevie off the dance floor without having to tell him then and there, in front of a packed room of celebs and quite a few journalists, about what she'd heard.

'It's Susie-Anne. She's here. On her own.' She stressed the last part of her sentence, but Stevie just stared at her like she was crazy.

'Great, so the Dolly Parton tribute act's arrived. So what? Jesus, honey, just because you haven't got a sex life, it doesn't mean you have to mess mine up too!' She wished Stevie would shut up for five minutes and let her explain. He'd probably get more turned on by the gossip she was about to impart than he ever would during a night of passion with the slightly paunchy and balding host of "Quick Wit or Twit?"

'No, that's not it. I overheard her in the toilet, talking about Tom.' She leaned in closer to him, aware that the place was buzzing with people who'd love to catch this snippet.

'And…?' Now she had his attention,

'And she's about to go home and shag Michael Cox.' The look on Stevie's face was a picture. 'On top of which, not sure that's the right phrase, but anyway, on top of which she's not even pregnant!'

'Jesus Christ, Tom will go apeshit if he finds that out. I mean he's marrying a walking ball of candyfloss for the sake of a non-existent baby. Jesus, he'll freak!' Stevie was completely animated, all thoughts of getting it on with the game show host seemingly forgotten.

'That's my dilemma. Do you think we should tell him?' She was still in shock but he gave her an are-you-mad sort of look.

'Are you completely insane? He already thinks we're a couple of idiots.' A grin flashed across his face. 'Anyway honey, I don't think it'll be long before he finds out. She's hardly being discreet.' He gestured behind Ashleigh and she spun round, just in time to catch Susie-Anne thrusting her tongue over enthusiastically down Michael Cox's throat, seconds before disappearing who-knew-where with him.

'Perhaps you're right,' She laughed and took a huge swig of her cocktail. 'Either way I'm out of here.'

It was almost a mile to the tube station. They could have gone to a nearer one, but it would have meant changing lines at the next station. Ashleigh wanted to walk for a bit and even Stevie hadn't complained for too long. The streets were unusually quiet and it was good to be outside, with the cool air on her skin.

'What do you think Tom's going to do when he finds out?' Stevie looked quite excited at the prospect.

'I don't know, but I don't suppose he'll be throwing a party. Although I still don't get what he sees in her.' Ashleigh sighed, it was none of her business, but it all just felt so wrong.

'Well there's the obvious fact that she's pregnant, but since this isn't the eighteen hundreds that doesn't really explain it.' He laughed, speaking in the sort of overly loud voice people use when they've had too much to drink. 'And not even you could make them look like a happy couple at the engagement shoot. His body language was screaming get-me-the-hell-out-of-here!'

'There's got to be more to it, but we'd better stay out of the rumour mill if we want to keep working for him.' Ashleigh held a finger to her lips. God knows what their new boss would do if he could hear this conversation.

'Even if he is marrying a drag queen!' They were still laughing when a noise behind them made her spin round and a figure ducked into a shop doorway. For a split second it looked like Jade, but it couldn't be. There was no way a gutter journalist, like Poison Ivory, would leave the party with the Susie-Anne and Michael show still going on.

Chapter Five

'Honey, I've just picked up the morning papers.' Stevie was out of breath and hadn't touched the Cornish pasty he'd been so desperate to get his hands on, from the corner shop.

'I take it the front page is full of Susie-Anne's antics?' She handed him a coffee and he dropped the papers onto the already cluttered worktop.

'Yeah, but there's something else and I'm not sure you're going to like it.' Stevie gestured towards the tabloid on top of the pile.

'Oh God, don't tell me my mother's posing naked on a plinth in Trafalgar Square again, protesting about the inequality of women in the workplace?' Ashleigh laughed. Her mother had a penchant for joining causes and the more outrageous the protest, the more likely she was to join in.

'No, but we're mentioned on the front page too - if not by name, at least by occupation.' Stevie was far less excited at the prospect than Ashleigh would have expected. 'Here, have a look.' He shoved the paper towards her and the headline was typical tabloid fare – WEATHER GIRL SCORES.

As she expected, the article was the work of Jade Ivory, who'd not only overheard Susie-Anne's confession but got photos of her doing things with Michael Cox to prove it. No surprises so far.

'Gross, no wonder it put you off your Cornish pastie!' She couldn't supress a smile. Susie-Anne's engagement to Tom had to be over.

'Have you got to the last couple of paragraphs?' Stevie was still looking serious. 'That's where poison Ivory mentions us.'

Ashleigh read down the article and went cold. "The state of Rushworth and Summers' relationship was being called into question by those closest to him even before last night's naughties, including the team involved in photographing the engagement shoot, who were overheard telling anyone who would listen how unhappy the soon-to-be-wed couple looked."

'Oh Christ, she must have followed us, unless she's actually progressed to bugging people.' The figure in the shop doorway had been Jade after all; she must have decided to tail them when Susie-Anne had disappeared with Michael. It was the perfect opportunity for her to drop them in it and get her own back for when they'd closed ranks after she was sacked. 'This makes it look like we deliberately sold Tom out.' Ashleigh sighed. If Jade Ivory had been hoping to ruin their day, she was doing a pretty good job.

'Let's not panic, I'm sure he'll be okay about it.' Even Stevie didn't sound convinced.

'You think? Do you remember the look on his face when he caught us talking about him and Susie-Anne outside his building?' She managed a rueful smile. 'And let's face it, he's hardly likely to be in the best of moods when he finds out the mother of his unborn child has been getting jiggy with some footballer, whilst we're quoted virtually saying we told you so.

I don't know about you, but I think I'm ready to head back to Kent for a few days, get away from this lot and put a bit of normality back into our lives. Not-withstanding my mother of course.'

'I'm up for it,' Stevie gave a shrug. 'I've got about a million calls to make to set up the outfits for Chloe's shoot anyway, so rather your phone bill than mine!'

'Do you want to go for a drink?' Angus was hopping from foot to foot and seemed to be offering Tom anything he could think off. He'd already given him one of those awkward bloke-hugs, thumping him on the back and telling him it would all be okay. It was sweet really, but Tom felt responsible for his discomfort. If only Angus knew.

'I think it's a bit early, even for us.' Tom shook his head, although a big part of him felt like cracking open the champagne. 'And like I said, I'm okay, honestly. Actually more than okay.' Susie-Anne's call in the early hours of the morning had jolted him awake, and her confession had woken him up to something else – just how trapped he'd begun to feel in a prison of his own making.

'Well, we have all thought it a bit odd,' Angus visibly relaxed. 'You and Susie-Anne being together that is.'

'Not as odd as me!' Tom smiled. He felt a lightness that hadn't been there for months. Yes, he had other worries, things that had triggered this whole chain of events, but it was looking stable on that front and the knowledge that there'd be no more coming home to find Susie-Anne waiting for him felt like Christmas had come early.

'But the baby, that bit must have upset you?' Angus looked uncomfortable again. He sat down and then immediately stood up, pacing like he was expecting a child of his own.

'Not nearly as much as I thought it would. Other people are more bothered about it than me, which says a lot.' The outpourings of sympathy posted on his *Twitter* page, following Susie-Anne's announcement on her own site that the pregnancy had been a 'false alarm', had shocked him. It certainly took her a long time to work that out, and funny how it coincided with her hooking up with Michael Cox, but all Tom felt was guilt. Guilt that people with enough to worry about in their own lives were out there feeling sorry for him, one person in particular. The impact of that was his only regret. He felt nothing for Susie-Anne at all. Perhaps he should have felt humiliated, but if he was honest he'd been more embarrassed about sleeping with her in the first place. Coming out of all this as the wronged 'good guy' was no bad thing. Better than the slaughtering he would have got in the press if he'd have been the one to walk out, after the baby was born, which had always been his intention.

'That's good then, I'm glad you're okay about it all,' Angus didn't sound convinced. 'Shall I cancel the spread we had planned for Susie-Anne's take on Thanksgiving? It's no skin off my nose and I can understand you not wanting to work with her.'

'God, no, absolutely not!' Tom's response was the strongest reaction he'd felt all day. 'I told her this morning that everything will carry on as normal, I'm still her agent. Her profile right now is higher than it's ever been and she's going to be in demand. There might as well be some upside to knowing her!' Tom laughed at the look of shock he'd provoked. 'Come on, don't tell me the editor of *Glitz* is getting confused between celebrity and real life?'

'Aye, I know I shouldn't be shocked at anything after all these years but…' Angus didn't finish the sentence.

'There's no buts, we signed up for this and sold our souls at the door.' Tom felt a fraction of his newfound lightness slip away. He might not be with Susie-Anne anymore, but the business meant that there were a thousand other Susie-Annes just waiting for their shot and prepared to do almost anything to get it. 'Come on, no more talking about my ex-fiancée, let's sort out this Chloe Nicholas situation instead. At least there's a girl whose soul we've got a chance of saving.'

Chapter Six

By the time they got back to Sandgate, Ashleigh had things in perspective. It seemed surreal that someone like Susie-Anne, who could pull a premiership footballer at will, would fake a pregnancy to try and trap Tom. She'd spent the first half of the train journey panicking about losing her job, until a family had got on at Ashford and she'd watched the dad talking to his excited little girl about their weekend away by the coast.

For the first time since the news about Susie-Anne and Michael Cox had come out, she'd thought about Tom and hoped he was okay. Up until then, it had helped her to dehumanise him, to take the edge off the attraction she didn't want to feel.

But she knew he'd wanted to be with the child he thought he was having, enough to offer to marry a woman he clearly didn't love. It put it all into context; there was a good chance she'd lost her most regular gig because of Jade Ivory, but she hadn't lost anything really important to her. Not like Tom.

Ashleigh and Stevie followed the promenade from the train station towards her flat at the end of Beach Road. The cliffs which faced the beach loomed up ahead, the cottage where her Mum and Step-dad lived prominent at their highest point.

Sandgate was where her heart was, she could breathe there, even if it did mean that her mother might descend on her at any moment.

'On my God!' Yanking Stevie's arm, she stopped him in his tracks. 'What the hell has she done now!' Even from the roadside, several hundred yards away, the twelve-foot high, homemade mural of the Nativity was obvious.

'Wow, that's so… Carol!' Stevie started to laugh and didn't seem able to stop.

'I was worried she'd do something like this.' Ashleigh shuddered. Still it wasn't the worst thing her mother had ever done. The thought of that life drawing class at Art College still made her skin prickle.

'I didn't realise she was that religious.' Stevie could barely get the words out and had tears streaming down his face.

'She's not.' Ashleigh shrugged. 'But the town council put an article in their newsletter suggesting that locals shouldn't put up outside Christmas decorations – in case it upsets anyone from another faith. You know no one has ever been able to tell Mum what to do. God only knows what will be up there in a couple of months' time, it's only October and she's already got enough decorations to put Blackpool to shame.'

'Christ. Literally!' Stevie tried and failed to stop laughing. 'I have to say it's magnificently awful and could only be your Mum's work! God knows I love your Mum to bits, but…'

'You wouldn't want her to be yours, right?' Ashleigh rolled her eyes as he nodded. 'It's my lucky day. Losing my job and coming home to a lovely reminder that at least half my genes were provided by a stark raving lunatic.' Despite herself, she laughed. 'Come on then. Let's go home and drown our sorrows. We can have a closer look at Mum's glorious art work later.'

Stevie had spent the afternoon making calls to the designers he thought might be most willing to loan him some dresses for the Chloe Nicholas shoot. Although Ashleigh secretly thought he was wasting his time, since Tom was bound to hold Jade Ivory's article against them. Pretending to work on enhancing some of the photos she'd taken for her London life collection, she'd really spent most of the time reading news feeds about Susie-Anne. By early evening they were both ready to relax and forget about work and everything else for a while.

'This is why I could never live in London full time.' A glass of wine helped to ease the tension from her back as she stretched her legs out in front of her, on the window seat at her flat. The view was always beautiful, whether it was miles of calm blue sea, or stormy grey waters smashing against the sea wall.

'Yeah, it's great, but seen one sea, seen 'em all.' Stevie was deadly serious. He'd like nothing better than for her to make the move to London and share a flat with him, so he could move out of the shoe box; he'd told her often enough.

'You're such a philistine!' Ashleigh couldn't reach the chair he was sitting in; otherwise she'd have given him a dig in the ribs. 'Do you think we should ring Angus and check if we're still on for Chloe's shoot?' The fall-out from Susie-Anne's indiscretions was never far away.

'I guess so.' Stevie curled his long legs underneath him on the chair and closed his eyes. 'I think I'll put it off until tomorrow though, have some more wine and a nice little sleep.' His glass of red was resting precariously on the arm of the chair until the mobile in the pocket of his jeans started to vibrate and he jumped, sending wine in a spray of red that made the flat look like something out of CSI New York.

'Oh shit, sorry honey.' Stevie leapt to his feet, the wine soaking into his jeans. 'It's probably ruined my mobile and your floor.' His phone stopped vibrating and he fished the soggy looking handset out of his pocket.

'Don't worry about the floor, I'll sort it out.' Ashleigh didn't fuss over things like a spilt wine; it was one of the reasons they'd make great flat mates – they were both walking disasters. 'Go and sort your phone, get changed and I'll pour you another drink.'

The kitchen in the flat was quite small, most of the floor space having been given up to the large open plan lounge and dining room with the sea view. Ashleigh was rummaging in the cupboard, where she kept her limited stock of red wine, when the doorbell rang.

'That better not be early trick or treaters or God help them!' In an effort to relax, she'd put on an old pair of PJs and some slippers in the shape of caveman feet, which her little brother had bought the previous Christmas and which she'd never dreamt of wearing before.

'Interesting outfit!' Tom was definitely suppressing a grin and it would have been less of a surprise if the Queen had turned up on the doorstep. 'Am I coming in?'

Considering he'd just had his heart broken, he looked great - wrapped up against the cold in a black sweater and grey jacket with jeans that fitted perfectly and accentuated his lean, muscular legs. Acutely aware of her tatty pyjamas, Ashleigh could do nothing to stop a blush creeping up her neck.

'Yes, come in. Can I get you a drink?' She gripped the new

bottle of red by its neck. Did someone like Tom drink £3.99 supermarket plonk? Probably not.

'I've got to drive back to London so I won't, thanks.' He followed her in to the small galley kitchen, the walls of which were closing in. It was as though he filled every bit of space and Ashleigh was scared to move in case she accidently touched him. 'I'd love a coffee though, if you have some?'

'You'd be forgiven for thinking that I'm an alcoholic, what with answering the door clutching my wine, but I do have coffee.' She moved across to the kettle, trying not to imagine Tom looking at the size of her bum in the hideously unflattering pyjamas. It was getting hotter still.

'Do you want milk?' Please let him say no, otherwise she'd have to reach down to the lowest shelf of the fridge and the bottom waggling would only get worse.

'No thanks, I'll take it black,' Tom leant against the kitchen work surface.

'Can I ask what you're doing here?' Ashleigh was damned if she was going to stand around exchanging pleasantries with someone about to sack her.

'Angus gave me your address,' She tried not to let the surprise show on her face as he spoke. 'I know, I know, it's not the done thing, but actually he was concerned about you. He thought you might be worried that I'd blame you for the Susie-Anne thing, given the fact that the so-called journalist seems to have you as a first-hand source.' He took a sip of the coffee. It must have been scalding hot, but his face didn't flicker as he swallowed. 'Anyway, I told him I had no issue with you and Stevie. I know you weren't part of the deal, just in the wrong place at the wrong time and I don't suppose you were the only ones to have an opinion on our relationship. You were just unlucky enough to be the ones overheard discussing it. You've got form on that front after all!'

'Thank you!' She was so relieved she kissed him on the cheek, the blush back with a vengeance. God, was she 28 or 13? 'Did you really drive all the way down here just to tell me that?' For some reason she was absurdly flattered.

'No.' He smiled nonchalantly, the feeling crushed. 'I was going to ring you, but when I spoke to Angus he told me you lived in Sandgate and I happened to be down the road in Hythe at the time, I thought I'd kill two birds with one stone.' He took another sip of coffee and she wished for about the millionth time that she too could perfect a devil may care expression, instead of constantly turning beetroot with embarrassment. It was just a coincidence that he'd been five minutes away, nothing more. A second before she'd been delirious just to know that she wasn't getting the sack. There was absolutely no reason to be disappointed.

'Why Hythe? Not exactly a well-known celebrity hang out is it?' Desperate to take Tom through to the lounge, Ashleigh was finding their physical proximity incredibly distracting. But the prospect of Stevie marching in naked and announcing that he couldn't get the red wine stain out of his Calvin Kleins was too much of a risk.

'I was visiting my mum. She lives there. Has done since before my father died over ten years ago, but they've always lived in the area.'

'Your mum? I never thought of you as someone who had family.' Oh God, the Tourette's was back, why the hell did she say these things?

'Did you think I was beamed down from Mars then?' There was that half smile at the corners of his mouth again.

'I'm so sorry.' The heat of the blush deepened further, she must look like she'd fallen asleep on a sun-bed by now. 'I just meant, you seem so business-like, I never thought of you like… that.' Digging herself in even deeper, she changed the subject. 'I'm really sorry about Susie-Anne too.'

'I'm not,' Tom turned to look at her. 'At least not about her. It wasn't just the Michael Cox thing. I expect you read all about it, but it turns out she's not even pregnant.' She couldn't read his expression, but there was no need to tell him that she'd been glued to her iPad for half of the day, following the reve-lations as they'd emerged. The beans had been well and truly spilt already. 'Sure, I'm disappointed about the baby, that's why I came down to see mum, to tell her in person that she won't be a grandma after all.' There was a note of resignation in his voice that was at odds with his usual demeanour. There would be plenty of girls out there only too willing to fill Susie-Anne's vacant spot in his bed and provide as many babies as he wanted, but perhaps the hurt was much deeper than he cared to admit.

'Maybe not this time, but I'm sure there's no shortage of girls who'd be happy to oblige.' It was crasser than she'd intended, but it was true; he could take his pick of women and, from what Zac had told her, he probably did.

'It's never been in my game plan.' Tom took another swig of coffee. 'I like my life as it is and so it wasn't something I've even thought about. Maybe the rumours about me are true, that I'm too ambitious for all that.' He gave a wry smile and Ashleigh did her best to feign a look of surprise that such rumours circulated. He paused, as though he was about to say something else, but his phone started to ring, looking at the screen, he ended the call.

'You can take that if you need to.' She didn't know why she said it; it wasn't as though Tom was the sort to ignore an important call out of politeness.

'No, it's nothing that can't wait.' He looked at her for a moment. 'What was I saying?'

'I think you were about to tell me why now and with Susie-Anne?' She just managed to stop herself adding of all people.

'Was I?' He laughed and gave a half-shrug. 'It was, shall we say, a surprise.' Something in his expression changed, another flash of vulnerability. For a long moment he didn't say anything. 'You know maybe I should sack you and give you the chance to find your true vocation.'

'Charming! There are people who actually think I'm quite a good photographer and that I might already have found my vocation.' She attempted indignation, but a slow smile had spread across his face and it was obvious his comments were no slight on her work.

'I'm told you're very good, but I think you might make an even better counsellor or maybe a priest. I don't know what it is about you, but I can't seem to stop telling you things that I wasn't planning to share.'

'So, tell me, how long has it been since your last confession?' She gave him a pious look and he took a deep breath, as if he really was about to confess some terrible sin. His phone rang again, but this time he turned it off.

'It's been far too long, but this isn't really about me.' He paused and took another deep breath, as though trying to control emotions bubbling uncomfortably close to the surface. 'Mum has leukaemia; the doctors say that they can manage it for now, but there's no cure and so it's only a matter of time. I'm an only child, so as far as her chance for a grandchild goes...'

'I'm sorry, I really am. I had no idea.' Almost unconsciously, she reached across and put her hand over his, the space between them disappearing in more ways than one.

'Why should you know? I don't really know why I'm telling you now.' For a second there was that look again; she caught a waft of his aftershave, it was subtle and expensive smelling.

Somehow her fingers had curled around his and, without saying anything, he kissed her. It was gentle and very, very good and she didn't ever want it to stop. Tom pulled away and looked at her, the tension between them palpable.

'I'm sorry, I shouldn't have done that, but I won't lie and say I didn't enjoy it.'

'Oh. Hello! Am I interrupting something?' Suddenly Stevie was framed in the doorway, wearing nothing but his lucky underpants. A familiar heat washed over Ashleigh. Just how much had he'd witnessed?

'Tom kindly came to tell us that we've held on to our jobs… again.' She'd snatched her hand away from his as soon as she'd seen Stevie.

'That's great, thanks mate.' Stevie clapped Tom on the back and appeared completely unfazed by the fact he was only wearing the skimpiest of pants. 'There's more good news too, honey!' He was bouncing with excitement. 'That was Angus on the phone. I called him back and he's given me Zac Starr's new number for you. Apparently his last fiancée has started stalking him, so he had to change his mobile. Angus has a message to pass on from him too. Zac said that the album shoot is yours, as long as you follow through with the shag you promised him!' Stevie threw back his head and laughed, oblivious to the sudden change of atmosphere in the room. 'Now get those hideous slippers off and your glad rags on, I'm taking us out to celebrate! You too, Tom, if you fancy it?' In a whirl Stevie was gone, unaware of the impact he'd had.

'Look, thanks for the coffee, I've got to go.' Tom's voice was clipped, all of the openness between them gone.

'It isn't true you know, I didn't promise Zac anything.' She tried to make eye contact with him, to make him see she was telling the truth, but he didn't look at her.

'It's really none of my business. Zac's a client, but he makes his own decisions. Just do me a favour and try to keep it out of the papers.' He was totally business-like, treating her as though she might give some kiss and tell interview at any moment.

'Thanks for the vote of confidence.' The ruthless Tom, the one she hadn't wanted to like until now, was firmly back in situ. 'You're right though; it really isn't any of your business. I think Zac's probably old enough to make his own decisions.' She couldn't quite believe what she was saying. Normally she went out of her way to avoid confrontation, but she was toughest when people weren't being fair.

'Zac always gets what Zac wants.' There was no trace of a smile as Tom spoke. 'If he wants you, then who am I to stand in his way?' She followed him as he made his way back into the hall.

'What about what I think?' It wasn't too late for him to turn round and apologise, but he opened the door and a blast of night air echoed the newly cool atmosphere.

'Thank Stevie for the offer of the drink. I'll see you both at some point to review the shoot.' Without even shaking her hand, let alone kissing her again, he shut the door behind him, leaving Ashleigh in the mood for anything but celebrating.

'Darling, what a surprise, I didn't think you were coming back again tonight.' Tom's mother was delighted to see him, as though she hadn't seen him for weeks instead of less than an hour before. 'Everything all right?' It was typical of Isobel Rushworth to worry about her only son, even in the midst of her own health crisis, and it was one of the many things he loved about her.

'I'm fine Mum, I just popped in to see a couple of colleagues from work and realised, when I left, that I feel too shattered to drive all the way home tonight,' He smiled. 'You don't mind do you?'

'Well, Bertie and I were planning to settle down on the sofa with some tea and cake and the latest episode of Downton Abbey, but I'm sure we can squeeze one more in.' Bertie was her adoring canine companion. He wagged his tail enthusiastically at the sound of his own name, and gave Tom a look, which said he was welcome to join them as long as he'd brought biscuits.

'Sounds great.' He meant it. If normality and genuine warmth was what he craved, his mother's house was the place to find it. She was the one person who wasn't interested in Tom because of what he could do for her.

'Are you sure you're okay, darling? You've been through a lot this week.' Isobel was already cutting him a huge slice of Victoria sponge; no small portions in her house. 'If you'd rather give Downton a miss, I'll quite happily spend an hour on a character assassination of Susie-Anne…several in fact. For a start, only oompah loompahs should ever be that colour!' Isobel winked, bitching about his ex-fiancée clearly entertaining her even more than her favourite TV show.

'Mum, that's not like you!' Tom laughed. She usually saw the good in everyone but, when push came to shove, she was on his side.

'I read it on a chat site when I Googled her.' There was a

hint of pride in Isobel's voice at having negotiated the vagaries of the Internet. 'And let me tell you, that's extremely mild compared to some of what was written.'

'You should never Google! If you read half of what was written about me it would horrify you.' Tom took a swig of tea and grimaced, his mother was prone to letting it stew and he'd taken cough medicine that was smoother.

'Oh I know, it's hilarious. I found out today that not only are you gay, but you've also had a hair transplant and bum implants!' Isobel laughed heartily. 'I haven't seen anything that funny for ages.'

'Am I going to regret getting you that iPad?' Tom smiled, even as exhaustion flooded his body. 'I can't be bothered to talk about Susie-Anne, she's not worth it.' The dog snuffled around the pocket of Tom's trousers as he spoke, impatient to discover if there were any biscuits on offer. 'At least Bertie makes it perfectly clear that he's only interested in me for the food I might be able to give him. I just wish other people were that honest.'

'Most of them are darling, but if you will go out with someone like Susie-Anne...' Isobel's lip curled as she said the name, 'then I'm afraid they'll always be after whatever is in your pocket.' Tom laughed again, an image of his ex-fiancée's none too subtle approach to flirtation flitting through his mind. Pocket snuffling might well be one way to describe it. His mother was right, Susie-Anne had been just as persistent as Bertie, only she'd been hungry for fame and didn't care what she had to do to get it. What worried him most was that he cared so little about losing the family he'd envisaged. Was he doomed to repeat his father's mistakes? As if reading his mind, Isobel put down her tea.

'The upside is that your lifestyle must have your father turning in his grave, so it isn't all bad.' She smiled, even after all these years it clearly gave her pleasure to rebel against her husband. 'But next time, just try to make sure your girlfriend stands a slim chance of beating Bertie at Scrabble.'

'You're right, I have had more interesting conversations with the dog and, despite his inclination to mate the odd visitor's leg, he's a lot more faithful!' As he spoke, Isobel snorted with laughter. He'd brought Susie-Anne down to see her a couple of times and to say they hadn't hit it off was an understatement.

It wasn't the Susie-Anne situation that was bothering him, but he didn't want to talk about Ashleigh. His feelings towards her were too confused. Why should he care if she was just another wannabe, willing to sleep with anyone who could advance her career? The last thing he wanted was his mother latching on to the name and planning a nice spring wedding in her fevered imagination.

'You just need to find yourself a nice girl.' Isobel patted his arm and he fought the urge to sigh. It was only ever a matter of time before she offered up this solution to all his problems. She'd so wanted to see him settled, he knew that, and the prospect of a grandchild had been enough to make them both look past Susie-Anne's obvious shortcomings. They both knew the clock was ticking for her and he'd been more than willing to sacrifice his own feelings to make his mother happy.

'It's a shame then that you were the last nice girl left.' He kissed her cheek, the compliment aimed at knocking her off track.

'If only the people who think you're a heartless workaholic could see you now, my caring boy.' There was a note of melancholy in his mother's voice. 'Although I don't suppose you want that do you? And plenty of girls on those websites seem to like the fact you've got the reputation of being tough.'

'I don't care what anyone thinks. When I sold the business to start the agency, I promised I'd follow Dad's example and I have.' Tom didn't miss the look of horror that crossed Isobel's face as he spoke. 'When it comes to business, I learnt from the best. Dad put it first and he was immoveable in getting what he wanted, that's why he was such a success. You know that as well as I do.'

'Yes, but look at the rest of his life.' She was still worried. 'Surely you don't want to replicate that too?'

'A personal life's just not a priority, that's all. Maybe I'm more like dad than either of us wants to admit. It's as though I still need his approval and I can get that by making the business a success, by putting it first. Although, Christ knows why I want his approval now he's dead, I certainly never got it when he was alive.' He took her hand. His words were obviously upsetting her, but he wanted her to understand that he wasn't missing out on anything, despite what she might think. 'In any case, if I let my guard down people would just try to take advantage. I can't let anyone know that at least a little bit of me comes from you.' He smiled, relieved that she was smiling too.

'I hope that bit of you takes over one day, I really do. I feel so guilty about the example we set you, but at least I've known love and I just want you to know it too.' She hugged him and he was suddenly aware how fragile she was, how much weight she'd lost. 'You know I only want to see you happy.'

'I know, Mum. Come on, let's hit the sofa and watch Downton.' It would be nice to immerse himself for an hour in a time when no-one had heard of reality TV and the only over-stuffed breasts on display would be presented on a silver platter. Not that he'd put that past Susie-Anne, if she thought it would get her on the front page of the paper. Trying not to think about Ashleigh, and whether she was telling the truth about Zac, Tom took another mouthful of the well-stewed tea. How had he got so old and cynical? Half his clients would be heading out to be seen in whatever club had the highest profile but he couldn't think of anything worse.

Chapter Seven

Sandgate in late October wasn't the most wild of towns and there were no high profile clubs to frequent, but Stevie was a one man Mardi Gras. They headed to Aubrey's, a wine bar on the seafront complete with dance floor and 70s throwback disco ball, liberally decked out with Halloween decorations for the annual party, which was just twenty-four hours away. He didn't seem to notice that Ashleigh wasn't as excited as she should be about sealing the deal to photograph Zac's album cover and, thank goodness, she'd managed to brush him off when he'd asked about Tom.

'He was in Hythe, so he thought it would be a good opportunity to talk me through the details of the shoot.' Ashleigh swallowed hard; she didn't want to think too much about the side of Tom he'd revealed to her during the few minutes they'd been alone in her kitchen.

'Did he seem upset about the Susie-Anne stuff?' Stevie poured two glasses from the huge pitcher of virgin mojitos he'd ordered, when Ashleigh had insisted that she couldn't face any more alcohol, and put the cocktail umbrella jauntily behind one ear.

'He didn't say much.' Ashleigh hated not being straight with Stevie, but if she told him what had happened she might end up telling him about the kiss. He'd never let that go and, since there was hardly likely ever to be a repeat, it seemed pointless even telling him. 'You know how Tom is. Very… business-like.'

'And hot,' Stevie grinned. 'You know, I've never really been in to the alpha male type before, but there's definitely something about our new boss that makes me want to rip off his cable knit sweater and see what's underneath.'

The group sitting in the booth behind them snorted with laughter and a chinless, pasty-faced guy in a wax jacket mumbled something about not realising it was *'poof's night'*. His three companions laughed loudly in response, as if he was some sort of wit rather than the complete arse he really was. Stevie, never one for discreet conversation, was his usual loud and proud self. Turning round to the two couples, who were clearly finding Stevie and Ashleigh's conversation far more interesting than their own, he leaned conspiratorially over the back of the partition separating the two booths.

'Trust me darling.' He addressed the girl sitting next to wax jacket man. 'You'd dump your bloke for our boss any day and, come to that, your bloke would definitely dump you for Tom. For a start he's got less facial hair. The fancy dress party's not until tomorrow, sweetheart, but you'll definitely pass for Chewbacca no bother.' Leaving them open-mouthed, Stevie knocked back the rest of his drink and pulled Ashleigh on to the dance floor.

'Don't let those idiots wind you up.' She was shouting over the music, but Stevie couldn't have looked less bothered.

'Oh honey, I couldn't give a toss about them.' Stevie was pulling some moves probably never witnessed before in a little seaside town. 'I really wanted *you* to have a great time tonight, to celebrate, but you seem on edge.'

'I'm sorry. I know I'm being boring, but I think I'd rather go home.' She should have realised that she couldn't really hide anything from him. He'd seen her through the messy break up with Liam and others before him. They'd been there for each other for the past ten years. She'd have to tell him something to explain why Tom's reaction had upset her so much, she just wasn't sure what.

'Come on then honey. Let's be boring old farts. I'll make us both a cup of tea and you can tell me what's really up.' Stevie disappeared into the kitchen as soon as they got back to the flat. From the window in the front room, the lights from five or six ships moored a few miles off the coast were visible in the otherwise inky black marriage of sea and sky.

'Spill it then.' Ashleigh jumped as he spoke. 'I know something isn't right. You should be dancing on the ceiling and you look like you've stepped in dog poo.'

'I think I annoyed Tom again, with the whole Zac Starr thing.' She swallowed a mouthful of tea he'd brought in, hoping it would push down the lump in her throat.

'He's just that sort. Mean and moody. He probably seems permanently naffed off, it's part of his charm.' Stevie put a biscuit in his mouth. He should have been twice the size given his penchant for biscuits, booze and Cornish pasties. 'Anyway, if the Zac thing works out, you won't need to worry about Tom anymore. You more or less said that *Glitz* is holding you back.' He dunked another biscuit in his tea and half of it broke off as he lifted it out, plopping loudly into the cup and sending tea and bits of wet biscuit all over the place.

'Yeah, but then I'd miss out on spending all my time with a sophisticate like you!'

'Don't change the subject. There's more to it than that isn't there?' He cocked his head to one side, his fringe flopping into his eyes, which he narrowed in the style of a maverick cop. 'You like him, don't you?' Stevie was bouncing with all the energy of Tigger on speed. 'Tom and Ashleigh sitting in the tree, K. I. S. S. I. N. G.!'

'Shut up! What are you? Twelve?' Ashleigh grabbed the cushion from behind her on the chair, not sure whether to hurl it at him or to cover the blush that was creeping up her neck. So Stevie could read her like a book; that didn't mean she had to fuel his adolescent hysterics. 'It's not that, I don't like the idea of him thinking I'd sleep with Zac just to get a job, that's all.'

'Yeah, of course, honey, it's just your professionalism speaking!' He smirked, ducking out of the way as she went with her impulse and decided to hurl the cushion at him. This wasn't good, though, she'd left crushes like this behind in the days of Bunsen burners and navy-blue gym knickers. If she didn't admit it to Stevie, maybe she could get away with it, if her face didn't give up the game first. The curse of the blush had haunted her since year nine when someone on the school bus had suggested that she had the hots for Mr Aspen, the biology teacher. Just because she'd offered to take the locusts home in the summer holidays. There was something creepily fascinating about them and the fact that Mr Aspen was a nice looking newly qualified teacher, at least 20 years younger than any of the other male staff, really had nothing to do with it. She'd tried to laugh it off, but a blush had taken hold and so she'd spent her final two years at school being taunted with the moniker 'Ashleigh Aspen'.

'You're always telling me I worry too much about what other people think, so I don't know why you're finding it so hard to believe.' She raised an eyebrow, daring him to deny it. Somehow she had to get Stevie off the scent and talk some sense into herself, before it was too late.

'If that's really all it is then stop worrying. I don't suppose he even cares about you and Zac,' Stevie winked. 'Although never say never, he might well fancy the variety of a woman with flaws and unregulated lumpy bits one of these days.'

'Well thanks!' She was laughing, though, off the hook. Now she could just forget it had ever happened, accept that she'd blown things out of proportion - made too much of the kiss and how it had made her feel. Most of the time she didn't even like Tom much. Next time she saw him there'd probably be nothing there, she was pretty much banking on it.

Chapter Eight

If seeing the guy who means nothing to you photographed arm in arm with another woman, two days after you've kissed him, makes you feel like you've been punched in the stomach by a heavyweight boxing champ, it probably means that you do quite like him, doesn't it? Ashleigh was forced to face up to it. Obviously the kiss had meant nothing to Tom, judging by his closeness to the doe-eyed blonde he'd been pictured with the next evening, splashed all over the late editions of the morning papers. But her reaction to seeing those pictures when she picked up a copy of one of the tabloids in the shopthe corner shop was proof enough that, if this was just a crush, then it knocked the one she'd had for Mr Aspen out of the park.

'Shall we go up and see her then?' Ashleigh spoke with her mouthful, as she emerged from the shop, already halfway through the packet of Rolos she'd bought as a direct result of seeing Tom's picture in the gossip section of the paper. She wished her occupation hadn't brainwashed her into automatically turning to that section of the tabloids first.

'Of course honey. You know I love Carol, she's always great for a laugh, but then she's not my mum.' Stevie winked. 'Looks like she's already driven you to chocolate and it's only ten o'clock.' Stevie got up from the bench outside the shop, where he'd been waiting and sneaking a quick cigarette.

'Always best to line your stomach before taking my mother on. She'll probably have made one of her organic chickpea concoctions that she'll want us to try. I swear to God that you could render a house with her homemade houmous.' She was happy to hide the real reason for her chocolate binge from Stevie.

The walk up to her mum's house on the cliff top always reminded Ashleigh how unfit she was. Half way up she and Stevie stopped and lent against the flint wall running around the perimeter of one of the neighbouring properties. Admittedly, her high heeled boots and woollen dress wasn't the most suitable of attire for a hill climb, but it was marginally more appropriate than Stevie's sequinned T-Shirt, paired with a tuxedo jacket and the obligatory skinny jeans.

'Nice arse darlin'.' The comment was shouted from the window of a red transit van and its originator had disappeared by the time they swung round to hear who'd said it.

'Whoa, do you think that was meant for you or me?' Stevie lifted his jacket slightly and wiggled his bottom, Beyoncé style.

'Yep definitely you!' She grinned. It might be totally against any feminist principle, but sometimes a random comment like that could make your day. Okay, so maybe Tom was right now in the arms of a gorgeous blonde, but the plumber fixing the boiler at number 32 had told her she had a nice arse. Unless of course he *had* meant Stevie. Although, in truth, they both knew his bum was virtually non-existent.

'Sweethearts, how lovely to see you both.' Carol enveloped them in an embrace, tangling Ashleigh's hair up with the rows of plaited bracelets she wore on each wrist. She smelt a bit like flowers and not the freshly picked kind, more like the aroma you get when flowers are ready to be moved from the vase to the compost heap.

'Mum. What's that smell?' Ashleigh managed to detangle herself from the bracelets and took a step back.

'Do you like it? It's my new perfume, I made it myself. It's full of pheromones.' Carol was obviously quite proud of her endeavour and Ashleigh silently prayed that she wouldn't be offered a bottle of the scent or, worse still, find one wrapped up for her under the tree come Christmas with the expectation that she should dab it on then and there. If it was full of pheromones, God only knew what was in it. Ashleigh just hoped it wasn't bodily fluids.

'So Carol, what's with the Nativity scene? Bit early isn't it?' Stevie took a sip of the disgusting rosehip tea, another home-made delicacy that had immediately been thrust into his hand. Ashleigh, who had tasted it before, artfully left her cup on the window sill.

'Well my love, I had to start early, it's a work in progress after all.' She'd ushered them through to the conservatory, which was really more of a lean-to and ran the length of the back of the house. From their position they could see the nativity scene in all its glory. Carol's artistic capabilities were probably on a par with her perfume blending skills. The head of the baby Jesus was at least twice the size of his mother Mary's and, in turn, she had been given thick spidery eyelashes that a drag queen might have written off as OTT. Never mind upsetting people of other faiths, Ashleigh couldn't help thinking that any Christian happening upon the scene would have far more cause to be offended.

'What else are you planning to do to it?' She barely dared ask. It was at least twelve feet high and the paint that her mother had chosen looked so lurid that she wondered whether it glowed in the dark.

'I'm thinking of putting some lights through holes in parts of the scene, but I need Geoffrey to use that puzzle-saw-thing-amajig of his to do it.' Carol wrinkled her nose. 'Have I got that right or is it a jigsaw? Anyway, he needs to cut the bits out before I can put the lights in.'

'Where exactly are you putting these lights?' The look on Stevie's face suggested he had no idea what was coming; unlike Ashleigh, who was only too aware that the chances of it simply being the star above the stable would be a given for anyone but her mum.

'I thought perhaps Mary's breasts.' Carol spoke without a hint of irony and Stevie looked like he was about to spit out his mouthful of rosehip tea.

'Mum you can't!' As much as Ashleigh was used to her mother's eccentricities, this was too much even for her.

'Why ever not? Breast milk is the giver of life darling and a woman's breasts should be lit up. Not just for a man's pleasure, although that can be divine too of course! I breast fed both my children until they were three you know?' Carol addressed Stevie, who was unable to hold back any longer and burst out laughing, almost choking on the revolting tea in the process.

'Mum, for God's sake! And you wonder why I never bring any boyfriends to meet you?' She pitied her little brother and her step dad, Geoffrey, being with Carol all of the time.

'So, is that why you never bring any of your boyfriends to meet me? I just thought you weren't getting any and that's why you're so snappy all the time. Sex is a fantastic stress reliever you know darling. You should try it! It's been over a year since you split up with Liam and I only ever see you with Stevie.' Carol leant across the table and squeezed his hand. 'Not that I don't love seeing you my darling.'

'There hasn't been anyone special enough to bring home, Mum. That's all.' Or anyone at all for that matter and, if there was anyone special, Ashleigh certainly wouldn't be racing to introduce him to Carol.

'Well, there is someone.' Stevie who had been idly flicking through the papers, in between choking on his tea, had happened across the picture of Tom and the mystery blonde. He clearly wasn't ready to let his theory about her attraction to their new boss go. 'This is Tom.'

'Ooh darling, what a hunk!' Carol grabbed the proffered paper from Stevie and squinted at the picture. 'Yes, he's definitely dishy!' She was probably the one woman left in the world who'd describe a man as 'dishy'.

'Don't get excited Mother.' Ashleigh struggled to look nonchalant, vowing to kill Stevie later. 'He's just our new boss, but that's Stevie's idea of a joke. Anyway it's obvious from the picture he's got a girlfriend.'

'And I thought you were a hip girl about town!' The time warp that was her mother's vocabulary never ceased to amaze. 'Don't you know who that is?' Ashleigh shook her head.

'It's Selly Medley. They say she's the new Germaine Greer and what's more she's just come out as a lesbian.' Ashleigh could have hugged her mother and would have done if she could have faced another embrace enveloped in Eau de Compost.

'Have you gone red, honey?' Stevie laughed. Although he

seemed to have realised that now wasn't the time to embarrass her further.

'No, I haven't!' She shot him a look she hoped would make it clear that it was definitely time to shut up. 'Where's Jamie? Out with his mates?' Ashleigh had been hoping to see her brother and was grateful of the chance to change the subject.

'Geoffrey's taken him to drama practice. He's going to play the lead in the Christmas show. You must come down for it, Jamie would love to see us out in force.' Carol had that scary animated look she always got when she was planning something. Ashleigh didn't know what it was, but she could bet that it was almost guaranteed to embarrass her little brother and probably her as well.

'I didn't even know he was in to all that sort of stuff?' Jamie was almost thirteen. The last time she'd seen him, he'd been waiting for the school bus and mooning over one of the girls, who was about the same age as him but didn't seem to realise he existed. Oh, she remembered that feeling well. Please don't say unrequited love was back to haunt her again in the shape of Tom Rushworth.

'Well I for one would love to come.' Stevie was genuinely enthusiastic. He'd always been fond of Jamie, who'd been just a toddler when they'd first met.

'Let us have the date and we'll be there.' She risked the Eau de Compost again and kissed her mother on the cheek. 'We've got to get back to London. There's a big shoot tomorrow with that girl who won that TV talent show last year.'

'That's not really my thing darling. Much as I adore the gossip pages, I never waste my time on reality TV stars.' Carol squeezed her hand. 'I prefer real singers, like Bob Dylan or Simon and Garfunkel, but I'm sure it'll be great.'

Ashleigh sometimes wondered how she'd ended up spending most of her working life hanging out with celebrities, when she'd been brought up in a house where lentils and mung beans were more revered than movie stars and she'd been the only person she knew whose family still had a black and white TV.

Chapter Nine

Chloe Nicholas was even more delicate and doll-like in person than she appeared to be on screen, but she had a huge voice that had won a legion of devoted supporters and some of her biggest fans were from the older generation. A week before the launch of her first album it had all hit the fan. Her childhood sweetheart had come forward, told all about the unwanted pregnancy that had almost put an end to Chloe's dreams when she was still at school. The papers must have paid him well for the amount of dirt he'd dished. The tearful last minute change of heart at the abortion clinic. The last goodbyes to baby Holly as the social workers took her away to a new family. The headlines screamed 'SINGING SENSATION DECEIVES PUBLIC. VOICE OF AN ANGEL OR GYMSLIP MUM?' and in that instant it looked like her promising career was over. Which it might have been if *Rushworth Associates* and *Glitz* hadn't stepped in. Now Ashleigh and Stevie were at the offices of Chloe's record company, which occupied every floor of a Georgian town house.

'Thank you so much for coming.' Chloe's voice was barely more than a whisper and her cheeks were pale; puffy red eyes indicative of sleepless nights and plenty of tears.

A team of make-up artists from *Glitz* buzzed around, trying to undo the damage that the recent revelations had done to her appearance. Chloe had insisted on having her own hairdresser though. Her mother.

'No problem, we were really pleased to get the assignment.' Ashleigh said and smiled, as a fresh crop of tears threatened Chloe's baby blue eyes.

'What are the chances of this working do you think?' It was as though Chloe couldn't look anyone in the eye. 'You know, to make the public and press like me again, instead of hating me?' She bit her lip, looking more like a frightened twelve year old than a pop sensation.

'I don't think anyone hates you.' Ashleigh crouched down at the side of Chloe's chair and laid a reassuring hand on her arm. 'And if they hate you for this, then that makes their opinion worth less than nothing anyway.'

'Arseholes!' Gilly was just as small in stature, but her body language bristled with more fight than her daughter's. 'Don't suppose any of them have done anything they regret, have they?' She spoke out of the corner of her mouth, whilst clamping hairgrips between her teeth and teasing Chloe's hair into a Grecian style up-do.

'Jesus! Regrets?' Stevie was incredulous. 'Sweetheart, anyone who hasn't got a regret, hasn't had a life.' He began sweeping through the outfits hung on the metal rail in Chloe's dressing room, loudly dismissing each one in turn. 'I've got this all wrong. I picked these for the remit *Glitz* gave me but now that I'm here none of the ideas I had seem to fit like I thought they would. No, it won't do.' Stevie exchanged a look with Ashleigh. Tom's brief for the photo-shoot had been that Chloe should look demure, but it seemed neither of them were convinced that the public would buy into it. They'd see it as fake. Chloe had been outed as a mature woman, with a past and flaws, just like everyone else, and pretending to be anything less just wouldn't wash.

'What do you have in mind?' Chloe eyes darted nervously between them and Ashleigh crossed her fingers that Stevie wouldn't suggest hot pants and a feather boa; no-one was ready for quite that level of image change.

'Look this isn't protocol, to completely change everything at the last minute, but I've got an idea. I'll need to source an outfit, but, as luck would have it, I think I know just the place.' He dropped one of his trademark lazy winks. 'Just give me ten minutes and I'll be back.'

'Are you going to let me in on this secret?' The whole focus of the shoot could change with Stevie's choice of outfit. 'I need to set stuff up, brief the make-up artists and Gilly, is this going to work best inside or out?'

'Non je ne regrette rien.' With another wink he was gone. Sometimes she could kill him. It was lucky she knew him as well as she did – and this might just work.

'Sorry Gilly, I think we might need to change the hair.' Ashleigh smiled apologetically. 'Tell me, how do you feel about Edith Piaf?'

True to his word, Stevie was back ten minutes later. With a dress draped over his arm and a victorious look spread across his unfeasibly handsome face.

'Where on earth did you get that? It's gorgeous.' Ashleigh touched the delicate lace overlay of the bateau necked black dress. With its ribbon detail at the waist and full skirt, it was perfect.

'You know that little dress agency around the corner, Clothes Line?' Stevie raised his eyebrows in question and Ashleigh nodded. She ought to know; he'd dragged her in there enough times. 'I hoped they might have something suitable, but they've outdone themselves with this.'

Gilly had restyled Chloe's inky black hair into the loose ringlets worn by 1930s singing icon, Piaf, and a slick of crimson lipstick perfected the look. They'd decided not to go for the legendary arched-to-within-an-inch-of-their-life eyebrows, but all in all the look was effective. Looking as fragile and half-starved as any artist in a Parisian garret, Chloe's vulnerability screamed from every pore. It was just down to Ashleigh to capture it as effectively on camera. No pressure then.

Two hours later she'd done it. Critical as she was of her own work, Ashleigh couldn't help feeling pleased.

'They don't look like me.' Chloe's voice was quieter than ever as she viewed the photos that Ashleigh had uploaded to her laptop. It was hard to believe that someone who spoke so softly, as if a gust of wind might snap her in two, could hit notes that even Adele might balk at.

'Don't you like them?' Ashleigh bit her lip. They'd taken a risk. Gone against Tom's advice and taken Chloe out of her comfort zone. Perhaps, subconsciously, they actually wanted to be unemployed.

'I love them!' Chloe threw her slender arms around Ashleigh. Stevie had disappeared somewhere; probably back to Clothes Line now that he'd hit a vintage jackpot. 'I can't believe I look so…'

'Grown up? Like a woman who's been through stuff?' Gilly interjected, wiping a tear away. 'I've heard that saying about a picture painting a thousand words, but I never thought it was true before.'

'We lost Dad, you see, when I was twelve.' Chloe slipped an arm around her mother's waist. 'When he died, it was unexpected and he didn't really have a back-up plan, so we ended up losing the house as well.' There wasn't a trace of self-pity in her voice, but Ashleigh understood more than Chloe could ever imagine.

'I was worse than useless.' Gilly shook her head when Chloe tried to protest. 'No, I really was. I was so wrapped up in my own self-pity that I couldn't see how much Chloe needed me. So she turned to friends, one boy in particular and one thing led to another.' Gilly was crying now. 'I didn't even know she was pregnant until close to the end. She went through all that alone, the abortion clinic. If I'd been there, if I'd been well, perhaps she'd have felt she had other options and we might have had Holly with us now.'

'Mum, don't.' Chloe hugged her. 'You've more than made up for it since. We did the right thing and one day maybe we'll get the chance to tell Holly why. Tell her that we're both survivors and I for one am not going to feel ashamed anymore.'

'Nor should you.' Tears stung Ashleigh's eyes. As quirky as her own mother was, Carol had always been there. No wonder Chloe looked so vulnerable. 'Are you okay for me to share these photos with Angus? He wants to select the final choices for release. If you can pre-approve that would be great.

'I love them all, but especially this one.' Chloe pointed to a reportage style image where Ashleigh had captured Gilly adjusting her daughter's hair. They were smiling at some shared comment, the warmth between them tangible. 'I know *Glitz* probably won't want to use it for anything, but I'd love a copy if that's okay?'

Ashleigh nodded and silently prayed that there were some photos from the shoot that the magazine would want to use. They undoubtedly looked their best in black and white, but *Glitz* was all about colour and bling. It was quite possible that not everyone was going to be as delighted with the results.

Isobel plonked the box file on Tom's desk and sat in the chair opposite. She was in London for a check-up at the Royal Marsden and he'd sent his head of security, Shaun, down to Hythe to pick her up, whilst he'd met with Angus about the proofs from Chloe's shoot.

'You shouldn't be carrying heavy stuff like that. Why didn't you get Shaun to do it?' Tom's attempts to protect her had evidently fallen on deaf ears.

'I'm not dead yet you know! Aren't you going to ask what it is?' She was shifting from side to side in her seat, like an excited child waiting for a present to be opened.

'I'm almost afraid to.' Tom lifted the lid, a knot forming in his chest at the sight of the picture lying on top of the pile of papers.

'It's your father's memory box.' His mother was turning the words over carefully, as if trying to make sense of them herself. 'Who knew?'

'Where on earth did you find this?' Tom couldn't move past the first picture. It was a Polaroid of him with his father, with that typically orange tinge that a lot of photos from the late seventies seemed to have. But it was nothing like the family photos that had been on display in his childhood. The stiff, posed formality, which mirrored the relationship he'd had with his father, had been carefully framed and hung on the walls. This slightly fuzzy image had been kept out of sight and it told a different story all together.

'It was up in the loft.' Isobel raised her hand as he began to protest. 'I know what you're going to say about me going up there, but what's the worst that can happen? It's not like it will rob me of years!'

'Mum, don't. You know I'm more than happy to come down and do any jobs like that or arrange for one of the staff to do it.' He picked up the photo, if he didn't know better he would have sworn it had been photo-shopped. 'Is that really me?'

'Well, who else's baby do you think he's got cradled on his chest?' Her tone was reasonable, but she must have been just as shocked when she first saw the photograph.

'But he's actually cuddling me and he looks…' Tom struggled to find the word that was so alien when talking about his father, '…happy.'

'I think your Aunt Hilary must have taken it when she was visiting. I remember her having one of those instant camera thingies, but it's too late to ask her of course.' His mother sighed. Aunt Hilary had died the year before, so any chance of finding out more had died with her.

'Do you ever remember him holding me like that? Looking at me like that?' Tom still couldn't get his head around it.

'No, but I always knew he loved you in his own way. That's what everything was about. He wanted to provide the big house for us, give us financial security. He just couldn't give us what we really needed; you know - affection, fun, his time, that sort of thing.' She smiled ruefully. 'But maybe this memory box shows that deep down he wanted to, but just didn't know how. I know one thing though, I've never felt as fond of him as I do right now.'

'What else is in here?' Tom finally set the photograph to one side and started to shift the papers, each new item in the memory box surprising him more.

'There's copies of your school reports, a postcard you sent us from a school trip and he must have kept the certificate you won in that spelling bee. There's a cutting from the paper when you raised all that money with the scouts and there's even one of your baby teeth in there.'

'I really don't know what to say. If he did love me, he had a very strange way of showing it.' It was incredible that the man who'd kept his son at arm's length, right up until his death, had secretly been proud of him. 'Are you sure these aren't things Aunt Hilary kept?'

'Positive. The box was with all the other things cleared out of his office and stored up there after he died. I thought we might need to look at some of it when we sold the business, but we never did, and it's been sitting up there gathering dust ever since,' Isobel paused. 'Anyway, I thought you should have it, in case it helped you to see things…differently.'

Tom said nothing. A box of keepsakes couldn't undo thirty-five years of feeling the way he had. He wouldn't put it past his mother to have put the box together herself, if she thought it would help him to change his outlook. Although she couldn't have faked the photograph, that was something else.

'Well I'll let you think it over and what it might mean.' Isobel smiled and shut the lid, pushing it to one side of the desk and revealing the proofs of the Chloe Nicholas shoot. 'Goodness, these are stunning.'

'They are, aren't they?' Tom seized the chance to change the subject.

'Who took them? They look much classier than the normal

photos in *Glitz*.'

'Thanks a lot!' Tom laughed, although he secretly agreed. 'The photographer was Ashleigh Hayes.'

'He's a genius, he's captured something of that girl that I bet even she didn't know she had.' Isobel scrutinised the photographs. 'Fabulous styling too.'

'I'm glad you approve, but that was down to Stevie.' His mother had always loved fashion and was still immaculately turned-out, even when she was only walking Bertie. 'They're a good team, Ashleigh and Stevie, but Ashleigh's a she not a he.' As soon as he'd said it, he realised he'd given her an opportunity to get started on her favourite subject.

'Is she pretty?' Isobel might be ill, but she didn't miss a trick.

'Very, but she's a lesbian.' The words were out of his mouth before his brain even registered what he was doing. Still it had worked well enough in putting his mother off her stroke when she'd got excited over the photos of him with Selly Medley.

'Oh, not another one.' She looked a little crestfallen. 'What about Stevie? I'd have plenty to talk about with a stylist over Sunday lunches.'

'Unfortunately, Stevie's a man and, despite what you've read on Google, he's not my type.' Tom laughed again, it was like a game of chess discussing his love life with his mother and that had to be double checkmate. 'But despite not being fodder for your matchmaking, I agree that they've pulled a genius stroke here. You can tell they've been together years.'

'Gosh, I'm getting confused now. So Ashleigh's bi-sexual. How interesting, that might keep you on your toes!'

'Mum! Where do you come up with these things?' Was there any line she wouldn't cross to see him paired up?

'Oh Tom, don't act so shocked. Your generation think they

invented sexual experimentation. Well, they didn't!'

'Enough, I can't listen to any more.' Tom held up a hand. There were some things you should never discuss with your mother. 'Anyway, just to clarify, she's not.'

'What bisexual or a lesbian?' Isobel fixed him with a steely stare. 'You better not be lying to me Thomas, just to shut me up.'

'Okay, okay, you've got me, but there are only so many times we can have the same conversation.'

'I'm not expecting you to get married and produce an instant grandchild, so you can take that look off your face, but I would like to see you have some fun.' As she spoke, she stood up and moved round to his side of the desk, placing a hand on his shoulder. 'And handsome and irresistible as your old mum believes you to be, not every girl out there is desperate to marry you.'

'Maybe if you stopped trying to marry me off to every girl I get photographed with, or brush past on the tube, I wouldn't have become such a paranoid ego-maniac.' He caught another glimpse of the proofs as he spoke. Ashleigh had captured something unique about Chloe; she had a real gift. Maybe his mother was right, it was time to take his head out of his arse and have some fun.

Chapter Ten

Four weeks after Chloe's photo-shoot, at the end of November, the issue of *Glitz* carrying her interview had hit the shops and Ashleigh was in Tom's office, about to find out how the change of theme for the shoot had really gone down.

'Can't the two of you ever just do what you're asked?' Tom stood with his back to her, a note of exasperation in his voice.

'I think they work.' Ashleigh was on the defensive. It was a chain reaction; get treated like a truculent teenager and you start to act like one.

'Luckily for you they do, circulation's up 120 per cent, but it would have been nice to have been consulted.' Tom turned to face her, his eyes meeting hers briefly. Her stomach did a weird sort of dip, like when you go over a humped-back bridge too fast. 'Where is your partner in crime anyway?'

'Looking at some wedding dresses by a new designer in Camden.' Ashleigh watched an unreadable expression cross Tom's face.

'Anything I should know about?' He seemed to visibly relax all of a sudden. 'Mavericks that you are, I don't want to wake up tomorrow to read in the papers that Stevie's helped Ryan

Murray come out as a transvestite and styled him in a vintage wedding dress just to make the point.' They both laughed. Ryan Murray was a reality TV star. A walking, talking, wall of testosterone and there'd never been a wedding dress made that could take the strain of stretching across his sixty inch chest.

'I don't think even Stevie would go that far.' She crossed her fingers underneath the desk so that Tom couldn't see.

'Mmm,' Raising an eyebrow, he looked doubtful. 'In that case, would you like to have lunch?'

'What me? Here?' She couldn't have been more shocked if Ryan Murray *had* turned out to be a wedding-gown wearing cross-dresser. Tom had his nice head on again. Good job he wasn't always like this; that would be dangerous.

'Yes, you. But, no, not here.' Tom was struggling to suppress a grin. 'How about *Grant's*?'

She nodded, still shocked at the invitation, when she'd expected a lecture about sticking to the brief. *Grant's* was a wine bar around the corner from *Rushworth Associates*. It had a laid back atmosphere, didn't try too hard to be trendy and the Spanish chef created tapas to die for. And, what's more, Tom was taking her there for lunch.

Ashleigh disappeared into the cloakroom of the restaurant as soon as they arrived, muttering something about the November weather playing havoc with her hair and telling him to go ahead without her.

Tom had no problem getting a table, even without a booking. Making a living from sorting out celebrities' lives had its downsides, but it opened a lot of doors too. He ordered a bottle of red wine and waited. The restaurant clientele were almost all trying to get noticed, one way or another. The women were well dressed in the main, although there were more than enough who were willing to wear a lot less to stand out from the crowd.

Ashleigh walked across the restaurant towards him; her red silk dress and knee-high boots were elegant and understated. Funny how tantalising a knee could be, when you were surrounded on all sides by women literally spilling out of their clothes. She was looking down at her feet, as though she wasn't worthy of making eye contact with the other diners. There was something incredibly sexy about her complete lack of ego. He was definitely up for having some fun, but there was no way of knowing if she was too. There was only one way to find out.

&

'So, how have you been?' Ashleigh fidgeted in her seat, a large glass of red wine taking the edge off the nerves that always seemed to come from sharing a space with Tom.

'What, apart from having a stylist and photographer who can't seem to follow simple instructions?' He was smiling though. 'I'm fine. To be honest, for the most part it's a relief. Susie-Anne isn't the most relaxing of people to be around.'

'Really?' Ashleigh feigned surprise. 'And there was me thinking she was low maintenance.'

'Talking of relationships. How's it going with Zac?' Tom kept his tone light, but there was an almost indistinguishable tightening of his jaw.

'It isn't.' Suddenly it was really important that he knew there was nothing going on. 'It never was. Of course I'm excited to be shooting his album cover and we've met up once or twice to discuss his ideas, but that's it. We're not…'

'Having sex?' He cut in. The thought clearly bothered him, although she couldn't understand why. Maybe he thought she'd be bad for Zac's image.

'I was going to say compatible.' Ashleigh grinned and tore off a hunk of bread. 'I don't think I'm really his type.'

'Somehow I doubt that.' Tom's voice was warm and, if it had been anyone else, she might have read something into the way he was looking at her. 'Has Zac even got a type? I don't recall any of his fiancées bearing a striking resemblance to one another. Although if he goes on much longer, he's bound to go full-circle eventually. Did it disappoint you?' He topped up their wine glasses. 'That you weren't his type, I mean?'

'No. Although given the fact that most women in my age bracket seem to have been engaged to Zac, perhaps I should be offended!' She raked a hand through her hair. Now wasn't the time to mention how Zac's hands always seemed to wander when they met up. Given the slightest inclination of interest, she could quite easily become Zac's type, for one night at least.

'I think you might challenge him too much. Conversation hasn't been top of his agenda in the past.' Tom didn't miss a beat; he must have known what she was thinking. After all, Susie-Anne wasn't exactly a noted raconteur.

They fell silent while the waiter laid the tapas out in front of them. The ambience of *Grant's*, and the warmth of the red wine, was starting to work its magic. She was less scared she might say the wrong thing and cause Tom to give her one of his infamous looks. He had an aura of power and there was no denying it was sexy, but, when he also had the power to decide whether or not you could make your mortgage payments, it was pretty scary too.

'Sorry!' She laughed awkwardly as their hands brushed reaching for the same plate of prawns. If it had happened before the wine, she'd have snatched her hand away and flushed to match the Spanish tomatoes on her plate.

'I'm not.' He laid his hand over hers and she didn't move away. They'd already kissed for heaven's sake; that ought to count for something. So why did she feel so much like a teenager on her first date?

'Is this a good idea?' Ashleigh spoke quietly, afraid of how he might respond. She couldn't drag her eyes away from his lips, suddenly wanting to relive that kiss more than anything.

'I don't know, but I don't care either. We're both adults and I need to be honest with you.' He waited until she made eye contact. 'If you're going into this thinking it might be love, then I have to tell you that I don't believe in all that. I like you and I'm really attracted to you, but I don't make promises I can't keep. I just have a feeling we could have some really good times together.'

'Right.' Ashleigh paused for a moment, not sure what to say. 'Well I'm pretty crap at relationships anyway, so perhaps a no strings approach is the best all round?' It was a daring thing for her. This wasn't like anything she'd ever done before, but with her track record she had nothing to lose and it was a long time since she'd had *that* kind of fun.

The food had completely lost its appeal and Ashleigh was relieved when Tom signalled to the waiter. 'In that case, would you mind if I got the bill?'

Within minutes they were outside the restaurant and Tom had hailed a taxi, giving the driver his home address. As they tumbled into the back seat, his mobile started to ring and he switched it off without even looking at it.

'It might be important.' She bit her lip again, the Dutch courage had dissipated and those first date nerves were back with a vengeance.

'Nothing's that important.' He moved towards her, taking her face in his hands. 'This isn't something I do all the time. I'm not Zac.'

'I know, I know.' She murmured until their lips finally met, their urgency and intensity apparent in the kiss. She was oblivious to everyone else in the world, including the cab driver sitting only a few feet away.

Funny how finding half the world's press camped on your doorstep could immediately cool things off. Pulling up outside his double-fronted town house, the huge wrought iron gates seemed to have grown human creepers, climbing to look into the garden and clinging to the metal work like ivy.

'For Christ's sake, what is it now?' Tom spotted the press pack, seconds before they spotted him. Dread prickled his scalp. What the hell were they all here for? He pulled out his mobile and listened to the urgent message from Francine, as photographers, journalists and camera crews began to surge like a tidal wave towards the taxi.

'Tom, Tom.' A young redhead in faded jeans, clutching a digital recorder hammered on the window. 'How are you feeling about Susie-Anne and Michael, now that there's a baby on the way?' Tom didn't respond. Even if he had it would have been drowned out by the shouts of the paparazzi, as they fought to get the scoop on his response to the news. His former fiancée getting knocked-up by a premiership footballer, barely a month after their split, would be front-page fodder.

'Just drive, before they swallow us up. We'll worry about where later. If we don't get out of here now, we never will.' Tom shouted to the cabbie, who performed wheel spins that an experienced getaway driver would have been proud of.

Chapter Eleven

'I've been trying to call you for over an hour!' Francine's irritation was palpable by the time Tom and Ashleigh finally made it back to his office. It was quite an art form, her ability to ostensibly ignore Ashleigh, while at the same time looking at her with obvious animosity.

'I know, I'm sorry.' Tom's voice was flat. Ashleigh knew they couldn't complain about press intrusion given his line of work. It was a side effect of his success that he'd become as newsworthy as his clients; but she'd bet right now he wished they'd all just sod off. She certainly did.

'I suppose you know now about Susie-Anne's… announcement on day-time TV?' Francine's mouth twisted, as though she found the whole idea of pregnancy distasteful, but her tone softened as she looked at Tom. 'The little fool confided in Ritchie Waters on *Morning Sunrise*. According to her latest *Twitter* posts, Michael's delighted with the news.'

'Great for them then.' Tom's sarcasm wasn't lost on Ashleigh and a frisson of doubt gripped her; perhaps he still had feelings for Susie-Anne after all.

'You heard how she did it?' Francine's nose wrinkled. 'She

took a pregnancy test out of her bag on live TV and brandished it in Ritchie's face.' Francine, who looked as though she would happily ban bodily functions all together, shuddered with disgust. 'I mean, she'd been to the toilet on that stick, can you imagine anything so awful? I certainly can't!'

Ashleigh said nothing, fighting the temptation to ask if Francine ever watched the evening news. If a bit of wee was the worst thing she could imagine, then she'd led a charmed life.

'So she'd only just found out?' Tom sighed. 'I suppose I shouldn't be surprised. Let's face it, Susie-Anne has always been gloriously indiscreet.'

'Apparently she did the test in the studio toilets just before going on air.' Francine was grimacing again, yet still managed to shoot Ashleigh a filthy look. 'I think we should prepare a press release Tom, don't you? I've cleared your diary for the rest of the day so once…' she pretended to struggle with Ashleigh's name and then deliberately got it wrong, '…er, Ashleen, finishes her meeting with you we can get to work.'

'Look, I think I should go.' Ashleigh half-hoped Tom would stop her. She wanted to reach out to him, but Francine was there – more than ready to be his sole support.

'You're right. You should go now and let us get on. I'm sure whatever you were meeting about can wait.' Francine's tone was clipped and she placed a hand firmly on Ashleigh's back, propelling her towards the door and away from Tom as quickly as possible.

'Well, okay.' Despite the pressure on her back, she paused. Tom still hadn't spoken, lost in his own thoughts as he stared out of the window. 'I've got to go and see Angus. So, call me later?' It was a question she needed the answer to. At last Tom turned to look at her, nodding his head.

'I'll call you tonight.' There, he'd said it, but whether he would or not remained to be seen.

'I thought she'd never go.' Francine put one arm along the back of Tom's chair, his mind racing. How on earth were they going to word the press release? As she leant in closer, it was obvious she'd undone a couple of extra buttons on her shirt, the top of her bra clearly visible. Not again. Why the hell couldn't Francine get the message without him spelling it out to her?

He should have been in bed with Ashleigh. He couldn't remember the last time he'd wanted something as much, it was a physical ache and the way she'd looked at lunch hadn't needed a deliberate flash of her underwear. He knew he hadn't been the only man in *Grant's* to notice her. There was so much vitality about her and she was getting to him.

'Tom, are you listening to me?' Francine straightened up, her frustration at his lack of reaction obvious. 'I can't understand why you keep getting involved with these sort of girls.'

'I don't think it's part of your remit to worry about my sex life, is it?' He was careful not to use the dreaded L word. It was just a physical thing.

'I just don't want to see you make the same mistake again. You and I both know that the business has to come first.' There was an unspoken suggestion that this should have made Francine his first choice. It was never going to happen; but she was right, the business was the priority.

'Don't worry, I've learnt my lesson and I won't be making any grand gestures.' As he spoke, a slow smile spread across her face.

'That's good to know.' She moved back to the side of his

chair and leant across him again, the attempt at seduction not yet over. 'Let's get this press release done.'

'What would I do without you?' Tom moved fractionally, so that her bony cleavage was out of his eye line. He wasn't deliberately leading her on, but he did need her – she was the most efficient PA he'd ever had. Business was business and she understood that. When all this stuff with Ashleigh was out of his system, things would go back to normal and losing Francine definitely wasn't part of the plan.

Calling into the *Glitz* offices on her way back to Stevie's flat, Ashleigh was met by a very excited Angus. Stevie was there too, the whole place buzzing with gossip about Susie-Anne and Michael Cox. Ashleigh gritted her teeth and played along as though it was news to her. She nodded and feigned interest when Angus went through the list of upcoming assignments. She forced herself to smile at the right times, until the strain of keeping up the pretence made her face ache and her head throb. It was hell. When she finally got the chance to escape to the *Dog and Duck*, with Stevie in tow, she could have given Usain Bolt a run for his money.

'So come on then, what's up with you? You've had a face like a slapped bum all afternoon.' Stevie put two pints of cider on the small table in front of her. It was going to be one of those evenings.

'I think I might have done something really stupid. I just wish he hadn't been so nice to me, then at least a little part of me could have carried on hating his guts.' She kicked the table and his pint jumped precariously close to the edge, but decided at the last minute not to topple onto the floor.

'Don't tell me you've made a pass at Angus?'

'We both know that the only one who has a chance with Angus is you. He giggles like a schoolboy whenever you're in the same room.' She managed a bleak smile. 'Think bigger.'

'Umm, bigger than Angus... are we talking physically or in terms of power?' He ducked away as she moved to slap him. 'Okay, okay, I suppose we're talking Tom Rushworth?'

'Yep, Tom.' Sighing, she stopped skirting around the issue and took a slug of cider. 'But I didn't make a pass at him, as you put it, I've just gone for the cliché of fancying the boss.'

'So what's new? You've been mooning over him for weeks and, after all, you've never had much taste in men.' Grinning, he put his arm around her. 'Except of course when it comes to choosing a best friend.'

'I'm starting to wonder about that too!' She was teasing. Stevie's gift for putting everything into perspective was working its charm; the only trouble was he didn't know the full story. 'I just wish I hadn't made it so obvious.'

'It's not that obvious.' Stevie pulled away and looked at her, his head on one side. 'I mean I can tell of course, but then I know you. Tom has women fawning all day long. I bet he hasn't even noticed.'

'Well, thanks!' She couldn't help laughing; Stevie also had a knack for bringing her back down to earth. 'But I think he has.'

'You didn't!' His eyebrows shot up, almost disappearing behind his fringe.

'Didn't what?'

'Tell him you fancy him? Ask him out? I don't know, make it obvious?' He looked shocked – this from someone who thought nothing of gyrating against a stranger in a nightclub, just to let them know his interest had been vaguely aroused.

'I didn't have to tell him.' She laughed again, as his mouth almost fell open. 'Oh for God's sake, I wasn't going to tell you but we kissed.'

'You didn't! When?'

'When he came to Sandgate to tell us we weren't sacked.' There was a second of guilt as they made eye contact. They shared everything, but she'd kept this from him.

'I knew something was up!' He smacked a hand against his forehead. 'That night when I came into the kitchen, you were as jumpy as hell. I thought it was just you worrying about the job.' The excitement had taken over and Stevie could barely sit still. 'So, come on then, was he good?' He didn't need to wait for an answer; the blush that had crept up her neck gave the game away. 'Oh not just good then, are we talking really good?'

'Really, really good.' A warm feeling curled in the pit of her stomach as she thought about kissing Tom.

'Okay, so he's hot, filthy rich and a great kisser. What's the problem?' Stevie was getting into the swing of things. 'Never mind your crush, I think I might have a crack at him myself.'

'It's never wise to get involved with someone on the rebound.' She attempted to mimic his jokey tone, but it didn't quite come off.

'Is that what you're worried about?' Stevie looked at her quizzically. 'Has there been something since the kiss then?' When she didn't answer, he moved in for the kill. 'Spill it Ash or I mean it, I will tickle you and I won't stop until you either 'fess up or wet yourself.'

'Okay, okay!' She twisted away from him, scared he might carry out the threat, even in a busy pub. 'I don't suppose there's any point in trying to keep it from you.' She took a deep breath, still in shock at how far things had almost gone with Tom. 'It isn't so much what happened as what almost did.'

'You were going to sleep with him!' Stevie was almost squawking. 'I mean I'm not bothered about the two of you getting together, but I'm supposed to be your best friend and you haven't even hinted that it's gone this far!'

'Well, it only really happened at lunch-time today, so I think you can forgive me for not filling you in straight away.'

'Could he not, you know… manage?' Stevie's eyes lit up, he still hadn't quite forgiven Tom for his off-hand manner and it clearly amused him to think that their boss might not be quite so powerful after all.

'Of course it wasn't that!' She'd expected to be embarrassed recounting the story, but her over-riding emotion was disappointment. 'Well, I mean we never actually got the chance to find out, but, you know, he seemed like he'd manage perfectly well.' Ah, there was the blush, back with a vengeance.

'So if it wasn't a performance failure, then what stopped you?' Stevie suddenly had a dreamy look on his face. 'I don't think I would have told Tom to stop. Yes, he's arrogant, but those eyes and that body…'

'Are you listening to me?' Ashleigh had lost him to a fantasy she'd rather he hadn't shared.

'Umm, sorry, yep, go on.' He grinned and Ashleigh shifted in her seat; if confession was good for the soul, Stevie wasn't making it that easy.

'Tom invited me out to lunch. I thought he was going to tear me off a strip for the Edith Piaf stunt we pulled with Chloe but…'

'He just wanted to strip you off instead!'

'Will you shut up? Or shall I just not bother telling you the rest?' He gave an apologetic shrug and mimed locking his mouth shut, throwing the imaginary key behind him. 'We got back to his place, just as the story about Susie-Anne had broken, and the press were everywhere. Tom seemed really upset and he just wanted to get back to his office, deal with the fall out and for me to disappear.'

'Oh honey. It was probably just a shock.' Stevie gave her a hug. 'Perhaps he was freaking out that he might not have escaped after all and he'd have to marry Susie-Anne.' He grimaced at the thought. 'I mean she's only been with Michael five minutes. The kid might not even be his!' Stevie, who could gossip for England, was lit up by the idea that there might be more to the story.

'I never even thought of that!' Great, now she had something else to worry about.

Chapter Thirteen

As it turned out, Tom kept his promise to phone her but the call had been brief. Stevie's attempt to prove he wasn't eavesdropping was as off putting for Ashleigh, as it might have been for a teenage girl whose dad was pretending not to listen into her phone call. There wasn't much to say, except that Tom was sorry that they'd had to cut short their lunch, as he delicately put it. Ashleigh had replied that it was fine, no problem, she understood. There'd been no talk of another date, not that there'd been a date as such in the first place, but it would definitely have made her feel better if Tom had suggested it. She was glad she was going home in a couple of days. There was just the small matter of Carly's hen night to shoot in London and then she could go home until Christmas. She had a few assignments booked for *Glitz* at some of the Christmas parties the celebs would trawl round and the rehearsal dinner and parties in the run up to the wedding, but none of them were in London and she could go home to her own bed every night. Putting some distance between herself and Tom probably wouldn't be a bad thing either.

'You ready honey?' Stevie looked more like the hen than the stylist by the time he'd got himself ready for Carly's big night. He was wearing sequinned jeggings, silver Ugg-style boots and a black silk shirt. There were hints of body glitter on his cheekbones and at the nape of his neck. There was no denying it, he was beautiful. No one else could pull off an outfit like that.

Stevie had already met with Carly on several occasions to plan her outfit and those of her hens. Ashleigh couldn't be persuaded to join in the bling-fest, as the two of them had termed it. Much as she liked Carly, she was working tonight and had on her habitual working uniform of Levis, boots and a long sleeved T-Shirt. Her long dark hair was pulled back into a high ponytail and only a hint of make-up attempted to mask her tiredness. She hadn't slept well since she'd last seen Tom and her concentration had been shot to pieces. Even watching mindless TV was hard to follow because her thoughts were elsewhere. Susie-Anne's news seemed to keep cropping up on the magazine shows that dominated the daytime TV schedules, which just served as another reminder.

'Ready as I'll ever be.' Ashleigh gave him a weak smile. 'I'm really not in the mood for this tonight. Carly and her posse of WAGs at their drunken worst is not something I'm looking forward to.'

'There's bound to be some gossip tonight or they'll create some of their own.' He enveloped her in his arms. 'And after all that you get to come home with me!'

'I suppose I should make the most of it.' She mumbled into his shoulder and sniffed self pityingly. 'Because at this rate it doesn't look like I'll ever have a hen night of my own.'

'Oh shut up!' He pulled away so that he could look her in

the eye. 'I'd marry you tomorrow honey.' He grinned as she rolled her eyes. 'No I mean it. So there'd be no sex, so what? We'd only be like most of the married couples around and I bet we'd be a whole lot happier. At least we really love each other.'

'Thanks Stevie. I do love you, you know that.' She began to gather up her equipment. 'And I might just take you up on that offer!'

Carly and the rest of the hens had spent most of the day in an exclusive spa in West London. Part of the photo shoot was to capture the 'fun and frolics', as *Glitz* would no doubt term it, of their day of pampering. Not wanting to spend the whole day trailing around after them, Ashleigh and Stevie had agreed to catch up with them at the tail end of the spa day. They were met there by Marco, the gorgeous Anglo-Italian hairdresser who'd just been short-listed for *Hairdresser of the Year* and Imelda, one of the regular freelance make-up artists working for *Glitz*.

'Ooh, you ain't 'alf looking tired girl.' Imelda was a stereo-typical cockney. Warm hearted and blunt in equal measure, she lost no time in appraising Ashleigh's care-worn appear-ance. 'What's 'appened? Nuffink's wrong is it?'

'Other than you telling me I look like crap?' Ashleigh laughed despite herself. 'I'm alright, honestly, just ready for the Christmas break. I think I've had enough of London for a bit.'

'But they say tired of London, tired of life, eh?' Marco swept her into an embrace, kissing her with gusto on both cheeks. Now there was someone who never got depressed.

'Well maybe there's a bit of that too!' She took in his appcar-ance, which would give Stevie a run for his money. He always seemed to fizz with excitement and he seemed more hyped up then usual. 'Anyway, it doesn't look like the same can be said of you.'

'Are the rumours true then?' Stevie submitted to Marco's attentions next. Although the hairdresser was a notorious womaniser, Stevie seemed to be making the most of the moment. 'Are we in the presence of a TV star?'

'Yes, it's true, it's true!' Marco clapped his hand together with excitement. 'I'm not supposed to say, but I stood in for George Lamore on *Morning Sunrise* this week and now I've got the gig for good!' His eyes twinkled and he definitely had the right look for TV. Viewing figures for *Morning Sunrise*'s makeover slot were going to go through the roof.

'Congratulations!' Ashleigh suddenly felt much more cheerful. She'd worked with George Lamore in her earliest career as a photographer and he'd been an egotistical pig back then; even before he'd won the coveted makeover slot and became a reality TV star. He'd since opened up his London salon, *La More, More, More,* to one of the satellite channel's cameras and its show of the same name. La Bore, Bore, Bore would have been more appropriate. The man took pride in belittling his staff and loved nothing more than revelling in other people's misfortune. He'd been one of the first to make public comment when Chloe's past had been exposed. Perhaps there was a God after all. George had lost his slot on *Morning Sunrise* and ratings for his satellite TV show had dipped to an all-time low.

'That's brilliant!' Stevie's gossip radar was on high alert after the events of the past few days. 'So come on, spill it, what's the silver fox really like? As nice as he seems?' He'd always had a bit of a crush on Ritchie Waters and Ashleigh knew that watching his Saturday morning TV shows as a kid had helped confirm for Stevie that it was definitely the un-fairer sex that set his pulse racing.

'Yes, he's great.' Marco nodded enthusiastically. 'All the presenters are and Ellie Summers is almost as gorgeous as our Ashleigh.' He glanced at her pale complexion and grinned. 'Well right now she looks a damn sight better than Ash!'

'Thanks, mate!' She wasn't offended though. It was good to be with people who knew her well enough to have a good laugh. It was managing to push thoughts of Tom, and the fool she'd made of herself, to one side. 'So everyone's great then? Bit boring on the gossip front aren't you?'

'Not everyone.' Marco wasn't known for his discretion. 'Some of the guests on the show are…' he seemed to wrestle for a moment to find the right words, '…complete pains in the arse!'

'Oh! Like who?' Imelda's eyes widened.

'Taylor Moore wouldn't come on set until she'd had a pedicure and quails eggs on toast.' They exchanged knowing glances. The daytime soap actress had walked out on her show to launch a career in Hollywood. The consensus of opinion was that she was much more likely to turn up next on one of the down-market celebrity reality shows so beloved of ex-soap stars.

'Hilarious!' Stevie was in his element. 'And did you meet the lovely Susie-Anne when she came in?' The raised eyebrows made it clear that he was hoping for some really juicy gossip. Ashleigh was praying that Susie-Anne had asked for five naked hunks, stripped to the waist, to provide a full body massage before she'd take her seat on the sofa. Anything that might further justify her opinion of Tom's ex-fiancée and give her a reason to believe that he might really prefer her.

'Actually, she was okay. Quite funny.' Marco was definitely the type to appreciate Susie-Anne's ample charms. 'Fair enough, she had a laugh like a hyena on helium that would drive me mad after a while, but I'd happily have spent a night or two in her company!'

'No histrionics then?' Ashleigh was disappointed; a laugh at Susie-Anne's expense would have been welcome.

'Well, she's no genius.' Marco shrugged. 'She was on top of the world about the baby and everyone got an eyeful of her two blue lines whether they wanted to or not.'

'It's Tom I feel sorry for though.' Imelda was well known for being soft hearted. 'I met 'im a few times working free-lance wiv 'is clients and 'e was always great to me, genuinely warm and like 'e was really pleased to see me. Any girl would be lucky to 'ave 'im and 'ow Susie-Anne could have let 'im go buggers me! 'e's such a lovely bloke. I'd never pick someone like Michael Cox over 'im.'

'I'm not sure she did either.' Marco was now laying full length on one of the leather sofas in the reception area of the spa. 'I mean we all saw the papers when she cheated on Tom, but she's a great one for telling you the ins and outs of every-thing and it seems he was already looking elsewhere.'

Neither Stevie or Ashleigh said anything and she didn't dare look at him. She wasn't quite sure if she could cope with hear-ing about someone else that Tom was seeing. Why couldn't she just get herself involved, for once, with a man who didn't have so many other options or at least one who didn't take those options up so freely?

'You guys might know more than me?' Marco gave them a knowing wink. 'Susie-Anne reckons he wasn't even bothered when the news came out about her and that footballer. She told me one of the receptionist's from Tom's office phoned and told her he was already seeing someone new from *Glitz*.'

'Probably Angus!' Stevie interjected quickly and Ashleigh was grateful he hadn't given the others a chance to put two and two together and work out that she was as likely a candidate as anyone.

'If Tom's gone for Angus, 'e obviously wanted someone wiv bigger boobs than Susie-Anne!' Imelda joined in the ribbing of their Editor, even though everyone loved him.

'They're ready for you now.' One of the masseurs had appeared from behind the glass door separating the reception area from the spa. Their reverie broken, the four of them headed into the steamy, almost jungle-like atmosphere of the spa. There were plants everywhere and Ashleigh's jeans instantly clung to her legs. She couldn't think straight, the heat and Marco's unexpected revelations had left her reeling. She couldn't even talk to Stevie about it. Did Susie-Anne know about her and Tom or was it just some coincidence? It wasn't as if they'd even kissed until after Tom had split up with her. Could there be someone else at *Glitz*? Obviously not Angus, but there were any number of pretty secretaries or journalists who might have caught his eye. God, she hated not knowing. The other side of Ashleigh screamed at her to 'get real'. She'd spent long enough surrounded by models and actresses to realise she was nothing special. Added to which they barely knew each other and they'd made a deal to keep it casual. She'd seen the way that Francine had looked at her, pegging her as just another vacuous airhead in the long line of hopefuls, and there was no way she'd give Francine the satisfaction of proving her right.

'What are you frowning at, bella?' Marco set himself up in

front of one of the full-length mirrors that lined one wall in the chill-out room of the spa.

'Nothing, just thinking.' The blush swept across her face immediately, but luckily it was well disguised by the pinkness of her cheeks brought on by the temperature in the spa.

'Well, stop thinking then. It makes you look miserable!' He squeezed her shoulder, seeming to sense that there was more to it than that. 'I'm thinking how the hell I'm going to do anything with the girls' hair in these conditions and it's making me pissed off too!' He threw his hands up in a typically Italian gesture.

Carly and the girls were in fine form and, despite his worries, Marco managed to make the girls' hair look natural enough for a day at the spa, but not plastered to their heads in the unflattering way someone might look in real life. One thing *Glitz* definitely didn't want to be was any mirror of real life. Imelda managed to apply some bronzing and basic makeup that didn't immediately slide off their faces. With the spa shoot over, all of the girls' hair and makeup was touched up again and they were despatched in groups of four by taxi. The cars were festooned with pink balloons, bearing Carly and Duane's names and wedding date, and ferried them to the next venue – a celebrity hangout called *Kitsch*. It was one of the hottest places in town to eat, run by Michelin starred chef, Anton Andrews, and his ex-model wife, Isabelle, but more than that it was *the* place for celebrities and wannabe celebrities, to see and be seen. Since Isabelle was one of Carly's hens, and a close friend from their modelling days, the party had been given exclusive use of *Kitsch* for the evening. Knowing that the paparazzi would be out in full force, and needing to keep

Glitz's exclusive as intact as possible, the taxis had stopped off in a car park around the corner. The absurdly glamorous group of women were then hidden in the back of a catering lorry that made its way into the yard by the back door to the restaurant kitchen. Anton and his staff, who were witness to bizarre celebrity behaviour on a daily basis, hardly batted an eyelid as the heavily perfumed entourage made their way through the kitchen, squealing with excitement.

'Champagne ladies?' Anton's young brother, Gerard, was Maitre'd at *Kitsch* and he immediately had the hens giggling and flirting with him as though their lives depended on it. The waiters weren't safe and neither was Stevie, but he was giving as good as he got, and wasn't averse to burying his face into a cosmetically enhanced cleavage given the opportunity. Ashleigh stood back from the throng and got some great natural shots of the party that captured the fun much more vibrantly than any posed shots would have done.

'Looks great.' She'd been reviewing the images on her digital camera and the voice behind her made her jump.

'Sorry, I didn't mean to startle you.' As she spun round, Tom placed a hand on her arm to steady her. 'I just thought I'd pop down to see how you were doing.' They both knew it was a lie and, as their eyes met briefly, she felt that familiar tightening in her stomach.

'That's nice.' She tried to stop looking at his mouth, determined to be cool and distant, but it was extremely difficult. 'It's going okay. Once they're done here, we're heading on to Carly's club to end the night and God help the blokes in there. They've been groping the waiters here and I've got plenty of evidence for any sexual harassment cases they might want to bring about.'

'How long will you be there?' His voice was low and soft.

'I'm not sure, not too long hopefully.' There was a grazing of stubble forming on his cheeks and she could smell his after-shave, it took her back to that first kiss in her kitchen. Was this really a good idea? She was rubbish at relationships and he'd virtually said he didn't really believe in them, so what was the point? Her brain and her body were having a battle over the whole thing. 'I just want to get a few good shots to finish off the piece. One of the journalists, Sally Grainger, is going to meet us there and take over. '

'Do you fancy going for a drink somewhere after you've finished?'

'A drink?' She smiled and he looked for a moment as though he might be going to say something else.

'Tom! What on earth are you doing here?' Carly's raucous shout cut through the narrow space between them and Ashleigh took a step back. Half the hens were represented by Tom's company and, ever the professional, he dragged himself away from Ashleigh to submit to the kisses and excited chatter of his clients and the rest of Carly's friends – whilst Ashleigh got on with her job.

Chapter Twelve

When the hen party finally decided to move on from the restaurant, Stevie and Ashleigh took a cab to the club, whilst Carly and the rest of the girls had a bone-shaking journey across London in the back of the van – although they were almost certainly inebriated enough not to feel a thing. Tom, who was being followed by the paparazzi in the wake of Susie-Anne's revelation, acted as a decoy and was dropped at the prominent entrance to an explosion of flash bulbs leaving Carly and her girlfriends to slip into the staff entrance unnoticed. When Stevie and Ashleigh used the front entrance a few minutes after Tom they didn't raise an eyebrow, never mind a lens shutter.

'You made it then?' Tom was waiting at the bar. His appeal to the hen party thankfully diluted by the presence of a host of other celebrities.

'Yes, I think the only interest we aroused was speculation about why somewhere like this would let people like me in, dressed in jeans and an old T-Shirt.' Ashleigh pulled self-consciously at her top.

'Don't worry, you look great. You look like you.' Tom poured her a glass of wine from the bottle that he had on the bar. 'Have you got much more to do?'

'I've just got to get a few shots here.' She took a sip of wine and the liquid warmed her throat. Maybe a few drinks would help; she could feel the nerves starting to bubble again. 'There's a cake apparently and the girls are planning a song or something, so I really ought to stay and get that at least.'

'I suppose you should.' Tom traced a finger along her jaw line. 'I wish you didn't have to, but you might get in trouble with your boss.'

'He's a tyrant, well known for it.' Ashleigh grinned and picked up her camera, pulling away from him. 'In fact I'd better get on, or he'll make me pay for it later.' She turned and headed towards the hen party, half of whom were busy with a shot drinking contest, whilst the other half were giving the dance floor good reason to be there.

Stevie, true to form, had been one of the first on the dance floor. For a gay man, he certainly had the dirty dancing moves and Carly was draped backwards over his arms in a move quite possibly good enough to score her a perfect ten on *Strictly*.

Ashleigh was confident she'd got some great photos and, once the cake arrived, she and Tom could leave. With the press camped out on the doorstep, maybe they'd be next in line for a bumpy ride in the back of the catering van.

Suddenly the music changed to Beyoncé's Single Ladies and the rest of the hen party descended on the dance floor, recreating the dance routine in a way that only people with plenty of time on their hands to practice, and the kind of confidence that most WAGs had, could. Moments later a huge cake was wheeled into the middle of the dance floor, it was almost five feet high and topped off with replicas of Carly and Duane, made from candle wax. It was about the tackiest thing Ashleigh had ever seen and all around the club people stopped to stare or started choking on their drinks. The Carly and Duane replicas were lit and looked eerily macabre as their faces started to melt. The wicks of the candles crackled with light, like sparklers on bonfire night. As the music and booty slapping reached a crescendo, the top of the cake burst open and an unidentified man, who Ashleigh assumed would turn out to be Duane, appeared from a crouching position inside. Lumps of sponge and icing ricocheted off the cake and with a huge Tarzan-like roar, the identity of the cake dweller was revealed.

'Shit, my fucking hair is on fire!' Capturing the action, even though she knew she'd never be allowed to use the pictures, Ashleigh watched as Zac Starr created havoc. One of the staff leapt across the bar and was on the dance floor in seconds, clutching a hand held fire extinguisher, which he quickly used to put out Zac's smouldering hair, along with the Duane and Carly candles which were doing their best to set fire to the dance floor.

'Interesting look Zac, are you hoping to start a trend to replace spray tans?' Tom was struggling not to laugh. Zac's face had turned an unappealing shade of red and the edge of his hair was actually singed. It smelt like a hairdressers during the 1980s, one that specialised in offering particularly severe poodle perms.

'It's not funny!' Zac was batting away the attempts of Carly and her friends to minimise the damage. 'I could have been killed, then you'd be sorry.' He was like a petulant child. His career might not be what it once was, but he still had an ego that matched its peak.

'The important question is are you hurt?' Ashleigh put her hand on Zac's arm in an attempt to calm him down. Now that the fire had been put out, and Carly's super-efficient bar staff had already cleared up the mess, the hen party had started to lose interest and drift back to the dance floor.

'It's a bit sore, but I'm more worried about whether my hair will grow back.' Zac was nothing if not vain and the amount of product he had on his hair had certainly helped ignite the situation.

'Maybe you should go to the hospital?' Ashleigh doubted there would be any lasting damage, but Zac obviously needed some sort of attention.

'Christ, no. The last thing I want is to be seen in public like this.' He looked at her as though she had suggested he streak naked down Regent's Street. She didn't like to tell him that she'd seen several of the partygoers filming the whole thing on their mobiles. Zac's flaming hair was set to be the next Internet sensation and would probably go viral within hours, but that was something best left for him to find out.

'Let's go through to the manager's office and work out what to do. I can hardly hear myself think in here.' Tom sounded every bit as frustrated as Ashleigh felt. It looked increasing like a giant Zac-shaped problem was going to get in the way of their plans. He ushered them through to the empty office, which was far enough away from the dance floor to have a proper conversation in.

'I could call Dr Hussani, I'm sure he'd look you over, put your mind at rest.' Tom already had his phone out and was scrolling through the contacts to find the number of the Harley Street clinic so beloved by celebrities. Plenty of Tom's clients were big fans of plastic surgery, so no doubt the doctor would be willing to offer a bit of after-hours care in the circumstances.

'I suppose that might work,' Zac chewed on his bottom lip. 'But I want someone to come with me, because I'm not going on my own.' There was the petulant child again. Zac was needy by nature and years of being pandered to as a pop star hadn't helped. Ashleigh wondered if it was why he drifted from one fiancée to another; he just didn't want to be on his own.

'The press are all over me at the moment,' Tom sighed. 'I'm not sure it would help you keep much of a low profile if I were to come with you.'

'Fucking Susie-Anne.' Zac's neck grew redder still.

'What you too?' Carly had followed them into the office and Ashleigh's hopes rose briefly. Maybe she would offer to accompany him to Dr Hussani's.

'God, no.' Zac grimaced. 'It's that silly cow's fault that Tom can't shake the press off and I wanted him to take me to get this checked out.' He gingerly touched the worse affected area and it crackled, revealing just how crispy the edge of his hair was.

'Borrow the catering van, that way the press won't even know you've gone.' Carly smiled benevolently. 'I won't be needing it again. By the time we've finished up here, even the paps will have gone to bed!'

The last chance of Tom being able to get out of accompanying Zac had disappeared, but Ashleigh couldn't blame Carly or even Zac; she knew it was Tom's job to make their lives easier, not the other way round.

'Maybe that is the best option.' There was an edge to Tom's voice. 'Get yourself sorted Zac and I'll meet you by the back door in a couple of minutes. Do you have anything more appropriate for him to wear?' Tom turned to face Carly. 'I'm not sure the cupid's outfit will help him blend into the background.'

'Yeah, I've got some spare bar uniforms out back. Come on Zac, let's get you changed, otherwise the party will be over before I get back to it.' Carly, who clearly thought he was making far too much fuss, dragged him away.

'I'm so sorry.' Tom caressed the back of Ashleigh's neck.

'Me too.' She managed a wry smile. 'I'm beginning to wonder if some greater cosmic force is trying to tell us something.'

'I don't believe in all that.' He frowned. 'It's just bad luck and bloody annoying! I'll get my driver to take you home, I don't want you getting a cab at this time of night.'

'Thanks Dad.' She smiled despite her disappointment; it was nice knowing that Tom cared about her safety. It was certainly different from most of the men she'd gone out with. His warm lips brushed against hers all too briefly and then he pulled away.

'I'll call you.' He was already turning to leave as he spoke and she barely resisted the urge to stamp her foot with frustration. Zac was in serious danger of being struck off her Christmas card list.

Ashleigh caught up with Stevie, who had disappeared into one of the club's private rooms in the wake of the cake disaster.

'Should I ask what you've been up to?' She gave him an appraising look; he didn't have the appearance of someone who'd just taken part in a wild orgy.

'Would you believe me, if I said playing cards?' He didn't sound that convinced himself.

'Nope, but I don't think I want to know anyway.' She suddenly felt really tired. Having missed out again on getting to know Tom better, the last thing she wanted to do was hear about someone else's sex life. 'I just wondered if you wanted a lift home?'

'I didn't realise you'd brought your push bike!' Stevie's reference to their student days brought the memories flooding back to her. Many was the time when one of them had ridden a pushbike home from the pub, with the other one perched on the cross-bar.

'Tom offered to lend us his car and driver.' It wasn't a lie, as such, and she couldn't face another cross-examination about why she and Tom never seemed able to get it together.

'That was nice of him, but why isn't he using it?' Stevie didn't seem too surprised that she wasn't heading off with Tom, no doubt just pleased not to have to hustle for a cab. 'Only I can't imagine Tom taking the tube home in some kind of selfless act of chivalry, no matter how much he fancies you!'

'He's taken Zac to the doctor.' Ashleigh was tempted to swing for him when he burst out laughing.

'What?' He grinned again. 'You've got to admit it was funny. Zac looked a right dick in that outfit, setting it alight was the only decent thing to do.'

'I thought you liked a man in lycra hotpants?' Zac's had been alarmingly tight, leaving nothing to the imagination, although she suspected that there had been some padding added. Either that or he had more than the usual number of testicles.

'Not when he's got a bouffant to match my Nan's.' He grimaced. 'Nope, if I were a woman, I definitely wouldn't be in the queue to audition as his next fiancée.'

'Will you stop whining?' Tom drummed his fingers on Dr Hussani's desk, as they waited for him to come back into the consultation room.

'Whining? He's just said I need surgery!' Zac was indignant and anyone would have thought the doctor had suggested an amputation rather than a minor op to help reduce the potential of scarring.

'He said you can have surgery if you want to speed up the healing process and remove some of the burnt skin, rather than just waiting for nature to take its course.' Tom couldn't keep the exasperation out of his voice, if Zac had been an NHS patient he'd have been sent home with a dressing and some aspirin at the most. 'Stop being a baby.'

'Is this how you speak to all of your clients?' He clearly wasn't going to be talked down from his moment of drama. 'If you're not careful, you'll only have Z-listers left.'

'Yeah and maybe they'll be grateful for the representation and give me less trouble.' Tom sighed. There was a copy of *Glitz* on the coffee table in Dr Hussani's office, with one of the photos that Ashleigh had taken of Chloe on its front cover. He couldn't stop thinking about her and the reminders that seemed to be everywhere weren't helping. He'd wanted to find a store cupboard at the restaurant or a cloakroom at Carly's and just bundle her into it, there and then. Only it seemed everything was against them.

'Don't be like that, you know you love me really.' There was a note of desperation in Zac's voice, as though he really needed Tom's reassurance that he'd be there for him. 'You will wait for me, if I have to have the op won't you?'

'I'll think about it,' Tom grinned, sensing an opportunity to get his own back. 'But if you make any more fuss, the first person you'll see waiting at your bedside when you come round will be Francine.'

Chapter Fourteen

The week between the hen night and the wedding passed in a blur. Ashleigh had been commissioned to take the pre-wedding shots of the bridal party at the hotel in their four day stay as part of the lead up to the big event itself. If a bride was ever buffed, puffed and waxed to the extreme, it had to be Carly. She'd tried out a number of hairstyles during her stay and had finally opted, with Stevie's input, for an up-do of tumbling curls, which stopped at just the point where her undeniably magnificent cleavage started. She did look stunning, if very slightly on the edge of *Big Fat Gypsy Wedding* styling.

Ashleigh and Stevie, whose budget didn't stretch to the minimum four hundred and fifty pounds per night price tag of the *Brewley Manor Castle Hotel*, the predictably lavish venue for the wedding, had spent the past four nights staying in a cosy bed and breakfast just down the road. They'd decided that their original plan of undertaking the two-hour drive back to Sandgate every night was pointless and probably more expensive, so they'd taken the train and booked into the homely B&B instead. As good friends of Carly's, she hadn't wanted them to be working on the big day and so another photographer from *Glitz* would have that responsibility. On the morning of the wedding they woke up to a delicious full English breakfast.

'Oh my God, these are the best sausages I've ever tasted.' Stevie leant back in his chair and groaned with pleasure, as he savoured the last mouthful of his breakfast.

'Shut up!' Ashleigh tried hard to suppress a grin. 'You sound like you're having an orgasm! If you ask me, it's about time you found yourself a new man.'

'You can talk. For what it's worth, I'm yet to meet a man who I've found more tempting than a good breakfast.' He tugged at his waistband. 'Anyway, if I keep on consuming the amount of calories I have been for the past few days, not only will I not be able to attract a boyfriend, they'll have to take a wall down to get me out of here. By the time I've eaten myself to the other side of Christmas, I'll need to employ someone in the New Year to rub cream into my folds of flab!'

'Um, you probably should worry.' This time she couldn't suppress the grin, given the look of incredulity on Stevie's face. 'If you're not careful, you might move up to a thirty inch waist.'

'Oh well, maybe it's inevitable, after all I'm about to hit thirty, so that's an inch for each year, not too bad.' Stevie obviously hadn't quite thought through the logic in the longer term.

'Okay, well let's see how you feel when you hit fifty and have a waist size to match!' Ashleigh laughed, but he was already reaching for another piece of toast.

'Oh whatever. Live fast, die young and all that.' Stevie really was living life in the fast lane, slathering his toast with butter and a thick layer of homemade blackcurrant preserve. 'So, are you finally going to let Tom into your knickers this weekend?'

'Wow! I know now why we're such good friends, it must be

the subtle nuances of our conversations.' That dreaded blush was sweeping up her neck. She wasn't about to tell him about the hasty trip to *Agent Provocateur*. Not wanting to tempt fate, she'd nearly just packed her usual extra support bras and the comfortable pants that helped to hold in her stomach. At the last minute she'd changed her mind though. Susie-Anne was probably the type of girl whose modesty, such as it was, would be covered either by just a layer of spray tan or perhaps two or three strips of strategically placed and ludicrously expensive satin and lace. The sight of Ashleigh in her slightly greying underwear, with skin that hadn't seen the sun for months, was unlikely to set Tom's ardour alight. Of course, a get together might not even be on his agenda, but the series of texts following Carly's hen night had suggested otherwise. They had gone from casual to sounding like they had a definite plan:

✉ From Tom
No lasting damage for Zac, although he moaned like a mule the whole time he was at the clinic. See you at the wedding, if not before.

✉ From Ashleigh
Glad to hear he was okay. Keep him away from YouTube or he might have a relapse – video was at nearly a million hits last time I looked! Looking forward to catching up.

There had been a few more chatty texts and she'd read each of her responses about fifteen times before replying. Should she add a kiss at the end or would he take that the wrong way? In the end, it was Tom who moved the conversation on:

✉ From Tom
Just to let you know, I'm staying at Brewley
Manor on the night of the wedding.

✉ From Ashleigh
Lucky you! It's a budget B&B for me and Stevie...
Time for a pay rise? ;)

As soon as she'd pressed send, she'd started to panic – what if he was annoyed about the mention of their salary or just decided she was an imbecile for putting an emoticon on her text message? An hour or so of hell had passed before his response.

✉ From Tom
Seems a shame for you to leave the hotel before
the real fun starts.

✉ From Ashleigh
Are you planning on a pillow fight?

✉ From Tom
Whatever floats your boat. So, is it a date?

✉ From Ashleigh
Sounds like it :)

In the end she'd risked another emoticon, it was safer than a kiss and it seemed, unless she'd totally misread things, that Stevie's prediction was spot on.

'Oh my God, you're going for it, aren't you?' Stevie knew

her too well and, even without the tell-tale blush, she might as well have been wearing a T-Shirt announcing her intentions.

'I'd like to spend some time with him, yeah.' There were proper butterflies in her stomach when she thought about it and it had been years since she'd felt that way. Maybe not since her first time, with Spencer, the sixth form rugby captain heartthrob, had she felt quite such anticipation. She only hoped that it would do more to live up to her expectations than that first time had, when she'd been left wondering if that was it, that was sex and what all the fuss was about.

'I thought so!' Stevie had that glint in his eye, which he always got when he'd somehow got one over on her. 'After all, I did wonder why Janice popped into our room this morning, to confirm the availability of the best room for your extra guest tonight!'

'Apparently she's not the soul of discretion I was hoping for.' The texts had hinted that Tom was planning on inviting Ashleigh to his suite at the hotel, but she knew from experience that they'd need to be discreet if they ever were going to get it together and Janice's B&B had seemed like a much better option. Although now, she was beginning to wonder.

'If it's any comfort, it's been bloody obvious anyway, the way your mobile phone's been buzzing day and night.'

'Okay, so we like each other. There's no crime in that, is there?' After all, it was only one night, just to settle these feelings and get past them once and for all. How involved could you get?

'Nope, no crime at all. It's great to see you having some fun for once and I have a sneaky feeling you'll have even more to smile about by this time tomorrow!' Stevie laughed far too loudly and she flicked him with her napkin. The middle-aged couple from the neighbouring table walked towards them and Ashleigh was sure they were going to complain about the noise she and Stevie had been making

'I'm sorry to interrupt, but I couldn't help overhearing your conversation.' The man addressed Ashleigh and she instantly felt the heat rising up her neck again.

'Sorry, we didn't mean…' As she started to apologise he cut her off.

'Don't apologise, my wife and I just wanted to give you our card, in case you were interested. You and your husband,' He gestured towards Stevie as he spoke, 'seem like just the open minded types we like.' Sliding a card across the tablecloth, he took his wife's arm and headed out of the restaurant.

Ashleigh turned over the card, not sure whether to laugh or cry.

'What is it?' Stevie whipped it out of her hand. 'Sussex Swingers' Nights?' He started laughing again.

'Not sure I'm tempted, but if it goes horribly wrong with Tom, at least I've got options!'

'Are you nervous?' Carly shook her head vigorously in response to Tom's question. She was glowing and it wasn't just down to the fake tan.

'No, I can't wait. I just needed to have five minutes away from everyone to get my head around the fact that in less than a few hours I'm actually going to be Duane's wife.' She couldn't stop smiling or fiddling with her hair.

'I can leave you to it then, if you want?' Tom had been Carly's agent for most of her career and he'd always been fond of her through all of it. She had that likeable quality that some celebrities seemed to lack.

'No, it's good to see you.' She gestured for him to join her on the tapestry love seat beneath the window in her room, where the sun shone in highlighting the bubbles in her champagne. 'Do you want a drink?'

'I'm okay, thanks.' He sat down beside her. 'It's not too late to call it off you know, run away.'

'What, with you?' Carly laughed, but there was no trace of bitterness. 'That moment passed a few years ago, but you know I would have done.'

'You mean all this could have been mine?' He squeezed her hand. He had good memories of the summer they'd had together and they'd stayed friends since. Even though Carly had clearly wanted more at the time, she'd accepted that Tom wasn't in it for the long haul and Duane had come along soon after. Carly and Duane were undoubtedly made for one another and, if Tom had believed in it, he might even call it love. 'Duane's a lucky man. I just thought I should give you the opportunity to run like hell if you wanted to. My grandfather said the same thing to my mother, but she went through with the wedding. I think it was something she regretted for years.' Tom knew that it was only his arrival that had allowed his mother to live with her decision. It was a memory she'd shared, something else that coloured his concept of marriage; but this was Carly's day.

'Thanks, Tom, it means a lot, but I really do love Duane you know.' She took a swig of champagne and looked at him. 'And you can't tell me it doesn't exist on a day like today, it's against the law.'

'Okay, I won't, not today anyway.' It was as far as Tom was prepared to go. 'Happy?'

'I am.' She leant across and kissed him. 'Now get your ugly mug out of here, I've got a wedding to get to!'

'Looks like a mafia reunion.' Stevie wound the window of the cab down slightly as it made its way up the long sweeping driveway of the *Brewley Manor Castle Hotel*. The security in place to protect *Glitz*'s exclusive magazine deal was worthy of that surrounding a president or a high-risk secure unit. Even Stevie and Ashleigh, who had worked with most of the security team for years, weren't ushered in without undergoing a check that was only one step away from a full body search.

'Can't be too careful love, sorry!' Shaun, the head of security gave Ashleigh a friendly wink as he rummaged through her handbag. His gruff Yorkshire accent and twenty inch neck circumference gave people the right impression. He needed to get the job done, but she knew he was a teddy bear really. 'Spare knickers eh love, what's that all about?' Shaun twirled round the itsy bitsy piece of fabric and lace, like the world's least attractive burlesque dancer, finishing his act with a flourish.

'She's a girl scout, always prepared.' Stevie stepped in just as the blush started creeping up her neck, realising she'd never manage to say something coherent put on the spot like that. 'Now, come on, equal opportunities and all that, I suppose you want to check my undies?' Stevie tugged at the waistband of his trousers, revealing the top of his very conservative boxer shorts.

'Nah you're alright mate, go on, go through, there's only twenty minutes 'til it all kicks off.' Shaun waved them in with a gesture of his short stubby thumb and Ashleigh sighed with relief.

'Thanks.' She squeezed Stevie's arm. 'Christ, he probably thinks I'm incontinent, but at least I didn't blurt out that I needed clean pants just in case I get an offer I can't refuse. I'm just glad he didn't find the toothbrush in the inside pocket.'

'You'd never make a spy, honey, or a thief. Guilt was written all over your face.' Stevie put his arm through hers 'But your innocence is one of the many things I love about you, so don't ever change'.

'Well, if things get messy, I might want to find another career, so I'll bear that advice in mind.'

They kept their arms linked as they rounded the corner of the manor house, the west wing of which was the original castle keep, complete with battlements and the later cosmetic addition of a Rapunzel style turret. It was completely over the top. Disney come to life and so 'Carly', it could have been built for her. Behind the main house was the chapel where the wedding would be held into which groups of guests were slowly drifting – some of them apparently reluctant to give up the frantic networking and flirting that made these kinds of events worthwhile, despite the biting December wind.

Ashleigh was conscious that her dress, which represented about a month's salary if she ruined it, and which had been borrowed from up and coming designer Samuel Horcross, was quite vulnerable amongst the moss clad walls of the manor house and chapel. It was camel coloured suede and clung to every curve of her figure as if it had been designed just for her. She felt good, thank God. She needed all the confidence she could get.

'Whoa!' Zac was standing in the doorway of the chapel, wearing a white suit and turquoise shirt and was looking surprisingly good, in a 1980s Miami Vice flashback kind of way. 'Don't I wish my girlfriend was hot like you!' He wrapped his arms around Ashleigh and planted a kiss on her lips. She pulled back and shook her head, to remind him of their agreement that he wouldn't overstep the mark. 'Sorry, I know, I know, I can look but not touch. Although you really do look great.'

'Not looking so bad yourself.' Ashleigh smiled, relieved that he didn't seem to be too offended by her gentle rejection.

'Yeah, you look hot.' Stevie drawled sarcastically, looking Zac up and down. 'Almost like you're on fire.'

'Piss off.' Zac didn't smile. He hadn't seen the humour of the cake incident on the night of Carly's hen party and he clearly still wasn't ready to see the funny side just yet.

'Come on boys, no fighting. It's Carly's wedding and it's nearly Christmas, the season of goodwill to all men. Let's go and sit together.' She couldn't help smiling, if she didn't know better she would have sworn they'd been on the phone to one another that morning. 'After all you do look well coordinated!' Stevie was wearing a turquoise suit, with an off white linen shirt.

'As long as you sit between us.' Zac pinched her bum and she struggled not to squeal. He had the vice like grip of someone who had spent years clutching either a microphone or a bottle of whiskey and had developed an eye-watering ability to pinch, and pinch hard, as a result. Her reminder that she wasn't interested in him obviously hadn't been entirely successful.

There were only minutes left to go until Carly was due to arrive and some of the burly security guards assigned by *Glitz* and *Rushworth Associates* were heading over to the chapel with large screens to protect the bridal party from the two helicopters which were buzzing overhead; circling like wasps around a jam jar, in the hope of capturing just one photo and making their fortune in the process.

The chapel was packed, there were a couple of rows of family and old friends at the front, but everywhere else there were recognisable faces, mostly from TV or the football pitch. There was enough surgically enhanced cleavage on display to rival the life's work of even the most prolific plastic surgeon.

Taking their seats towards the back of the chapel, Ashleigh suddenly caught a glimpse of Tom. Unlike the flamboyant apparel of Zac and Stevie, his grey suit screamed class. She could admit to herself now that she'd been attracted to him from the second they'd met and all the waiting and near misses had only served to intensify those feelings.

'Bloody hell honey, you're crushing me.' Stevie yanked his hand away from hers. She hadn't even realised she was holding it.

'Sorry, I was a bit distracted.' She met his gaze, silently willing him not to say anything in front of Zac, who was to discretion what Charlie Sheen was to sobriety.

'Can't say I blame you.' Thank God, Stevie was whispering. 'Tom really does look great today and if I knew I'd be getting a shag from him later I wouldn't be able to control myself either.' He winked at her and then grimaced as she squeezed his hand again with all her strength. 'I'm glad you're finally over that prick, Liam. Let's face it, he wasn't even in the same league as Tom. And I would offer to keep my fingers crossed that there are no other similarities, but since you appear to have crushed all the bones in my hand you'll have to take your chances!'

Carly's fiancé, Duane Johnson, was already at the front of the Chapel with his best man, Michael Cox, at his side. Susie-Anne was a couple of rows back, decked in a weird feather clad ensemble that made her look like a plus-size ostrich. She was stroking her non-existent baby bump and announcing to anyone who was interested, and most of those who weren't, that she was having to drink a bottle of Gaviscon a day to ward off crippling indigestion and had an uncontrollable craving for *Krispy Kreme* doughnuts.

'Poor Tom.' Ashleigh wished she was sitting closer to him, so that she could see if he was okay. Ever the professional, you would never know from the way he was acting that there had ever been anything between him and Susie-Anne. It must have been hard to hear though. He was supposed to be the one rushing out for *Krispy Kremes* as a small price to pay for impending fatherhood. She wondered if Michael dragged his gaze away from the mirror for long enough to tend to Susie-Anne's needs. He hadn't stopped looking at himself in every reflective surface, including the mirrored handbag of the bride's mother, since he'd got to the front of the chapel. Susie-Anne, who didn't have an ounce of shame in her body, was either unconcerned or unaware of any discomfort that Tom might be feeling as she regaled tales of her pregnancy within his earshot.

'Yeah, poor Tom.' Zac's tone was heavy with irony. 'He looks devastated with those women on either side of him desperately trying to brush up against him.'

Tom was sitting next to two of Carly's modelling friends and they were giggling over-enthusiastically and touching his arm at every available opportunity.

A frisson of nerves gripped Ashleigh's stomach. Maybe she'd got the messages all wrong. Then he turned and a smile lit up his face as he spotted her.

'Shit.' The word was barely audible, but Stevie heard her curse.

'What's up?' Thankfully Zac was busy gossiping with a group of fashion journalists sitting behind them.

'I've just realised I'm in way over my head.' She'd felt something and it wasn't good, but Stevie was looking blank and she knew she'd have to explain it to him. 'I can't believe I've been such an idiot.'

'What's up, forgotten your condoms?' He was trying to lighten the mood, but this wasn't the time. 'Honey, I'm sorry, what is it?'

'I've convinced myself there's absolutely no possibility that I stand the risk of falling even a little bit in love with him. But what if there is, when he's made it clear that's the last thing he wants?' Ashleigh furrowed her brow. 'Or maybe it's just the wedding atmosphere getting the better of me.' She attempted to smile, but it went a bit wobbly.

'Shit's right. I knew you had it bad honey, but I think you're over reacting.' Stevie squeezed her hand. 'Don't worry about it, you've not slept with him yet. It might well all be over after that.' A slow grin spread across his face and the corners of her mouth started to twitch too. 'After all, you must remember…'

'Gary!' They both spoke at once and said the name so loudly that people in the row in front turned to look at them.

She felt instantly better. Gary had been a lecturer at their art school. Forbidden fruit, both she and Stevie had experienced crushes on him at various points during their studies. Finally, after years of her day dreaming about it in boring lectures, Gary had made a move on Ashleigh at the graduation ball. By that time, she'd built up the fantasy so much in her mind that she was expecting fireworks, a symphony and to run off into the sunset hand in hand the morning after. She hadn't expected beery breathed kisses and a tongue that probed her throat so deeply she was left wondering if he'd performed a tonsillectomy with it. Against her better judgement, she'd gone ahead and slept with him. Three minutes of missionary position action and a scary sex face on his part and it was all over. Stevie was right, she'd spent so long being afraid of getting hurt, of letting herself have feelings, that she was blowing what was really just physical attraction out of all proportion.

'I love you.' She snuggled into the crook of his arm. Whatever happened they'd have each other.

'I love you too.' Stevie kissed the top of her head.

'What about me?' Zac had finished gossiping with the row behind and evidently wasn't enjoying feeling like the third wheel.

'Sorry love, you're not really my type!' Stevie puckered his lips all the same and blew him a kiss. Zac's response wasn't quite so polite, but it was lost as the first strains of Mendelssohn's Wedding March heralded Carly's arrival, along with an entourage of eleven bridesmaids.

Carly sobbed throughout the wedding ceremony and by the time she'd swept away most of her make-up on a sea of tears, she looked even more beautiful than she had before.

Chapter Fifteen

There was no way that any photographs could be taken in the grounds of the castle. As well as the helicopters circling overhead, there were paparazzi and members of the public poking telescopic lenses through hedgerows. Instead the guests were bundled along a man-made corridor of white sheeting, into the main castle. The reception hall was dominated by a huge Christmas tree, decked out with baubles and lights matching Carly's wedding theme and had a bride instead of an angel as its topper.

'God, I needed that.' Stevie had grabbed two champagne cocktails from a passing waitress, given one to Ashleigh and drained his in seconds. 'Another one?'

'No, I'm trying to keep a clear head.' She took a sip, longing to drain the glass, but somehow knowing that it wouldn't turn out well if she got drunk before she saw Tom.

Groups of guests were called up in turn to take part in the photo shoot, whilst the rest of the wedding party got stuck into the champagne and canapés. The focus was on the celebrity guests of course; it was their faces that would sell copies of *Glitz*, when teasers of the wedding photos were printed on its front cover. Ashleigh had already seen Tom disappear to be included in some of the main shots. He'd probably be in demand for ages, so there was plenty of time for her nerves to continue twisting her insides. Zac had been called to be photographed too, much to her relief. Although she really liked him, Zac and Stevie were no better than a couple of bickering kids and it was very difficult to take when you were as on edge as she was.

'Having a good time?' Tom was suddenly at her side. She could sense the eyes of people all around, staring at them. They all wanted to speak to him, to get his attention; but he seemed oblivious to them.

'Yes. Better now.' So much for being subtle. It was no use pretending; there was no comparing Tom to Gary, the artless art lecturer.

'Shall we go for a walk?' His eyes searched her face, as if daring her to come up with some reason why she couldn't.

'Won't people notice or need you?'

'I couldn't care less about people noticing and I think I deserve half an hour off?' Tom grinned and instantly lost the no-nonsense look that he wore so well. It was sexy and confident but Ashleigh preferred his softer side. The one she'd first seen in her kitchen that night back in Sandgate, when they'd shared their first kiss.

Outside, the castle's famous rose garden was a shadow of its summer self. However, the wedding organisers had strung masses of tiny lights everywhere and they twisted like tiny glowing rosebuds between the barren thorn bushes that wouldn't bloom again for months.

'I've been looking forward to today, but not because of the

wedding.' Tom took her hand in his and the simple gesture sent adrenaline rushing through her veins.

'Me too.' She couldn't look at him, couldn't trust herself not to leap on him in front of the entire wedding party.

He led her towards a small wooden gazebo, the sides of which were covered in heavy-duty trellis and which offered some protection from any unwanted attention. If it had been summer, honeysuckle would have been draped in fragrant swathes from the trellis and would have completely hidden them from any prying eyes.

'I can never understand why people want to get married in the depths of winter.' Her teeth were chattering, but she wasn't entirely sure that it was down to the cold.

'Please tell me you're not one of those people who've had their wedding day planned out since you were eight years old? Time of year, venue, colour of bridesmaid dresses, everything.' The corners of Tom's mouth twitched and a familiar rush of blood flooded Ashleigh's cheeks.

'I didn't mean that, I'm not some desperate wannabe bride.' She was stuttering and growing redder by the second, wishing for the millionth time that her emotions weren't so readily on display.

'I'm shocked!' Tom's eyebrows shot up with a look of mock horror. 'You look great when you blush by the way.'

'I doubt that.' She struggled to regain her composure and leant with her back against the side of the gazebo, trying and failing to sound nonchalant. 'So what are we doing out here? I didn't have you down as a frustrated gardener.'

'There's only been one frustration of late.' He crossed the gazebo in two strides and placed his palms on the columns, either side of where she stood. Somehow her hands found their way into his hair and her body was pressing against his as if her life depended upon it. The kiss was even better than before. 'I've wanted to do that from the moment I saw you today.' When he finally pulled away from her, they were both breathless. Any thoughts of the cold had long since disappeared and the only thing Ashleigh was aware of was the sensation of her mouth tingling and the desire to finish what they'd started. The anticipation was starting to drive her mad.

'I hope it didn't disappoint.' She shot him a flirtatious look, confident that she'd been able to feel his interest when their bodies were pressed together.

'It'll do.' He ran his fingers gently down the side of her face and neck. 'I wish we could just slip away now.'

'It might be a bit obvious.' Ashleigh's tone was reasonable, although part of her was terrified that, if they didn't seize the moment, it would be lost and she couldn't take that again.

'I don't want to rush it.' Tom's fingers continued their journey down her arm, until they were entwined with hers. A horrible thought crossed her mind. What if she turned out to be the female equivalent of Gary and Tom thought she was useless in bed? Oh God, she had to work with him after all this…

'I think we should go back to the wedding.' Suddenly the desire to rip off her clothes and leap on Tom had subsided. 'Before anyone misses us, well more accurately you.'

'Promise me that we'll carry on where we started off then?' He seemed to sense the change in her mood. 'I'm not going back in until you do.'

'Okay. Maybe we can meet up tonight?' Her mind already turning over a hundred excuses for ducking out of the wedding and out of their plans.

'No maybes.' He kept his fingers curled around hers as they

headed back to the manor. The last of the photos would be coming to an end and the guests beginning to slip into their seats for the wedding breakfast. As they got closer to the manor they passed a garden store, where the team of gardeners no doubt stopped for tea breaks and listened to whatever sporting event was being broadcast that day. There were no grounds staff about, though, so the strange groaning noise coming from the shed was unexpected.

'Should we take a look?' As Ashleigh spoke, Tom's mouth started twitching again. 'It sounds like someone's in pain.'

'I don't think it's pain.' He was laughing now, but she still wasn't sure why. 'But if you're worried, we can check.' She shook her head as the groaning reached a crescendo. All at one, it was obvious exactly what kind of groaning it was. Yanking Tom by the arm, she pulled him behind a holly bush and crouched down slightly as the door of the garden store opened. The first to emerge was one of the bridesmaids, hastily smoothing down her coral pink dress and brushing leaves and bits of dried grass off around the knee area. Ashleigh held her breath; it wouldn't have surprised her if Zac had appeared next. After all, he was well overdue to hook up with fiancée number eight. The breath left her body in a rush as it became clear just who the bridesmaid had been giving so much pleasure to. It was future father of the year, Michael Cox, looking even more smug than usual, hastily zipping up his fly as he slipped out of the shed un-noticed – or so he thought.

'Oh God.' Ashleigh shivered, suddenly aware of the cold again.

'He apparently thinks so. Well, God's gift to women anyway.' Tom's tone was light, but there was no way of knowing what he was really thinking.

'Poor Susie-Anne.' Even though she'd treated Tom appall-
ingly, Ashleigh wouldn't wish that on anyone. There was
something incredibly tacky about the kind of man who
shagged around and made a fool out of his pregnant girlfriend. Especially the type of man who did it at a wedding, in
a garden shed.

'She knows.' Tom sounded as though the whole situation
were entirely normal.

'About Michael and that girl?' Nothing should have
surprised Ashleigh, after all she'd been working with celebrities for years and they had a whole different code of ethics
from most people. Yet she was shocked and a little bit sickened
by it.

'I don't know if she knows about that particular girl. I have a
feeling that Michael didn't even know about her before today
and probably doesn't know her name even now.' Tom still had
hold of her hand and they were almost back at the main part
of the manor house. 'But she rang me in tears a week or so ago,
to say that she'd found pictures on his mobile phone and some
video of… well I expect you can guess the rest.'

'But they're still together.' Ashleigh had never been able
to understand how some women could share the men they
professed to love. She tried not to think about how casual she
and Tom were planning to keep things.

'She was upset.' Tom shrugged his shoulders. 'But she likes
the lifestyle. She said that it happens, he's ten times more
famous than he was a year ago and he gets offers all the time
– sometimes he just can't turn them down. Michael told her it
didn't mean anything and so she's just going to turn a blind eye
to it. She was more worried it might get out to the press and
ruin this image she's trying to create of a perfect little family

in waiting.'

'What about you? Are you okay?' Did it hurt him more than he let on that Susie-Anne had left him for a piece of work like Michael Cox?

'I couldn't give a toss what Michael Cox does.' He pulled her into his arms, even though they were now in full view of the house. 'Or what Susie-Anne chooses to put up with. I can't even judge him.'

'Well I can, he's a total bastard.' She bristled. 'Please don't tell me you think it's okay too, just because he's a footballer and these things are the norm?'

'Whoa, calm down.' He kissed her lightly on the lips, but she pulled away. 'All I meant was that I can't judge him for cheating on Susie-Anne. Not when I've wanted you since the day you walked into my office and tried to make me drape myself across the window seat with Susie-Anne on my knee. When I was engaged to her and thought she was having my baby, I still wanted to know what it was like to sleep with you.' He gave her a rueful grin and suddenly looked like a naughty school boy. 'So there you are, that makes me just as much of a bastard as Michael Cox.'

'I don't think you would have done it though, even if you thought about it.' It was absurd to be pleased that Tom could compare himself to Michael Cox, but the fact he'd wanted her from the start was more important than any comparison he might make.

'It doesn't matter now.' He kissed her again, but they couldn't put off going back to the throng of wedding guests for much longer. 'I just want you to promise me that nothing will stop us today, not even Zac setting himself alight.'

'Stop us doing what?' She was teasing him, but already dizzy at the prospect.

'The pillow fight you promised me. What else were you expecting?' He dropped her an entirely casual wink and started walking towards the house.

'I take it all back.' Feigning indignation, but with a smile like a lottery winner, she called after him. 'You are a bastard after all!'

Chapter Sixteen

'Where the hell have you been?' Stevie looked genuinely irritated when she arrived at the table where they'd been seated for the wedding breakfast. 'I've had to make conversation with these two and I've already agreed to go to the polo with them and hook up in Marbella in May.' He gestured towards two predatory looking women in their early thirties, who were making their way back to the table with another bottle of champagne.

'More bubbly lovely? Couldn't wait for that blasted waiter to get his finger out and serve us. A person could actually die of thirst in this place!' The taller of the two women, who had poker straight hair and an alarmingly horsey appearance, sloshed champagne into Stevie's glass and across most of the table. No wonder the poor waiter had been unable to keep up, it looked as though she'd knocked back several bottles already.

'Oh no. Who are you?' Horsey's friend was staring point-edly at Ashleigh, clearly horrified to see that another woman had moved in on her territory. She had a sulky mouth, which might have rivalled Angelina Jolie's had it been turned up at the corners, instead of turned down like a semi-deflated tyre.

'You didn't say you had a girlfriend!' The lips deflated some more.

'Girlfriend?' Ashleigh laughed and Stevie gave her a quick kick under the table. 'Oh no, we're just friends. Stevie hasn't got a girlfriend.' The kicking was growing more vigorous. 'Hasn't had one for as long as I can remember.'

'Oh goody!' The taller woman thrust out her hand towards Ashleigh, bon vivre fully restored. 'I'm Hortense, pleased to meet you.' For a moment, Ashleigh genuinely thought she'd said her name was 'horse sense'.

'Lovely to meet you Hortense.' She turned the word over carefully as she spoke, knowing just how easy it would have been to make the slip of tongue that was screaming inside her head.

'And I'm Mandy.' Tyre lips thrust out a bony hand. 'We're friends of Carly's. We meet up with her every New Year in Barbados, that's how we first met. We can't bear to see her in January surrounded by grey weather and miserable, over-weight people.'

'Great to meet you, I'm Ashleigh. I expect Stevie has already told you how we know Carly and I'm sure he's also revealed how single he is?' She kept the smile on her face even as Stevie whispered in her ear that he was going to kill her.

'Don't you just love weddings?' Hortense, having happily discerned that Ashleigh was no threat after all, sloshed champagne into her glass with the same sense of abandon that she seemed to be applying to her hunt for a man. 'Such a fabulous way to meet people I always think.' She winked at Stevie, who visibly shuddered.

'Sorry, someone just walked over my grave. Probably a traitorous friend.' He was grinning though.

'Ooh, I hate it when that happens. I can think of much nicer things to make the body shudder.' Hortense laughed and Ashleigh felt strangely disappointed that it wasn't more of a bray. Although, the large floppy straw hat she was sporting did make her look scarily like one of those donkeys on a seaside postcard.

'Sex?' Ashleigh couldn't fight the bubble of laughter any longer. 'Oh yes, that could definitely make Stevie shudder all over again!'

'Yippee!' Hortense giggled, seeming to accept that as a confirmed invitation. 'We've been watching *Four Weddings and a Funeral* by way of preparation for today, haven't we Mandy?' Hortense was obviously the talker of the twosome; Mandy just gave a small nod and a twitch of the resolutely down turned mouth. Ashleigh wondered if she ever smiled. It was going to be a long afternoon.

๛

After the meal and what felt like hours of uncomfortable silence from Mandy and inane conversation from Hortense, the dancing finally started. The newly weds took to the dance floor first, but that was where tradition started and ended. Carly had changed into a gold two-piece outfit, which Ashleigh could have sworn she'd last seen in a Shakira video. The top of it was a crystal-encrusted bikini top and the bottom half was a mini skirt with a row of tassels made from strings of gold beads, which flicked around in all directions whenever Carly moved, and boy was she moving. Duane was positioned on a chair in the middle of the dance floor and, to all intents and purposes, his new wife was performing a less than private lap dance for her husband.

No doubt every straight guy in the room would happily

have changed places with him at that point. Although it did creep Ashleigh out when Carly's uncle, who was also seated at their table, was as enthusiastic about it as the rest of them.

As the dance routine reached an end, other people started to move towards the dance floor. Predictably, Zac Starr was one of the first up and soon had his arms around the waists of two of Carly's bridesmaids.

'God, that man's a dick.' Stevie had a rare curl of the lip as he spoke.

'Looks like he's got fiancées eight *and* nine both lined up together!' Ashleigh grinned. Zac had finally firmed up the plans for her to shoot his album cover later in the week, so he could do no wrong as far as she was concerned.

'Shall we hit the dance floor then?' Stevie tugged at his waistband again. 'I've got to do something, I must have consumed about ten thousand calories today.'

'About eight hours of solid dancing should take care of that then.' She smiled and held out her hand. Sometimes knowing how many calories it took to work off one chocolate cheesecake wasn't a good thing. 'Come on, let's show them how it's done.'

They took their position near the edge of the dance floor and it wasn't long before Zac had dumped the bridesmaids and edged his way across to join them. If there'd been such a thing as a brush-off dance, Stevie was doing it. The more Zac tried to dance next to Ashleigh, the more Stevie positioned himself to block Zac's attempt.

'Mind if I cut in?' Tom was suddenly standing next to them. The thought that he'd been watching her dance moves was mortifying.

'Yeah, go for it Tom, I need a drink anyway.' Zac gave him

an amiable dig in the ribs. 'Watch out though, she's hot stuff tonight.'

'I'd noticed.' Tom's expression was unreadable and Ashleigh thanked God that the Latin beat of the band's second song had subsided and been replaced by their version of *Have I told you lately?* by Van Morrison.

'I'll let you two tackle this one on your own.' Stevie winked. 'Just don't do anything I wouldn't do.'

'This is my favourite song.' She breathed in the subtle scent of Tom's aftershave as he pulled her towards him. 'I know you don't believe in it, but I think this song is exactly what love should be all about.' He was a less flamboyant dancer than Zac or Stevie, but he could move and there was an intensity in the way that he held her that was a thousand times more intimate than all Zac's hip thrusting could ever be. She could easily have been lost in the moment, if she'd let herself. The dance floor had cleared a little and conversation was more possible, so she tried to concentrate on that instead.

'Still enjoying yourself?' He pulled away from her for a moment, looking at her so intently that she had to glance away.

'The best bits of the day have had you in them.' She buried her face in his shoulder, so that eye contact was impossible.

'You seemed to be really enjoying yourself with Zac.' It was a statement rather than a question.

'You know Zac and Stevie, we were just having a laugh.' His body relaxed a little as she spoke and he pulled slightly away again.

'Is this a laugh too?' His face was unreadable. 'Only as far as I knew we had firm plans for tonight and I'd rather know now if you want to back out.'

'Do you want me to sign a contract?' She tried to make light of it, suddenly struck by the thought that there might be a first reserve already waiting in the wings, and she didn't want to think about that. It was like contemplating the flight home from your holiday when you were only just packing your case to go.

'No contract, I'll take your word for it.' Tom's lips brushed her lobe as he whispered in her ear. 'Can we go now?'

As they made their way out into the main stairwell of the hotel, they bumped into Stevie, charging past the huge Christmas tree in the other direction, with the perfect outline of a hand print, in stinging red, emblazoned across his cheek.

'What happened to you? Are you alright?' Ashleigh was full of concern as Stevie gingerly touched the area of his face where he'd been slapped.

'Yes, I'm fine.' He gave her a sheepish smile. 'I was just kissing someone and they were kissing me back. I think it took us both a bit by surprise though and they obviously felt like I'd taken advantage.'

'Are you sure you're okay?' He wouldn't want to say too much in front of Tom, so she didn't press him about the mystery recipient of the kiss.

'Yeah I'm fine, just a bit shocked about both the kiss *and* the slap!' He grinned, reassuring her he was okay. Either way, Tom might have given Stevie more than a slap if she'd disappeared to sort out his problems. 'I'll tell you all about it tomorrow. Let's just say that if I sang *I kissed a girl and I liked it*, you wouldn't be any more surprised.' He leant forward, giving her a quick kiss of her own. 'Now go and have fun for God's sake!'

Chapter Seventeen

The staircase sweeping up towards the first floor of the hotel was straight out of 'Gone With The Wind'. Tom took her hand and began to lead her up the first few steps.

'What are you doing?' Ashleigh stopped on the third step and refused to move any further. The whole point of booking the bed and breakfast had been to ensure discretion and a little bit of privacy away from the wedding party. 'What if someone sees us?'

'Frankly my dear, I couldn't give a damn.' There was that easy wink again. 'Look, desperate as I am to get you into bed, I was planning to take the time to shut the door.'

'I meant in the morning.' He was teasing her, but what if she'd got the etiquette wrong and he wasn't planning on her spending the whole night with him? It was all so complicated, like a game of chess she didn't really understand. It was no wonder Stevie had been the only man in her life for so long.

'Are you ashamed of me then?' When he smiled, there was no way to resist. He pressed himself against her, until her back was up against the balustrade of the banisters. His lips brushed against her mouth and a jolt of desire shot down her spine.

'Not ashamed no.' She smiled and would have attempted a wink herself, if it didn't end up making her look like a stroke victim. 'Only my mother wouldn't approve of us kissing in public like this.' It was a lie of course. Had her mother been in Ashleigh's shoes, she'd probably have taken half her clothes off by now and left them on each stair on the way up, like some kind of gingerbread trail announcing to the world that she was on her way to this gorgeous guy's room to have sex.

'Good, because I couldn't care less who sees us.' He paused for a second to kiss her again.

At least she'd had the foresight to get a bikini wax, she couldn't risk Tom bursting out laughing the moment she whipped off her pants. Or he did. Panic rose in her throat again, her mind was a blank; she'd completely forgotten how these things worked, just who was it that did the knickers removal?

With each step, she was more tempted to make a bolt for it. What if she really was boring in bed, as Liam had suggested? Her mind was whirring. Would Tom be waxed in anticipation of their night too or was he the hairy natural type? She was all for a bit of chest hair, but she wasn't quite sure how she would react if he had hair from his shoulders to his buttocks like a silver-back gorilla.

By the time they reached Tom's room, she was shaking. Had she been in a different state of mind, she might have appreciated her surroundings more. The suite was dominated by the mandatory four-poster bed set in the middle of the circular room, positioned in *Brewley Manor*'s turreted wing. There was also a huge, squashy sofa, a table laden with fruit, a bottle of chilled champagne and one of the biggest boxes of chocolates that Ashleigh had ever seen. Tom hadn't touched them, not a single one. If she and Stevie had been given the room, the chocolates would have been devoured within minutes, with only the Turkish delights and rock hard toffee centres left. That must be the difference when you had money and were used to this sort of thing all of the time. It wouldn't be nearly as much of a treat for Tom.

'What are you thinking about?' He cupped her chin gently until her gaze finally met his. Probably best not to tell him that she was thinking about chocolate.

'You.' Well it wasn't a lie, she was thinking about him, at least about how he'd been able to resist the chocolates. Her brain seemed to be trying to distract her, albeit temporarily, from panicking.

'That's good, because I've been thinking about you far too much from the day you first walked into my office and began ridiculing my choice of fiancée!' He was grinning though and the dimples were back. God, he was sexy.

'I'm sorry about that.' She couldn't suppress a grin either. 'Well, okay, I'm not sorry. It's just she didn't seem like your type.'

'But you are.' It wasn't a question. 'You have no idea how gorgeous you are, do you?'

She dropped her gaze again, she couldn't look at him when he was saying things like that to her. A sudden sound, like hundreds of fire crackers outside the bedroom window made her jump.

'It's the fireworks. Carly said they'd be having them at nine o'clock, it's when they first met. She told me she doesn't even remember it, but Duane never forgot.'

Tom's arm circled her waist and he led her to the window, as thousands of pounds worth of fireworks exploded into the night sky. 'When we first met, I wondered whether you and Stevie were a couple. I suspected he was gay, but then the way you looked at each other made me think I might be wrong.'

'And I thought you hated me.'

'I think I tried to convince us both of that, it would have been a hell of a lot easier than what I was really thinking.' He gave her a rueful smile. 'There I was with my pregnant fiancée, wondering what the photographer taking our engagement photo looked like without her clothes on.'

'So… do you want to find out?' A familiar blush swept across her skin, but for once she didn't care.

'Right now, there's absolutely nothing else I'd rather be doing.'

Tom moved towards her, the fireworks still crackling outside. This was it. It was really going to happen. Just like the first time they'd kissed, as his lips pressed against hers again, Ashleigh found herself rooted to the spot. She wanted this, and him, but part of her wanted to run too, before it really was too late to turn away from the risk she was about to take.

His hands moved up from her waist, finding the zip on her dress without hesitation, the silkiness of her new underwear helping it slide to the floor with ease. Finally able to move, as he drew away, she undid a couple of buttons on his shirt – her hands so clumsy it was almost like they belonged to someone else. She was aware of his eyes on her body and she tried not to wonder what he was thinking; she was supposed to be sexy and confident, not blushing like a first-timer. The decision she'd made to keep a clear head and stay sober suddenly felt like the wrong one. All of this would have been much easier with her inhibitions dulled.

At last his shirt was undone and she knew she'd risk anything to sleep with him. Seeing him half-naked, she couldn't have backed out even if she'd wanted to. The smell of sandalwood clung just delicately enough to his skin. Subtle notes of the distinctive aftershave that always made her think of him, were left too; a heady combination which, with the sight of his bare chest, left her unable to resist running her hands down it towards his waist. Fumbling with his belt buckle, she dropped her gaze.

'Are you sure you want to do this?' Tom's voice was gentle, his hands over hers – he must have been able to feel her shaking.

'You know I do, I'm just a bit worried that I'll…' He raised a finger to her lips before she could finish.

'Trust me. There's nothing to worry about. This is all about having fun, so you can leave your angst at the door. There's no rush either.' She finally looked at his face; the intensity in those dark blue eyes said as much as his words. It might be casual and it might be fun, but this didn't feel like a one-night stand any more. He slid off his unbuttoned shirt and removed the rest of his clothes as she watched him, until only his boxer shorts were left. Thank God he wasn't the sort to keep his socks on.

Leading her towards the sofa, they sank down together and his hands moved expertly across her body as they kissed again, discarding her underwear with considerable skill. She wasn't going to think about just how many times he'd done this before, though. His mouth moved to her ear and down her neck, his breathing deepening. She could hear how much he wanted her, her more than anyone at that moment. She slid her hand inside the waistband of his shorts and the physical confirmation that she'd wanted was obvious.

The warmth of his skin against hers felt natural, her nipples grazing his chest as his mouth moved slowly towards the base of her neck.

'Have you got something?' She was panicking again, aware she was being swept away by his touch. But, if he was like Liam, there'd be expectations within minutes – things she was supposed to do; things she didn't want to do without knowing they were both protected.

'Stop worrying, it's sorted. Just relax.' Tom's breath on her neck made her shiver. Easy for him to say. As his lips found her collar bone, and continued their journey down, her whole body stood to attention. Okay, the sex might not turn out to be fabulous, but so far it was… An involuntary gasp escaped her, as his tongue slowly circled her nipple. Parts of her she hadn't known had any connection to that area of her body rushed with blood; even the soles of her feet began to tingle as he closed his mouth around her and she responded – a million sensations flooding through her.

'I want you…' She couldn't help saying it; in a thousand years she wouldn't have said it out loud if she could have stopped herself. What he was doing wasn't unchartered territory, but what it was doing to her was. Ashleigh wanted to feel the weight of his body on hers. It was crying out for him.

He stopped and looked at her, drawing upwards until their heads were level again. 'That's good to know, because I've been feeling that way about you for a very long time now - much longer than I wanted to wait.' Tom's eyes seemed darker than ever as he smiled, the anticipation created by their near misses heightening the moment. 'Please tell me you haven't just thought of some emergency that means we've got to stop? I'm not sure I could take it again.' He raised an eyebrow and, without replying, she began to slide down his body. – it was her turn to satisfy him. This was always how it had been before, you got a little bit and you gave a little bit. Only Tom was stopping her, his hands on her face, gently guiding her upwards until they were level again. 'Not this time. It's your turn tonight.' He pressed his body against hers so that she was left in no doubt and smiled again. 'Just promise me you'll relax and let me show you how good this can be… for both of us.'

She nodded. She'd already decided to go along with it, pretend it was the best sex ever if she had to; she'd done it before. Liam did sex by numbers, as though he'd been programmed to repeat the same routine every time. His fingers prodding at her or moving in circular motions quicker and quicker, as if he just wanted to get that bit over and get on with the bit he really enjoyed. She'd faked enough orgasms to be pretty convincing. Although she'd be frustrated as hell, since Tom's touch was proving to be like nothing she'd ever experienced.

His mouth was moving away from hers again, travelling slowly back down her neck and finding the other nipple, bringing back that sensation that made her want to beg him, her body arching for what it wanted. This time, when Tom stopped, he didn't work his way back up her body. His lips brushed the skin across her abdomen, his tongue dancing across her hip bone and then kissing her outer thigh, moving about half way down before shifting his head slightly so that his tongue was travelling up her inner thigh. The anticipation and teasing of his mouth against her skin so intense it was almost painful.

'Tom…' He didn't stop at the sound of his name, it was clear he didn't want to and finally she let herself believe it, his hands moving upwards until they were holding down her arms. It wasn't that she couldn't have escaped if she'd wanted to, but she didn't want him to stop either – not for anything.

Finally he was at the point where those million sensations she was experiencing met and as the tip of his tongue swept across she almost screamed. He'd released his grip on her arms, and she found herself scrunching handfuls of the sofa cushions, as her body arched towards him again. Each sweep and circle of his tongue built the intensity. If he stopped now, she might actually die. But he didn't and at last her body took over from her mind, giving itself up to pure pleasure, leaving no room for anything else. She must have made a noise, but she didn't hear it. Everything was centred on that one point and the rest of the world slipped away. It wasn't that she hadn't done that before, but it had never felt this good, not even a tenth as good.

Tom moved backwards, until he was sitting further down the sofa. Taking her hand in his, he pulled her towards him, and she moved so that she was straddling his legs.

'If you want me to stop, tell me now. Because the way I'm feeling at the moment, if I touch you again there'll be no going back.' Tom kept his eyes on hers as he spoke, even as he reached across to the coffee table and slid a foil packet out from its hiding place.

'I don't want you to stop.' She just managed to stop herself adding the word "ever". Waves of sensation were still pulsing through her body, but she wanted to feel that intimacy that only the next step could bring. She took the condom out of his hand, her earlier clumsiness replaced by newfound confidence. Sliding it on, she kept watching him, his eyes closing as her fingers moved up and down.

'It's not that what you're doing doesn't feel great, but I'm so ready for you that I don't know how much longer I can hold out.' His words rushed out with gasps of breath, as he ran his hands up and down her back, and she knelt up, moving forward slightly before lowering herself down again. The feel of him was another sensation all together, as powerful as she'd known it would be. His lips found her nipple again as she moved on top of him and he moaned in response. This bit was supposed to be about him, but the places he touched made her lose control and within minutes she was shivering again, with new intensity, as those million sensations once more found themselves exploding together. She couldn't have stopped for anything. Even as she wanted to pull away, as the pleasure and pain of such feelings began to merge, she found herself moving with him once more and for a third time she gasped throwing her head back as he finally let go and joined her, almost lifting her off the sofa with the intensity of the moment.

For a second neither of them spoke, and she didn't move. Not wanting to break the connection she felt of him being part of her.

'Okay?' Tom cupped her chin, so that she had to look at him again.

'More than okay. You?' He smiled at her words, so that Ashleigh knew exactly what his answer was going to be.

'Oh, definitely. A very good start.' He was teasing again, but the rise and fall of his chest and the catching of his breath told the real story. Putting his hands around her waist, he drew her gently upwards. 'I'm going to grab a shower,' he paused for a second, grinning again, 'Interested?'

'Very.' In that moment, she didn't even pause to grab a cushion or something else to try and cover up her nakedness.

Taking his hand she followed him to the bathroom, knowing that something in her had changed forever.

Ashleigh was having one of those weird experiences where you wake up and don't know where you are. She looked down and saw her own smooth white leg curled around Tom's browner, much hairier one. Despite the reassuring manliness of his legs, Ashleigh had been thrilled to discover that Tom's back was delightfully hair free and he had quite the most magnificent buttocks she had ever seen in real life. She gingerly lifted the covers to have another sneaky peek.

'I hope you're not looking at my bum.' Tom turned on to his back in a vain attempt to protect his modesty, only the manoeuvre back fired slightly, as he was clearly more than ready for a repeat performance.

'Come here.' He didn't seem able to stop touching her and she wasn't complaining. 'You really don't know how beautiful you are?' He smoothed a tendril of hair behind her ear, as she shook her head. 'I wish you could see what I see.'

'Thanks. You'll do for now too. Until we both get bored of course.' It was what he wanted to hear, so she said it, and he pulled her towards him again. Conversation, it seemed, was the last thing on his mind.

'Oh no, is that the time?' Ashleigh sat bolt upright, two hours later. After having sex again, she'd fallen sleep in his arms and now it was almost eleven o'clock.

'Are you worried you've missed breakfast?' Tracing the curve of her breast with his finger, Tom gave her a lazy smile.

'It's not that.' She darted under his arm to escape as he tried to kiss her again. If she let him, she knew she'd have to write off the rest of the day. 'Although I am absolutely starving.' Her stomach decided to echo the sentiment by giving a rumble worthy of an approaching thunderstorm. 'It's just if I miss Joseph singing his solo love song to Mary my life won't be worth living.'

'Okay, I definitely have to get you something to eat.' He placed a hand on her forehead and pretended to take her temperature, giving her a look of mock concern. 'You appear to be delirious.'

'It's my brother's solo, in church this afternoon, he's playing Joseph in a musical version of the Nativity.' She frantically tried to stay wrapped in the bed sheets, whose hospital corners appeared to have been welded to the bed and didn't want to move with her, as she searched around in a fruitless attempt to locate her underwear.

'Do you want me to come with you?' Tom unhooked her bra from its resting place on one of the bedposts and handed it to her. 'I could drive you down. Maybe we could meet up afterwards or I might even be willing to come to church if you made it worth my while.'

'God no!' Ashleigh shuddered and then, seeing the look on his face, shook her head again. 'If I turn up with you, my mother will go into hyper drive that I've got a sex life at last. It wouldn't be pretty, trust me.' She'd finally found her knickers, which shimmered like a small satin puddle under one side of the bed. 'Stevie's coming with me. He's known the family for years, so the fact that they really are all bonkers, especially my mother, won't faze him.' She desperately tried to cover her modesty, even though they'd hungrily explored one another's bodies just hours before.

'Ah, mothers, always best to keep them out of things.' He

grinned and she wasn't sure if it was the sentiment, or her struggle to get dressed without him seeing, that was amusing him so much.

'Definitely one of the upsides of keeping it casual.' Having wrestled back into her underwear whilst still half-wrapped in the sheet, Ashleigh allowed him to pull her back into his arms. 'It's nearly Christmas and that makes it my crazy mother's maddest time of the year and if I don't turn up, Jamie will get it all.' She could feel herself weaken as he began kissing her neck and she had to stand up before she changed her mind. 'Sorry Tom, it's not that I don't want to stay.' Her words were muffled as she slithered back into the soft suede dress that she'd abandoned with such pleasure the night before. 'But I can't leave the poor little sod to cope with my mother all by himself.'

'Okay, okay, I concede.' Tom pulled her to him for one last kiss. 'But I want to see you again soon. Are you back in town before Christmas? Or can I come to your place?' He wasn't a man to play games. Somehow she knew if he said he was going to call that he would. After someone like Liam, it made Tom even more attractive. Was she mad to leave him to go to a Christmas service in a draughty church battered by freezing December winds?

'Call me tonight?' Ashleigh smiled, she could guarantee there'd be plenty to tell him about her mum's behaviour in church. She could only hope Carol wouldn't be dressed as the Virgin Mary.

'Only if I can see you tomorrow.' It might have sounded needy from a different man, but coming from him it made her feel incredible to be so wanted.

'We'll see.' Trying and failing to sound casual, she grinned and scooped up the huge box of chocolates that she'd admired the night before. 'I'll just take these in lieu of breakfast.'

Tom had a hot shower and ordered some food from room service. He'd wanted Ashleigh to stay, but was glad that she had her own life to live. Maybe they'd be together for six months, like he and Carly had been, or even a bit longer. The photos Ashleigh had taken of Chloe had been the game changer. She didn't need Tom to raise her profile, her talent was enough. So there was no reason why they couldn't stay friends and, even more importantly, work together once the rest was over.

Tom finally switched his phone back on twenty minutes after Ashleigh had left and it immediately rang, the number on the caller display all too familiar. 'What's up, Francine?'

'It's Ryan Murray, he was drunk and high on a chat show and used the word "fuck" three times before the watershed.' Tom could just imagine Francine's pained expression as she spoke, it was a bit like hearing your Nan utter the F-word.

'Is he okay?' Tom sighed. The rumours about Ryan's alleged drug taking were probably true and they'd had a few problems with him before, but he'd been dealt a rough hand in life, from his troubled childhood in and out of foster care.

'I expect he's got a sore head this morning, but it serves him right.' Francine knew about Ryan's past too, but it clearly hadn't touched the block of ice that passed for her heart. 'I think we should drop him from our representation. It's not like he's a big earner.'

'No way!' Tom was adamant. Ryan needed help instead of being unceremoniously dropped; everyone deserved a second chance in life. In any case, Tom was in a good mood, better than he'd been for a long time, which made him much more forgiving. 'Get him booked into *The Priory* and issue a press release on his behalf, apologising for his behaviour and confirming that our medical team suspect it's the result of a reaction to some prescription medication.'

'I don't think we should make excuses for him. I don't like it.' Francine sounded sulky; Ryan's fame, as a reality TV star, was the type of celebrity that she loathed most of all.

'Well that's our job, like it or not.' Tom's knuckles tightened around the mobile phone; he wasn't in the mood for Francine's histrionics.

'You know best.' Her tone belied the statement. 'When will you be back?'

'I'll give you a call, but I might go and see Mum.' Before she could reply he ended the call. There was nothing like a conversation with Francine to bring your mood down.

Creeping in through the front door of the Bed and Breakfast, Ashleigh was mortified to see the landlady, Janice, smiling merrily at her from behind the reception desk.

'Looks like you had a good time luvvie.' The old lady gave her a wink, making her acutely aware she was wearing the same clothes as she had been the day before.

'Er, yes I did thanks.' She needed a hot shower. Stevie darn well better not have hogged all the water.

'Christ, you look even worse than I do.' She was shocked to see Stevie still lying in bed. The shadows under his eyes made him look like a vampire from the *Twilight* movies. A crop of angry purple bruises spanned much of his neck on one side, the remnants of a night of snogging, the like of which Ashleigh hadn't seen since her teenage years. Did people really still give each other love bites?

'Which of us looks worse is a matter of opinion.' Stevie grinned. 'Although I might have to borrow a bit of foundation to cover these up.' He touched his neck, wincing as his fingers made contact with the bruises.

'Who the hell did that, Henry the Hoover?' She dropped her bag onto the bed and kicked off her shoes. The shower could wait five minutes; she had to know who had given Stevie love bites requiring that level of suction.

'That's the worse part.' It was completely out of character for him to look embarrassed, if she hadn't known better she would have sworn he was blushing. 'I honestly can't remember.'

'You tart!' She was teasing him, but she just hoped he'd been careful. She'd known him to get drunk before and take risks that in the cold light of day hadn't seemed like quite such a good idea.

'Hey you can talk!' He pulled her on to the bed and she rested her head on his shoulder. 'At least I ended up in my own bed.'

'Yes, but who with?' Had he seriously woken up with some bloke and not even bothered to ask his name.

'I came back here in the early hours… alone.' His tone was somewhere between righteous indignation and disappoint-ment. 'I take it that you and Tom finally got it together?'

'Uh ha.' Ashleigh slid towards the edge of the bed and stood up. 'I've got to grab a shower and head down to Jamie's show.' Keen to change the subject, she didn't want to cheapen the time she'd spent with Tom by sharing every lurid detail – not even with Stevie. 'Are you still coming?'

'Yeah, yeah.' He stretched and gave an excruciatingly long yawn. 'I'll jump in the shower after you. But don't think you're getting out of it that easily. You can give me the gory details on the way down there'.

Chapter Eighteen

Janice had come to their rescue and given them a lift to the station in time to catch the one p.m. bullet train to Kent. By the time they reached the church, groups of parents were already jostling for position to see their little darlings perform in the show. It was the week before Christmas, but festive spirit went out of the window when it came to bagging the best seat in church. Predictably, Carol had ensured that she wouldn't be outdone. She was lying on the second pew from the front, stretched from edge to edge to make sure that no-one even thought about trying to take one of the seats she was working so hard to save. Not that anyone in their right mind would choose to sit next to her. She looked like one of those wild eyed weirdos who manage to keep the four seats surrounding them free on public transport, by virtue of the fact that no-one wants to sit within a ten foot radius of them.

'My darling girl, at last!' As Carol rose from her seat, a wave of her homemade perfume rose with her and Ashleigh coughed slightly as it hit the back of her throat. Carol was wearing a red sequinned dress at least two sizes too small and her hair had been dyed an alarmingly lurid shade of magenta.

'And Stevie, sweetheart, you look divine!' She enveloped them both in a vigorous hug and her eye-popping cleavage threatened to escape as a result of her enthusiasm.

'Love the matching roll necks, so 1960s!' She stepped back to get a proper look at them. Stevie had borrowed one of Ashleigh's jumpers, to hide the crop of love bites that Carol would have been far too excited about.

'Hello Mum, Geoffrey.' She kissed them both on the cheek, her mild mannered stepfather colouring at the show of affection. 'How's Jamie bearing up? Is he nervous?' They shuffled up the aisle, leaving one seat spare at the end.

'Only about whether I'll show him up!' Carol broke into noisy peals of laughter, drawing yet more attention to herself.

'As if!' Stevie squeezed her knee, provoking another outburst of hysteria and exasperated tutting from some of the other parents seated in the row behind.

A few minutes later the curate turned off the lights at the back of the church hall, leaving just the stage floodlit. The young vicar had obviously decided to adopt a modern take on the nativity, telling it from the point of view of Joseph, meaning that Jamie had the lead role.

For someone who wanted to be a scientist and who believed staunchly in evolution, Jamie gave a convincing performance. He had a great operatic voice and Ashleigh had to sniff back tears at one point.

'Thank God for that!' The interval clearly couldn't arrive quickly enough for Stevie who, suffering from a monster hangover, had drunk four pints of water in an attempt to assuage his raging thirst – resulting in a bladder that was ready to burst at any second.

'I didn't realise you'd be quite so delighted to see me!' The slow drawl was recognisable enough and, since he was wearing sunglasses indoors on a damp December afternoon, it could only be one person

'What the hell are you doing here?' Stevie's tone was unusually aggressive. Ashleigh, aware that they'd never quite hit it off, quickly squeezed past Stevie, risking setting his bladder off in the process and kissed Zac on the cheek.

'If you remember, Stephen,' Zac stretched out the syllables of his name, so that even saying it sounded sarcastic, 'when I said I wanted to take Ashleigh out to dinner to discuss the shoot, you told me what you were both up to today.' She hadn't felt more like piggy in the middle since she'd been at school, when the twins, Sadie and Kirsty, had fought until blood was drawn over who Ashleigh's best friend was. 'So you came all the way down here to see if I was telling the truth?' Stevie couldn't have looked less pleased to see someone if he'd tried.

'Why don't you nip to the loo?' Ashleigh gave him a beseeching look, she loved Stevie to death but there was no way she could afford to lose the chance she'd been waiting for to get her big break. Zac might be a massive pain in the bum, but photographing his album cover could be the start of something new.

'Yes, why don't you pop off? There's a good boy.' Zac's voice was dripping with undisguised animosity. They certainly weren't going to make things easy for her.

Stevie bit his lip and stood up, squeezing past like a determined pensioner desperate to bag the last seat on the bus, elbows out.

'What's his problem?' Zac raised an eyebrow and, spotting her mother, held out his arms. 'You, my darling, must be Ash's sister?' It was the cheesiest chat up line in history, but Carol still shrieked with pleasure and happily folded herself, cleavage and all, into Zac's ready embrace.

'Silly!' Carol pinched his bum; if there was ever a meeting of minds it was these two. 'I know exactly who you are of course.'

'I suppose Ashleigh's been talking about me non-stop?'

'Not really.' Inadvertently taking the wind out of his sails, Carol was nonplussed. 'I just love the gossip pages of the papers and you always give them something to write about!'

The second half of the show was quite a lot shorter and Ashleigh had positioned both herself and her mother in between Stevie and Zac to minimise the chances of a slanging match breaking out.

Carol and Geoffrey were taking Jamie out for a fish and chips supper at *Triviani's* to celebrate his success. Since Jamie's mates seemed to love Carol as much as Stevie did, they were also taking several other twelve and thirteen year old lads out with them. Tempting as the offer to join them was, Ashleigh declined. She had a good excuse; Stevie, appalled by the lack of festive cheer at her flat, had made her promise he could decorate it ready for Christmas. In truth, she just wanted to make sure she was back in time to take Tom's phone call. The thought of speaking to him had been keeping her going all afternoon. After all, he knew exactly what Zac and Stevie were like and might be the only person in the world who'd appreciate why she'd been left feeling like an exhausted school teacher.

Hanrahan's was an old fashioned hardware store that had a small nursery out back. They sold the most fabulous Christmas trees, which bushed out with generous foliage and whose pine aroma drifted down the street. The shop was officially closed, as it was a Sunday evening, but Pete Hanrahan would be in the pub next door, ready and waiting to serve any local who popped in, offered him a pint and wanted to do a quick bit of after-hours shopping.

Stevie lined up a couple of pints for Pete on the bar of the *Lord Nelson* public house and was rewarded, in return, with a set of keys to the back door of the nursery. Having known Ashleigh for years, he was more than happy to trust them with the keys to his empire, as Zac trailed along behind. Stevie was like a whirling dervish in the shop, picking up armloads of decorations and selecting an oversized Norwegian Blue pine. He tallied up the bill and expertly ran the transaction through the till, charging the cost to his own credit card. That Saturday job at Top Shop in his teens hadn't been a waste of time after all.

'Let me pay.' Ashleigh didn't want Stevie to bankrupt himself with false bravado in front of Zac. She'd seen the bank statements at his flat and he could ill afford to splash the cash.

'No, consider it an early Christmas present.' He winked and they shared a private joke. 'That way, you won't get any nasty surprises on Christmas day.' Every year, Stevie bought her something to wear in the vain hope of persuading her to embrace the latest trend, regardless of whether or not it suited her voluptuous shape. Over the years, she'd opened and never worn a range of items ranging from rah-rah skirts to harem pants.

'Only diamonds would do for someone like you.' Zac flicked open his wallet ostentatiously to reveal a stash of credit cards in gold and platinum.

'Yeah, well, they don't sell those here, mate.' Never had the word *mate* been uttered with less sincerity. 'Only diamante baubles. Perhaps you could use a couple of balls though?'

'Okay, are we done?' Ever the peace-maker, Ashleigh scooped up the bags of shopping, leaving Zac and Stevie to argue over who was going to demonstrate his manliness by being the one to carry the Christmas tree home.

Having dropped the keys back to Pete in the pub, the three of them began to trudge along the increasingly frosty pavement of Sandgate high street, towards the flat.

'Shall we leave the tree outside while we work out the best place to put it?' Ashleigh didn't fancy witnessing a tug of war between Zac and Stevie, whilst the tree turned from a lovely bushy specimen into a crispy brown twig, with pine needles carpeting every inch of her floor.

'Okay.' Zac grudgingly relinquished possession of the tree and propped it up in its temporary home, outside the entrance to her flat.

'How about here?' Inside the flat, Stevie indicated the corner in front of the large picture window that gave the best view of the sea. 'Imagine it all lit up, twinkling against the back drop of the lights from the boats out there.' Stevie's face was glowing. His first love had been interior design and Ashleigh sometimes wondered if he'd be happier doing that. After all, sitting rooms didn't answer back or moan that sea breeze blue really wasn't their colour.

'You're right, it would look fabulous there.' Zac's voice was low and quiet, almost as if he couldn't bear to be heard agreeing with Stevie about anything.

'There it is then.' She wasn't going to argue with them. If they'd managed to reach a consensus then that was good enough for her.

'Great, well you two bring it in and I'll start sorting out which decks to put on where.' Stevie had taken over and was in his element, bossing them about as though they were a couple of interns sitting in on one of his photo shoots for *Glitz.*

Outside the sudden drop in temperature caught Ashleigh's breath, the frost on the step making her stumble slightly as she leant forward to take hold of one end of the tree, causing her to canon into Zac who had been about to bend down to pick up the other end. Catching her mid fall, he steadied them both for a moment, before pulling her towards him and kissing her as though his last chance of oxygen depended on sucking it out of her. The kiss couldn't have been more unexpected, yet at the same time predictable. If she'd been asked to guess what kind of kisser Zac was, she would have described the experience down to a tee. He'd clamped his lips so firmly over her mouth that she was finding it difficult to breathe, even through her nose. The kiss was forceful, yet somehow passionless and he was sharing more than a little bit too much of his saliva for her liking. Hadn't she made it clear enough that she wasn't interested? Perhaps a knee in the groin was called for.

'I appear to be interrupting something.' The voice was dismissive, exactly as it had been that first day in his office. She extracted her lips from Zac, with a noise not unlike plunging a blocked sink. There was a muscle going in Tom's cheek. 'I thought I'd pop in and surprise you.' He fired the words like bullets, through clenched teeth. 'Only it seems like I'm the one who's got the surprise.'

'It isn't what it looks like!' Even as she protested, she was aware the words sounded trite. Wasn't that what everyone said in these circumstances, having been caught out? She turned to Zac for some back up. He had to explain it had been a spur of the moment thing and entirely his doing to instigate the kiss. Zac, who was looking a bit embarrassed, had almost shrunk into the shadows, clearly deciding that saying nothing at all was the best policy in this situation. 'Oh for Christ's sake!' Ashleigh grimaced, he had less backbone than the average garden worm. 'Nothing's going on. Zac just seems to have got caught up in the Christmas spirit, that's all.' Surely he'd see that she wasn't remotely interested in Zac? But Tom was already turning away from her.

'Whatever you say. Look, this was obviously a mistake on my part so I think I'll just leave you to it.' He strode back towards his car, her protestations vanishing into the night air as he disappeared from view. Either he hadn't heard her or didn't want to. She suspected the latter. Tears of frustration at the unjustness of it all, which she absolutely refused to cry in front of her new nemesis Zac, burned at the back of her eyes.

Tom thumped the steering wheel of the car. What the hell was wrong with him? Christ, if he reacted like that in nego-tiations on behalf of his clients, he would have gone out of business years before. It wasn't like he and Ashleigh had prom-ised each other anything and she wasn't the sort to fall into Zac's arms hours after she'd been in his bed, which made his reaction all the more illogical. Much more likely that it was Zac's doing, an aging rock star trying to prove something to himself. So why had he reacted like a schoolboy? If this was jealousy, he didn't like it – no wonder people said it was an ugly emotion. Whatever it was he was experiencing, he'd never felt it this strongly before. So why the hell had it started now? He hit the steering wheel again at the exact moment his phone began to ring.

'What?' He'd seen Francine's number flash up on his phone and the last thing he wanted was another lecture about what a mistake he was making with Ashleigh. Francine would be in the know, the gossip about him and Ashleigh at the wedding no doubt spreading like wildfire between the staff at Glitz and *Rushworth Associates.*

'It's Chloe.' Francine wasted no time with niceties. 'She's about to lose us millions of pounds, if you don't get back up here and sort her out before she chucks her career away.'

'What's wrong?' Responsibility weighed him down. There were always someone else's problems that had to take priority over his. Chloe was a girl with genuine talent and vulnerability, probably the one client he would prioritise before making things right with Ashleigh, but it was typical of Francine to put the money before the person. How much of that had come from working with him? It was a depressing thought.

'Her mother had a heart attack and evidently Chloe's lost the plot and been wandering around semi-naked.' There wasn't a trace of empathy in Francine's voice. It was all about the business, same as ever.

'Oh God, is Gilly okay?' Tom swallowed hard. Chloe relied on her mum and, like him, had few other people she felt she could trust.

'I'm not sure.' Francine sighed. 'Does it matter? Regardless of that you need to get up here and sort Chloe out, the business needs you.'

'Yeah, but will it keep me warm at night and make me laugh?' Chloe wasn't the only one losing it.

'Are you drunk?' Francine's tone was sharp. 'Look, I'll send a car if you need one, you just need to get back here.'

'I'm not drunk and I'm on my way.' He shook his head, attempting to dislodge the thoughts that were clouding his judgement. Maybe it was for the best that Francine had called;

something was happening to him and he didn't like it. Perhaps she was right about what was important. People would come and go in life and more often than not they ended up letting you down, but work was his one constant. It was a sentiment he repeated to himself all the way back to London.

Following Tom's departure, Ashleigh had left Stevie and Zac to bicker over the best way to decorate the flat. No doubt Zac had given Stevie his version of what had happened and Ashleigh had retreated to her bedroom with a box of apple pies, three *Kit Kats* and her mobile phone. She'd sent Tom a text to tell him what had really happened and was determined that she wouldn't contact him again if he didn't reply. Three apple pies later and her resolve, like the pastry, had started to crumble. By the time she'd eaten all three *Kit Kats*, she'd sent him no less than six texts without a response. The texts had got progressively more abusive. Fuelled by her frustration, and the lack of response, she'd ended up telling him he was a bastard and calling Zac even worse names. Now she not only had the waistband of her trousers cutting into her, and what looked threateningly like a spot about to break through on her chin, she'd probably come off looking like a psycho and certainly not employee of the year material.

'Morning honey.' Stevie was stretched out along the window seat, next to the newly decorated Christmas tree, which any editor of *Homes and Gardens* would have been proud to include in the December special.

'Where's Zac?' She wasn't sure she wanted to know. As much as shooting his album cover was pivotal to her career plans, right about then she'd have been happy to do time for his murder.

'Gone.' Stevie sounded equally relieved. Even in her abject misery it was obvious that the atmosphere in the flat was lighter for Zac's absence. 'A chauffeur driven Merc turned up about midnight last night and whisked him off. He said he'd see you on the twenty-third.' Stevie suppressed a grin. 'Oh and he said chin up or something equally uplifting.'

'Pratt.' Just the very hint of a smile threatened for a second. She could well imagine Zac saying something that crass. Who the hell did he think he was anyway, assuming she'd still be willing to turn up for the shoot on the twenty-third after all that had happened? Okay, so she was willing to, but he had a damn cheek for making that assumption. She drained her first cup of coffee without taking a breath and poured a second cup from the pot that Stevie had thankfully had the foresight to make.

'So, I suppose he told you what happened last night?' She could hardly bear to think about it. Tom had over-reacted and, if she'd cared less about him, she might even have written him off for the way that he'd behaved. Susie-Anne's betrayal must have had more of an effect on him than even he realised and he didn't seem to trust anyone. Now she and Zac had made things worse.

'Yeah.' Stevie gave her a rueful smile. 'Zac told me, well his version of it anyway.'

'Let me guess? I pretended to trip so he could catch me in his arms and I'd get the opportunity to leap on him, irresistible sex god that he is of course?' There was a desperation about Zac that was much more of a turn off than Tom's brief flash of insecurity. Yet there were still plenty of groupies lining up to spend a night with him and perhaps get the lifestyle that would go with becoming fiancée number eight. If she hadn't been so angry with him, she might have felt sorry for him. Despite the seven fiancées, it was quite possible he'd never really been in love or had anyone really love him. He loved himself, of course, but in the long run and with the gradual diminishing of his fame that might not prove enough.

'Yeah, it was along those lines.' Stevie put a slice of bread into the toaster. 'I know you probably don't feel like eating, after that mountain of chocolate you consumed last night, but you look like you could do with it. You've got a greenish tinge to your face, which really doesn't complement the festive décor that I worked so hard to create. It's altogether the wrong shade!' Stevie ducked as she threw a scrunched up *Kit Kat* wrapper at him, which had been stuffed into the pocket of her jeans. 'Hey, take it out on Zac, not me! He said Tom seemed really pissed off and stormed off before he had a chance to explain.'

'Zac never even opened his mouth, except to clamp it over mine and virtually suck the teeth out of my gums.' She shot Stevie a look and he grimaced. 'I think things are pretty much over with Tom.'

'He's obviously the jealous type. Are you sure you want to be with someone like that?' Stevie put his arm around her shoulders as she heaved a sigh.

'I think it's probably a moot point.' At least she still had Stevie. What would she do without him? 'I can't say that I wouldn't have reacted the same way had the boot been on the other foot. If I'd seen Tom kissing someone else yesterday I'd probably have reacted a damn sight worse.'

'If he's got any sense, honey, he'll realise you're not that sort of girl. He probably feels like a prize dick right now.' Stevie squeezed her shoulders.

'I'm quite insulted he thinks I'd go for someone like Zac. I'm definitely not *that* sort of girl.' They both jumped as the bread popped up from the toaster.

'Oh right and who exactly is that sort?' Stevie raised an eyebrow quizzically and handed her a plate from the drainer.

'Airheads, who don't have any brains for him to suck out with his turbo-powered snogging technique.' They exchanged a look and she smiled for the first time.

'Susie-Anne!' The name was spoken in unison. Stevie laughed and then an unreadable expression crossed his face. As always, being with him made everything, even last night's disaster that little bit better.

Chapter Nineteen

The festive cheer in the run up to Christmas was lost on Ashleigh. She'd kept her promise and resolutely refused to contact Tom again. Having driven herself mad for the first forty-eight hours constantly checking and rechecking her phone to see if he'd decided to apologise, she realised there was only one thing for it. Changing her number might cause her some problems, but at least then she could stop expecting Tom to call or text since he didn't have her new number.

It was more difficult to get away from reminders of him, though, as Chloe Nicholas had hit the number one spot in England and America and it looked like she'd be there until Christmas. Dogged by tragedy her whole life, the papers had reported that Chloe was found wandering barefoot, three streets away from her flat in the early hours of the morning, the day after her single was confirmed as number one. The papers were full of Tom stepping in to sort out the situation and there were photographs of him with his arm around her fragile shoulders, shielding her from the worst of the media onslaught that had resulted.

Stevie had stayed with Ashleigh for the first two days,

but then he'd had to go back to town, as he typically hadn't even begun to think about buying Christmas presents. His poor Nan was probably in line for a pair of skinny jeans or a block-coloured ensemble in orange, sky blue and purple.

Having spent as much time as she could bear with her mother, she was relieved when the twenty-third finally rolled around. There'd been a couple of brief moments in the middle of the night, since that ill-fated kiss, when she'd seriously considered telling Zac to stick the photo-shoot up his cosmetically enhanced bum. He had more junk in his trunk than Ashleigh personally found attractive in a man, unlike Tom whose bottom had been nothing short of a work of art. But she couldn't think about that. The dawning of the days had sobered her up each time. There was no point throwing her career into the same skip as her personal life. It had been a pretty disastrous year all in all.

Zac was unlikely to feel any guilt as a result of her pulling out of the shoot, so she'd just be cutting her nose off to spite her face. It was something to focus on, something positive that might come out of this whole mess. Knowing Zac had to have some upside. His greatest hits album was guaranteed to be an international bestseller. Despite the wane in any new success over recent years, the market for re-mastered versions of his old hits was as strong as ever.

Ashleigh borrowed her mother's ancient Land Rover, which was liberally decorated with dog hair and mud. Its tank-like quality meant it wasn't the most aesthetically pleasing vehicle in the world, but she'd been relieved to find that it actually had a reasonable turn of speed. Admittedly, the old girl whined a bit when she hit seventy miles an hour, but she made surprisingly good time and reached Zac's country pile in Sussex a full forty-five minutes before she'd been due to do so. He'd insisted that the shoot take place at home, as he wanted the album cover to reflect who he really was. Having had so much cosmetic surgery, it was impossible to be sure who Zac really was. There would be a series of shots, one for the front of the CD and some for the inlay inside, including one of him 'at work' in his studio. Fans downloading his album would also be able to access copies of the artwork for a small additional fee, from which Ashleigh would receive a percentage.

She punched the code Zac had given her into the security gates at the foot of the half-mile long gravel driveway, which swept up to the front of his Georgian manor house. The outside remained classic and beautiful. The inside, however, was a different matter and it had been well and truly Zac'ed over the years. Each room had a theme and it felt more like a film set, or a Disney hotel, than it did a home. She'd done several photo-shoots at the house before, so pretty much knew her way around.

Ashleigh gave the old-fashioned bell pull a good yank, the sound echoing in the hallway inside. Having got no response after five minutes of trying, she took out her mobile and scrolled down to Zac's number. She might actually kill him if he'd stood her up. Thankfully the phone was ringing some-where just inside the front door, so at least he hadn't gone out and forgotten about the shoot. He never strayed far from his iPhone. Typically narcissistic, he'd downloaded one of his own singles as the ring tone.

Walking round to the back of the house, where the pool and gym were, Ashleigh sighed. Zac definitely wasn't in her good books of late. There was every chance he'd be having a last minute workout, or ten minutes on his sun bed, to make sure he looked his absolute best before the shoot: too self-centred to worry about letting her know where he was.

'Hello?' She poked her head around the door of the gym. Every wall was mirrored. The thought of seeing herself red faced and sweating, whilst attempting to operate the machines that looked like they had been designed by NASA engineers filling her with dread. But Zac needed to be within a head turn of a mirror at all times. The gym was empty, but music was playing and every light in the place blazing. He obviously belonged to the non-believers camp when it came to global warming.

Ashleigh edged around the gym equipment, the handles of which threatened to skewer her at any moment should she make one false move, and headed out through the solarium towards the indoor pool.

Zac was in the water, but he wasn't alone. He had his hands in the hair of the latest recipient of his patented super-suction snog, but they were obscured by the back view she had of Zac, who to her horror didn't appear to be wearing any trunks.

She cleared her throat, but the snogging was too full on to be infiltrated so easily. Ordinarily, she would probably have discreetly slipped out and waited until Zac, and the latest candidate for fiancée number eight, emerged from the pool. However, since he'd caused her so many problems recently, she wasn't about to afford him that level of courtesy.

'Coo ee, Zac!' Oh God, she was turning into her mother, the only person she knew who still used expressions like 'Coo ee'. Worries about turning into a clone of Carol paled, as Zac finally broke off from kissing his latest conquest.

'Ashleigh! I'm so sorry, I didn't want you to find out like this.' It wasn't Zac who had spoken; he was still staring open-mouthed in her direction.

Stevie was already wading towards the edge of the pool, leaving Zac where he was.

'So when were you going to tell me?' Ashleigh was vaguely aware of sounding like a wronged wife. How had she not seen it? She'd thought they hated each other and if Zac's persona had all been an act, then she was an idiot for believing it. 'How long has it been going on?'

'Carly and Duane's wedding.' Stevie hauled himself out of the pool and wrapped one of the white fluffy towels around his waist to hide his nakedness. 'I'm sorry, I wanted to tell you.'

'So the love bites, they were him?' She should have known. Having been on the receiving end of Zac's suction technique, it should have been obvious who had inflicted the bruises on Stevie's neck. 'So why the hell did you feel it was necessary to kiss me and mess up things with Tom?' She was shaking as she turned on Zac. He had finally edged his way over to the side of the pool, but apparently elected not to get out; clearly feeling very vulnerable in his naked state, especially in the wake of Ashleigh who was trembling with rage.

'I'd always fancied you.' For once in his life, Zac had the grace to look a bit sheepish. 'At least I thought I had. When Stevie kissed me at the wedding I was horrified.'

'He slapped me in fact, but the opportunity just presented itself and it felt so right, I couldn't help it. We'd been bickering, as usual, and then he looked at me in a way he never had before, so I had to take the chance that my hunch might be right. When he kissed me back I knew.' Stevie looked like he wanted to put his arm around her but he didn't, as if sensing that she was still too angry to be comforted.

'Yeah, but I was horrified by how much I liked it.' Zac sighed.

'After the slap, I wanted to run off, but I couldn't stay away from him. I've never felt like that before and I knew then that all the girls over the years had just been an attempt to suppress what I'd wanted all along. We spent most of the evening talking and… other stuff, but I still wasn't ready to admit how I felt, even to myself. I deliberately started a row with Stevie and told him I never wanted to see him again. By the next afternoon, at the church, I'd convinced myself that it had just been a one-off and that it didn't really mean as much as I thought it had.'

'So what, you thought by kissing me that Stevie would get angry and the problem would be solved?' She sat down with a thud on one of the sun loungers; her legs no longer seemed to hold her up.

'Not exactly. I thought if I kissed you and enjoyed it, I could go back to being straight after all.' Zac attempted a wry grin. 'Only it didn't quite work out.'

'So you used me?' Nausea washed over her. Not only had Zac ruined things with Tom, but it turned out she'd just been part of an experiment.

'He's sorry, we both are.' At last Stevie moved to sit next to her on the sun lounger and took her hand in his. 'Up until the night of the wedding our attraction to each other had been masked by us both, so much so that we couldn't bear to be in the same room. It was hard for him to admit how he felt. He just wanted to be sure. To be fair, Zac had no way of knowing that Tom would see it all.'

'Fair?' She snatched her hand away. 'What would be fair would be for you to tell Tom what you've told me.'

'I have.' Zac finally emerged from the pool and caught the towel that Stevie had thrown in his direction. 'Not exactly the whole story, but at least I told him that none of it was your doing.'

'So what did you tell him?' Ashleigh bit her lip. If Tom knew the truth and he still hadn't got in touch with her that was even worse.

'I told him that I instigated the kiss, gave you no choice.' Zac moved on to the lounger next to theirs.

'Yeah, so that bit's true, what else?'

'I told him I did it to test my feelings for someone else, I just didn't say who.' Zac stared at the ground and sympathy stirred in her, despite all the trouble he'd caused. Regardless of how strong his feelings for Stevie were, it didn't look like he was ready to admit them to the world. For a man who had built his career on a certain reputation it was going be a huge thing to reveal.

'And what did Tom say?' She wasn't sure if she was still angry with Zac or if it was Tom she most wanted to slap.

'He said I was a complete arse and… oh yeah, and that everything I say is bullshit, I think those were his words.' Zac grinned at the memory. 'I thought for a moment that he might even punch me!' Tom had quoted one of the texts she'd sent him almost word for word.

'Nothing else?' She couldn't stop shaking, everything was changing so fast. Stevie was obviously in love for the first time in all the years she'd known him and the partnership that had always sustained her looked like it might be about to change for good.

Chapter Twenty

An hour later, only ten minutes after they'd been due to start, Ashleigh had begun to get over finding Stevie and Zac locked in a passionate kiss, at least enough to think about where to start the shoot.

Zac had requested a 'moody look' for the album cover because he thought it would help his music reach a new audience. She didn't think Goths and Emos would ever buy Zac Starr's *All the hits and a few new bits* album, but it was his call. He emerged from his bedroom, after a quick change, looking like an extra from a film about medieval knights, in a weird black cloak trimmed with fur over leather trousers and knee high boots.

'I can see the influence you're having on him already.' Ashleigh managed a weak smile in Stevie's direction.

'Shut up!' He returned the smile, their ability to banter still intact at least. He'd looked almost as shocked as she'd felt finding them together and there'd be a lot of adjusting to do. 'That outfit has nothing to do with me. Lust has just made me blind to his appalling dress sense I suppose.'

Zac had swept out towards the stable block, where the groom

was preparing one of his horses to be part of the photo shoot. He admitted to Ashleigh and Stevie that he only got around to riding sporadically and it was blatantly obvious that he didn't enjoy it much. Despite that, he couldn't resist showing off for the shoot and was soon mounted on the most impressive of his horses, a five-year old white stallion called Tempest.

The horse was quite flighty, sensing that his rider was less than confident in the saddle. Ashleigh clicked away with the camera, hoping that she'd get a few decent shots where Zac's face didn't portray the panic he so clearly felt.

'Right, what's next?' Having taken shots from as many angles as possible, including Zac perching on the low branch of a huge horse-chestnut tree in Tempest's paddock, Ashleigh had exhausted the scope of his medieval knight theme. Hoping they might move to the studio next, to give her a chance to capture a few reportage style shots, she waited for his response. He didn't get a chance to reply, as a large brown hare shot out from the undergrowth right in front of Tempest. The horse spooked violently, leaping first to one side and then swiftly changing direction, unseating Zac as smoothly as butter off a knife.

'Oh my God!' Stevie had sprinted over to where Zac had landed, almost before Ashleigh had put her camera down.

'I'm all right. Although I think I might have broken my arse or at least burst one of the bags of collagen I've had stuffed into it.' Zac struggled to his feet, Stevie fussing around him like an over-protective mother. The groom quickly caught Tempest, who was likely to be for sale in *Horse and Hound* magazine within the week. Zac, who seemed to be quite enjoying the drama and the level of Stevie's concern, put an arm around each of their shoulders and allowed them to support him as they made their way back to the house, like some wounded soldier from the battlefield.

'Oh dear, not interrupting again am I?' Standing on the steps at the front door of the manor house, looking ridiculously handsome, was a smiling Tom. Suddenly aware of her flushed face and tousled hair, Ashleigh cursed that she wasn't one of those woman who looked effortlessly groomed at all times; the sort who emerged from planes looking like they'd just had an appointment with their hairdresser, instead of as she did with hair like Russell Brand.

'Zac's had a fall, we were just helping him back to the house.' He'd put her on the defensive again. After his reaction last time she wasn't taking any chances and being falsely accused in the first place had got her back up. She had in her grasp the opportunity of wiping that smug look off his face by revealing that Zac was more likely to be interested in him, but that wasn't an option. Neither Zac or Stevie were ready to make their relationship public yet, nor were they willing to trust Tom with their secret. She didn't owe Zac any favours, but she'd never betray Stevie.

'Should I call an ambulance?' Tom descended the stairs in two strides and immediately relieved Ashleigh of the burden of supporting Zac's weight.

'Nah, I'm fine, just a bit of a bruised bum that's all.' Zac didn't seem keen on giving the paparazzi another chance of snapping him in A&E. Rock stars weren't supposed go to hospital for a few bruises.

'I'm not sure, I think he should get checked out.' Stevie was struggling to keep the emotion out of his voice. Apparently Zac wasn't the only one who had fallen hard recently.

'Ooh all this concern! I think I'll have to fall off my horse more often, but I'm okay, honest.' Zac laughed, wincing as it shook his bruised frame. 'Although I must say, I much prefer having a hot woman like Ash tending to my wounds than you mate.' He winked and a warm sensation crept up Ashleigh's neck. It was a response to the lie, but thankfully Tom was none the wiser. Would Zac ever break the habit of a lifetime and stop acting the lady-killer he was expected to be? And where did that leave Stevie if he couldn't? Despite his deception she cared about him more than he'd ever know and she couldn't bear the thought of him being hurt.

Zac disappeared to his bedroom and Stevie went with him, on the pretext of helping him select an outfit for the next stage of the shoot. Resorting to the typically English pastime, as a response to any kind of trauma, Ashleigh made tea and found herself alone with Tom.

'How have you been?' His voice was full of concern.

'Yeah, I've been good, thanks.' If she sounded unconvincing, she couldn't help it and she busied herself putting teabags into four mugs so she didn't have to look at him.

'Ash, I'm so sorry, I really am.' He caught hold of her elbow and she turned to face him.

'For what?' She looked down, suddenly awkward in his presence, as though the night they'd spent together had never happened.

'For reacting like I did when I saw you and Zac.' He cupped her chin with his hand, forcing her to meet his gaze. 'I wanted to come straight back to the flat when I realised what an idiot I'd been.' He grinned and she pressed her lips together, willing herself not to let him off the hook too easily. 'I was about to get back out of the car when the call came in about Chloe. Then, when Zac called and I still couldn't get hold of you on the phone, I decided to drive down and see you. But he told me you were coming here and I thought mutual ground might be safer.'

'Is Chloe okay?' Ashleigh had liked the fragile young singer, but if she was the real reason why Tom had chosen not to get in touch she wasn't sure she wanted to know. Chloe was beautiful and successful, just the sort of girl that people would expect him to be with.

'She's okay.' Tom frowned slightly. 'Her mum, Gilly, had a mild heart attack and I think the shock was worse for Chloe than it was for her.'

'Oh God, will she be okay?' Guilt immediately flooded Ashleigh; there were more important things in life.

'She got to hospital as soon as she started having chest pains, so they were able to treat her really quickly. The signs are good, but it's been a tough time for them both with Chloe in the spotlight so much at the moment.' Tom took her hand. 'But I don't want to talk about them, I need to know if we're still… friends?'

'Friends is good.' She hoped they would be, whatever else passed between them. It was time to let him off the hook. 'I can understand how it looked, but really Zac has never been someone I've been interested in like that.' She shivered as he pulled her towards him.

'You didn't return any of my calls, I've been trying to get hold of you for the last three days.' Their faces were inches apart. 'Once I'd got Gilly and Chloe admitted to hospital, the first thing I wanted to do was sort things out with you. When you didn't call me back, I really thought I'd blown it.'

'I changed my number.' She didn't say why, it seemed so stupid now.

'So, can I have your new number?' There was a teasing tone to his voice and she nodded. He moved forward a fraction and their lips met. The kiss was hungry, five days of longing and wondering if they would ever get the chance to do it again had ensured that there was no shortage of desire. His hands slipped inside her jumper and roamed up and down her naked back, making her body arch in response to his touch.

'My turn to ask if we're interrupting anything, I think?' Zac was grinning from ear to ear as he and Stevie came into their kitchen. Love was all around or, at least, lust. From their flushed appearance, it was obvious that Stevie and Zac had been involved in a similar exchange upstairs.

Ashleigh sprang away from Tom, but his arms were firmly locked behind her back, preventing her from going too far. Unlike Zac, he seemed more than happy to go public with his relationships, whoever they were with and however long they lasted.

'This gorgeous girl was just demonstrating that she forgives me for being a total idiot.' Tom's good mood was infectious.

'Well, it's more than you deserve, but I'm glad I made that call now.' Zac was still smirking, having no doubt decided that not only was he now absolved of any blame, but he was also a hero for getting Tom to come over and sort everything out.

'Don't think I'm not grateful.' Tom certainly seemed in the mood to forgive. 'But I'll be even happier if you can let her finish the shoot, so I can take her home and apologise properly.'

'What, all night long!' Zac roared with laughter and whacked Tom on that back. 'Nice to see you finally hooking up with a woman with an IQ bigger than her bra size.'

'And I suppose all your fiancées had PhDs?' Ashleigh played along with the joke. She wanted to keep Stevie's counsel and any animosity she'd felt towards Zac had long since melted away.

'Maybe not, but perhaps I should try it.' Zac winked again, the secret unspoken between them. 'Let's have the cup of tea you promised me and we can get the shots in the studio and chapel done so we can call it a day.'

Never able to resist taking a photo when the opportunity arose, Ashleigh took twenty or thirty shots of the three men just in the time it took for them to drink their tea and demolish a packet of chocolate *Hobnob* biscuits. There were at least two shots where Stevie and Zac were exchanging looks that needed no words. Tom appeared none the wiser, however, as he barely took his eyes off Ashleigh. Every time she glanced at him he had already been looking in her direction. He probably wouldn't even have noticed if one of them had been sipping their tea stark naked.

The shots in the studio were relatively straightforward. Zac looked reassuringly normal in a black shirt and a pair of Levi jeans. Ashleigh told him to just carry on as though she wasn't there and he played a couple of the new tracks from his album to the captive audience. All of the posturing and posing of the horse riding scenes were forgotten and he became the musician so rarely noticed behind his rock star facade.

There was another costume change before they took the final shots of the day in the tiny chapel that formed part of the manor house's estate. It was a beautiful flint building with ivy trailing up the walls towards the small tower with its single bell.

'This would be a great place for a wedding.' Tom had his arm around her waist as they followed Zac into the building, who by now was resplendent in a pair of purple crushed velvet trousers and a deep V neck jumper with nothing underneath.

'I've always preferred the idea of Vegas for a wedding myself.' It was a total lie, but nerves had fluttered at his words – was he trying to test her? Like most girls, Ashleigh had imagined what her wedding might be like from time to time and she'd always pictured the church that looked out across the sea from the top of the cliffs in Sandgate. She was never quite sure how to read Tom, though. Even his planned marriage to Susie-Anne had been more of a business deal than a romance, and she didn't want to scare him off by making him think she was already planning the guest list for their wedding.

'Bride's prerogative, but you could have had a wedding here and all this could have been yours…' he made a sweeping gesture with his arm, 'if you'd just kissed Zac back.' Tom was grinning, but it was impossible to tell if he was joking or not, so it was probably better to say nothing at all.

Unfortunately, Zac was back to his old self in the chapel shots. He insisted on not only lying on the altar for one shot, but also posing like Christ on the cross and lounging against a tombstone in the tiny graveyard at the back of the chapel. Whilst Ashleigh doubted that many of his fans would be committed Christians given the lyrics in some of his songs, he couldn't have been more likely to cause offence if he'd tried. Half an hour later the shoot was over.

'That's a wrap then?' Tom had been watching her work and he seemed to approve.

'I think that's enough for today.' She smiled. 'Zac's going to pick the photos as the record company want them by the second of January, so I'll email them over tomorrow. Let's just hope there's enough here to please his lordship.'

'Is Stevie making his own way home?' It was obvious from the way that Tom was looking at her that he was banking on the answer being yes. Thankfully she'd managed to snatch five minutes with Stevie for a private chat in the bathroom at the recording studio. They'd previously arranged to spend Christmas together, but things had changed quite drastically for both of them since. The look of relief on Stevie's face, when Ashleigh had asked if he minded Tom joining them, had spoken volumes. Grinning, he'd said he didn't want to be a gooseberry and he was happy to take up Zac's offer of staying with him. Perhaps that had been Zac's motivation for getting her and Tom back together all along. It didn't matter now; for once everything seemed to be going right.

'Yes, he's staying with a friend for Christmas.' She kept her tone light, hoping that Tom wouldn't ask any questions. It wasn't a great idea to lie to your boss, or the person you were sleeping with, but even worse when they were one and the same.

'Great!' She needn't have worried, Tom clearly couldn't care less who the mystery friend was.

'Are you sure you don't mind being on your own with me?' Ashleigh was suddenly confident enough to do the teasing, but she didn't get an answer. He just kissed her, making his feelings perfectly clear.

The drive back to the flat was frustrating for Tom. He couldn't persuade Ashleigh to leave her mum's car at Zac's until he could get someone from *Rushworth Associates* to drive it back. Her reasoning had been that the old girl was temperamental and he'd assumed that she was talking about the car rather than her mother, although from what he'd heard about Carol he wasn't too sure. As a result, they'd been forced to drive back separately and he'd much rather have had her to chat to, to laugh about the outlandish nature of Zac's costume choices and generally put the world to rights. He was beginning to realise he missed having a friend like that; it was another sacrifice the business had forced him to make. He'd put it absolutely first in the old days, working day and night to get it going and networking his socks off in between to get a client base started. His only social life had been work related, mixing with the people he needed impress and letting his old friends and university buddies fall by the wayside. Sometimes he wondered what they were doing now, but never for long enough to get in touch, and the next crisis at work had always been enough to fill his time. Looking at Stevie and Ashleigh, though, he could see what he might be missing. Maybe he'd make a New Year's resolution to look up some of his old mates, or at least reply to the telephone messages that were intermittently left at his mum's from them. Just maybe.

His car had a much quicker turn of speed than the elderly Landrover, but he was worried about Ashleigh driving such an old tank, especially as the weather was turning icy and the gritter lorries were out in force. He checked his speed and slowed down again until he saw her car finally appear behind him. The internal light of the Landrover had come on as soon as she had started the engine, which she'd said it did from time to time, dodgy electrics a sign of its age and just one of its many quirks. As a result, when he let her get close enough, Tom could make out Ashleigh in his rear view mirror. Her dark hair was falling loose around her shoulders, the memory of how it felt against his skin almost tangible.

It was no good, he had to stop looking, it wasn't helping his concentration or his driving technique and the last thing he wanted to do was to get pulled over by an over-zealous traffic cop. He turned his rear view mirror down slightly so that he couldn't see her anymore and slid the disk that Francine had given him into the CD player. It was from a group called *The Xcess*, who'd just been signed by one of the big record labels and were keen on having *Rushworth Associates* represent them; at least it gave him something else to think about. Even the clashing sound of the band's Thrash Metal style was more conducive to his concentration than catching sight of Ashleigh in the mirror. It was going to take a while to get her out of his system.

Chapter Twenty-One

Waking up on Christmas Eve next to a gorgeous naked man took some beating. Ashleigh stretched like a contented cat, as winter sunlight streaked through the window, the warmth of Tom's body next to hers a welcome sensation. He was breathing in a soft regular rhythm, clearly still asleep.

Pushing one leg out from under the duvet, she tried to slip out without waking him. It would be fun to play the domestic goddess and whip him up a gourmet breakfast. Well, bacon and eggs at least. Her stomach gurgled at the thought. They hadn't eaten the night before; falling into bed the moment they got through the door, with food the last thing on their minds. Her stomach gave another loud grumble at the prospect of a crispy bacon sandwich. Creeping around to Tom's side of bed she was home and dry, until a warm hand shot out from under the duvet and grabbed hold of her thigh.

'Where do you think you're going, gorgeous?' Tom looked annoyingly unruffled and her hand immediately shot up to smooth her own wild mop of hair.

'I was going to make you some breakfast.' Smiling, she let him pull her down on top of him. She wasn't *that* hungry after all.

An hour later, the rumbling in her stomach couldn't be ignored any longer.

'Have you got your washing machine on spin?' Tom grinned and placed a hand on her stomach. 'It's like a scene from *Alien* in there.'

'Well, we would have eaten ages ago if it wasn't for you.' Most of the women who moved in Tom's social circle probably ate no more than a salad with a sprinkling of speed to take the edge off their appetites and motivate them for yet another marathon workout. As long as Tom didn't expect the same of her, one missed dinner and her stomach was already making a very vocal protest.

'Oh for God's sake, I don't believe it.' Opening the fridge door a few moments later, it was obvious that her mother had been down to the flat. The bacon and bread had been taken out and probably chucked in a bin somewhere along the high street. Instead there was a loaf of Carol's homemade soda bread, which could easily double as a doorstop and needed an industrial strength saw to cut it. There was also some of her homemade bean dip, which resembled the contents of a sick bucket and didn't smell much better, and some Ostrich bacon.

'Umm, looks lovely.' Tom walked up behind her and put his arms around her waist.

'It's my mother.' She sighed, there was no way that she could serve this up. She'd had years of her mother's cooking and 'healthy eating' experiments and she still couldn't stomach the stuff. She'd had delicious soda bread and bean dips from the deli in Sandgate in the past, but her mum's home-made attempts to replicate the recipes would have been better suited to supporting a DIY project than they would to creating a decent meal. 'She's decided to make over my fridge with her idea of a healthy diet for me. I wish I'd never given her a key in the first place.'

'Don't worry.' His voice was soothing and his breath warm against her neck. 'I'll nip down to the shops, pick up the papers and get some new supplies.' He turned her round to face him. 'I need to check on news of Chloe anyway and see what they're writing about her now. Just let me jump into the shower and you can make me a list of what we need.'

By the time he got back from the shops, Ashleigh was all the better for having had a nice warm shower too. She'd sent the photos to Zac and had laid the table in a way that would make any 1950s housewife proud. She'd even found the little toast rack that her Auntie Alice had given her 'for her bottom drawer' as she put it, when Ashleigh had first been planning to move in with Liam.

'God that bread smells good.' The crusty farmhouse loaf was still warm. 'Anything much in the papers?'

As she spoke, Tom dropped the pile of tabloids on the table with a heavy thud.

'I picked up a few phone messages from Francine about something, on my way to the deli. All seems okay on the Chloe front though.'

'So who is on the front page then?' She mentally crossed her fingers that it wasn't an expose about Zac and Stevie. It would only take one pap to get shot of the two of them kissing and the lid would be blown off their affair and possibly off Zac's career.

'It's Susie-Anne.' He sounded more exasperated than anything. 'It's nothing I need to get involved with though. I might still have an interest in her career, but her personal life is her own.'

'Can I have a look then?' Ashleigh waited and, after a few seconds, he reluctantly handed her a paper from the top of the pile.

STORMY OUTLOOK FOR WEATHER GIRL. The headline dominated the front page. Scanning the top couple of paragraphs, Ashleigh's appetite started to fade.

'Shouldn't you call her?' Although she'd never warmed to Susie-Anne, the photos of her tear-stained face splashed across the front pages of the tabloids would have stirred even the hardest of hearts. It was made all the more poignant by the fact that she was pregnant.

'Most of my female clients have been dumped at some point in their careers.' There was that nonchalant tone again, as though he were trying far too hard to be off-hand.

'Yes, but I take it not all of them were pregnant or former fiancées of yours?' Why was she pushing him when who knew what might happen if he met up with Susie-Anne in that vulnerable state? Maybe she was testing him, at least that way she'd find out if he meant what he said about always being honest.

'That's true, but I'm not responsible for her and we all know how Susie-Anne loves a drama.' Tom moved to crouch down beside Ashleigh so that he could make eye contact. 'It's you I want to be with right now and I'm not going to give that up to go chasing after a client, even one who I was briefly engaged to, who could well be back with Michael again by tomorrow.' The words 'right now' framed the sentence, but she wouldn't let it bother her. She'd wanted to enjoy just living in the here and now and this was her chance.

'Okay, if you're sure, but I don't want you to think that you can't be there for her just because we've slept together a couple of times.' She was trying for nonchalance, but it came out sounding like she didn't care.

'Okay well thanks, I'll bear that in mind.' Tom's dark blue eyes searched her face. Disappointment reflected in his own, but she couldn't for the life of her imagine why. The last thing he wanted was another Susie-Anne; he'd told her that often enough. Of course, he wasn't to know just how much effort it was taking on Ashleigh's part to convince herself she felt that way too.

She finally started on breakfast at what turned out to be far closer to lunchtime and Tom busied himself trying to stuff the stack of tabloids into the tiny kitchen bin.

'Honestly it's fine, don't throw them out, I want the TV guides anyway.' It was a less than subtle lie on her part and he roared with laughter.

'And there was me thinking that we were going to have this red hot Christmas and you're all set for the *East Enders Omnibus* and the *Strictly Come Dancing* Christmas Special!'

'I might forgo *Strictly* if you make it worth my while.' She grinned as she put breakfast on the table.

'What did you have in mind?' Tom didn't comment on the broken eggs and over-cooked bacon. She might not be able to cook, but he evidently had other priorities.

'Shopping?' She'd realised with some horror that, without a shopping trip, Christmas dinner would consist of Findus Crispy Pancakes and oven chips. Worse than that, she had absolutely nothing suitable to give him as a Christmas present.

She had the lime green sweater she'd bought for Stevie, who she wouldn't now be seeing until after Boxing Day, but it was about as far removed from being Tom's kind of thing as possible and two sizes too small to boot. So even desperation ruled that out.

'Not quite what I'd hoped for, but okay.' He attempted to spear a piece of bacon, which promptly shot across the table and on to the floor. 'And maybe we should think about getting you a dog while we're at it.'

Chapter Twenty-Two

The shops were horrendously busy, just as they'd expected and having spent £300 in the supermarket and overloaded the trolley so much that even Tom could barely push it in a straight line, it was as much as she could do to persuade him to drop her off in Sandgate High Street to 'pick up a few last minute bits and pieces'. Giving him the key to her flat, she'd dashed up and down the high street in a wild-eyed panic. What on earth could you buy the man who had everything when the extent of your options were limited to a handful of small independent shops in a quaint little seaside town? After almost buying him a whisky decanter – she wasn't sure if he even drank the stuff – and a ridiculously over-priced digital photo frame she finally found something suitable in Sands art gallery. It was a small seascape, probably only twelve inches by ten inches, but something about it drew her in. It pictured tempestuous grey skies and inky blue water, capturing the malevolence of the sea in the eye of a storm. There was the back view of a young woman in the foreground of the painting, watching the storm unfold from the shoreline. It was difficult to date, her clothing could have been from the Fifties or, with the cycle of fashion, it might have been painted a week ago.

'I don't know much about it to be honest love. That's why it's only eighty quid.' Jim Clutterbuck, the owner of Sands, shrugged his shoulders as she handed over her credit card. 'Sonny got it from a house clearance this week; I reckon it's a few years old and I had to clean it up a bit. It's signed by an R Thomas, never heard of him though, so don't buy it if you're hoping to take it on the *Antiques Roadshow* in a couple of years' time!' He let out a raucous laugh, as though he'd just told a filthy joke to the rugby team first eleven.

'Thanks Jim, but it doesn't matter who it's by, you're still a life saver.' Giving the shopkeeper, who had made a pass at her mother a couple of years before, a quick peck on the cheek she dashed out of the shop and headed up the road to home, hoping against hope that Tom wasn't the sort of person who snooped through your underwear drawer when left alone in your flat. There were some very un-sexy greying bras in that drawer, which were headed for the bin at the first available opportunity.

Tom had, in fact, resisted the urge to go searching through her drawers. He'd made a couple of phone calls, including one to his mum to tell her about Ashleigh. He admitted to Isobel that his ruse about Ashleigh being a lesbian had been just that, but their relationship was very casual and that she shouldn't get any ideas, or her hopes up, whatever she might read in the paper. He would definitely see his mum at some point on Christmas Day and he was tempted to take Ashleigh with him. His mother's theory rested solely on the premise that he hadn't found love because he hadn't met a nice girl. Once Isobel met Ashleigh, her whole argument would be undermined – if anything she was too nice for the business they were in. If it hadn't happened with someone like Ashleigh, his mother might finally accept it never would, she might also realise it didn't have to stop Tom enjoying himself and she could quit worrying.

After he'd finished his calls, Tom spent a while looking around the flat and at the bank of photos on one wall of the living room, which seemed to depict every major milestone in Ashleigh's life. Stevie was in most of them, but she clearly wasn't the sort to display pictures of ex-boyfriends.

Unpacking the shopping whilst he waited, he noticed how simply she lived. It was amazing that she'd remained so unaffected by the celebrity nonsense they'd both chosen for their professional lives. He hadn't wanted to admit how much he'd missed being around her when she wouldn't return his calls. The deluge of texts she'd sent him on the night of her kiss with Zac had freaked him out a bit, but he felt reassured by what he saw. There was no evidence in the flat that she'd misunderstood their no-strings agreement, no wedding magazines stuffed behind the cushions on the sofa or half written love letters that she hadn't got round to sending. It must have been relief he was feeling, but it was a strangely hollow sensation. Perhaps it was just shock, after being with someone like Susie-Anne who had suffocated him planning their 'lives together'.

Tom checked the latest stream of messages on his phone, which had appeared as soon as he'd turned it on. Ignoring them all, he switched it off again. He needed a break from the other nonsense and everyone deserved one day off, didn't they? More than anything he wanted to spend that day with Ashleigh.

Staying in her flat, he could sense her warmth even when

she wasn't there. He liked her, really liked her, she knew the importance of honesty. It was the thought that he might have been wrong about her that had caused him to over-react when he'd seen her kissing Zac, nothing else. The intense physical attraction aside, he actually enjoyed her company and it was no more or less than that. Having given himself a good talking to he set about creating a Christmas concoction to make the atmosphere in the flat even warmer.

The aroma of Christmas greeted her as soon as she opened the front door. Tom was seated by the window watching the afternoon light fading to grey, warming his hands on a cup of cinnamon coffee. Shoving the painting in the hall cupboard, she sat opposite him, accepting the drink he already had waiting for her.

'This place has you written all over it.' He smiled and she searched for something self-deprecating to say in response, it had become a bit of a defence mechanism over the years.

'What a bit tatty and in need of a make-over?'

'I think it's beautiful and the view is breath taking.' Tom drained his coffee and moved his armchair until they were side by side, taking her hand in his. 'I could more than happily look at it for a very long time.'

'I loved it the moment I saw the place.' Ashleigh fiddled with a loose thread on the arm of the chair; she may as well bite the bullet sooner than later. 'My mum has a great view from her place too.'

'It's the cottage up on the cliffs by the church, isn't it?' Tom smiled as she widened her eyes. 'It's okay, I haven't been stalking you. Zac told me about it when he rang up to explain what really happened that night.'

'Oh.' She could just imagine how that conversation had gone. 'Well, anyway, I was wondering if you wanted to see the view from up there?'

'Are you inviting me to meet your mum?' A look of surprise flitted across his face and she was anxious to reassure him that she didn't have any ulterior motive. 'Well I wouldn't put it as formally as that.' Ashleigh shrugged. 'But I'm going up to the service at the church tonight and they'll all be there. I mean you don't have to come or anything, you're welcome to hang out here or there are probably other things you want to do.' She was rambling now, but she couldn't seem to stop herself. 'Except if you do come with me, they'll expect us both to go back for a drink, that's all.'

'Well, I can't say church is my usual priority on Christmas Eve or any other time, but I have to admit I'm tempted if only to find out whether your mother is as eccentric as you say she is.'

'Trust me, she's way worse than I've painted her.' She grimaced slightly at the thought.

'In that case, how can I say no?' He smiled again. 'But only if you do me a favour in return. My mum's invited us for breakfast tomorrow, before she goes to her sister's for the rest of Christmas and New Year. She's got this theory that all I need to do is meet a nice girl and I'll suddenly realise that love isn't a crock after all.'

'So, I'm your social experiment, is that it?' She tried not to let the reason for the invitation upset her. It was nothing if not honest and that's all he'd ever promised.

'No, what you are is much more than the nice girl she was asking for.' He kissed her neck. 'But it still doesn't change the situation and I want her to know I'm happy with things the way they are, so she can be too.' His lips brushed her neck and she knew she'd be powerless to say no to him at that moment, whatever the question.

'Are you sure she'll want me there?' Nerves swelled in her stomach at the thought of meeting Tom's mother, even though it was just to prove a point. One upside was that she wouldn't have to subject Tom to another of her burnt offerings. Added to which there'd be no chance of Carol press-ganging them into breakfast at the cottage, with her Heston Blumenthal inspired menu of roast marrowbone and nettle porridge.

'Trust me, Mum will love you'. He grinned and her stomach flipped again. The shops were already shut, so what the hell was she supposed to buy his mother?

Having spent the rest of the afternoon in bed, they almost missed the Christmas Eve service at the church. The six p.m. timing was aimed at families, with the midnight mass a more adult affair, give or take the immature behaviour of those in the congregation, who made a last minute decision to attend on the way home from the pub. As a result, the nativity service featured a real donkey and an ensemble of local children dressed as shepherds, angels and even the odd Mary and Joseph.

'It's beautiful, don't you think?' A thirty-foot Christmas tree totally dominated the nave of the church, decorated with just rows and rows of tiny white lights and a single star. Breathless from the dash up the hill and the emotion of being in church on Christmas Eve, Ashleigh caught her breath.

'Yes, it's lovely'. Tom winked. 'If you like that sort of thing'.

'I'm sorry, maybe I shouldn't have made you come'. A burning sensation stung the back of her eyes. He couldn't know how important it was to her. 'It's just I always come to this service on Christmas Eve, it's a kind of tradition.'

'Hey, Ash, I was only joking.' Tom furrowed his brow; he must think she was mad. 'You're not crying are you?'

'I'm sorry, I really thought I'd be okay this time.' Her words were punctuated with sharp intakes of breath, as she struggled to keep hold of her emotions. 'It's stupid, but it just makes me feel close to my dad to be here, he brought me every year without fail.'

'I don't think you've ever told me what happened to your dad.' Tom placed an arm around her shoulder and she allowed him to usher her into an empty pew towards the back of the church, the last thing they needed right now was an audience.

'He died when I was fourteen, not long after the last time he brought me here.' He might as well know everything. If she didn't tell him, her mother was bound to get maudlin after a few drinks and the whole thing would come out in a dramatic monologue. 'It was New Year's Eve and he and Mum had another blazing row, just the latest in a series of many.' She paused and he squeezed her hand. 'He'd had more than a few drinks and got in his car when he shouldn't have. He took a bend on the coast road far too quickly and went spinning off it and into the garden wall of some poor family just seeing in the New Year. Thankfully no-one else was hurt, but he was killed outright.'

'Oh God, I'm sorry I was flippant, no wonder this is so difficult for you.' His voice was monotone, as though he couldn't really connect with what he was saying and found her show of emotion uncomfortable. 'You and your mum must have been devastated.'

'We were.' She hesitated for a moment, perhaps she should

just gloss over it, but she couldn't pretend she felt nothing. It was hard enough pretending to Tom that she was entirely comfortable with the whole 'friends with benefits' thing they had going on. In for a penny, in for a pound.

'In truth, Mum's heartbreak was borne out of guilt more than anything.' Ashleigh sighed and ploughed on. 'She was already seeing Geoffrey on the side. She and dad would never have got married if she hadn't got pregnant with me. They stayed together for nearly fifteen unhappy years and I think they both had affairs to be honest. It was all so messed up.'

'It sounds like your parents set you the same example as mine did for me, but at least it's made us into realists.' He gave her a wry smile, but didn't elaborate on his own dysfunctional parenting. Perhaps that was why he'd been attracted to her, recognising her as someone who didn't automatically assume that all relationships ended with the couple skipping off into the sunset to live happily ever after. 'It also explains why you thought I was making such a mistake with Susie-Anne, apart from the obvious personality defects of course.'

'Maybe they were just doing the best they knew how to do.' Ashleigh waited for him to say something, uncover a little bit more of himself, but the church organ burst into life at that moment with a somewhat wobbly rendition of *Silent Night*. The congregation rose to their feet to belt out the hymn, the most vocal of all was a woman at the front wearing a foot-high hat in the shape of a Christmas tree.

'No-one could accuse her of having a Silent Night!' Even as he said the words, a look of horrified realisation spread across Tom's face.

'My mother never does.' Ashleigh laughed, causing two of the regular church members to turn around and shush them.

'It must be my day to put my foot in it.' Tom grimaced. 'Perhaps your mum is the one who needs a warning about my big mouth, rather than the other way round!'

'It's okay, honestly.' Ashleigh giggled, earning another tut from their neighbours in the pew in front. Tom's eyebrows shot up in shock as Carol's Christmas tree hat was suddenly illuminated by her switching on the battery-operated fairy lights at the crescendo of the song. 'At least you know what I was talking about and meeting her won't be quite so traumatic.'

The service wasn't too long and the kids in their nativity outfits looked incredibly cute, with proud parents and grandparents on hand to capture every precious moment on film. There was a faraway look in Tom's eyes a couple of times as if he might be thinking about the baby who never was and the fact that his mum might never get to see a grandchild of her own. Of course, Ashleigh couldn't know that for sure, it might have been something different altogether, but Christmas was a time when emotions ran high. The tension was broken towards the end of the service when the children followed the donkey down the aisle towards the mocked up stable at the far end of the church. Albert, the elderly donkey, had slightly less control over his bowels than in previous years and decided to leave an unexpected gift halfway through the procession. Several of the children were a bit too close behind and, when the manure hit the slate floor of the church, there were more than a few in its line of fire. Much screaming of little girls and hysterics from the adults ensued as a result. Tom's ludicrously expensive suede shoes hadn't escaped the onslaught and Ashleigh began to giggle, until there were tears streaming down her cheeks. To Tom's credit he started to laugh too, not remotely fazed by the fact that his shoes were probably beyond rescue.

'That's why I live in London, you might have to dodge the odd pile of vomit on the pavement but I can honestly say that I've never been sprayed with donkey shit before.'

Chapter Twenty-Three

Carol's house was literally a stone's throw away from the church and half the congregation had been invited back for Christmas Eve drinks. Ashleigh for one was pleased; it meant that they'd be able to slip out after a little while without her mother noticing. There were so many people crammed into the small cottage that she had to get more intimate with the vicar than she'd ever planned to, just to get into the kitchen and find herself and Tom a drink to make the ordeal more bearable.

'Ashleigh, my darling, I thought I saw you lurking at the back of the church.' Carol enveloped her in a theatrical hug. The Christmas bauble earrings she was wearing bashed against Ashleigh's cheekbones.

'Mum, this is my friend, Tom.' Having extricated herself from her mother's embrace, she pulled Tom forward by his wrist and propelled him into the Lion's Den. Never one to hang back, Carol flung her arms around him in a similar fashion.

'You're right, he *is* gorgeous.' Her mother howled with laughter, whilst a familiar warmth flooded Ashleigh's face; she'd said no such thing.

'Pleased to meet you Mrs Harper.' Tom smiled as he disentangled himself from Carol's clutches and reached out to squeeze Ashleigh's hand briefly.

'Ooh, Carol, please.' She threaded her arm through his and propelled him away from Ashleigh, ensuring that his full attention was on her. 'You're much nicer than that last one she brought home. That rock star fella.' Carol, who must have had a fair bit to drink even before the church service, struggled to remember his name. 'I mean what kind of bloke wears bloody sunglasses in a church when it's dark?' Ashleigh, desperately wishing the ground would just open up, said nothing. If her mother knew how much trouble Zac had caused her that night, even she might have shied away from talking about him.

'The kind that's a total prat,' Tom said, much to Carol's delight.

'Exactly. Now come on darling boy, let me introduce you to the verger, she's got a hilarious story about losing a sticking plaster in the Christmas pudding that you absolutely have to hear!'

Ashleigh, who had zero chance of rescuing Tom from her mother's clutches until she'd finished with him, decided to leave him to his fate. If there were ever a woman who might challenge his business-like approach to giving unwanted introductions a quick brush-off, then it was her mother.

Taking her mobile out of her bag, Ashleigh scrolled down to the number that she should really know by heart.

'Honey!' Stevie's breathlessness suggested that he'd only just managed to grab the phone before the voicemail connected. 'Everything okay?'

'I'm fine.' Ashleigh went hot at the thought of what she

might have interrupted. Stevie normally leapt on the phone at the first ring, so he must have been otherwise engaged. 'Sorry, I shouldn't have called, I'm just missing you a bit.'

'Me too.' Stevie's tone was serious and she knew he meant what he said. He was happier than he'd been in years, which was great, but she still wished he could give her a hug. He was the only person in the world who understood how she'd be feeling tonight. He'd sat through countless nights with her, talking about her mum and dad's messed up relationship and helping her get through it all.

'So how's it going with Zac?' She hoped Stevie would spare her the lurid details, which he'd always been able to prise out of her in the past; but not this time, not with Tom.

'Great!' There was a smile in his voice and it made her grin too. 'We were just in the pool when you called, synchronised swimming.'

'What?' Ashleigh laughed. Maybe that was a euphemism for something else, but now he mentioned it she could hear splashing in the background.

'Yep, apparently Zac's always loved it, right since he saw an old black and white movie when he was a kid.' Stevie was laughing too, the splashing in the background growing more frantic. 'Then he got completely hooked after the London Olympics and he's been having lessons from that troupe who were on *Britain's Got Talent*. So there you go, Zac does have some hidden depths after all. Pun intended!'

'Oh my God. How did one of us not realise he was gay ages ago?' A sudden mental picture of Zac and Stevie with nose clips and matching frilly bathing caps had Ashleigh on the verge of hysteria.

'Less of the stereotyping there you!'

'Sorry, I'm sure it's all very macho.' He was only teasing, but she went hot again all the same. There were probably plenty of straight guys who loved synchronised swimming, but it just didn't go with Zac's image as a player with seven fiancées in his wake.

'Oh honey, I'm only kidding.' Stevie's tone was gentle and more than ever she wished he were there to give her a reassuring hug. 'He's like the underwater version of Louie Spence, I've never seen anything so camp!'

'I'm glad you're having a good time, you deserve it.' She meant it. What she had with Tom might not even make it until the New Year, but there was every chance Zac and Stevie could make it all the way.

'Hey, don't go yet, I haven't asked you how it's going with Tom?' He'd clearly heard the note of melancholy in her voice and this year it was more than just regret about her dad.

'It's great. We're at Mum's tonight though and she's kidnapped him and taken him to meet the verger.' Ashleigh paused as Stevie burst out laughing, only too aware what kind of social events Carol's soirees were. 'So I'd better go and rescue him, before he's press-ganged into becoming a campanologist or the hymn book monitor!'

'He'd better not be, she promised that job to me last year!' Stevie blew her a kiss down the phone. 'Happy Christmas, honey.'

'You too, babe.' Ashleigh slipped her phone back into her bag and headed into the house, still smiling at the image of those frilly bathing caps.

'Tell me about you and Ashleigh then. She must be a bit of a departure from your usual girlfriends, being so… ordinary.' The verger leant in towards Tom, so close that the red wine and cigarette smoke on her breath was inescapable.

'She's anything but ordinary, have you seen her work? She's amazingly talented.' The woman, who had no boundaries about personal space of any kind, was becoming increasingly irritating. At any other kind of party, Tom would have made his excuses and moved away from this overbearing, self-opinionated bore. He could walk away and never have to see these people again, but Ashleigh would have to live with the consequences of his actions. So he forced himself to remain polite, unsure how much longer he could keep it up.

'Oh, I'm sure she is, if you like that sort of thing.' The verger was dismissive and spoke with her mouth half-full of pork pie, flakes of pastry crumbling on to her button-down top, which strained across an ample bosom and even more fulsome stomach. 'I meant her looks really. She's pretty enough in an understated sort of way, but you must meet some absolutely stunners. I can never understand why Ashleigh hasn't got a bit more about her. After all, look how vivacious Carol is! I know it frustrates her mother that she doesn't follow in her footsteps more.'

'Well, there's no accounting for taste I suppose.' Tom wanted to tell the verger to *go forth and multiply* and he couldn't keep the edge out of his voice. Anyone with an ounce of emotional intelligence would have picked up on his meaning, but he hammered the point home any way. 'I've always preferred elegance to brash, but that's just me I suppose.'

'You're right, there is no accounting for taste!' The verger guffawed loudly and Tom suspected she had one of those really loud singing voices that members of the clergy often seemed to possess.

'Well, it's lovely to meet you, but I must make sure I have a chat with Ashleigh's step-dad before we head off.' He shook the verger's sweaty hand, barely resisting the urge to wipe his palm on his trouser leg.

'Ooh, going to pop the question are you?' Her flushed face grew redder still at the prospect.

'I'm afraid she's far too good for me.' Tom was already moving away from her, his only chance to escape. If the verger responded he didn't hear it. Thankful for the throng of people to disappear into, he let the crowd swallow him up. He was glad Ashleigh had brought him here. It explained a lot about the way she was and he liked her even more because of it.

Ashleigh headed back into the kitchen, which was practically wall-to-wall corduroy on one side. Her stepfather Geoffrey's friends discussed the double-dip recession and their latest golf scores with the sort of passion that other men reserved for debating the merits of their favourite football team. Reliable but dull, that was Geoffrey and his ilk. How he'd got together with her mother, Ashleigh would never know.

Unlike her stepfather, Carol didn't collect friends who were clones of herself, in fact quite the opposite. This was possibly because there was no one else quite like her mother, but mostly because she didn't like sharing the limelight. Every time Ashleigh or her brother had been in danger of glimpsing it for themselves, their mother was there in some ridiculous outfit or, worse still, in nothing at all.

Carol's friends, who were thronged in the hallway and sitting room, were a far more eclectic bunch. There was the 'God Squad' as she affectionately called them, from St Mary the Virgin, the church perched high on the cliff-side only a few hundred feet from her mother's front door. Carol wasn't actually a believer. In fact, for a long time she'd been a die-hard Atheist, but she loved the social side and had told Ashleigh that there was noth-ing quite like the church get-togethers for a good gossip. Then there were the activists. Carol liked nothing better than a cause and it didn't really matter what it was; at least that was how it had seemed to Ashleigh over the years. There were friends of her mother's from the latest anti high-speed rail-link group, and families whose livelihoods were threatened by EU fishing laws, in support of whom her mother had posed wearing a ridicu-lous mermaid's outfit on Sandgate beach. She'd worn a hideous synthetic blonde wig to hide her exposed nipples and given everyone within a ten-metre radius a static electric shock. There was also a group from the Countryside Alliance who were pro hunting and with whom her mother had got involved after her third lot of chickens had succumbed to Freddie the Fox. It was typical of her mother, who'd previously been firmly in the hunt protestors' camp, to switch allegiance when the mood suited her. Back in her hunt protesting days, she'd been known to hide in hedgerows dressed like the lovechild of a ninja and a tramp, ready to jump out and hopefully unseat one of the 'blood thirsty murderers'. That all changed when she'd found half of Betsy, her favourite hen, on the doorstep one morning and the rest of the chickens slaughtered indiscriminately in the upturned coop. Within a week, Ashleigh got a text from Jamie, to tell her that their mother was going to be on the evening news. Carol, having joined the Countryside Alliance march in London dressed as a chicken, had ended up being arrested for brawling in the street with a man dressed as a fox, who turned out to be the leader of her former anti-hunting posse.

Geoffrey and his brother Cliff had performed a pincer movement and trapped Tom in the corner of the conservatory that led out from the sitting room. Set out along one wall, partially obscured by the overgrown vines that snaked their way across the brickwork and dangled from the roof of the conservatory, was a table groaning with food. There was a surprisingly good selection, which could only mean that Carol and Geoffrey's friends had brought a plate of food each.

Ashleigh smiled, her mum was right, Tom really was gorgeous and it was hard not to keep looking at him. His clothing was casual, but screamed quality. The midnight blue shirt a marked contrast to the tie-died T-Shirt that Geoffrey was sporting, with his trade-mark cords, probably under the misapprehension that it made him look younger, rather than slightly deranged.

'So, you're a boob man then?' Ashleigh's stepfather, who was enthusiastically interrogating Tom about his passion for breasts, clearly hadn't seen her approach.

'He must be!' Cliff, his creepy older brother, sprayed chewed-up cashew nuts into the air, laughing like it was the funniest thing he'd ever heard. 'I mean Ashleigh's are huge, but the rack on that Summers girl is to die for.' Cliff was actually drooling at the thought.

'I can't say it's my main priority.' Tom spotted her and gave her a look of amused exasperation, not bothering to explain to Cliff that his attraction to Ashleigh wasn't based on the size of her breasts. At least she hoped not, she'd never compete with Susie-Anne on that basis. Cliff had made that perfectly clear.

'I love tits.' Geoffrey's announcement was emphatic. This had to be the most embarrassing thing ever to happen to anyone in the history of the world. Horror flooded her body as Carol placed her hand on the small of her back and propelled her into the group.

'Mum!' Ashleigh protested to no avail. Carol was determined to join the conversation.

'He certainly does, can't leave them alone!' Her mother laughed merrily. Carol had always called herself a feminist, but had never been the sort to burn her bra and was much too proud of her double D cup to risk them descending too far south. As far as she was concerned, feminism wasn't about acting the same as a man and if you could use what nature had given you to your advantage, then why not? Puberty had been a nightmare for Ashleigh.

'For God's sake, do we have to have this conversation?' She could only imagine what Tom must be thinking. She hadn't met his mother, but she was almost certain that Mrs Rushworth wouldn't be the sort to discuss anyone's passionate desire for her boobs.

'Oh loosen up, darling!' Carol grabbed the underwire of Ashleigh's bra and yanked it up until her breasts almost spilled over the top of her grey woollen dress. 'You should make more of your assets and let someone enjoy them.' Carol looked pointedly at Tom and Ashleigh officially wanted to die.

'I think she looks great as she is.' Tom manoeuvred himself so that he could slip an arm around her waist and he must have felt her shaking. 'It's been lovely to meet you all.' He smiled warmly, practised as he no doubt was at disguising his emotions. 'But we've got an early start in the morning and I think perhaps we ought to head home.'

After the inevitable embraces from her mother and half the guests at the cottage, with assurances that they would pop in before heading back to London, they finally managed to escape into the crisp, still night just after ten p.m. Midnight Mass might even make the news, given that the vicar, the verger and a number of other key church members were, at that point, doing a conga in her mum's back garden.

'I'm sorry about my mother, well all of them really.' As she spoke the cold night air stung her throat.

'Don't be sorry.' His fingers entwined with hers and he squeezed her hand. 'She's just as you said she would be. Although Geoffrey and his brother were somewhat of a revelation!'

'Oh God, I know, so embarrassing. I never thought I'd hear either of them use the word *rack*.' She shuddered at the thought.

'Does your mum always try to…' Tom stumbled for the words, as if trying hard not to make her feel worse than she already did, '…um, encourage you like that.'

'I think I'm a constant disappointment to her in lots of ways.' Ashleigh hated coming across as a victim, but she might as well be honest. He'd already met her mum and there was no hiding the fact that their relationship was what all the self-help books called 'dysfunctional'.

'But surely she sees your success and is proud of that?' Tom's voice was unfamiliar, almost defensive.

'I suppose she is, in her own way.' She smiled ruefully. Tom's mum was probably beside herself with pride at her boy's achievements and she had every reason to be. 'But she'd rather I was photographing meaningful stuff, like the latest protest march for whatever cause she's adopted.'

'What about you, is that what you want?' He sounded genuinely interested, not just wondering if he needed to find a replacement photographer.

'Sometimes.' She didn't tell him about the 'street life' photographs that she'd begun to compile; that was something she hadn't told anyone but Stevie. The idea of putting a book together might seem laughable to Tom and she wasn't really up for anyone laughing at her dreams tonight. 'I know I'm lucky to have the breaks I've had though. Mum loves the whole celebrity thing too, don't get me wrong, but she just thinks I don't do that properly either.'

'What do you mean? Your shots are always the best thing about *Glitz*.' Tom's unexpected praise, genuine since he definitely wasn't the sort to offer false flattery, almost made her cry. It was a good job there was only a weak glow from the streetlight illuminating the inky night.

'She thinks I should get more involved, make the most of it, if that's the world I've chosen to live in.' She smiled, back in control of her emotions. Her mother certainly practised what she preached. 'When mum moved to the cottage she joined the church, even though she was an atheist, and suddenly she's non-stop socialising with them and they're happily congaing around her back garden.' They were so different. Ashleigh faded to grey in her mother's shadow, envious of her relentless confidence, even though her eccentricities were a constant source of embarrassment.

'Don't try to be like your mum. You're perfect as you are.' The last part was barely audible and what he said next surprised her even more. 'I know what it's like to have a parent who wants you to be something you're not.'

'Really? I assumed your mum would delight in everything you do.' If it sounded bitter Ashleigh hadn't meant it to, but Tom's openness had shocked her.

'Not Mum, my father. Before he died, I could never live up to his expectations, almost from the day I was born.' He was matter of fact about it, as though the emotion it evoked had long since been dealt with, or locked away in a metaphorical box. 'Anyway, that's the past, but don't let your mum change who you are.'

'Ooh, this is like the *Jeremy Kyle Show*, you giving out sage advice and lifestyle coaching!' There was no point probing further about his father, he'd probably already told her more than he'd planned to.

'Jeremy bloody Kyle!' Tom feigned indignation, as though glad of a chance to change the subject. 'I thought I was a cut above that and might at least get Oprah.'

'Nope, you'll need to work on that.' Ashleigh grinned, the lightened atmosphere taking some of the weight from her shoulders. 'You need a tag-line to close your statement if you're going Oprah-style, something like "You have to know what it is you want to be true to, before you can be true to yourself". You know, deep and meaningful!'

'I'll work on it!' Tom was still laughing as they reached Ashleigh's road, no doubt thankful that their own deep and meaningful conversation was over.

When they got to the flat, Tom wanted to check on Chloe and her mother. Leaving him to make the call Ashleigh disappeared into the spare room, which doubled as her office. She'd been struck with an idea about what to give Tom's mum for Christmas – that was if any of the photos she'd taken the day before were good enough. She scrolled through the uploaded photos of Zac's shoot and allowed herself a moment of satisfaction at how well they'd turned out. Amongst the shots were some of Stevie and Zac together, the chemistry between them as obvious as her instinct had told her it would be. There were also a few of Tom that she'd taken when he wasn't aware and one of them stood out from the rest. He'd been laughing in the studio, at some silly remark Stevie or Zac had made and he looked gorgeous. As much as Tom's mum would adore it, it was a moment she didn't want to share.

Switching the computer off, she opened the wardrobe and pulled out a small stack of paintings from the back. She selected one of the back-view of a child on the beach at Hythe, near to where Tom's mum lived. Ashleigh had painted it a few years before and been pleased enough with it to get it framed, but she'd decided it was narcissistic to hang it up and perhaps it wasn't that good after all. So she'd stuck it back in the wardrobe with the rest. Still, there were much worse paintings for sale in the gallery where she'd bought Tom's Christmas present. Hastily wrapping the painting, which she wasn't planning to confess was one of her own, in the same paper as Tom's, she leant it against the wall beside his. Satisfied that Christmas was finally sorted, she smiled to herself and went to find Tom.

Chapter Twenty-Four

'Happy Christmas.' Tom was propped up on one elbow watching her as she opened her eyes.

'That's a bit off putting you know.' She smiled lazily; there really wasn't much to complain about waking up next to his naked form. 'A girl doesn't like to be looked at too closely right after waking up.' As long as she hadn't been snoring or dribbling, or doing something else even more embarrassing, whilst he'd been watching her.

'Well, waking up with you isn't the worst start I've had to a Christmas.' He stroked the back of her neck, making her shiver.

'Not the worst start?'

'Well there was that time when I was eight and I didn't get the *Scalectrix* I had set my heart on…' Ducking as she threw a pillow at him, he slipped an arm under her back and pulled her down on top of him.

'No chance!' She pinned his arms above his head and planted a quick kiss on his lips. 'Sorry, not this morning, there's no way I'm being late for breakfast with your mum.' Leaping off the bed, before he could stop her, she switched on the shower in the ensuite. 'Your present is in the other room.'

Tom was waiting for her when she emerged, the painting still wrapped. On her side of the bed was a Christmas stocking, stuffed with a selection of small parcels.

'I wanted us to open them together.' He handed her a glass of freshly squeezed orange juice and she leant back against the plumped up pillows. Every gift she took out of the stocking was fantastic and she felt more and more embarrassed about the £80 painting, although she stood no chance of being able to compete with Tom. There was designer perfume, gift cards for *Harrods* and *Harvey Nicks* and tickets to several of the top shows in the West End. They were exactly the sort of gifts she expected *Rushworth Associates* to buy for its clients and corporate partners, so putting together something like this was a lot less thoughtful than it looked. Not that she wasn't grateful, but being with Tom was all she really wanted anyway. Well, that and the beautiful pair of silver and amber earrings he'd given her, somehow much more personal than the other gifts, the amber uncannily close in colour to her eyes. She'd like to think he'd chosen them for that very reason. As if, despite their no-strings label, she mattered enough to him to notice the little details.

'Everything is fabulous, thank you.' She kissed him slowly on the mouth, whatever he said and whatever her body was screaming at her to do, they definitely didn't have time for sex before leaving for his mum's. 'You may as well open mine.' She smiled shyly as she pulled away from him. 'It's not much in comparison, but I hope you like it.'

For a long moment after he peeled back the paper he didn't

say anything, his face unreadable, and she was certain he was horrified by her gift.

'I bought it at Sands in the High Street.' Ashleigh couldn't quite bring herself to admit that it had been a last minute purchase the day before; she didn't want him to think she was thoughtless as well as lacking in taste, but then she hadn't even known they'd be together again for Christmas.

'It's fantastic.' He laughed and she couldn't tell if he was joking. Only he must have been because there'd been a horrible mix-up.

'It's okay, you don't have to pretend. You've opened the wrong painting.' She braced herself for more embarrassment. 'I painted that. I was going to give it to your mum, as it's meant to be the beach near her house and, frankly, I was desperate.' There was that reliable old blush again, just as likely to turn up on Christmas Day as Santa Claus himself.

'My God, you honestly don't realise do you?' Tom really was grinning like a kid. 'It's brilliant, can I keep it?'

'Look it's okay, you can stop messing about. I know I'm not the world's greatest artist and you don't have to pretend to spare my feelings.' Ashleigh smiled weakly. Gary 'the disappointing in bed' art lecturer had made it clear that she should stick to photography.

'You should know me well enough by now to realise that I never tell lies to spare someone's feelings.' He grinned again, as if reading her mind. 'Although there's no harm in a bit of spin if it puts a client in a good light.'

'And there's money to be made.' It had crossed her mind that Tom might not be entirely delighted if Zac decided to bring his relationship with Stevie out in to the open. From a marketing point of view it would make no sense at all.

'True, but this is my personal life and I'm always honest about that. You're really talented, in lots of ways.' A brief smile played around his mouth. 'I just wish you'd realise it.'

'Well, thanks. If you're sure you want to keep it then you're more than welcome.' Ashleigh found compliments difficult to handle, but tried to be gracious. 'Only there's no changing your mind later when your mum opens the one from Sands and you realise you've missed out.'

'I rarely change my mind.' He held the painting at arm's length again. 'Anyway, I really do love it. It reminds me of days at the beach with my mum when I was a child and Dad was away somewhere. They were always the best days.' There was that touch of vulnerability, the hint that there was more to Tom than met the eye, and then he shut down again. 'Right, well I don't know about you, but I'm starving.'

As Ashleigh expected, Isobel Rushworth's home was a grand Edwardian double-fronted house with a sweeping in and out driveway. It was as far removed from Carol's cliff top cottage, complete with hippy style décor, as it was possible to be. The old lady herself – and she was old, having had her only child late in life – was surprisingly tiny, given Tom's stature, and incredibly elegant. Her hair was perfectly coiffured and her make-up immaculate. She wore a suit, silk blouse and an unexpectedly towering pair of high-heels. Ashleigh, who was in her usual winter uniform of Levis, knee high boots and, as it was Christmas, a red silk shirt, felt alarmingly under-dressed.

'Happy Christmas my darlings.' Isobel embraced Tom and smiled warmly at Ashleigh. 'I've heard a lot of good things about you.' She winked with all the ease of a seasoned entertainer and Ashleigh began to relax.

'I hope Tom hasn't been using his famous spin and I disappoint!' Much to her surprise, she was comfortable enough to gang up with his mother to tease Tom.

'Hmm, well he has been known to exaggerate.' There was that casual wink again. 'But since the last girl he brought home had the personality and IQ of a fridge magnet, I think we'll give him the benefit of the doubt this time!' Isobel peeled into infectious laughter. There was no hint that she was unwell; if Ashleigh hadn't heard it from Tom himself it would have been very difficult to believe.

'Alright, alright, enough you two I think!' Tom was smiling, pleased that the two women liked each other.

'Okay darling, if you must spoil our fun.' Isobel pinched his cheek affectionately, just as she might have done when he was a toddler. 'Present time I think.'

They moved through to the drawing room and the elegant sash windows allowed the winter sunlight to give the room a pale glow. The furniture, as expected, was made up of elegant period pieces. The room was homely though, rather than a museum piece, like it had seen life.

'I brought you a little something, it's not much but I hope you like it.' Ashleigh handed Tom's mother the parcel and she carefully pulled out the painting that had originally been intended for her son.

'Where did you get this?' Isobel traced the signature in the corner of the painting with her fingers and, when she looked up, there were tears in her eyes.

Horrified for the second time that day at the reaction to a present, Ashleigh stumbled over her words. 'A gallery… in Sandgate… I'm sorry, I can take it back.' The blush was back with a vengeance; paintings were far too personal to give as presents to people you barely knew.

'Oh no, I love it.' It was almost a carbon copy of Tom's reaction and suddenly Isobel's small hand was over hers. 'It's just it was painted by an old friend of mine and I've wanted to try to track down one of his pictures for years. I honestly can't believe you've found one. It's like a one in a million coincidence.' Glancing briefly at Tom, who was busy pouring Bucks Fizz into glasses on the other side of the room, she leant conspiratorially towards Ashleigh and whispered. 'The girl in the painting might even be me!'

Regaining her composure and beaming as if the painting really was the best present she'd ever had, Isobel handed out her gifts. There were diamond cufflinks for Tom and a beautiful silk scarf for Ashleigh. She was thrilled with the cruise tickets that Tom gave her for a trip to Alaska with her sister Maureen and she insisted on seeing the photograph, which Tom had taken on his iPhone, of Ashleigh's painting of the beach at Hythe.

'Beautiful and talented too. About time Tom picked himself a good one.' As Isobel leant forward to kiss her cheek, the paper-thin fragility of her skin was a shock to Ashleigh.

'Now come on son,' Isobel gestured to Tom insistently. 'Let's treat this lovely young lady in the way she should be. Help me bring breakfast through. She deserves to be waited on.'

A moment or so after they disappeared into the kitchen, Ashleigh's mobile beeped. As there was no one around to witness her checking it, or to think she was rude for doing so in company, so she took a quick look. Maybe it would be Stevie filling her in on how ostentatious Christmas with Zac was turning out to be, but the text was from her mum.

✉ Mum
Happy Christmas darling. Hope U & Tom R
having fun, wink, wink! As requested Geoffrey
has bought me a voucher 4 the tattoo & piercing
parlour in Canterbury for Christmas & so I'm
going 2 get my nipples pierced next week! xx

Unlike Ashleigh, Isobel had served up a breakfast in the dining room that any TV chef would really have been proud of. Mid-way through, and just as Ashleigh had put slightly too much bacon in her mouth, there was a violent battering on the door. Seconds later her chair was vigorously pushed from behind, almost causing an unintentional Heimlich manoeuvre.

'Bertie, no!' Isobel shouted at the chocolate Labrador, who by now had his head on Ashleigh's knee and was gazing up at her with soulful eyes, just begging for the tiniest scrap of her breakfast. 'You're supposed to be in the kitchen, you naughty boy.' Even as she chastised him, the affection in Isobel's voice was as tangible as it had been when she'd greeted Tom.

'I don't mind. He's lovely and he certainly seems pleased to see us.' Ashleigh sneaked a piece of bacon rind beneath the table and fed it to the delighted Labrador, who rewarded her with a trail of saliva across one leg of her Levis.

'Oh, I'm so glad you like dogs too! Susie-Anne seemed to be horrified by Bertie, that's why I left him in the kitchen.' Isobel clapped her hands with delight. 'Such a mark of a person, if you ask me, liking dogs that is. We've always had them, even before Tom was born. Let's see there was Robbie, Bert, RoRo and first of them all was plain old Robert, the light of my life just like his namesake.'

'I sense a theme!' Ashleigh returned her smile. 'Was that

your husband's name?'

'Oh no!' The older woman shook her head with conviction. 'He was Clive, such a dull name, nothing you can do with that at all.'

Tom, who appeared unsurprised to discover that another man had been the one to light up Isobel's life, said nothing. The heat of a blush swept up Ashleigh's neck and across her cheeks, she'd really put her foot in it.

The rest of the breakfast passed in easy conversation, with the odd nudge from Bertie checking whether there was any more bacon rind going begging. Isobel had been a delight. She was easy-going and loved to recount tales of Tom's childhood, including the time he'd swallowed three hotels from his *Monopoly* game to stop his cousin snatching a late victory, and had ended up in Accident and Emergency as a result.

'I should have realised then that nothing would stop him from being a success!' Isobel's laugh really was infectious, she was an attractive woman even in her late seventies and Ashleigh had no doubt she'd been stunning in her youth. Meeting her was an unexpected pleasure. The buttoned-up side of Tom indicated that his upbringing had lacked warmth, or been terribly formal, but there was no trace of that with Isobel.

After she'd insisted on clearing the breakfast plates herself, resolutely spritely, Isobel played the card that was surely guaranteed to ensure Tom's compliance.

'Tom, darling, I'm feeling the effects of my tablets a bit this morning, you wouldn't be an angel and walk Bertie for me before you go would you?' Isobel leant against the back of her armchair with a weak smile. 'I know your Auntie Maureen won't want to do it later; she'll be too busy fussing about the security of the turkey. Just because Bertie licked it a bit last year when it was still frozen. Honestly, there was no harm done at all!'

'We'd love to, wouldn't we? Ashleigh can show me the part of the beach in my painting.' Tom, obviously suspecting exactly what his mother was up to, attempted to head her off at the pass.

'Oh no, you're not taking Ashleigh with you.' Out manoeuvring Tom with a verbal checkmate, she added. 'After all, you wouldn't want to deny a dying old woman a bit of company on Christmas morning would you?'

Within a few minutes, and after Bertie had leapt about attempting to catch his own tail, whilst Tom struggled to attach his lead, the two males of the household were on their way to the beach, Tom striding out purposefully beside the eternally bouncy Bertie.

'He really likes you, you know?' There was no beating around the bush with Isobel, who, in so many ways, had no time to waste. 'The fact that he brought you here and was interested enough to meet your family tells me that. Only he doesn't even know how much himself.'

'We enjoy each other's company.' Ashleigh shifted uncomfortably in her seat. She could hardly tell Tom's mother that they would never be any more than friends who were currently enjoying the best sex of her life.

'I know he's not good at showing his emotions when it comes to girls.' Isobel sighed, genuine sadness in her voice. 'It's entirely mine and Clive's fault we completely messed up, setting him the worst possible example of what a relationship should be like.'

'I'm sure that's not true.' Ashleigh wanted to reassure her, to tell her she'd wished more than once over breakfast that her own mother was a bit more like Isobel, but she struggled for what to say. 'Tom adores you, anyone can see that.'

'True, we do adore one another.' Isobel was smiling. 'Only I could barely stand his father and I shouldn't have put Tom through that.'

'I think Tom and I get on because we both realise how complicated families can be.' Ashleigh took a deep breath. 'My parents only stayed together for me and my mother was always, how can I put this, a free spirit. It wasn't the most harmonious of households.'

'Ah, but if they rowed at least there was passion. Here it was like stone.' Taking Ashleigh's hand in her own, she went on, as though desperate for her to understand. 'I never really loved Clive, it was sad for him, always in the shadow of Robert. Robert and I were teenage sweethearts, went everywhere together for almost five years. He was an artist, the painting you bought was one of his.' She smiled warmly at Ashleigh. 'I feel it was fate that you bought the painting and I knew the moment I opened it that I had to tell you the story I've shared with so few.' Pausing she took a sip of her drink. 'Robert and I had a passionate relationship like you've never known, huge rows and oh, such wonderful times making up… We had one row, the biggest we'd ever had and I told him I wouldn't make up with him this time and that I would marry Clive. Clive worked for my father in his import and export company and was busy climbing the ladder to success, desperate to date the boss' daughter as the cherry on the cake. I thought he was boring and a stuffed shirt, but I knew that saying it would really hurt Robert, as he so wanted us to marry, but we both knew my family would never approve.' A single tear snaked its way down her cheek. 'I didn't mean it of course, I would have made up with him in a heartbeat, only he went roaring off along the coast road on his bike, took the bend too fast and…'

'Oh, my God, please don't tell me he died.' Ashleigh clasped a hand over her mouth, there were echoes of her father's accident and so many tragedies in the name of love. It was beginning to make sense why Tom so fervently rejected it.

'Instantly.' Swallowing the emotion even nearly sixty years later seemed difficult. 'I think that was the hardest part, not getting the chance to say goodbye. For three years afterwards I spent nearly all my time crying and in the end I settled for Clive, thinking it was better than being alone.'

'But it wasn't?' Ashleigh squeezed the other woman's hand

'No, my darling, you're right it wasn't. Clive was always less than second best. It really wasn't his fault.' She appeared to be struggling to think of something positive to say. 'He was a good provider, grew my father's business four-fold and he loved me, I really believe that, only his love was like cold ash compared to the fire I'd had with Robert.'

'But you had Tom and that's what kept you together?' Ashleigh was beginning to understand him, just as his mother had planned. Her reaction was to search for the love that her parents had never had, but Tom's had been more clinical – deciding to dismiss even the possibility that it might exist.

'Well, in a way, but actually Tom's arrival made things more difficult in some respects.' Isobel shook her head vigorously. 'Not that he was in any way unwanted – I wouldn't change his arrival for the world, not even to have Robert back. He truly was and is the best thing ever to happen to me. It just made things with Clive even more difficult; there were now two men in my heart who outranked him and he was jealous. Little did he know that I was finally plucking up the courage to leave him and find out if there might be more to life when I discovered I was pregnant.' She sighed again. 'Perhaps it would have been kinder to both of them to leave anyway, but it wasn't the done thing in the circles we moved in and with the business and everything our lives were so intertwined, it was complicated.'

'So Tom and Clive didn't get on?' Some of the comments he'd made in his vulnerable moments had hinted at that, but now it was starting to piece together,

'Clive was jealous of Tom and I made it worse, I suppose, by releasing all of my pent up emotions and pouring all the love I had into this baby. He must have seen that I'd never had any of those feelings for him. Added to which, I insisted on calling him Thomas, which was Robert's surname, as a link to him. Sometimes I'd fantasise that Tom really was his baby, ridiculous as that sounds.'

'It's not ridiculous at all. I think we all have those kinds of fantasies, a way of making our dreams come true.' Ashleigh had imagined a hundred times what her father might say if they could have one last conversation. She'd have given anything to have that chance. He was the one person who would have understood how challenging being the object of Carol's attention could be. Her brother Jamie could empathise, but, like Geoffrey, he had a way of letting it all go over his head – whereas she took it to heart.

'Clive did love Tom in his own fashion. I didn't realise how much until recently. I found a memory box he'd kept of Tom's things and it made me so sad in a way, about how much missed opportunity there'd been for us all.' The pain was etched on Isobel's face.

'I know what you mean. I wish my mum and dad had felt

able to separate, they'd both have been happier and dad might still be here now.'

'Thank you for understanding, somehow I knew you would.' Isobel visibly relaxed. 'I would never have said these things to Susie-Anne; I never have to any other girlfriend of Tom's. When he told me she was pregnant and that he was planning to marry her, I was horrified.' Another tear began a familiar path down her face. 'Of course I was delighted that Tom would have a child. For so long I was afraid that Clive's resentment and treatment of him, and the mistakes I'd made over the years, had put him off fatherhood and that he would never get close enough to someone to experience that joy. Yet, on the other hand, I could see history repeating itself: a loveless marriage where Tom would dote on the child but his relationship with its mother would be damaging to them all, just as Clive's and mine was. I was scared, realising that he was probably doing it for me, much more than for himself. He sees how much I love my sister Maureen's grandchildren and he wanted to give me that last gift, I know.'

'I think you should go easier on yourself, he's not turned out so bad.' They exchanged a wry smile; in so many ways Tom's life was an unprecedented success.

'True, but he chooses to pretend that love doesn't exist. It's easier for him to think of relationships like they are business deals and he's happy to work in partnership with someone for a while, but if they show any interest in a long term merger then the deal's off.' Isobel smiled again, pleased with the analogy she'd drawn.

'Perhaps, but he's always honest about that and I know exactly where I stand, I'm perfectly okay with that too.' She smiled brightly in return, keen that Tom's mother wouldn't see her as desperate or sad, pining away the hours clinging to the unlikely scenario that he might one day declare his undying love for her.

'I know and I'm glad of that, but I'd like to see him realise that love really does exist and leave this world knowing that at least he has the chance of finding it…' Isobel hesitated, '…with someone like you.'

'I think you can feel reassured.' Flattering as it was to Ashleigh, the compliment was undoubtedly driven by the fact that time was running out for Isobel. 'After all, he loves you and he should be capable of replicating that when the right girl comes along.'

'Just promise me you'll remember what he's been through, what it is that has shaped his responses, if you are the right girl and he misses the chance to show you what's really in his heart?' Isobel's eyes pleaded with her. It was a big gesture to make such a promise, but it was such an unlikely scenario that it barely mattered.

'Okay, if that time ever comes, I promise I'll remember.'

'You don't know how happy that makes me.' She returned Ashleigh's squeeze of the hand. 'The chemotherapy tablets I'm taking have bought me a little more time, but before much longer they won't be able to stop the inevitable.'

'I'm so sorry.' There was nothing Ashleigh could say that would make a difference.

'Don't be, I'm ready to see Robert again, I so hope I will.' Isobel closed her eyes briefly, as though imagining the possibility and choosing not to consider that it might be her late husband, Clive, waiting for her when the time came. 'I'll miss Tom though and he's all I worry about, but less so after today.'

The beach was largely deserted, save for an elderly couple who were wearing pristine coats, which looked like they might just have been unwrapped. The wind whipped at Tom's scarf, making him wish he'd worn a hat.

'Come on Bertie, you must have had enough by now. It's freezing!' The Labrador was gambling amongst the icy waves, as though it was a warm August day, and they had nothing better to do. But Tom didn't want to give his mum any longer than was necessary to fill Ashleigh's head with the sort of nonsense she almost certainly would.

Just as Bertie was about to comply and head in Tom's general direction, a golden retriever came charging across the water's edge and the two dogs began a merry game of chasing one another, making handbrake turns that sent them skidding across the sand.

'Oh, bless them, aren't they sweet together?' The elegant blonde coming towards him on the beach caught Tom by surprise. 'Suki so loves having a playmate, perhaps we could exchange numbers and arrange a date for them on a regular basis?'

'He's not actually my dog.' Tom gave her the benefit of his 'professional' smile, her breath-taking forwardness a shock even to him. She was attractive, but he wasn't interested in making pointless conversation; there was a disaster to avert.

'I'm Helena by the way.' She held out a gloved hand. 'And I know who you are!'

Right. So that's why she'd been so keen to give out her number to a total stranger.

'And who might that be?' There was only one way out of this situation quickly and he'd used it many times before.

'Tom Rushworth of course!' Helena gushed and moved uncomfortably close to him.

'Not another one!' He used his equally well-practised

'professional' laugh, the sort he adopted to humour his clients. 'I'm afraid you're not the first person to mistake me for him.' He shrugged his shoulders, as if apologising for her mistake.

'You do look *awfully* like him.' She looked him up and down, the disappointment as apparent on her face as it was in her voice.

'Like I said, I'm sorry about that.' He moved a step closer to Helena, who had begun to back away. 'But I'd still love to take your number.' He didn't really want it, of course, but there was a theory to test.

'Sorry, you're an attractive guy and all that, but I don't make a habit of giving out my number to strange men on the beach.' Helena didn't appear to sense the irony in her words, suddenly looking distinctly uncomfortable. 'Come on Suki, we've got to go.'

Watching her disappear along the beach, Tom sighed. Had it always been like this? Grabbing Bertie before he could escape again, he clipped on the lead. He had to get back. If his mother said what was on her mind, everything with Ashleigh might change. He wasn't ready for their friendship to end just yet, because, whatever else it might be, at least he knew it was real.

Isobel's sister Maureen arrived to collect her and the dog for the remainder of Christmas and New Year just as Tom got back with a wet, but considerably calmer Bertie. In a flurry of hugs and protestations from Auntie Maureen about the smell of wet dog in the back of her husband's Nissan, Ashleigh and Tom headed off with promises to visit Isobel again soon.

'I take it Mum told you about Robert?' Tom kept his eyes on the road, as he drove away from his mother's house and back to the flat. 'I suppose you know now why all of our dogs have had such similar names?'

'Yes.' She didn't know what else to say; any remark she made would sound flippant.

'It's just a fantasy that kept her sane in an unhappy marriage. If Robert had lived, I'm sure she'd eventually have realised that those feelings don't last, except in films with saccharine sweet endings.'

Ashleigh just nodded. It was pointless getting into a debate with Tom about love.

'I'm glad she liked you as much as she did though.' He grinned suddenly, the famous dimples making an appearance. 'She told me I'd finally proved that I don't waste all my good sense on making business decisions!' He paused, glancing at her, as she struggled not to show any reaction to his mother's words. 'But don't read too much into anything she says, she's just desperate to see me settle down.'

'Don't worry, I won't.' Ashleigh kept her voice even. Buying into Isobel's theories could be very dangerous indeed.

They spent the rest of the day just enjoying each other's company, curled up on the sofa watching old movies and having a secret cry at *It's a Wonderful Life*. They had a somewhat unconventional dinner of lobster and demolished most of a tin of chocolates, like millions of other couples on sofas in front of their TVs all over the country. They spent most of the afternoon in bed and watched the sky turn pink over the sea as Christmas day began to ebb away. If she'd wanted to buy into Isobel's theory that Tom was secretly in love with her, then she could have done. It was such a perfect day, but, just as Tom had always so fervently insisted, perfection wasn't meant to last.

Chapter Twenty-Five

Boxing Day was a milder, much greyer day than the one before. Mist hung in the air and the dampness made Ashleigh's hair far curlier than she wanted.

'What's wrong?' Tom's expression had changed almost as soon as he'd switched his phone back on.

'It's Susie-Anne.' He widened his eyes. 'Francine has sent me about a million messages, apparently it's all over the Internet too.'

'What is?' Ashleigh shivered, Tom was still hesitating. Whatever it was, it wasn't good.

'Michael took to *Twitter* and he's told the world that he can't be sure he's the father of Susie-Anne's baby.'

'Oh God, don't tell me she pulled that trick again!'

'No, she's definitely pregnant, only it turns out that she also got friendly with at least one of Michael's team mates.'

'And we thought we were Jeremy Kyle material! So can she narrow it down to two, do you think?'

'I wouldn't put it past her to carry out a DNA test live on air if she thought it would raise her profile.' He managed a rueful smile; it was a distinct possibility.

'What happens now? Will you need to issue a statement or something?' Even as she spoke, his phone started to ring.

'Sorry, it's Francine, I'm going to have to take it.' Tom put the phone to his ear and walked through to the kitchen.

Suddenly vulnerable and exposed, in just a vest top and a pair of lacy knickers, with the real world flooding in, Ashleigh wanted to turn back time. She put her clothes on like a suit of armour – if only it were that easy to protect herself.

'Now what?' Could there be anymore? It was like she'd been caught up in a soap opera storyline that she couldn't escape from.

'Susie-Anne's in hospital. They think she might be having a miscarriage.' Tom's voice was emotionless, as though he didn't know how to react. After all, Susie-Anne had lied to him and made no attempt to spare his feelings, but deep down there was a vulnerable side to almost everyone and, regardless of who the father turned out to be, there was a baby at the centre of all this. If Ashleigh was struggling with it all, it must be a hundred times worse for Tom.

'You've got to go.' The finality of Ashleigh's words weren't lost on her, but what he said next took her breath away.

'Not without you.' He searched her face, waiting for her to respond. She'd be well within her rights to tell him to get stuffed and she very nearly did.

'I don't think that would go down too well with Susie-Anne, me turning up at her bedside!' She managed a half smile, her humour bleak. Everything about the world they'd be going back to was tarnishing things, as though the last two days had just been smoke and mirrors too.

'Just come with me, please? She's been taken into hospital in Brighton.' He stood up, wrapping his arms around her waist. 'Although knowing her it will be a false alarm for added drama.'

She hesitated, it would be much easier to stay at home, let Tom go and text him later to say it had been fun, but they both knew things would run their course eventually and that now seemed as good a time as any. Only the thought twisted her insides even more than the prospect of pitching up at Susie-Anne's bedside. Despite her best attempts, she hadn't managed to keep her feelings for Tom in the friendship zone. Part of her was hoping that Isobel might be right and she hated herself for it.

'Okay, if you really want me to, then I'll come.' They wouldn't be far from Zac and Stevie if she needed to bolt, and that was what tipped the balance. 'But I'll borrow Mum's car and follow you down in that, so if you need to hang around I can head off.'

The drive down to Brighton was interminable, not helped much by the bone-shaking nature of the ancient Land Rover. Thankfully, Carol, who was still in the midst of a very merry Christmas, didn't ask too many questions about why she wanted to borrow it. Tom was waiting in the car park outside the hospital's maternity unit, pacing up and down much like any other expectant father.

'I thought perhaps you'd changed your mind.' He kissed her lightly on the lips. Was she just a PR pawn, there to make sure Tom didn't look like a victim to the photographers who were bound to be hanging around?

'Are you sure this is a good idea?' He'd been right to worry about her turning up. Twice she'd almost taken the slip road off the motorway and headed straight back to Sandgate.

'It'll be fine.' Tom was insistent.

'I'll come in for a bit.' She didn't want to carry on the conversation in the middle of a busy car park, whilst relatives laden with *IT'S A BOY!* balloons and bunches of flowers walked past, happily eavesdropping on their conversation.

Tom didn't respond but he took her hand, leading her into the foyer of the maternity unit where Francine was already waiting.

'Tom, how are you?' His uber efficient PA was just as deadly when it came to getting Tom's undivided attention. Without even acknowledging Ashleigh's presence, she literally swept her aside and embraced him with odd stiffness.

'I'm fine.' Tom stepped back and immediately glanced around, almost certainly checking whether any journalists had managed to get inside. The newspaper stand outside the hospital shop was laden with tabloids; the Susie-Anne and Michael Cox debacle front-page news. 'I thought Susie-Anne was booked to go to the Portland Hospital?' Tom was irritated; it would obviously have been easier for him to control things there.

'She was.' The private hospital was *the* place to give birth for the good, the great and anyone with a high profile. 'But she was taken ill at her cousin's place in Brighton and so they brought her here, in case it was serious.' Francine spoke as though the whole thing were an illness that needed to be 'got over'.

'And the press?' Tom frowned, but there was no sign of anyone hanging around in the foyer as far as Ashleigh could tell.

'Seems like they haven't got anyone inside the building.' Francine smiled briefly, but it definitely wasn't the kind that lit up her whole face. 'Although I suspect it's only a matter of time. Especially as you've decided to bring… outsiders.'

'Right, well, we'll go through then, whilst the going's good.' Tom appeared to let Francine's comments drift over his head, no doubt her abrasive personality often came in useful; she was bound to be excellent at dealing with unwanted press interest for a start.

'You're *both* going in?' Francine raised a perfectly arched eyebrow, her mouth twisting into a sneer.

'Yes. Have you seen her yet?' He didn't acknowledge her comment and Ashleigh could only imagine Francine's bedside manner. Somehow she doubted it had brought Susie-Anne much comfort.

'Briefly. Apparently the doctors are trying to…' Francine appeared to be grasping for the right words; the term 'miscarriage' with all of its gory connotations not something she was willing to say '…stop things until it's the proper time.'

'Thanks. Are you okay to hang around?' Tom's tone was expectant. As if it were perfectly reasonable to ask someone to give up their time on a day that, for most people, was devoted to spending time with loved ones. Taking in Francine's sharp business-suit, Ashleigh suspected she was only too happy to work rather than make merry.

'Yes, happy to help.' There was that tight smile again. 'I'll be out here when you need me, Tom, and *everyone else* has gone.'

Susie-Anne was in a private room and was almost unrecognisable with her white-blonde hair scrapped back and not an ounce of make-up on her face. Despite being hooked up to a drip and devastated by the events of the last few days, she was doll-like and much prettier than Ashleigh remembered.

She should go without make-up more often.

'Oh, Tom, I'm so sorry.' Susie-Anne clasped his hand, like a drowning woman clinging to a life raft. 'I'm so glad you're here.' Ashleigh shrank back into the corner of the room by the door, hoping that Susie-Anne wouldn't see her. It felt so wrong to be here, like she was intruding in someone else's life and, in a way, she was.

'Is that the photographer?' Susie-Anne, who clearly knew exactly what had been going on between Ashleigh and Tom, was playing the innocent. 'Thank you darling, I know my fans will be anxious to know how I'm doing, but I don't think photographs right now are a good idea.'

'Ashleigh's not here for…' Tom started to explain, but she cut him off.

'Susie-Anne's right, I should go.' She held up a hand to stop Tom, as he moved to come towards her. 'Give me a call when you're ready for those photos. I hope it goes alright and the baby is okay.'

Out in the corridor, she just wanted to escape. She wouldn't cry, not here. The last thing she wanted was to give Francine the satisfaction of seeing that.

'Ashleigh, don't go. Wait for me in Reception, I won't be long.' Tom was behind her, his hand on her shoulder, and she turned around to face him.

'It's best if I leave. Without Michael, she needs you. Even as her agent you owe her that, despite whatever else has gone on.' She dropped her eyes, not giving him a chance to make her weaken. 'Just call me when you're ready, we can talk then. Goodbye Tom.'

'Are you okay?' He tried to touch her face, but she turned away and began walking to the double doors that led back to the Reception area. Susie-Anne was calling his name and, when she glanced back at him, he was torn for a moment, before the inevitable happened, his business head took over and he turned towards the hospital room. She just kept walking.

Chapter Twenty-Seven

Ashleigh decided to take the long way out of the hospital, unable to face bumping into the journalists who'd be hanging around outside the building by now. If Tom had used her as a pawn she could deal with that, it might even make the decision she was considering easier to stand by, but she wasn't about to make the job of the leeches who drew their life blood from this sort of situation any easier.

The hospital, like most big city hospitals, was a maze of corridors and wards. In an attempt to find an exit as far away from the maternity unit as possible, Ashleigh ended up passing the cardiac unit, just as the double doors to one of the wards swung open. She nearly bumped straight into a couple emerging from the unit, who were giggling and holding hands, oblivious to the world around them.

'Ashleigh, my goodness, fancy meeting you here!' Chloe Nicholas, with a glow about her like one of the new mums in the maternity unit, let go of the hand she'd been holding and threw her slender arms around Ashleigh's waist.

'I've just popped in to see a friend.' It was a bit of a stretch to describe Susie-Anne in that way, but it wasn't a lie to say she'd *popped in.* Driving this far for a two-minute visit would definitely hit that classification. 'How's your mum doing?'

'Brilliantly!' Chloe was beaming, almost unrecognisable as the fragile young woman that she and Stevie had met a few weeks before and who'd been found disorientated and wandering the streets in the early aftermath of her mother's heart attack. 'And it's all thanks to Hugo.' Shyly she reached out her hand to draw the man behind her slightly forward. 'He's the doctor who saved Mum.'

'Well, I wouldn't go that far!' Hugo to his credit blushed slightly, two crimson dots colouring his cheeks in a way that Ashleigh herself would have been proud of. 'There were lots of us who treated Mrs Nicholas, although it was never really life threatening as such, and we're all delighted that she's on the mend.'

'He's fantastic! Mum and I realise that, even if he doesn't.' Chloe rose to her tiptoes, planting a kiss on his cheek, making him redder than ever.

'I think all doctors and nurses are amazing, so I'm with Chloe on this one.' Ashleigh smiled, immediately warming to Hugo, her kindred spirit in the blushing stakes.

'Well I'll take that then, two beautiful ladies singing my praises.' Hugo beamed. He was obviously modest enough to take their admiration as a real compliment. 'But I'm afraid I will have to love you and leave you, as I've got to have a chat with the clinical lead before he goes on his rounds.' Hugo and Chloe exchanged a brief but meaningful kiss on the lips, leaving no doubt that theirs was more than a doctor and grateful relative's relationship.

'Have you got time for a coffee? There's loads to tell you!' Chloe had publicly credited *Glitz* with saving her fledgling career – allowing people to see her as she really was and to fall in love with her all over again. She'd written to Stevie and Ashleigh telling them as much and sending them both a crate of Champagne. So perhaps it shouldn't have been such a surprise that she seemed so thrilled to see Ashleigh again.

'I've got plenty of time.' The prospect of sharing a coffee with Chloe was infinitely preferable to driving home, or over to see Zac and Stevie and having to explain everything. She didn't want to do that anymore than she wanted to go back to the flat straight away and begin turning over the rest of the day's events in her mind and analysing things to death, as she was so prone to doing.

The hospital cafeteria was largely populated by exhausted looking relatives, who had probably spent their Christmas at the bedside of very poorly loved ones and for whom the tinsel festooned, neon-lit room's *festive atmosphere* was quite likely to be the very definition of irony.

'I'm so glad your mum is okay.' Ashleigh wrapped her hands around the polystyrene cup of coffee, thankful for the warmth it proffered, despite the taste.

'God, me too. They say once her pace-maker is sorted she should make a complete recovery and it should prevent any recurrence.' Chloe couldn't stop beaming. 'And Hugo… it's like he was sent to save us both. I spent a night in rehab, as Tom was so worried about how I was coping with Mum being ill and then I came back here. Hugo's been my rock.'

'I take it you two are an item?' Chloe's excitement was infectious, how could Tom not believe in love when it made this amount of difference to someone's life?

'It's been mad, so intense and so quick, but I can honestly say I've never felt anything like it.' Chloe dropped her gaze slightly, as if she was still coming to terms with her own feelings. 'I know it sounds cheesy and crazy because we've only known each other a few days, but I feel like he's my soul mate.'

'Life is mad.' Ashleigh grinned. 'My cousin, Sally, got engaged to her fiancé when they were at Uni and they finally got married twelve years later, in June this year. Mum sent them a Christmas card at the beginning of December and got a letter back from Sally to say they'd split up, it turns out they weren't suited after all. So who's to say that just because something is quick and intense, that it's any madder than a slow burn? If it's meant to be it will be.'

'I love you more every time we meet!' Chloe clasped her tiny hands around Ashleigh's. 'I just knew you'd understand. I'm writing a song about him! It's so great to be able to write a happy song for once, and we've already told each other we think it's love.'

'He seems like a lovely, genuine guy. I should probably tell you to be careful, but I'm a sucker for a romance and life is for living. You and I both lost our dads at a young age, so we know that more than anyone.'

'True, and don't worry, Tom will no doubt be the voice of reason!' Chloe, who didn't seem to have any idea that Ashleigh and Tom were together, pulled a face. 'You know what a stickler he is for the business and I'm sure he'll tell me not to get carried away.'

'I think you can bank on that,' Ashleigh struggled to keep her voice level, 'and do you think you'll listen to him?'

'For now, but not because of the business. I just don't want the press to taint things.' Chloe sighed, for the first time more like the frightened and fragile girl that Ashleigh had met at the photo-shoot. 'I know only too well how it works. They'll find something to dig up about Hugo – some girlfriend from university who wants to pay off her student debt by sharing an exposé on him. It sucks and I don't want that to touch what's so perfect for us at the moment. So if we keep it quiet that will be the reason.'

'That side of things does get to you after a while doesn't it?' Ashleigh for her part was exhausted by it all.

'Definitely. If singing wasn't my dream I'd quit tomorrow. But there's nothing else I want to do right now, so I just have to try to find a way of balancing it.' Everything Chloe had been through had made her wise beyond her years and her words resonated with Ashleigh, who wasn't really living her dream. Now there was even more to think about on the journey home.

❦

'So what's going on between you and the photographer, sugar? I hear you two have been getting quite cosy?' There was an edge to Susie-Anne's voice, as if she was jealous. Had she seriously expected him to pine for her and stay celibate in the hope that things might not work out with Michael? Surely even Susie-Anne wasn't that deluded.

'Does it matter?' It wasn't often that Tom hated his job, but today came pretty close; both Francine and his ex-fiancée had pushed him to the very limits of his patience. He could have been in Ashleigh's warm flat and… He tried not to think about the rest, it only made him more irritated.

'I guess not, but we're friends aren't we? We can still care about each other.' Susie-Anne was using the little girl voice that she mistakenly assumed was endearing, but which frankly made Tom question how he'd ever managed to spend more than half an hour in her company.

'What about you and Michael, isn't that a more pressing

issue right now?' Tom changed the subject. He'd never been friends with Susie-Anne and never would be. He liked her less and less every time they came into contact. So the last thing he wanted was to have a cosy chat with her about his personal life.

'Oh he's just an arsehole who can't keep it in his pants!' Susie-Anne's accent was stronger than it had been in months, her anger at the alleged father of her unborn child tangible.

'You knew about that before, though.' Tom raised an eyebrow and resisted the urge to ask Susie-Anne just how many men she'd helped out of their pants, to see if they could narrow down the growing list for the DNA testing.

'Yes, but he's been jumping anything that moved and he's got the cheek to question my fidelity.' She looked completely affronted at the thought and Tom wanted to laugh out loud. Susie-Anne taking the moral high ground was a paradox of epic proportions.

'And is the baby his?'

'What if I told you that the baby might be yours?' There was the little girl voice again and she glanced up at him through ridiculously long eyelash extensions that wouldn't have been out of place on a pantomime cow.

'Then I'd know you were bullshitting.' She'd fooled him once, but he wasn't in the frame this time and he was more thankful for that than she'd ever know.

'Pity, but you can't blame a girl for trying.' She really had no shame. 'So is it love with you and the photographer then?' Susie-Anne clearly couldn't believe there'd be any other reason for Tom turning her down. Apparently she *was* that deluded after all.

'You of all people should know there's no such thing.' His

patience was now completely exhausted. 'We're friends, that's all'

'Friends with benefits? Does she know that's all you are?' Susie-Anne feigned a sympathetic look. 'Poor girl, she's obviously crazy about you.'

'You've barely said ten words to her in your whole life, so just keep out of my personal life and I'll pick up the pieces of yours, okay?' Despite his strong rebuttal, Susie-Anne's words had hit the Achilles heel they'd been aimed at, creating a sense of unease. He needed to speak to Ashleigh, iron things out, make sure they were both still on the same page. Tom could understand her not wanting to hang around in the same room as Susie-Anne, he wouldn't do it himself unless he was getting paid for it, but she'd definitely been upset. He hoped she wasn't developing feelings for him that could ruin what they had together, because, if Tom was honest with himself, he wasn't ready for things to end just yet either. He'd sort the Susie-Anne situation, work with Francine on a press release and then call Ashleigh. Prioritise and keep everything in his life within the parameters he'd set for them, just as he always had.

Chapter Twenty-Eight

Ashleigh decided not to call in on Zac and Stevie on the way back from Brighton. She figured that the last thing they wanted was her arriving as a human antidote to their first heady days of love, moping around following the decision she'd reached to end things with Tom.

She'd realised something at the hospital. As much as she'd tried to understand Tom's commitment to the business and his total rejection of a real relationship because of Isobel and Clive's cold marriage, she couldn't live with his willingness to live a lie and manipulate the world into believing something – just to turn a profit for his clients and *Rushworth Associates*.

It was fair enough for Tom to reject love, he'd been honest about that from the start and Isobel's sharing so much with her had touched Ashleigh. In a way it had made her feel like she knew Tom better than most people. But he'd told Chloe to lie about her relationship too and she'd realised he would always put the likes of Susie-Anne and the business first. Now she wondered if anyone, least of all her, knew the real Tom at all. She did know herself, though, and that if she didn't call things off now, she'd be the one to get really hurt.

For his part he'd called or texted every day, Susie-Anne had been put on bed rest due to her threatened miscarriage and they were keeping her in hospital for monitoring as her blood pressure continued to spike. Chloe's mum, Gilly, had been released from the same hospital and there were lots of photos of Chloe in the papers, being shielded by Tom, his arm around her shoulders looking every inch the protector.

She couldn't tell Tom why she needed to finish things over the phone, she'd been tempted on more than one occasion just to text him, but she'd hate that if the situation were reversed. Christmas Day had been so perfect and they had shared so much on Christmas Eve and that deserved more than a phone call. After all, she was the one who hadn't been able to stick to the bargain they'd struck.

Tom had headed back to London, but had called to say he'd be down in Kent on the thirtieth and that he'd like to see her. Steeling herself to face up to the situation, Ashleigh had arranged for him to meet her at the flat. He wouldn't make a scene; in fact she wasn't even sure how bothered he'd be. Although she suspected he was the one used to finishing things.

'You look pale.' Concern tempered Tom's voice and he kissed her slowly, with a tenderness that twisted her heart just a little bit more.

'I'm fine, I've just had a few things on my mind that's all.' She pulled away from him, the familiar scent of his aftershave and their close physical proximity momentarily weakening her resolve. 'Can I get you a coffee or something?'

'That would be great, thanks.' Tom headed through to the lounge and she busied herself making drinks in the kitchen, running through what she wanted to say in her head, as she had done so many times over the last couple of days.

'So how is Susie-Anne?' She handed Tom his coffee, drawing him back from whatever it was he'd been thinking about. He'd been staring out at the grey sea, which was lashing the sea wall; a cruel mistress indeed.

'She's okay, living out every second of her hospital stay and her personal life on *Twitter*.' Tom sighed. 'Against mine and Francine's advice of course. And she's very emotional at the moment.'

'I guess that's understandable.' Ashleigh allowed herself a half smile, imagining Tom and Francine discussing the ridiculousness of all that emotion, when there was business to think about. 'And Chloe and her mum, are they doing okay?'

'Yes, Gilly's had a pacemaker fitted and Chloe is really upbeat at the moment, writing new songs. She seems to have turned a corner.'

'I understand some romance might be on the cards.' Ashleigh held her breath; it was Tom's reaction to this that would be most telling. Her brain told her exactly what he'd say, but her heart still held on to the tiniest grain of hope that he might surprise her, make her think that their relationship was worth something to him after all.

'What this?' Tom picked up a copy of the paper, which Ashleigh had left on the coffee table with a couple of other tabloids.

'There's nothing going on with Chloe if that's what you mean. I promised I'd be straight with you and I always have been.'

'I bumped into her when we went down to see Susie-Anne.' Ashleigh took a swig of coffee. 'I met Hugo, he's lovely.'

'I see.' He paused for a minute, wrong footed. 'Yes, he's a nice enough boy, but it won't last.' Tom laughed as Ashleigh pulled a face, not realising he'd said the very words she knew he would. 'It's just that Doctor effect, where a good bedside manner can look like love. I've told her to keep things discreet, but she's writing soppy love songs. If Chloe being photographed with me allows the papers to make false assumptions, and put someone else in the frame, then that's great. It's not like I've hidden my relationship with you, but that won't sell papers and so they prefer to print that Chloe and I are together.'

'So you'd rather let the world think that Chloe's love songs are aimed at you?' Ashleigh furrowed her brow, what difference did it make who the press thought Chloe was writing about? If it ended with Hugo, it ended. It was hardly as though Chloe and Tom would skip up the aisle one day either, not unless someone performed a lobotomy on him and he had a complete change of personality.

'We can control that story, play it out to Chloe's advantage. If the world finds out about her and Hugo, she risks the same exposés made by her previous boyfriend when it finishes. Her new image is not about playing the victim.' He was like a frustrated parent having to explain something to a child for the tenth time over.

'So it's about control?' Ashleigh was every bit the child whose opinion didn't seem to matter to anyone. She wanted to shout that he didn't understand what she was trying to say and to slam a few doors for effect. 'What if Chloe and Hugo really have found love, how are you going to control that?'

'What, after a week of knowing each other?' Sarcasm dripped from Tom's voice, his every reaction, as she'd known it would be. 'Get real Ashleigh. I don't know why we're having this conversation, what is it that you expect me to say?'

'Oh, I don't know, maybe that it's nice to see Chloe so happy, that you hope she's found someone as great as Hugo seems to be.' Holding back the threatened tears she forced herself to look him in the eyes. 'You know those normal kind of responses.'

'I think I should go.' There was a hint of emotion in Tom's voice, but she couldn't be sure if it was anger or something else.

'I think you're right. I know we agreed there were no strings, but this isn't working for me anymore and we always said we'd get out at that point, didn't we?' Her voice was calm, unlike the rest of her.

'I think those were the terms.' Tom picked up his keys. 'In that case, I'll see myself out.'

Ashleigh, whose stomach was in knots and whose throat was aching with the effort of bottling up her feelings, trotted out a well-practised last line, perhaps the business-like delivery would impress Tom. 'I hope this won't affect our professional relationship.'

There was a suggestion of something in Tom's eyes, as though he wanted to respond differently to the question than he did. 'Of course not. I'll have Angus get in touch about some assignments in the New Year.'

Ashleigh didn't respond. The lemony scent of his aftershave lingered in the air as she sank down on the sofa, finally allowing the tears to flow, as bitter as the now cold coffee on the table beside her.

'No Ashleigh today then, darling?' Isobel greeted Tom at the front door of her sister's house with a warm hug, but disappointment that he was on his own was evident on her face.

'Not today. It's just a flying visit I'm afraid.' Tom wasn't about to stand on the doorstep and tell her that Ashleigh had called things off. His aunt's neighbours weren't adverse to a bit of eavesdropping. The middle-aged couple, who lived next door, had come out as soon as he'd arrived and were making a great show of examining a rosebush that wouldn't sprout a leaf for months, probably on the off chance of hearing a bit of juicy gossip. Curtains were no doubt twitching all around them.

He was already in a bad mood and a well-meaning enquiry from a nosey neighbour might well have tipped him over the edge. For days he'd thought of little else but spending the afternoon in bed with Ashleigh, and he'd cursed himself on the drive to his aunt's. It was always going to be difficult for someone like her not to get more involved than he wanted.

'That's okay darling, I'm just thrilled you weren't coming to tell me that the two of you had split up.' She fixed him with the kind of steely glare that she'd once reserved for getting him to do his homework. 'You know that sort of news could literally kill me don't you?'

'Where's Auntie Maureen anyway?' Tom changed the subject; he wasn't keen to lie to his mum, so the less said the better.

'They've gone for a look around the sales.' Isobel grimaced. 'So Bertie and I have taken the opportunity to have a cuddle on the sofa. We're not normally allowed!'

'Why don't you just go home then?' How his mum and her sister had emerged from the same gene pool was a mystery to Tom. 'Do you think I'm allowed in?'

'Yes of course darling, but probably best to take your shoes off, just in case she gets home before you go.'

'Got to love Auntie Maureen, she'll have us all shuffling around like psychotic inmates who can't be trusted with their own shoelaces.' Tom followed his mother into the house, which ironically had quite a few similarities with a padded cell. There were thick, white shag pile carpets, which he'd assumed had gone out in the Seventies, and white walls. Only the glass chandeliers and coffee tables, with ornate marble columns supporting their weight, offered any contrast in the room. Homely it wasn't.

'So, how was the rest of your Christmas? Romantic I hope!' Isobel's eyes lit up. It wasn't going to be easy for him to get out of talking about Ashleigh.

'It was great, the best one for years.' It was true. Of course it didn't mean anything, but they'd had a good time; even he couldn't deny that.

'I'm so glad, darling, you'd be an absolute fool to let Ashleigh go.' Patting the dog's head she smiled. 'Bertie sensed it straight away and dogs are an excellent judge of character. Call it a mother's intuition, but I really think she could be the one.'

'We'll see.' He couldn't bring himself to shatter her illusions, it could wait until the New Year and maybe there'd be another candidate for his mother's romantic fantasies by then. After all, just because a dog and an elderly woman thought so, it didn't mean he'd really lost something important, did it?

Twenty minutes after Tom left there was a knock at the door. Maybe he was back, coming to tell her he'd got it all wrong. Ashleigh's heart thudded; let it be him. But it wasn't. Instead Carol was framed in the doorway, swathed in crushed purple velvet and looking very much like she'd rummaged through Dumbledore's closet.

'Mum.' She couldn't inject any enthusiasm into the word. 'What are you doing here?' She'd have to let her mother in, otherwise she'd draw even more attention to herself. Carol began waving the object she was holding in the air, the feathers, shells and weird tassely bits jerking about as she did so.

'I've brought you a dream catcher!' Her mother continued to make it dance in the air and Ashleigh automatically folded her arms across her chest. A dream catcher? Right. Useful.

'Are you stopping?' She did her best not to make it sound like an invitation.

'I can't really, darling, I'm going to my path to tranquillity classes.' Carol breezed past, despite saying she couldn't stop. It was almost certainly best not to ask what the 'path to tranquillity' classes were.

'What are you doing?' Ashleigh asked the question even though it quickly became obvious, as her mother began throwing open every window in the flat. A more appropriate question might have been to ask why.

'There's a lot of negative energy.' Carol gave her a look, which suggested that Ashleigh had brought it on herself. 'And it smells worse than my five bean pot roast in here.' When Ashleigh started to protest, her mother cut her off. 'Oh, I know you all think I'm daft and that I don't know what you say about my cooking. Yes I know the five bean roast stinks when I'm cooking it and that it gives you gas like a warthog, but it's very good for the soul… and the bowel come to that.'

'Mum, please, do you have to make everything about bodily functions?' Ashleigh was exhausted and, despite her protestations, too weak to really fight her mother on anything. She could only hope to God that Carol didn't pick up on that, or she'd be dragged along the path to tranquillity too. There was no way she was going to confide in her mother about finishing with Tom either. The last thing she wanted was to find herself press-ganged into a date with Nigel, the sweaty bell-ringer who she'd caught staring at her several times during her mother's party, before you could say campanologist.

'Oh relax, will you darling, you need to get out more – physically and mentally – you spend far too much time in your own head. You really should mediate with me, such a shame I don't have time before I go.' Carol wavered for a moment.

'Yes it's a shame, but you really have got to go.' Ashleigh stopped short of actually shoving her mum through the door, but it came pretty close.

'Okay, darling, well another time, definitely.' The promise was akin to a threat. 'And don't forget this.' Thrusting the dream catcher into Ashleigh's hand, Carol swept out of the flat, almost running down the path to tranquillity by now.

'What the hell am I supposed to do with this?' Ashleigh spoke out loud in the empty flat, setting down the unwanted gift on the coffee table. One by one she shut the windows that her mother had just opened. Dreams only set you up for disappointment and, right now, the only thing she was in danger of catching was a cold.

Chapter Twenty-Nine

Given that she'd only sent muted responses to his texts inviting her over to see him, and sidestepped his questions about how things were going with Tom, Ashleigh wasn't completely shocked when Stevie turned up on her doorstep, late in the afternoon of the thirty-first. Although she wished he hadn't; it wasn't fair on Zac to lose out just because she was a walking disaster when it came to love.

Resolving not to be pathetic and cry, Ashleigh recounted the events of Boxing Day, her decision to finish with Tom and the resulting conversation the day before. Predictably, after some tea and sympathy from Stevie, her resolve was soon broken. It was a mixture of the break up and it being New Year's Eve again, the anniversary of her dad's tragic accident, that did it, tears blurring the lines between the two things.

'Right, there's only one thing for it.' Stevie stood up and pulled Ashleigh to her feet. 'It's New Year's Eve tonight and we're going out to get very, very drunk.'

'Oh no, Stevie, please, I really don't want to.' She did her best to sit down again, but there was no way he was letting go. 'You should be with Zac anyway, not keeping a miserable idiot like me company.'

'Honey, no arguments, not tonight. Forget about Tom and let's have a drink to your dad's memory instead. Zac's on his way over anyway and we're taking you out.' He propelled her towards the bedroom. 'Get changed and I'll pour us both a huge drink.'

By the time Zac arrived, they were well on the way to getting plastered. Ashleigh had squeezed into a midnight blue body-contour dress that Stevie had bought her the Christmas before. Having miraculously lost half a stone since Boxing Day, the dress finally clung to her in all the right places.

'Heartbreak obviously suits you, babe.' Zac hadn't quite relinquished the Casanova act and he pinched her bum enthusiastically. 'Come on then, let's get this party started.'

Aubrey's wine bar was heaving with people, it was certainly too closely packed to catch someone's eye across a crowded room and, as a result, not many people realised that Zac Starr was among their number. Ashleigh wasn't in the mood for getting caught up with fans wanting an autograph. She just wanted to get drunk and wipe the past few months out of her mind so that she could forget all about Tom, at least until she sobered up.

At some point, someone, it must have been either Zac or Stevie she supposed, decided it would be a good idea to move on to tequila. The boys hit the dance floor not long afterwards, but couldn't persuade Ashleigh to join them – the tequila holding far more appeal by that stage. After the fourth shot, she was becoming more numb than emotional, when he suddenly appeared, a face from the past.

'Wow, Ash, baby. You are looking hot!' Liam hadn't changed

a bit. He was still as slimy as ever and the way he was looking at her made her flesh crawl. Had she really been in a relationship with him for all that time and not noticed what a vile human being he was? 'And you've lost weight.'

'Thanks.' She wished she could be one of those people who could casually tell someone else to 'piss off', but she wasn't. Even though she gave Liam no encouragement whatsoever, he wedged himself tightly into the seat beside her. She was too drunk to care that almost the entire side of his body was pressed against hers, so she didn't bother moving – mistake number one. 'No Millie tonight then?' His librarian lover was nowhere to be seen.

'We split up at the beginning of the month.' Liam leered at her, as if expecting her to be overjoyed.

'What was up? Didn't you want to fork out for a Christmas present!' Ashleigh swayed forward, laughing a bit over enthusiastically at her own joke, which gave Liam an excuse to put his arm around her, drawing her back into her seat.

'Don't be like that babe, you know how generous I can be.' He winked at her and she shuddered slightly at a memory she'd rather not have had. He'd always gone on about how hard he worked to make sure she had two orgasms. His workmanlike approach to the task was somewhat off putting, however. More often than not she'd faked at least one of them, just to make sure the determined poking and prodding had stopped. Yet with Tom it had been so different. But she wouldn't think about it, couldn't let herself weaken. It was far better to end it now.

'So, what was the problem then?' Ashleigh wasn't even interested, but somewhere in the foggy, cotton wool wasteland of her brain, it seemed a good idea to keep him talking;

at least that way he wouldn't be able to stick his tongue down her throat.

'She kept on about rings constantly. It was all she wanted for Christmas, some big engagement scene in front of all of her family.' It was Liam's turn to shudder. 'You know me babe, commitment, mortgages and all that stuff, it's just not for a free spirit like me.' He flicked his hair, probably thinking it made him look cool. But, having grown it to shoulder length and added heavy blond streaks since his split with Ashleigh, he was uncannily like Miss Piggy.

'Hi Ya!' She mimed the Muppet's famous karate move and got a blank look in return. She was definitely drunk. 'Sorry, not sure what came over me there. Was Millie, very upset?' Maybe he'd left another poor girl to struggle with a mortgage alone.

'Yeah, judging by the twenty texts a day I received for the first couple of weeks, I'd say so.' Liam gave her a self-satisfied smile. 'You know what it's like to be on the end of that kind of heartbreak yourself though, don't you babe?' There wasn't a hint of irony in his words and Ashleigh struggled not to laugh, to tell him he'd been a minor bump in the road. It wasn't until Tom that she hit the big pothole and understood what her break up with Liam should have felt like, if she'd ever really loved him.

'So back with your mum are you?' Ashleigh smiled. Martha, Liam's mum, had been one of the nicest things about him. She was a warm homely kind of woman, who fussed around after Liam, taking great care of the girls who passed through his life too, and still referred to him as her little prince.

'Yeah, for now at least.' There was a suggestion that, if she played her cards right, she might get a new roommate.

'Right, so really living that free spirit life then...' Laughing again, she nearly choked as she took another huge slug of tequila. Zac had persuaded the barman to sell him a couple of bottles, so that he didn't have to queue with the masses for drinks. He and Stevie were still dancing, and looked vaguely like they were practising their synchronised swimming moves on dry land, so it was down to Ashleigh to keep necking tequila for the team.

'What about you babe, how's your love life?' Liam ignored her snide comment, either too thick or too drunk himself to notice. 'Any action, or are you still missing these hips?' He swivelled his pelvis in what he probably assumed was an alluring manner and a wave of pure disgust swept over her.

'Oh my God, don't please!' She took another swig of tequila to push the nausea back down her throat. How could she have slept with someone like Liam? She'd wanted to live with this man, really? Maybe one day she'd bump into Tom at work and have the same reaction, but she very much doubted it. 'I've just finished with someone actually, but I don't want to talk about it.' Liam was absolutely the last person on earth she would choose as a confidante.

'Oh shame, dumped again.' He seemed to think it was fate, a golden opportunity to get Ashleigh into bed and he gave her thigh a painful squeeze. 'You know your problem, don't you babe?'

'No, I don't actually.' Ashleigh wasn't about to correct his assumption that she, as he so eloquently put it, had been dumped. 'But I'm sure you're about to tell me.'

'You're damaged goods.' The bluntness of his response shouldn't have shocked her, but it did.

'What you mean because I'm still so heartbroken over you?'

She gave a brittle little laugh. If only he knew.

'No, well, at least not at first, I don't suppose it helped though.' Liam patted her leg almost as though he might be sorry for what he'd put her through. 'You've always been like it, at least as long as I've known you. I reckon it's to do with your mum and dad and everything, you're just so needy.'

'Needy?' She struggled not to shout the words and tears began prickling at the mention of her dad tonight of all nights, Liam had clearly forgotten the significance of New Year's Eve.

'Yeah, you've got no self-esteem babe. You need constant reassurance that you're doing your job well, that you look okay, that the person you're with really loves you, blah, blah, blah.' He blew out his cheeks with a long breath, like a marathon runner at the end of a race. 'Frankly babe, it's exhausting.'

'Fancy a tequila?' Ashleigh, who'd expected to value Liam's opinion about relationships as much as a sumo wrestler's advice on healthy eating, suddenly really needed another drink. She didn't want to admit that he might be right. Sloshing more tequila into two of the empty glasses on the table, she took another huge slug and then another. After that, her recollection of the evening all went a bit hazy...

'Oh Christ. My head.' Something like sawdust was lining her tongue and her skull was on too tight. Trying to turn over in bed she hit something solid – the wall. Except she wasn't in bed, but seemingly in some impossible yoga move with her legs almost behind her head, curled into one of the armchairs in the front room. There was a lumpy outline on the sofa next to her. Something lumpy and snoring. 'Liam?' She leant over the sofa and shook him by the shoulder.

'Morning gorgeous.' He reached out a hand, which, like a

homing pigeon, made instant contact with one of her breasts.

'Er… morning.' An involuntary groan escaped her. Had she really been that drunk? She had no memory of getting back to the flat and certainly no memory of inviting Liam back there. Her hand shot downwards, she still had her Spanx on. They'd been an essential pre-requisite to wearing a tight dress the night before. Thank heavens for small mercies and big knickers. 'We didn't… you know?' She shuddered again, horrified at the mere possibility, despite the reassurance she still had her pants, a fresh wave of nausea sweeping upwards.

'Sadly not babe, just a bit too much tequila came between us.' He leant towards her, obviously ready to give her another one of his tongue-twisting kisses, his morning breath as repellent as the rest of him. 'Shall we have a go now?'

'Look, I'm sorry. I should never have invited you back or let you think there was a chance I was interested in some kind of repeat performance.' Ashleigh slumped back into the armchair, her arm wrapped across her breasts, in a too-little-too-late attempt at modesty.

'Hey, no hard feelings babe.' Liam whipped back the blanket covering him, revealing his naked body and a reasonably impressive hard-on. 'Or maybe just the one.' He certainly hadn't lost his touch for sexual innuendo.

Getting up, he pulled on his discarded jeans and shirt. There was no sign of his pants. Whether he'd had any in the first place wasn't a question Ashleigh could answer and she wasn't about to ask. 'It was great catching up babe. I'll see you around.' Dodging his attempt to kiss her on the mouth, their cheekbones banged awkwardly and he ended up kissing her on the ear. Sitting on the recently vacated sofa, she put her head in her hands. This must be it – her all time low.

'You okay, honey?' Stevie poked his head around the living room door.

'Yeah, great.' She could barely lift her head to look him in the eye and, if he laughed, she swore to God she'd kill him.

'I think your boyfriend left these behind.' Zac, looking unnervingly chirpy, appeared at Stevie's shoulder twirling a pair of red thong underpants around his index finger. 'They were on the lampshade of the hall light'

'That's it. Can someone just kill me?' Ashleigh groaned. Like two naughty schoolboys, their lips pressed tightly together in an attempt not to laugh. 'No offers? Call yourselves my friends?'

At that moment, Liam's thong flew through the air and landed in her lap. 'You could always hang yourself with lover boy's knickers elastic.' Zac had given way to laughter now and she shot him a look before a familiar sensation swelled in her stomach.

'Oh God, I think I'm going to be sick…' A wave of nausea took hold of her body. Suddenly Zac wasn't laughing and nothing in her line of fire had escaped.

After a change of clothes and hot showers all round, Ashleigh finally stopped wishing for death. Picking at the corner of the piece of dry toast, which Stevie had insisted on making for her, she groaned again.

'I'm sorry guys, it's just Liam said some stuff to me last night and I was already upset about Tom and Dad, so I think somewhere in my subconscious I decided to try and drown myself in a bottle of tequila.'

'We've all been there honey.' Stevie kissed the top of her head and she grimaced, even her scalp was tender, bruised by the hangover from hell. What on earth had she put her body through? 'We can forgive it all, just thank God you didn't sleep with that dickhead Liam!'

'We saved you by taking the bed I think.' Zac grinned, acting like a noble gentleman, even though he'd made it clear that he didn't *do* sleeping on sofas or floors. 'What did that prat have to say to you that made you so upset anyway?'

'He said I was needy, that I had to be reassured and told I was loved all the time.' She glanced at Zac, her eyes so dry and sore that they ached with the effort. 'The worst thing is I think he was right. All this time I've been thinking it was Liam's fault we split or that there was something wrong with the way Tom acts and it was probably just my issue all along. I don't think there's a man out there who could put up with me.'

'Bullshit!' Zac and Stevie spoke in unison and exchanged a smile.

'As my old nan used to say, there's a lid for every pot and someone out there will be perfect for you, you just have to keep on keeping on.' Zac moved beside her and put an arm around her shoulders. 'Look at me, it took me seven fiancées before I got Stevie and I've never been happier in my life.'

'Maybe I should go for a woman then?' Ashleigh managed a smile. 'Unless you guys fancy a threesome, without the sex of course!'

A member of the local press struck gold later in the day, when he took photos of Zac, Ashleigh and Stevie on the beach at Sandgate. The accompanying article speculated who Zac's mystery girlfriend might be and whether the girl he was seeing in the New Year with was likely to be his eighth fiancée. If only that journalist had realised how close he was to a much bigger scoop, and had not cut Stevie out of the photo, his career might have been made for life.

Despite the story barely even being newsworthy, it shared the headlines on the showbiz page alongside an 'exclusive' chat with Susie-Anne Summers, which the journalist suggested lifted the lid on her on-going close relationship with Tom Rushworth. The report claimed that Susie-Anne was devastated not to be able to accompany Tom in his moment of need, keeping a vigil at the bedside of his elderly mother at the Coast and District Hospital in Kent – where she'd been taken in a life threatening condition after slipping on some ice in the early hours of New Year's Day.

Chapter Thirty

'Is there anyone you want me to call for you?' The nurse set the tea down next to Tom in the relatives' room. Why was it that tea was seen as a cure all, regardless of the crisis you found yourself facing? Tea wouldn't make things any easier for him to bear and it certainly wouldn't help his mum.

'No, it's okay thanks.' He wished, not for the first time, that he had a brother or sister. Someone else in the world he could share moments like this with, someone who would understand how he was feeling.

'Okay, if you're sure?' The nurse hesitated. 'I'm afraid I can't give you any more definite information about your mother's condition at the moment. When the doctors have finished assessing her, we'll come to see you and explain the options more fully then.' With that she was gone, escaping from the oppressive atmosphere in the room. Tom knew he would have been just as eager, given half the chance.

She'd said that they'd explain the options. It didn't sound like a particularly positive word in that context. Options usually meant choosing the thing you most wanted to do and that would have been getting his mum home safely as soon as possible. The dread creeping over him suggested that particular option was no longer open. He was on his own and never more so.

'Are you sure this is the right thing to do, honey?' Stevie, who'd insisted on driving Ashleigh to the hospital, had spent the entire journey trying to talk her out of it, as she'd known he would. Pulling into the hospital car park, he switched off the engine and turned to look at her.

'He might not be delighted to see me and I'm not daft enough to think this will be some romantic bedside scene.' She laughed as Stevie wrinkled his nose and gave her a pitying look. 'It's okay, I know you think I'm crazy. I just wouldn't feel right unless I at least tried to find out if there's anything I can do. Since Tom has clearly switched off his phone, there's not much else I can do other than just show up, is there?'

'You could have phoned Francine and asked her to pass on a message.' Stevie winced as she dug him in the ribs.

'Yes or I could have done my Paul McKenna impersonation and used the power of my mind to send Tom a telepathic message.' Ashleigh mimed the action, screwing up her face in mock concentration. 'It would have more chance of getting there than any message that I passed via Francine.'

'Fair point. Am I at least allowed to wait for you?' Stevie grinned at the group of nurses, who'd stopped to admire Zac's shiny new Porsche and were now checking out the driver with undisguised excitement.

'If you wait here you'll have been mobbed by the time I get back.' Ashleigh leant over and gave him a quick peck on the cheek. 'I think it might be better all round if you head back to mine to pick up Zac and spend a bit of quality time with your boyfriend.'

'But you'll call if you need us, won't you honey?' Stevie pushed a loose strand of hair behind her ear and gave her the earnest look he always did when he wanted her to promise him something.

'I will.' She smiled, if only all of the relationships in her life were as perfect as the one she had with Stevie. 'But I won't need you. You and Zac are like my surrogate parents. You've made sure I've got enough money for a cab to the station and my train fare back home if Tom tells me to sod off and I promise that I won't talk to strangers!'

'Okay, okay!' Stevie held his hands up, finally accepting defeat. 'Good luck, honey, and I really hope the papers are wrong about how poorly Isobel is.'

Inside the sterile environment of the hospital, Ashleigh's bravado began to fade, growing weaker and weaker with every step she took towards the ITU department. The interview with Susie-Anne had claimed Isobel was in intensive care, but since Ashleigh highly doubted Tom's ex really knew any more than she'd heard from second hand gossip, it was hardly gospel. Angus had confirmed that Isobel was in hospital, when Zac had rung him, but even he hadn't been able to reach Tom since he'd first got the news – so she didn't really know what she was going in to. Would they let her in, would Isobel even turn out to be there and, if she was, what reception was she likely to get from Tom?

Forcing herself to walk through the double doors that led to the nurses' station in the ITU, Ashleigh spotted Tom before he saw her. He was sitting at the end of a row of plastic chairs, his head in his hands. Normally immaculate, his clothes gave the distinct impression of having been slept in and there was a layer of dark stubble on his cheeks.

'Tom.' Crouching down beside him, she instinctively put a hand over his, as he lifted his head to look at her.

'Oh God, Ash, she's really bad…' There were no recriminations, no questions about why she was there. The navy blue eyes were red-rimmed and there was total despair in his voice. 'I've never felt so out of control, so helpless.'

'You're here and that's all you can do, all she would want you to do.' Ashleigh hoped she wasn't saying the wrong things. As if there was anything she could say that would make the slightest bit of difference to how Tom was feeling.

'And you're here too. It's crazy. She's been asking where you were and I didn't have the heart to tell her.' Tom looked utterly distraught. 'I was going to go down and see her on New Year's Day, let her know that we'd decided we're better off as friends.' He grimaced. 'Not strictly true I know, but she liked you and she'd want to think we could at least have that. I didn't want to tell her over the phone and I couldn't bring myself to tell her when we first split up.' Tom's voice broke on the last words and he took a breath to regain his composure. 'Only she insisted on coming home from Auntie Maureen's on the morning of the thirty-first. It would have been Robert's eightieth birthday apparently. She spent New Year's Eve watching TV and then, just before midnight, for some bizarre reason, she decided to take Bertie for a walk down to the sea front. She'd barely got to the end of the road when she slipped on black ice. The people who eventually found her said Bertie was sitting next to her, licking her and desperately trying to keep her warm, barking like crazy to try and get someone's attention, but there were parties nearby in full swing and no one heard him, or if they did, they didn't bother to go and see what the fuss was. By the time someone eventually found her, she was so cold they thought she was already dead.'

'Oh my God.' It was horrifying. At the same time as Ashleigh had been fighting off Liam's advances and downing tequila like her life depended upon it, Isobel had been lying on an icy pavement and Tom was getting the kind of phone call that nightmares are made of. 'How is she now?'

'Barely hanging on, but it's only a matter of time.' Tom's jaw was set in a grim line. 'I've earned more money over the years than I could ever spend, but none of it means anything now. It's all pointless, it won't help Mum, nothing can.'

'Isn't there any chance?' It felt surreal. A little over a week earlier Tom's mum had been defiant of the leukaemia, like she might fight on for years.

'She's conscious, speaking with difficulty, but I can see her fading. She broke her hip in the fall and developed pneumonia, either from the shock of the fall or the cold. She's too poorly to operate on and so it's just a waiting game.'

'I'm so sorry.' She didn't want to say the words, they were bland and pointless, but she said them anyway. 'Is there anything I can do to help out? Get you a change of clothes, anything?'

'She'd like to see you. I know...' Tom swallowed hard. 'I know it's a big ask, but can you do me a favour please, don't mention anything about us splitting up?'

'Of course not.' She longed to stroke Tom's face, offer him some comfort. Hard as she'd tried to fight it, she'd fallen in love with him during the vulnerable moments, where he'd let down his guard and revealed the chinks in the armour that both protected and restricted him. Never had he seemed more vulnerable than at that moment.

Willing herself to stay strong for him, Ashleigh followed Tom into his mother's hospital room. Isobel's skin was barely distinguishable against the crisp whiteness of the sheets. There were wires connecting her to a monitor, an oxygen tube in her nose and a morphine driver to relieve the pain.

'Got myself into a bit of a state.' Isobel's voice was a hoarse whisper and as she tried to smile she managed to dislodge the oxygen tube, causing one of the machines to start bleeping erratically, as her heart rate dropped, until one of the nurses pushed it back into place.

'Now don't be letting her talk too long.' The chubby Irish nurse smiled at them; no doubt as aware as they were that their last chance of speaking to Isobel was slipping away, like grains of sand in an egg timer. But, still, she needed to do her job.

'Give us a minute for some girl talk, Thomas.' Isobel used the long version of his name, as though she meant business. 'Get yourself a coffee, you could use it I'm sure.' Isobel closed her eyes until Tom left the room, opening them again seemed to take the kind of incredible effort required to scale a mountain.

'I'm glad you're here. You love him don't you?' Every word was a battle and Ashleigh didn't want her to struggle on, so she just nodded. 'And he loves you, but you realise he might never show it? Will it be enough for you?'

'It's okay.' Ashleigh fought to find the right words. While she could admit to loving Tom with a clear conscience, she wasn't sure if she could lie to a dying woman and give her false hope. 'As long as Tom feels it, even if he can't say it or show it, it will be enough for me.' It was true after all. The moment she'd seen him in the hospital, she couldn't pretend that there'd ever been anyone else who'd meant as much to her as Tom did. If he wanted her, then she'd be there. So it might not be perfect, not like the movies or books said it should be, but she wanted to be with him and if pretending it wasn't love was what it took, then she could do that. She was sure she could.

'Thank you. I can go now and be happy.' Isobel's body visibly relaxed, the pinched look on her face less obvious.

'Don't talk like that...' Ashleigh wasn't sure what else to say; she was dying, what good were words?

'Robert's waited long enough, we both have.' Her voice drifted off and she closed her eyes. For a moment she was so still, her breathing so shallow that Ashleigh was sure she had gone. Realising that the heart monitor was still beeping with clinical regularity, Ashleigh stopped holding her own breath. Please God, don't let Tom be long, he should be here for this.

Perhaps the Paul McKenna style telepathy was working after all. The door to Isobel's room swung open and Tom looked across at Ashleigh, in a way he never had before, as if some boundary between them had at last been crossed.

'Tom...' Isobel opened her eyes again for the briefest of moments, as he took the seat beside her and placed a hand over hers, '...I love you so much, you've been my greatest achievement, my greatest joy.' Every word was punctuated by a struggle to breathe. So wanting to get the words out, even though they were literally killing her.

'I love you more.' The devastation in Tom's voice would

have touched the hardest of hearts.

'But I love you most.' It was fitting, Isobel having the last word and these her very last of all.

Sadly, as Ashleigh had already acknowledged, real life is often completely divorced from that depicted in the movies. Death, it seemed, was no different. It would have been beautiful, in its own way, if Isobel had slipped away in Tom's arms following that last declaration of love, but tragically and painfully it was far more ugly and brutal than that.

Despite the protestations that she couldn't wait to be with Robert, something in Isobel just wouldn't allow her to let go. The doctors said she had the heart of someone half her age, despite the leukaemia and its gruelling treatment. All those long walks on the beach with Bertie and his predecessors had clearly kept her fit. Ironic, then, that the same routine should eventually hasten her death.

The young Irish nurse had instructed Tom on how to administer the morphine and had told him not to overdo it. There wasn't quite a 'wink, wink' or a 'nudge, nudge' with the instruction, but the implication that the regular administration of morphine might speed up the inevitable and offer the ultimate form of pain relief, was apparent none the less.

Twelve interminable hours passed and still Isobel held on. When the time came to change shifts and the pretty, Irish nurse headed home, a humourless staff nurse began trying to move Isobel's position in the bed. Despite being in a coma, she whimpered in pain.

'What the hell are you doing that for?' Tom's face was red, a muscle pulsing in his cheek.

'If we don't move her she'll get bed sores.' The nurse spoke to him as though he were a child.

'For Christ's sake, she'll be dead by tomorrow, so what difference will bed sores make?' Tom moved between his mother and the nurse.

'Mr Rushworth, please, I'm just trying to do my job.' She looked like someone who knew from bitter experience when to back away from irate patients or relatives. Her austere bedside manner no doubt resulted in more than an average number of altercations over the years.

'We know and we're sorry.' Ashleigh suspected she was the sort of nurse who might respond best to a bit of flattery. 'We're so very grateful to you all and we know how much you've done for Isobel. But she's dying, and she's so peaceful when she's not being moved, couldn't you just leave her please? ' She hesitated, as the nurse seemed to consider her suggestion. 'I know that a nurse like you, someone with your wealth of experience, must have made these kinds of decisions before.' She was laying it on thick, desperate for Isobel and Tom not to suffer any more than they had to.

'Well it's not protocol, but, as you say, as a senior nurse I can use my discretion.' She tapped the side of her nose, as though she'd just given away a state secret or let Ashleigh in to some insider trading. 'I'll leave you all in peace then.'

As the nurse left, Tom turned to Ashleigh. 'Thank you. I know I handled it badly, but I just couldn't stand it. I don't know how I would have got through all this without you.' He was beyond despair and it was obvious he'd barely slept since his mother's accident. 'I might even have ended up being carted off by security for slapping her if you hadn't stepped in.'

'It's a normal reaction. If someone I loved was hurting I'd go in all guns blazing too.' Ashleigh took Tom's out-stretched hand; she'd done just that very thing, but protestations of love were the last thing he needed to hear.

Those last few hours with Isobel felt like the longest of Ashleigh's life. There were no other visitors. Tom told her that Maureen had been in when Isobel was first admitted, but couldn't bear to see her sister like that and he'd insisted that his mother wouldn't want her friends or other relatives to see her in her state either. Ashleigh had asked Tom if he wanted to be alone with his mother, but he'd told her that he wanted her to stay. Needed her to. The three of them held hands as the hours dragged on.

Isobel's lungs had filled with fluid and continued to do so, despite the medical staff's attempt to drain them. A sickly sweet smell, like rotting petals, filled the air.

The morphine driver working overtime, Isobel finally took her last breath as the sun rose. The monitors droned and nursing staff took over, whilst Ashleigh and Tom waited outside the room so that the tubes could be removed and the body made ready for its final journey.

'Thank you for being here. You'll never know how much you've helped and how much it means to me.' Tom pulled her into his arms, the strength of his embrace taking her breath away.

'I wanted to be here for you, if you needed me.' Her words were muffled against his chest; he was still holding her as though he couldn't let go.

'I did need you, I still do.' It was as close as Tom had ever come to declaring his feelings and his usual control was put to one side. 'Do you think you could bear to come back in with me… to say goodbye?' He drew back slightly to look at her. It would be difficult, but she sensed he couldn't do it without her.

'I'm here, as long as you need me.' Ashleigh's words echoed her promise to his mother from hours before. It was hard to believe that she was gone, a scary reminder of how fragile everyone, and life itself, really were.

Isobel looked serene by the time they re-entered the room. Her eyes were closed and crisp white sheets, folded neatly across her chest, with her arms by her side, made it appear for the entire world like she was sleeping. Only her chest was still and her skin was already colder as Tom took her hand in his. Silent tears slid down his face. He'd lost the only woman in the world he had ever loved and it was almost too much to bear.

Ashleigh sat next to him, her arm around his shoulders offering some comfort as the tears turned to sobs. They didn't speak and there were no final words he wanted to say to his mother. He'd said all he needed to before the light in her eyes had gone out and now he'd never get another chance. They just sat for a long time until his eyes were raw from the outpouring of sorrow that had shocked him with its intensity. He knew there would be fresh waves of grief washing over him as relentlessly as the tides at Sandgate, for months to come and he wasn't sure if he could stand it.

Chapter Thirty-One

Tom couldn't face going back to his mother's house that first day. He'd eventually have to, start making decisions; not least about Bertie, who was currently staying with the neighbours and to whom his Auntie Maureen had reluctantly offered a home. Sending Bertie there would be like an elderly childless-by-choice relative taking on an orphaned child. His days of freedom, sofa surfing and gambling merrily along the beach would be over, likely replaced by an enclosure in the garden, an electric anti-barking collar and perhaps the odd walk around the block if he were lucky.

They spent that first night in the flat. Hollowness filled the space where his heart used to be. It was as if he'd been given a numbing injection, just enough to take the edge off and allow him to keep on breathing. Insisting that he needed to eat something, Ashleigh had prepared her speciality of toasted cheese sandwiches and they'd eventually fallen asleep side-by-side on the sofa beside the fire.

The next morning the numbness started ebbing away. It was a relief at first, to feel something, but there was a lump in his throat that no amount of coffee could shift and a growing realisation that this was the first day of many without his mum in his life. They'd both been fairly independent, not living in one another's pockets, but each had always known that the other was there.

He'd been glad of the powerful jets of water in the shower, washing away the fresh tears that hit, unexpectedly, just because Ashleigh used the same brand of shampoo that his mother always had. They had a lifetime of memories together and, if something as mundane as a brand of shampoo was going to set him off, Tom was terrified he'd never stop crying.

'Do you want me to come with you?' Ashleigh, who had woken early and managed to extricate herself from Tom's tangle of arms and legs on the sofa, was already washed and changed and pouring him another cup of coffee.

'Would you mind?' His eyes, red-rimmed as they were, were still one of the best things about him. He had a way of looking at her like she was the only person in the world he wanted to look at. It was what made her believe they could make it; hopeless romantic that she was. Who needed words of love when a look said so much more? She'd promised Isobel that it would be enough to feel it and not hear it and she wasn't about to break that promise. 'You must have a million other things to do. I'm probably stopping you working as well.'

'I have an understanding boss.' They exchanged a brief smile. That first meeting in Tom's office, finding out he effectively had the power to determine her career, felt like a lifetime ago.

The journey from her flat to Isobel's house took less than ten minutes. On the way Tom pointed out landmarks that triggered more memories of his mum and told Ashleigh their stories. There was the cafe on the seafront where she took him every Friday after school, come rain or shine. Isobel always had a pot of Earl Grey tea and Tom an ice-cream sundae. There were the public baths where she'd taught him to swim and the park where they'd fed the ducks, walked Bertie's predecessors and she'd taught him how to ride a bike. It seemed all his happy childhood memories were of the two of them and they were everywhere he looked.

Going into Isobel's house felt warm and welcoming, like she was there in spirit. In truth, the heating was on a timer and the winter's chill had been banished with clockwork regularity. Her newspaper, folded on the arm of the chair with the reading glasses still on top, added to the feeling that she was still present. Tom turned away to wipe his eyes and Ashleigh longed to hold him; it was going to be a difficult day.

Seeing the man she adored so devastated was much harder than she would ever have believed. Swallowing her own emotions like boulders in her throat, she took control – deciding that too much too soon would be more than he could stand. The bare essentials had to be done and the rest could wait for another time. This wasn't a day for making big decisions about the house, for writing to let people know or for clearing the decks and taking bags of possessions to the charity shop. There was time enough for all of that later. What they had to do was to choose an outfit for Isobel, which Tom could take to the appointment at the undertaker's, to turn off the heating and water and, most importantly of all, to make a decision about Bertie's future. Thankfully, Tom's Aunt was picking up the death certificate from the hospital and going to register the death. She would also meet Tom at the undertaker's and had then offered to set about contacting everyone who needed to know.

They decided against anything formal for Isobel to be buried in. Tom said he thought she would want to spend eternity in something comfortable. They chose some black trousers and an apricot coloured cashmere jumper, as Tom couldn't bear the thought of her being cold. He'd also decided to give the undertaker Isobel's locket, which had been taken off at the hospital. There was a picture of Tom on one side and Robert on the other and she had worn it close to her heart every single day.

The couple who lived next door to Isobel – Graham, an architect, and his wife Karen, a dentist – had willingly taken Bertie in. They'd done so not only to help out, but with the vested interest, Karen explained, of seeing how the children were with a dog in the house, having nagged their parents to get a puppy since the Christmas before.

'Wow, it's the first time he's reacted to anyone.' Karen raised her eyebrows in astonishment as Bertie greeted Ashleigh like a long lost friend, licking her hand and recognising her as the supplier of bacon from Christmas Day. 'He's been pining terribly, the kids tried to get him to play but he just sat in his basket looking sad.'

'We're so very sorry about your mum. Isobel was such a lovely neighbour to have, she doted on the kids you know, such a shame she never got to have grandchildren of her own.' Graham shook Tom's hand and Ashleigh flinched. His well-meaning words would have hurt Tom, just as they had unwittingly tightened the lump in her throat. 'We would offer to keep Bertie for you, but he just seems so unhappy here.' Graham coughed awkwardly. He didn't give the impression he was keen on the idea of getting a dog and the prospect of having a clinically depressed Labrador moping around the house clearly wasn't something he relished.

'Don't worry, thanks anyway, but I'm going to take him home.' Tom was already clipping on Bertie's lead.

'Really?' It was the second time that Karen had expressed surprise. 'I wouldn't have thought your lifestyle lent itself to all that.' She smiled. 'I know you probably didn't have me pegged as a *Glitz* reader, but I always flick through copies of the magazines that my receptionist buys for the waiting room at the surgery. She says that reading about celebrities helps to keep the patients' minds off their impending root canal treatments!' She laughed, as if the thought of root canal surgery gave her genuine pleasure. 'So I know all about your lifestyle! Although, now that you've got a partner, there'll be someone to share the load and help look after Bertie.' Karen smiled again.

'Ashleigh and I don't live together, so it will just be Bertie and me but I'm sure we'll manage.' Tom's bald statement winded Ashleigh. Yes, it was true, they didn't live together but the bit about 'it will just be Bertie and me' was so final.

'It was lovely meeting you and thanks again for having Bertie.' Ashleigh's voice cracked on the words, but she held herself together just enough to kiss Karen on the cheek. Tom was already halfway to the front door with a reluctant Bertie, who appeared not to want to go anywhere at all unless Ashleigh was with him.

In the days that followed, Ashleigh listened to her heart and not her head, convincing herself that the throwaway remark about it being just Tom and Bertie meant nothing. In any case, the two of them had taken up permanent residence in her flat, at least until after the funeral, when she guessed they'd both be headed back to London. They hadn't talked about it or about any kind of future, but they were together all of the time.

As Ashleigh didn't have a garden at the flat, they took several long walks each day with Bertie. They talked about anything and everything and sometimes nothing at all. The only time they spent apart was when Tom met Isobel's sister to make the funeral arrangements and Ashleigh went alone to stock up on supplies for Bertie, who seemed to eat more than the two of them put together. It was on these occasions that she would phone Stevie for some light relief and listen to the gossip about the latest craze that Zac was into, including the belly dancing lessons he'd roped Stevie into trying.

On the third night after his mother's death, Tom had led her into the bedroom and the tenderness between them had been something new, as though there really was a deeper level of connection.

By the time the day of the funeral dawned, crisp and frosty but under a bright blue sky, she really believed that what they'd shared had changed things. He needed Ashleigh more than ever and it was a burden she wanted to bear.

Bertie was as devoted to her as he had been since the first exchange of bacon on Christmas Day and, as they set off for the church in Hythe together, the dog included, they were like a proper little family.

Mourners were packed into the church, filling the pews on both sides of the aisle, including Angus, who'd cut short a trip back to Scotland to give Tom his support. There were a handful of photographers outside, too, no doubt hoping to capture the grief on Tom's face, which would guarantee to sell some papers the next day. It was that human nature thing of rubber-necking, an insight into someone else's misery could somehow make you feel better, putting your own troubles into perspective.

Tom was in his body but not really there. He couldn't remember getting dressed, but of course he had, and everything was happening on some weird kind of autopilot; the numbness he'd felt in the first hours after her death was definitely back. It was a kind of coping mechanism, he supposed, to make the grieving process survivable. He'd need it to continue if he was going to get through the eulogy he'd written.

The vicar welcomed the congregation, his golf shoes just visible beneath his cassock. He'd squeezed Isobel's funeral in, telling Tom that January was always the busiest month, the cold weather claiming so many of his elderly congregation. With the departed having a celebrity son, the vicar had decided it was worth it, suggesting to Tom that a sizeable donation would be welcomed by the church and a fitting tribute to his mother.

'Isobel was a vibrant member of the community, loved by many as is apparent here today.' The vicar cleared his throat and smoothed his hair, sporting a comb over that wouldn't even convince the dead he still had a full head of hair. 'Although her visits to church were intermittent, Isobel expressed her faith on the occasions that we met and her belief that she would be reunited with those she loved.' Adopting a look he evidently felt would comfort the most heartbroken of mourners, the vicar made eye contact with Tom. 'And we can give thanks not just for Isobel's life, but that she will now be in God's glorious kingdom, reunited with her own parents and her beloved husband Clive.'

Tom and Ashleigh exchanged a look and he managed a half smile. Only she really understood how ironic the vicar's comments were.

There were several bible readings and a hymn before the vicar finally called upon Tom to pay tribute to his mother.

Standing in the pulpit in his black suit, shirt and tie, Tom fought hard to stay in control, although no one appeared to have noticed that he was shaking – as though giving a eulogy at his mother's funeral was something he could just take in his stride. He didn't care what people thought. If anyone assumed he wasn't torn up by his mother's death then they didn't know him at all. Ashleigh was the one person who really knew the agony he was going through and that was all that mattered. The muscles in his face tightened as he struggled to hold it all together, just wanting to be alone with her again, so that he could be himself and let the emotion out.

'Isobel Rushworth was a philanthropist, working tirelessly as a volunteer for her favourite charities right up until her death. She was a good neighbour, friend and partner and to me she was the best mother a child, a boy and a man could ever ask for. My mother taught me everything in life that is important, how to swim, read, ride a bike, how to play, laugh and have fun. Without my mother I would be nothing and her loss is the hardest thing I have ever had to bear.' Tom swallowed hard, shuffling the papers on the stand in front of him, as he forced himself to regain his composure. 'I have been and will always be thankful, every day, that I am Isobel Rushworth's son and I will love her whole-heartedly for the rest of my life.'

Returning to his seat, Tom took Ashleigh's hand, wondering for the hundredth time how he would have got through it without her.

There was hardly a dry eye in the church by the time the service ended, but there was an added heaviness in Ashleigh's heart as they filed out of the church. She was a terrible person, selfish and self-centred for the way she was feeling about Tom's words, the undeniable outpouring of love for his mother. After all, who could be jealous of a dead woman?

Only Ashleigh, Tom, his Auntie Maureen and her family attended the private burial. The vicar's words at the graveside brought forth a fresh crop of tears.

The rest of the congregation had made their way to the *Imperial Hotel* on the seafront at Hythe, where Tom had booked the wake.

By the time Isobel's immediate family joined them, following the burial, the rest of the mourners appeared to have made good use of the bar and were regaling each other with tales about Isobel and laughing at shared memories of the woman whose life they had come together to celebrate.

'So nice to see you again, Tommy Boy!' An elderly man, who could have made a good living as a Colonel Sanders' lookalike, slapped Tom heartily on the back. 'Your mother was so proud of you, you know.'

'Thank you Fred, it's good of you to come all the way back here for the funeral.' Tom shook Colonel Sanders' hand. 'Ashleigh, this is Fred, Mum's best friend Doreen's husband, they retired down to Cornwall ten years ago.' Following Tom's introduction, Fred wrapped Ashleigh into a warm embrace, like they were long lost relatives on one of those shows that reunite families.

'My word, so you're the famous Ashleigh.' Fred drew back to look at her. 'Isobel telephoned Doreen on Christmas night to say how thrilled she was that Tom had finally found himself a lovely girl and my goodness she didn't exaggerate.' There was a twinkle in his eye, suggesting he'd been an out and out flirt in his day and hadn't entirely lost the knack. 'Might I need to buy a new hat?'

'I think a fascinator might be more your thing Fred.' Tom gave him a stiff smile 'Although the question of Mum's capacity for exaggeration is open for debate.'

'Shame. Still living in sin can be awfully good fun, eh?' Fred nudged Ashleigh enthusiastically, sloshing his drink on her in the process.

'We don't live together, never have and probably never will.' She spoke before Tom could jump in and give his own forthright response. 'It's been lovely meeting you, Fred, but I must go and walk Bertie. He was so good at the church and we've had to leave him in the car, so I've promised him a walk.' Leaning forward to kiss Fred on the cheek, she didn't look back and just kept walking.

It was freezing on the stretch of beach that ran along the coastline from outside of the hotel towards Sandgate. The one benefit of the inclement weather was that there were no other dog walkers to spoil their splendid isolation or to fall victim unwittingly to Bertie's shower of grit and spray as he greeted every stranger like an old friend. The wind whipped at her hair and her eyes streamed with a mixture of emotion and reaction to the weather.

Ashleigh must have walked at least a mile in the direction of home; the sharpness of the wind and the physical pain, as the cold made her ears and throat ache, a welcome distraction from the pain of knowing that no matter how much she didn't want to, for her own sanity, she had to break the promise she'd made to Isobel. The fresh air woke her up and she was suddenly aware of the truth, the fog of delusion that had shrouded her during her isolation with Tom blown away.

She couldn't deny it any more, not even to herself. She wanted 'forever' and it was something that Tom would never be able to give her. It might mean making the hardest decision of her life, but it was what she needed to do, even though her heart was suddenly heavier than a beach full of stones.

Completely inappropriately dressed, in her smartest black dress, she turned back towards Hythe, finally accepting that she had to stop running from the truth. She had to explain things to Tom and, if Isobel were listening, up there in the ether somewhere, then perhaps she would understand and be able to forgive Ashleigh too.

Could she go through with it, today of all days? In truth, she had no choice. She couldn't go back into the hotel and risk hearing one more comment that might send her over the edge. She loved Tom so much that it hurt and she was shattered, exhausted from pretending. Guilt at ending it on the day of Isobel's funeral tore at her insides, but it would be far worse for Tom if she went back inside the hotel with him and ended up making a scene. His heart had been broken by Isobel's death and her leaving was almost nothing in comparison. He might even be relieved. She was drowning, though, and she had no choice but to save herself, however terrible it might make her feel.

Ashleigh and Bertie were within a couple of hundred feet of the hotel when she saw him, staring towards the headland and then scanning back along the beach until he spotted them walking towards him.

'Thank God, I was getting worried. I thought something might have happened to you.' As Tom spoke she shivered. She hadn't stopped to retrieve her outdoor coat from the hotel's cloakroom before grabbing Bertie and had walked away as fast as she could, desperate to get out before she lost control. 'Put this on, you must be freezing.' He draped his coat over her shoulders. The sudden warmth against her body, and the faint hint of his familiar aftershave on the collar of the coat, almost made it feel like he had his arms around her. 'Are you okay?'

'Yes… No, I'm not hurt or anything if that's what you mean. Well, not physically anyway, but there's something I need to say before I change my mind.' Ashleigh's words were falling over each other as she struggled to get them out. She'd been rehearsing what she had to say all the way along the beach and back and she needed to say it while it was still clear in her head. 'I'm sorry to do this to you, especially at a time like this, but if I don't do it now I might never do it. I think we both know deep down that we ought to call it a day, we don't want the same things out of this and I don't want to become the sort of person who is desperately clinging on to something in the hope that it might one day turn out to be more than it is.'

'Is this because of what Fred said?' Tom had that exasperated, we've-been-through-all-this-a-hundred-times-before look on his face. 'Were you expecting me to tell him we'd asked the vicar to book us a date for the wedding, at the

same time as arranging the funeral, on a two for one deal?'
His sarcasm was almost as biting as the wind.

'Of course not. That's not what I mean at all.' The perfect
speech she'd practised was all going a bit array. 'It's just I
realised today, what I've known all along really, that you are
capable of loving someone. Only that someone isn't me.'

'I've been honest with you about my feelings from day
one.' The exasperated expression was dissipating, replaced
by something else, sympathy even. 'But you are the person
I feel closest to right now and who I want to be with. I just
can't promise it will always be that way or when either of
us might want out. It's not just that I don't love you, I don't
believe it exists in a romantic sense, that's all.' That's all! It
was like he was just expressing a preference for red grapes
rather than green ones, so matter of fact, so decisive.

'I know you've always been honest and I can never regret
the time we've spent together.' Ashleigh silently congratulated
herself on her composure; elements of the well-rehearsed
speech were starting to filter back into her consciousness.
'But I want to be honest with you too. Someone who loved
another person as much as you loved your mother will
always be capable of love again, romantic or otherwise, and
one day someone will come along who knocks you off your
feet and throws away all your preconceptions about love. But
I know now that someone won't be me.' She put her hand up
to stop him saying anything; she had to get this out. 'And I
need to move on for my sake. Try as I might to buy into your
theory, I can't deny it to myself or to you any longer. I do love
you. And, as much as that hurts right now, I'm glad that I've
admitted that to both of us so that I can start to move on. I
don't want to be some sad person looking out for signs that

you might feel the same and treading on eggshells around you or when people ask questions about our relationship.' She moved towards him and brushed her lips against his one last time, letting his coat fall off her shoulders. 'Take care of yourself and Bertie. I'll miss you both.' Thrusting Bertie's lead into his hand she kicked off her shoes, picked them up and turned around, running along the sea wall, thankful once more that there was virtually no one around to witness this mad woman jogging towards Sandgate in her stockinged feet.

'Ashleigh, stop, let's talk about th…' Tom called after her, but his words were lost on the wind, mingling with Bertie's howls. The dog's distress at losing his own true love for the second time in a matter of weeks was obvious, but Ashleigh kept running.

ॐ

Watching her leave, it was as though Tom's skin had been peeled back and his insides exposed. Emotion gripped his throat making it difficult to swallow, but he couldn't be sure what he was feeling. Maybe it was anger, or shock at the fact she'd left him when he'd needed her support, but he didn't have the right to be angry. He was glad she'd been honest; it was the only thing they'd ever promised each other. The timing wasn't ideal, but it was the right thing for Ashleigh to do. He couldn't expect everyone to be like him, turn off their feelings if they started to get out of hand. The rest of the world didn't seem to realise that love was an illusion, even when they'd tried as hard to see it for what it was as she had. And she'd really tried. If he was honest with himself, it was obvious she was struggling with it almost from the beginning. His mother's death had affected him in a way he never dreamt possible and Ashleigh leaving had just heightened that. At any other time it would have felt different. He didn't try to convince himself that he wouldn't have been bothered, he could admit he liked her enough to care, he'd been hurt the first time they split up, but this unbearable feeling of loss was just tied up with his mother, it meant far less on its own.

Bertie was still whining when Tom reached the car, having had to drag the dog behind him and away from the beach. He wouldn't go back to the wake, he couldn't face talking to anyone, couldn't speak – not even to comfort Bertie. The dog would get over it, they both would. Life went on, whether you wanted it to or not.

Chapter Thirty-Two

The days after saying goodbye to Tom following the funeral were the worst that Ashleigh had ever experienced, even more terrible than when her father had died. It was an awful comparison to make, but the guilt made it all so much worse. She'd seen films where people were sick with shock or at bad news, but she'd never believed it could happen in real life.

She'd left Tom when he needed her, and Bertie too, all because she was too selfish to put her own feelings to one side. She'd had no control when her father died, but she'd chosen this and the guilt tore at her from the inside out.

Almost as soon as she'd got through the front door, she'd run to the toilet and thrown up, over and over again.

'What on earth's happened, darling?' Ashleigh scraped open her eyes, her mother looming over her. Carol had obviously let herself into the flat and if there'd been an ounce of energy left in Ashleigh's body she'd have jumped out of her skin. As it was she lay, like a lump of rock, on the sofa in her front room, where she'd spent most of the last twenty-four hours.

'Why has something got to be wrong?' The effort of speaking

scratched her throat. Was it too early for a drink?

'Because you're sleeping at two o'clock in the afternoon.' Carol sat on the edge of the sofa, forcing Ashleigh to turn on her side. 'And because I saw the dream catcher I bought you hanging up at the window. You hate all my new age stuff, you've told me often enough.'

Ashleigh squinted, the light burning her eyes, which were desperate to close again. Had she really hung that thing up in the hope it could live up to its promise and filter out all the bad thoughts? Slowly she focused on the window. There it was, in its lopsided position, looped over the window opener.

'I'd forgotten I did that.' She shifted into a different position. 'But I hardly think it calls for an intervention.'

'Darling, when you start buying into my theories and taking my advice, trust me, I know it's time to panic.' Carol smoothed back her hair and Ashleigh realised, to her surprise, that she wanted her to stay.

'I've been having a bit of a rough time and I was willing to give anything a shot last night, just to get some sleep.' Every time she'd closed her eyes she'd seen Tom standing there, watching her leave him. The wind had been blowing straight off the sea for half the night, too, howling like Bertie and not letting her sleep, even when she'd buried her head under four cushions.

'Is it Tom?' Her mother squeezed her hand. It was quite unnerving her being like this, almost like a normal mum, and all she could do was nod. 'Do you want to tell me what happened?'

Ashleigh wasn't sure she could. How could she explain something she could barely rationalise? 'He doesn't love me.' The words escaped all by themselves in the end and hot tears trickled from the corners of her eyes.

'Well, then he's not worth crying over.' Carol, who was usually so laid back that nothing bothered her, had gone red in the face. 'You deserve so much more than that.'

If Ashleigh hadn't been so acutely aware of the pain in her head and her chest, she would have sworn she was dreaming. Her mum hadn't said anything like that to her in… as long as she could remember. 'But I love him.' She tried to keep the emotion out of her voice, but it was like holding back the tide. 'It hurts, Mum, so much.' She was half-sobbing and sucking in huge gulps of air.

'Pain is the body's way of telling you something's wrong. Maybe, in this case, it's Tom that's wrong.' Carol moved so that she was lying next to Ashleigh, wrapping her arms around her daughter. 'He might see sense and realise how special you are but, if he doesn't, that will be his loss. But you deserve to be loved, you know that, don't you?'

Ashleigh nodded and let herself relax in her mother's arms for the first time in years, Carol's yak-hair jumper scratching her nose. It was a weird mixture of comfort and terror… when her mother started to make sense, she was right, it was definitely time to worry.

Stevie and Zac had sent flowers to the funeral, separately of course. They'd wanted to pay their respects for Tom, but had stayed away from the funeral itself at his request that it shouldn't be turned into a media circus. After the funeral, Stevie spent two days intermittingly calling Ashleigh on her home and mobile phones. She didn't answer, couldn't bring herself to admit what she'd done to Tom, even to Stevie. She texted, though, to say she was fine and that he absolutely wasn't to come over, but of course he did. She'd heard the key turning in the lock, the spare key she'd given him when she first moved in. She couldn't move to get up and greet him; she was a sodden, tear stained lump on the sofa and it was all she was good for.

'Go back to Zac's, Stevie. I'm fine.' Lying on the sofa, still wearing her pyjamas at four p.m., Ashleigh wasn't fooling anybody.

'Yeah, you look it.' Stevie sat on the end of the sofa and stroked her leg. 'Come on, honey, tell me what's up.'

Sympathy was quite the worst thing Ashleigh could have been given and she dissolved into noisy sobs, relaying the whole sorry tale. Her misery was such that one thing just melted into another and in the end she was crying about the fact that she would never do what she wanted with her career and that she might as well work in the make-over photo studio where she really belonged.

At least Ashleigh had the luxury of time to think about what it was she actually wanted to do. Zac, who had been delighted with the album shots had paid her enough money to cover her mortgage and the rest of her bills for a good six months. She told Stevie that there was no way she was accepting any work from *Glitz*, she couldn't even bear to see a copy of the magazine while she was passing the newsagent's window. That had been enough excuse to keep her holed up in the flat since the funeral. It was giving her far too much time to think and Stevie told her he wasn't going to risk leaving her there. Throwing some of her clothes into a suitcase, he bundled her into one of Zac's many cars and drove her back to the manor house, dismissing her protestations. Standing in the hallway of Zac's gilded and glitzy house, she was exhausted by it all.

'I feel like an alien in another world.' Her shoulders dropped as she spoke. 'Like grey, lumpy porridge trying to look at home in a bowl of exotic fruit. I don't know why you want me here.'

'Because we love you.' Stevie didn't have to say anymore, he'd brought her home and he obviously wanted her there – that was enough.

Zac took in Ashleigh's pale appearance and gave her a hug; for once the Romeo act was on the back burner. Stevie had phoned him and filled him in on what had happened, when they'd stopped at the services en route. Ashleigh had pretended that she needed the loo, although all she'd really wanted was to have a cry in private.

'I think a cup of tea and some biscuits are in order.' Zac took her hand and led her through to the expansive kitchen. He was more down to earth than before, as if he was growing to like the mundane – making his own tea, cooking for them. It was real and Ashleigh had never seen him look happier. 'Flick the TV on babe. There must be something terrible going on in the world somewhere that will make you feel better about all this.'

'Good idea, let's hope for some horrible disaster.' Stevie grinned and Ashleigh didn't miss the look they exchanged, which needed no words.

Zac had been right, the twenty-four hour rolling news from Sky didn't disappoint. There was a plane crash, a flood and even a fatal shark attack to help put her troubles into perspective. There were also the lighter hearted pieces, including one about a family in Bradford who claimed they had seen the face of Christ in their *Shredded Wheat*, as well as some entertainment news. The newsreader smiled broadly as he announced Susie-Anne's release from hospital after three weeks of bed rest, over footage of her cradling her stomach and clutching on to the arm of an impassive looking Tom like her life depended on it.

'Well, that was… nice.' Zac's cup of tea hovered in mid-air.

'Do you think they're back together?' Stevie barely whispered the words, as if saying it out loud might push Ashleigh over the edge.

'It doesn't really matter.' Exhaustion washed over her again. 'If they are, I feel sorry for her. It won't be because he loves her. It might just be a pretence to help her career, but it doesn't matter either way because the only thing he does love at the moment is the business.' A frisson of worry prickled her scalp. 'I wonder who's looking after Bertie?'

'Will you call, see if he's okay and check on Tom too?' Stevie looked over at Ashleigh. 'I know he's been an arse, but part of me can't help feeling for the bloke. His mother's just died and he still has to put up with the likes of Susie-Anne and deal with all the crap that comes with it.

'I think it's best left alone.' She put down her cup and stood up, her head was full of concrete. 'It's all such a mess. He made his feelings clear and they're hardly going to change, are they? I think he's made that blatant enough, even for someone as hopeless as me.'

'Are you sure?' Zac put his hand over hers. He was suddenly acting like an expert in love, after years of messing everything up, as if he wanted to fix things for everyone around him too. 'You don't want to have any regrets.'

'You know the worst part of it all?' She couldn't stop the tears, any more than she could control how she felt about Tom. 'I know he can feel love, real love. I saw how he was with his mum, so I can't even say it's a problem with him. He just doesn't love me, that's the simple truth. Like Liam said, the problem with me is…' She didn't even finish the sentence. 'I'm going to have a lie down, if that's okay? It's been a long couple of days.' She sniffed and Zac nodded, letting go of her hand.

♥

'Will you stop looking at me like that? I've told you before there's nothing I can do about it.' Tom addressed Bertie and the Labrador whined again, his misery since Ashleigh had left knew no bounds.

Tom tried again to get him to eat. He'd cooked some chicken breasts specially and sliced one up carefully for the heartbroken dog. Back before Isobel had died, Tom would have risked losing a finger if he'd dangled chicken in Bertie's face and the Labrador would have swallowed it whole, hardly tasting the food. Since Ashleigh had left, Bertie scarcely bothered with his food and, as Tom had no appetite either, the seagulls at the landfill site were doing quite well out of them.

'What do you expect me to do?' Bertie looked up as Tom spoke, his big round eyes a picture of sorrow. 'She left us you know, not the other way round.'

Tom put the bowl down and Bertie had the decency to sniff the chicken before rejecting it and curling up in his basket.

'I know you think I've been a complete idiot and maybe you're right, but we've only got each other now, so you need to buck up.' Tom took a bite of the chicken sandwich he'd made for himself and then pushed it aside, in much the same way Bertie had reacted to his lunch. It was like wool in his mouth. If this was how it was going to be now, maybe he should just curl up on his bed and take Bertie's approach to the rest of his life.

'How about a walk, boy? Maybe that will cheer us up?'
Bertie moved his head less than an inch off the base of the
basket and sighed heavily, before sinking back down into the
tartan blanket that lined his bed.

'You're right, I doubt it would work either.'

Tom took a bottle of bourbon out of the fridge and poured
himself a generous slug. If losing a friend felt this bad, he was
more grateful than ever that he'd never been in love.

Over the years, there were members of the paparazzi who
had lived off Zac's exploits. He'd been their bread and butter
and provided enough stories to pay off the mortgage on at
least one reasonably-sized family home. As a result, there
were members of the tabloid press inclined to hang around
outside the gates of Zac's estate and to poke their telescopic
lenses through any gaps in the hedgerow that provided the
slightest opportunity. One such lowlife would be paying for
his summer holiday on the strength of the pictures he'd taken
of Zac holding Ashleigh in his arms in front of the chapel
in the estate's grounds. It served to fuel the rumours about
Zac building on his budding New Year's romance with a little
known celebrity photographer, who was surely set to become
fiancée number eight.

Accustomed as they were to the tabloid's tenuous relationship with the truth, the three of them decided to ignore it.
They'd got into a routine, not unlike Ashleigh and Stevie's old
student lifestyle, of staying up late, drinking and putting the
world to rights, getting up just in time to catch the start of
Morning Sunrise.

The usual presenters were all either on holiday or covering
high profile stories for their other presenting roles. As a result,

Dominic Hargreaves, former boy-band front man, turned wannabe presenter, had been given his big break, alongside, of all people, Susie-Anne. Her recent high profile, and the historical pattern of weather-girl-turned-daytime-TV-presenter made her a natural choice for a trial shot on the show – which was no doubt a dream come true for her.

'O.M.G… Shall I turn it off?' Stevie couldn't have looked more horrified if they'd given the job to a serial killer.

'Christ yes!' Zac had his head in his hands, the shock of seeing Susie-Anne on screen apparently making his head too heavy to hold up without support. 'Her voice is grating on me already.'

'Hold on, don't switch off yet!' Ashleigh grabbed the remote and turned up the sound, making Zac wince more than ever. 'Look, they're talking about us!' Susie-Anne and Dominic were chatting to the presenter of 'The Viewer's Voice', and the topic of the day's phone in was serial engagements, with Zac and Ashleigh the celebrity case study.

'Isn't that the girl who was going out with Tom Rushworth until recently?' Dominic turned to Susie-Anne with a smug, you-ought-to-know, sort of smile.

'Yes, and I'm glad she's moved on, just as we all have.' Susie-Anne smoothed down the material of her dress over her neat, almost non-existent bump. 'With the baby coming we want to concentrate on the future rather than the past. I just hope that Zac really means it this time.' Her saccharine tone might convince people that she really cared, unless you actually knew her of course. She'd conveniently forgotten that everyone who'd read a tabloid paper, or who followed her on *Twitter*, knew that Tom wasn't the father.

'Yes, you're right, let's hope Zac's serious this time. Although what an average-looking wedding photographer has that a string of models don't, I'm not sure.' Dominic gave a wry, man-of-the-people type smile and pointed at the camera, directly to his audience at home. 'Just saying what you're all thinking!'

'Okay, enough already.' Stevie grabbed the remote back from Ashleigh and flicked off the TV.

'I think I might go back to bed.' Leaving the sofa without another word, Ashleigh beat a now familiar path up the stairs to the guest room. There were no tears anymore; she just curled up on her bed, staring at the ceiling wondering what the hell she could do to ever get away from all this. There was one solution, but it meant leaving her best friend, just like she'd left Tom.

Chapter Thirty-Three

Exhaustion washed over Tom. If the old adage were true, that being tired of London meant you were tired of life, then he was more than ready to curl up in a corner and hibernate until summer.

'There are some press cuttings here that need your attention.' Francine entered his office without knocking, her cloying perfume reaching him before she did. If anything, he'd been colder to her than ever since his mother's funeral, but Ashleigh's disappearance seemed to have given her renewed hope. She was wearing bright red lipstick and had the look of Joan Crawford about her, hard and scarily ambitious.

'Thanks.' He couldn't summon up any enthusiasm for work and even less so for his humourless PA.

'There's some urgent stuff amongst it, most notably about Zac and Ashleigh. Seems she's as much of a bed hopper as he is!' Francine raised an arched eyebrow, as his hands clenched the edge of the desk – his knuckles turning white.

'She's nothing like Zac and I don't *ever* want to hear you spreading that sort of gossip.'

'I can't understand why you're still defending her. She left you at your mother's funeral, I think that says all you need to know about the girl.' Francine knew nothing about the situation, had no idea how hard Ashleigh had wrestled with the decision; but Tom did.

'I don't want to talk about it, least of all to you. But I meant what I said and I don't want to hear you talking about Ashleigh again.' He was tempted to tell her to get out, but he had to work with her *and* Susie-Anne, had to pretend the things that had driven him for the past ten years still mattered. Didn't he?

⊗

Ashleigh opened the email for what was probably the hundredth time since it had arrived in her inbox, the words "at least a year" swimming in front of her eyes. Six months earlier the offer contained in the short and to the point message would have been a dream come true, now it felt like her only option, but, if she took it, would she just be running away?

'Not bad news, is it?' Zac was suddenly behind her. He might play the eccentric rock star, but he didn't miss a trick. He must have noticed the logo of the hotel emblazoned across the email and everyone had heard of *The Golden Rock* in Las Vegas.

'No, just a job offer.' She hadn't planned to tell Zac or Stevie. For once in her life she wanted to make a decision without seeking someone else's approval, break the mould, but it was such a huge thing it was almost a relief that Zac had caught her out.

'Please tell me that you're not thinking of taking a job as the official photographer in the hotel foyer? *The Golden Rock* might be fantastically OTT and the sort of place that Stevie would love, but you can do way better than that.' Zac was unusually serious and, to her surprise, Ashleigh had to supress a smile. At least things hadn't got that bad.

'No, not quite. The email's from Calvin Welch, I don't think he bothers appointing those sort of staff.'

'Calvin! Wow, if he's been in touch then it must be a serious job offer. He contacts me every so often to see if I fancy a stint in residence, but I'm not that old yet.' He grinned and pulled up the chair next to her, craning to try and read the email on her iPad. 'Apparently he'd been a fan from the days when I was still in my first band and Tom told me at the time that I should be flattered Calvin got in touch direct, normally everything comes through his assistants.' Zac clamped a hand over his mouth. 'Sorry, I forgot we weren't mentioning he-who-can't-be-named.'

'Don't worry about it.' She shrugged, they'd talked the situation to death, there was really nothing else to say. 'That's how Calvin found me. He said in the email he looked me up after he saw the shots of your album cover and tracked down my blog. I've been posting a few photos I took in London, which he loves.' Ashleigh swallowed hard, Calvin saying that had been the best news she'd had in a long time. She'd never told anyone but Stevie about her hopes for those photos, but Zac was a massive part of his life now and, by default, of hers. 'I've been working on some photos of life on the streets, from city bankers and shopaholics on Regent Street, to those who have no homes to go to. I've always had this stupid dream about doing a book, seeing it on display in a shop window.'

'It's not stupid.' Zac put a hand over hers. 'You're brilliant at what you do. It's about time you start to realise that. So what does Calvin want you for?'

'He's made me two offers. He wants me to photograph the shows, the VIPs, guests and the celebrity performers, to help the hotel keep its number one spot on the strip. In return he'll give me my own exhibition, Vegas in Black and White, which he'll put through his publishing company – so I'll finally get that book.' It still didn't seem real. She'd always imagined the euphoria she'd feel at that sort of offer – instead she just felt numb because of the price tag it came with.

'A man with a finger in many pies, that one.' Zac squeezed her hand. 'It's an amazing offer, especially to come from the man himself.'

'It is but it's a long way from you and Stevie and…' She didn't finish. There was no 'and' anymore, but it was still there – in her heart.

'We'd miss you, but it wouldn't be forever and maybe it would do you good.' Zac squeezed her hand again. The old Ashleigh might have worried he was just trying to get rid of her, so he could have Stevie to himself, but she knew it wasn't that. 'Who knows, you might meet someone with more balls than Tom, balls enough to love you.'

'That many balls? I'm not sure I could handle it. I'm off relationships for good.' Ashleigh managed a wry smile. 'So, if Calvin Welch is after a fling in return for his offer, he's barking up the wrong tree.'

'I think you're quite safe on that front. He's happily married,' Zac paused for a moment, that trade mark grin back in place, 'to his fifth wife and, at twenty-nine, you're too old to become number six. I think the current one is four years younger than you!'

'Listen to you, Mr seven fiancées!' She nudged him in the ribs.

'I know, I know, but now I've found my Mr Right and I just want you to be happy too.'

'Do you think I should take the job?' Even as she said the words, her hand shook. 'The contract, to get the exhibition and the book deal in return, is for a minimum of a year.'

'Stevie will freak…' He paused again and nodded. 'But this isn't about him or me or what we'd want you to do. If this really is one of your dreams, then I think you've got to grab it with both hands. How many people have one of those come true?'

'Not many.' Hitting the reply button before she changed her mind, she started to type.

'I would say I don't think much of your PA, but she's a marked improvement on the last one.' Angus bent down to pat Bertie, who lifted his head in a half-hearted way and then took up his default position, flat out underneath Tom's desk. 'Although he's about as pleased to see me as Francine always was.'

'He's been like that…' Tom caught himself, he didn't want to talk about Ashleigh. That was over. 'Since mum died.' He changed the subject, although it led back to her in one way or another these days. 'Is there anything in the press I need to know about?' He didn't elaborate, Angus would know exactly what he meant.

'No. It's all quiet on the Francine-front. Susie-Anne has put something on her website about new representation, but it seems they're all sticking to the rules. Obviously I got your message, but do you want to tell me exactly what happened?'

'It wasn't my finest morning.' For a second he almost smiled. He didn't regret any of it, but it was still hard to explain how it had all come about. 'Something snapped when Susie-Anne turned up with that idiot Dominic Hargreaves in tow, she'd brought him into the offices to see if I'd represent him.' He didn't mention that he'd heard, an hour before Susie-Anne's arrival, that Ashleigh had left for Las Vegas and his mood had been less than charitable as a result. He'd seen the clip of *Morning Sunrise* with Susie-Anne's inference that Tom was somehow still part of her life, as well as Dominic's comments on Ashleigh. They were both idiots. It was like a light bulb had been switched on when he watched it and he knew there was no way he could stand to be associated with her anymore, not even in a professional sense.

'How did you get her to go quietly? She's not exactly known for taking rejection lying down.' Angus laughed. 'Although maybe I should rephrase that!'

'I told her if she didn't make a fuss, I'd arrange for Toby Goldstein to sign her and her latest lap dog, Dominic, to his new agency.' It had been like a weight had lifted from his shoulders. 'Do you remember Toby? He used to work for me, but he moved on to set up his own agency last year. Even though he'd represented some of our major clients, they all decided to stay with me after he left. So he was more than happy to sign the two of them up and I couldn't wait to get shot of her. I got Francine to sort out all the paperwork before she left.'

'Aye, now that's the bit I'm really struggling to get my head around. I still can't quite believe you sacked the Rottweiler.'

'It wasn't quite as dramatic as that. The legal bit cost me a small fortune but it was worth it. I couldn't sack her, but we reached a 'compromise agreement'. Truth be told I paid her off, otherwise she'd have gone for unfair dismissal, but there was no other option in the end.'

'You said in your message you'd put the wheels in motion for that, even before you shifted Susie-Anne off your books?'

Angus gave him a quizzical look. 'I thought she was destined to be by your side, one way or the other, for the long haul.'

'That was the problem, so did she - especially after... everything. I couldn't stand the I told you so look on her face.' Tom sighed. Had he cut off his nose to spite his face? Francine had been good at her job, but he couldn't live with the way she'd judged him – or Ashleigh – any more.

'You might have to sack me next then.' Angus looked unusually serious.

'What do you mean?' Tom couldn't imagine Angus telling him how wrong he'd been to get involved with Ashleigh. He thought the world of her; that much was obvious.

'How many celebrities do you think we have in this thing over the course of a year?' Angus held up a copy of the latest addition of Glitz and then let it fall on to the desk in front of him.

'I don't know, all told, with parties and everything? Well over a thousand, at a guess.'

'At least that. And there's you, finding something real, something worth having among a thousand stars who parade across the pages of this thing, and you let it go.' His brogue came through strongly when he was passionate about something and right now it sounded like Angus had never left Glasgow.

Tom shook his head. 'It was never meant to be anything serious, and according to Zac she's chasing her dreams in Las Vegas now. So although your advice is pointless, I won't be sacking you just yet.' He managed another half-smile. 'It's far too expensive!'

Chapter Thirty-Four

Ashleigh fumbled for the clock on the bedside table, which seemed to be about a mile away. The blackout curtains and jet lag meant she had no idea what time it was. It was her seventh day in Vegas and she was hoping she might have finally cracked the time change thing. Five thirty a.m., not bad. It was nine thirty in the evening in England. Stevie wanted her to call every Friday; in fact he'd made her promise.

When she told him she was leaving, there'd been a few tears – mainly his – but he'd understood and even told her she was right to follow her dreams. He'd only tried to talk her out of it once, when they were out of earshot from Zac, and she would probably have been offended if he hadn't. His insistence that it was the right thing to do hadn't stopped him texting her twenty times a day and he could still be relied upon to impart the gossip from back home. The night before hadn't been any different.

✉ From Stevie
What R U doing? Partying hard with dancing girls & magicians who've got orange skin & bigger hair than U? xx

✉ From Ashleigh
I'm doing some research about Lake Mead. Party central here! What are you guys up to? Xx

✉ From Stevie
Glad U R making the most of Vegas! Only U could work so hard somewhere like that. Life of leisure can be quite boring but big goss 2day! xx

✉ From Ashleigh
And? Xx

✉ From Stevie
Tom's got rid of Francine and Susie-Anne. Angus thinks he's having a break down! Xx

✉ From Ashleigh
Doubt that. It will be a financial decision. Speak tomorrow. Love you Xx

She didn't respond to his follow up text. She wasn't interested in hearing about Tom, it was the rule she needed to live by. Knowing Stevie, he'd have forgotten the thread of those texts by now anyway and moved on to something or someone else to talk about. She picked up her iPad and put through the FaceTime call

'Morning gorgeous. It is morning there, isn't it?' Stevie's face filled the screen, but then he grimaced. 'Christ honey, you could have brushed your hair before you called!' Zac leant over his shoulder as he spoke and joined in the laughter at her expense. God, she missed them.

'I need a stylist.' She was only half-joking and she bit her lip to stem the emotion bubbling to the surface.

'What's on the agenda this morning, more Lake Mead research?' As Stevie spoke, Zac cut across him.

'What he really wants to know is whether you've got any gossip, Stevie's run the well dry this end.'

'I'm having breakfast with Calvin Welch's assistant, although I've not seen much of the big man himself yet.' Ashleigh raked a hand through her hair as she spoke. Stevie was right, a brush definitely wouldn't go amiss.

'Like I said, he's got his fingers in a lot of pies, you don't get to amass his kind of fortune otherwise, but remember he wanted you enough to track you down and write to you personally and he'll honour your deal.' Zac was quite partial to pep talks lately and she smiled. He was totally different to the man he'd been before Stevie. They were jostling each other to get closer to the screen and she couldn't work out what room they were in; there were so many of them at Zac's place they could have been anywhere.

'Oh I'm not worried and his assistant is lovely.'

'Not like Francine, then.' Stevie shuddered at the thought.

'No, nothing like Francine.' Marcus couldn't have been less like Tom's ice-cold PA if he'd tried. He'd been so helpful, taking her to places where she could capture aspects of Vegas that most tourists didn't get to see.

'Thank Christ for that. Although she might well be on the lookout for a new boss now, so if Calvin's got any jobs going you two could be roomies!' Stevie laughed a bit too hard and Zac had to hit him on the back.

'Are you trying to give me nightmares?' She couldn't help smiling. She didn't care what Tom did, but the thought that he'd finally given Francine what she deserved was strangely cheering. 'Much as I love the abuse you two give me, I've got to go!" Ashleigh blew them both a kiss and ended the call. Time to get ready for the hotel's famous breakfast.

The hotel foyer was typically Vegas, over the top and opulent. The gold theme was everywhere, from the huge statues that flanked the entrance to the flower displays taller than Ashleigh. She'd miss this when she moved out to her rented apartment, but she had to stop pretending she was on holiday and get on with her new life.

'How are you doing today?' Marcus stood up from the table where he was already waiting and kissed her on both cheeks. 'Over the jet lag and the change of climate yet?'

'I am. I feel almost human today and I'm ravenous too!' Ashleigh moved towards the buffet. At one end the grill chefs were offering freshly cooked steak, but that was a step too far – even for her.

'I've got a few hours to spare and I thought maybe we could check out some more sites off the strip?' Marcus loaded his plate with fresh fruit, as she speared some bacon. A rasher shot across her plate and she couldn't fight the memory of that breakfast with Tom at Christmas, as it hit the floor, when he'd said she needed a dog. Bertie would love it here, a mountain of bacon would be his idea of heaven. Pushing the thought away, she turned to look at Marcus.

'That would be great and I've got my first shoot at the theatre later, I think?'

'Yes, we've got a new act, Bill Desire, coming in to do a fort-night of shows while Melindra is on a break. If it goes well, he might take over when she finishes her residency.' Marcus looked delighted and Ashleigh couldn't bring herself to confess that she'd never heard of Bill. They seemed to do a line in country and western singers at *The Golden Rock*, who she was loathed to admit she'd never been into. Melindra Meadows was a huge star in the States, but that genre of music had completely passed her by.

'Where were you thinking of heading today?' It was probably safest to steer the conversation away from music. They'd been into the desert the day before and it had been amazing, although exhausting.

'I'm thinking of Paradise,' His warm brown eyes crinkled in the corners. She knew from their conversations that his grandparents, on his mother's side, were originally from Mexico, and he'd clearly inherited their olive skin tone and dark hair.

'Paradise? Now there's an offer I can't refuse.' It was a town on the outskirts of Las Vegas, largely ignored by tourists, she knew that much.

'I thought the campus at the University of Nevada might give you some fodder.'

'It will, but are you sure you've got time?' She could find it, that's what cabs were for, and Marcus must have better things to do than to babysit her.

'For you, yes.' He gave her a lazy smile as they returned to their table.

'Won't Calvin mind?' Ashleigh couldn't imagine someone like him assigning so much of his assistant's time to help her out.

'He can't complain really. He gave me the day you arrived to help you settle in, but I've been on annual leave since then.'

Ashleigh ran through some of the shots she'd captured on her camera and couldn't help smiling. Marcus had been right.

The university had been a rich source of inspiration, but her favourite photos were of the elderly professor who'd been lecturing outside, talking to his students about the origins of the pioneer wall. His face was an illustration of wisdom, each deep line drawing his mouth upwards. His students were rapt, looking at him as though he were some sort of evangelist. When people thought of Vegas, they thought of showgirls, neon lights and roulette wheels – not this – which was exactly why it was so brilliant.

'Did you get some good material?' Marcus addressed her, but kept his eyes on the road. The traffic on the strip was crawling slowly forward and the engine of the car, which was one from the staff fleet at *The Golden Rock*, hummed in quiet impatience. Next to them was a pink limo, almost bouncing along the road with the volume of music coming from inside.

'I really did, thanks so much for taking me. I think I might even have one or two that could make it to the final exhibition and the book.' As she spoke, there was a 'whooping' sound from the limousine in the neighbouring lane and suddenly a pretty girl in a cheap wedding veil popped out of the sunroof where she was quickly joined by two other young women wearing shot glasses around their necks.

'They seem to like the sound of it!' Marcus looked at her briefly, but the bumper-to-bumper traffic drew his eyes back to the road almost instantly.

'Looks like they're ready to party. Do you ever find it too much, living in a party place like this?' A man dressed as a Roman Centurion strolled past on the pavement as their car inched forward.

'As you're finding out, you can find a hundred different versions of Vegas if you look for them.' The car pulled to a stop at the intersection and for the first time he turned to look at her properly. 'But it can be ironic, being single in the wedding capital of the world.' There was another whooping from the pink limo. 'Not to mention the bachelorette parties.'

'I'm sure…' Ashleigh faltered; not knowing what it was he wanted to hear. 'It's okay, I've been building up the nerve to ask you to dinner, but you're giving out quite obvious messages that it would be a bad idea.' Marcus went back to looking at the road ahead, the traffic moving again but still crawling unbearably slowly towards their destination.

'It's not you.' She wasn't going to tell him about Tom, rake all that up again, it was bad enough every time Stevie mentioned him. The last couple of days she'd even started to wonder if Tom had been right all along and that work was the only thing that could be truly fulfilling. At least she'd felt something close to love for her new job when she'd been at the university. A fling with Marcus might have given her a temporary boost, that someone wanted her, but Liam, of all people, had it spot on – she had to stop looking for someone else to make her feel worthwhile, in the end it was down to her.

'You don't need to explain.' Marcus smiled, he was so sweet. 'I've enjoyed watching you work, I wasn't expecting anything in return.' They both jumped, as a scream from the limo pierced the air. 'Jeez, I hope they aren't heading to *The Golden Rock*. Just in case, I think I'm going to drop you off, dump the car and head straight home. Not sure I can face much more screaming.' If her gentle rebuff was the real reason for his quick getaway, he was doing a good job of hiding it. 'How are you feeling about your photo-shoot with Bill Desire by the way?'

'I still can't get over that name!' She'd finally admitted to

Marcus at the university that she didn't know who Bill was and that she'd made a rule never to Google the celebrities she worked with beforehand, even if she had no idea who they were. She wanted to find a way of photographing them that wouldn't be influenced by what others had done and getting drawn into viewing endless images of them online wasn't the way to go. It was what Calvin Welch had written in his email, he loved the photos of Zac because she'd captured him in a different way than everyone else. Now that she didn't have to jump through *Glitz*'s hoops anymore to fit their formula, she was going to make the most of it.

'Sounds a bit like he should be a crooner of love songs, doesn't he?' Marcus finally pulled into the hotel and carried on into the underground staff car park.

'He does, or an erotica writer!' Ashleigh laughed as she spoke, unclipping her seatbelt as the car came to a stop. 'I'm building up this great mental picture of what he looks like, so I just hope I'm not going to be disappointed.'

'Oh you won't be!' He dropped a casual wink, suddenly reminding her of Stevie, and she felt another brief pang of homesickness.

'I'm not quite sure what to expect now!'

Marcus grinned. 'You'll see. And if you change your mind about dating, remember what happens in Vegas stays in Vegas.'

'I'll bear that in mind. Have a great evening and thanks again for today.' Closing the car door, she gave him a quick wave and walked towards the hotel, sadly what happened in London wasn't playing by the same rules, no matter how hard she tried to forget.

Chapter Thirty-Five

'Come on Bertie, this is getting old now.' They were on the beach, it was so cold that the pebbles were almost crystalizing, with tiny specks of ice glistening on their surface. The wind blowing off the sea towards them was making Tom's ears ache and he wondered why he'd bothered.

Get away for the weekend, Angus had said, so he'd come down to his mother's house to sort through the rest of her stuff before it went on the market. It had been a mistake. It was grey and cold and matched his mood perfectly.

Bertie was sitting at the base of the stone steps, which Tom had virtually dragged him down, his soulful eyes staring out to sea. If a dog could really frown, then he was doing it.

'I'm not here for my own enjoyment you know.' Going home to his old house was supposed to be helping Bertie, but if anything it had made him worse. He'd been excited at first, dashing from room to room, his wagging tail slowing and drooping further and further down as he realised that none of them contained Isobel or Ashleigh. 'We might as well go home if you're going to be a baby about it.' Now they were just cold as well as miserable.

There was hardly anyone around and Tom shivered as he took the road back up to Isobel's house, which was on a steep incline. The last time he'd walked Bertie up the same way it had been Christmas Day and things had been good. He hadn't realised it then of course, but now so much had changed.

He was lost in contemplation and jumped as a voice interrupted his thoughts. It was Karen, his mother's next door neighbour – the dentist who'd looked after Bertie with her reluctant husband, straight after Isobel's accident. He toyed with pretending that he hadn't heard her but his mother would have hated that, so he turned to look in her direction. It was obvious she'd been crying, but he hadn't caught what she'd said.

'Sorry, Karen, I didn't get that. Are you okay?' Tom put a hand on her arm. Looking at her now, she was pale, her eyes darkly rimmed with red.

'Graham left me. On his fortieth birthday, last week. He's been seeing his personal trainer on the side for the last year and it turns out she was giving him the work out of his life.' Karen tried to smile, but it morphed into a sob before she could stop it.

'I'm sorry. I thought you seemed so settled when we met. It must have been a terrible shock.' Tom wasn't sure what to say. This woman, a virtual stranger, was telling him her inner most secrets out on the street and he'd never been exactly skilled at dealing with emotion.

'I thought so too.' Karen's eyes were brimming again. 'The kids are devastated, but the bastard has bought them a puppy at his new flat with… her.' She almost spat the word. 'He wouldn't let us have one here and I supported his decision and all the time he was probably scheming this.'

'Where are the kids now?' Tom looked anxiously towards her house, the front door was open and he could here Adele's *Someone Like You* blaring out from inside.

'With him and Jessica. She's barely ten years older than the children and she's got a stomach like a washboard.' Karen's voice cracked again. 'I used to have one of those. Maybe I shouldn't have let myself go.'

'This isn't your fault.' Tom didn't really know enough about Karen or her husband to know if that was true, but he had to say something to her. 'I don't think you should stay on your own. Is there anyone you can call?'

'I don't want anyone to know.' Karen sniffed back a sob. 'Not yet, not while there's a chance…' She'd given into the crying now and they couldn't just stand out in the street; he couldn't leave her either, even if he wanted to.

'If there's really no-one else you can call, why don't you come for a drink at Mum's?' If it was odd to refer to the house that way, he couldn't help it - it would never be anything else for him.

'Are you sure you don't mind?' Even as Karen spoke she was walking in the direction of Isobel's house, until he put his hand on her arm again.

'Maybe it will do us both some good and Bertie could certainly do with some cheering up. Only I think it might be an idea for you to shut your front door first.' She smiled weakly in response and turned towards her house.

It had all the warning signs of a huge mistake and he wasn't even sure why he was doing it, he was hardly the counselling type. But it was like Isobel was inside his head, telling him to do the right thing for once. If misery really loved company, they were on to a winner.

Bill Desire was sitting in the middle of the stage, with a guitar slung over one shoulder when Ashleigh walked into *The Golden Rock*'s *Phoenix Theatre*. He was wearing an over-sized cowboy hat, the hair that emerged from beneath it long enough to rest on his shoulders, and huge sunglasses even though the theatre was almost in darkness.

'How ya doing darlin'?' Bill looked up as she got closer; at least Ashleigh thought he had, it was hard to tell behind those sunglasses.

'It's lovely to meet you.' She joined him on the stage and he kissed her on both cheeks, just as Marcus had at breakfast, his beard brushing her skin in a way that seemed somehow over familiar.

'You too, sugar.' He sank back on his chair and began strumming his guitar and humming, disappearing into a world of his own so that she was almost afraid to disturb him. Maybe not finding out more about Bill before meeting him was a mistake…

'Have you got any preferences about how I handle the shoot?' She lifted her camera to take the first shots, but Bill just shook his head and started to sing about the dog he'd had as a child. This was why she'd never got into country and western music. Did people really like this stuff? His voice rose suddenly and then cracked when he sang about the poor hound's death. It was maudlin and cheesy and she might have laughed out loud if it hadn't made her think about Bertie again, so that tears stung the back of her eyes instead.

'I'd like you to get some pictures of my lady if you don't

mind, sugar?' Bill smiled and she wished he'd stop saying
sugar. It had made her think of Susie-Anne and even missing
Bertie like mad was better than that.

'Of course. My remit is to capture the real you, to let *The
Golden Rock*'s audience into some insider information. So
seeing you with your wife would work perfectly.' Heat prickled Ashleigh's skin all of a sudden. Bill hadn't said wife, he'd
said 'lady'. What if she was his girlfriend, or worse still his
mistress? She might have crossed the Atlantic, but she was
still more than capable of putting her foot in it.

Bill's 'lady' sashayed across the room, she had long blonde
hair and legs that seemed to go on forever – although she
would have had a shot in a knobbly knees competition. Wearing matching dark glasses, she said nothing as she took Bill's
guitar off him and laid it on the floor, before perching herself
on his lap and nuzzling his neck. Now this wasn't just embarrassing, it was getting downright weird.

'This is Steffi, my fiancée.' Bill almost fell off the stool as Steffi
kissed him enthusiastically and Ashleigh fought the urge to
sigh. It was like being back at *Glitz* and everything she'd loved
about the job in Vegas so far seemed a million miles away.

'Congratulations.' Her voice was flat, but she went through
the motions. Years of working for the magazine had trained
her well; she could feign interest in the life of celebrities she
couldn't care less about. 'So when's the wedding?'

'Depends when our bridesmaid can get an evening off work.'
Bill's deep-south accent suddenly sounded distinctly odd.

'So what do you say, honey, when's it gonna be?' Steffi spoke
for the first time. Except it wasn't Steffi at all – it was a voice
she'd know anywhere.

'You bastards!' Ashleigh threw herself into Stevie's arms,

as he got up from what she could only assume was Zac's lap, dislodging his blonde wig in the process.

'Surprise!' He swung her around in a circle and she just caught sight of Zac peeling off his beard, his hat and wig already long gone.

'What are you doing here? I only spoke to you this morning!' Ashleigh was breathless with shock, but the two of them were grinning like naughty schoolboys.

'Well, we came to see you, mainly, but Calvin persuaded me to do a two-week stint starting at the end of this month to give me a taste of what it might be like if I agreed to be the performer in residence for a while,' Zac took hold of her hand, 'suddenly there was a much bigger draw for me to give it a whirl. We were already in our suite, two floors above you when you called. My jet lag was so bad I almost had to cellotape my eyelids open.'

'There was one other thing we came for, wasn't there?' Stevie grinned again, 'We've got some planning to do for this.'

He passed her his phone, there was a picture of him and Zac in matching blue T-Shirts, holding hands. The slogan on Zac's T-Shirt read: 'I'M WITH HANDSOME' and Stevie's said 'NOT FIANCÉE NUMBER 8, FIANCÉ NUMBER 1!'

'That's incredible!' Ashleigh hugged him. 'Are you really getting married?'

'We are, but if I can hardly believe it, there's only one way of convincing everyone else.' He smiled, happiness written all over his face. 'We want to let the world know that this isn't just another one of Zac's engagements.'

'So, you've told everyone?' Ashleigh was still recovering from the shock that they were both here and now this. It was so much to take in, but she couldn't have been happier for them.

'Not yet, but I want to shout from the rooftops just how much he means to me.' Zac shrugged. 'I know everyone's going to assume this is just another of my crazy stunts but this is the real deal and afterwards we'll release the photos so everyone knows I'm serious and this time it's forever.'

'And then he gets to be centre of attention for a second time when we do it all over again and have a blessing at home.' Stevie put an arm around them both. 'But tonight's mission, honey, is to find a venue. So are you up for it?'

'Just try and stop me!'

Chapter Thirty-Six

'How do we look?' Stevie did a twirl, when she met them in their suite an hour later.

'You both look great, although you do have the perfect figure for that dress you were wearing earlier – apart from the knees!' Ashleigh looked around their suite as she spoke. Calvin Welch might have wanted her, but he clearly wanted Zac a darn sight more. The room they stood in had a highly polished chocolate-brown marble floor and a wall of glass, which looked directly out on to the strip. There was a curved bar area in one corner, with bottles of champagne lined up and a huge box of chocolates, the like of which Ashleigh had only seen once before. Why did everything have to remind her of Tom?

'What's the plan for tonight?' She watched an unreadable expression cross Zac's face.

'Well, we were going to ask you for one last favour, before we go public with all of this. We want to be able to pick a wedding venue without the world breathing down our necks and revealing what we're up to before we're ready.' Zac headed towards one of the other rooms in the suite as he spoke.

'So that's the plan, look at a few venues and then go out for dinner to celebrate with our beautiful bridesmaid!' Stevie swept her into his arms again.

'And what's the favour you want from me?'

Zac emerged from the other room, sporting his stick on beard from earlier and a pair of dark glasses. 'I thought it might be best to go incognito, whilst we're keeping things under wraps, so I wondered if you'd mind pretending the wedding was for you and me – at least until we decide on the venue.'

'This has an oddly familiar feeling about it.' Ashleigh raised an eyebrow. 'But what's a bit of fraud between friends?'

'What do you think?' Zac leant over the replica of the Rialto Bridge in *The Venetian Hotel* and gestured towards the bride and groom being punted in a gondola along the faux river towards them.

'I love it!' Stevie hadn't stopped grinning all night. It was no surprise, after all Vegas was his spiritual homeland and he'd loved all the other venues – the replica of the Eiffel tower, the helicopter, the grand staircase at the *Luxor Hotel* and the courtyard over-looking the fountains at the *Bellagio*. He just wanted to marry Zac, Ashleigh could see that, and he didn't give a damn where.

'They're all brilliant options for the two of you, but maybe this one is a bit public?' She raised an eyebrow, as they were pushed up against the side of the bridge by other people wanting to get a glimpse of the new bride and groom in their finery. 'Do you really want to wear that fake beard on your big day?'

'True. You know I liked The Crystal Room at *The Golden*

Rock, it was so intimate and like something out of Narnia.' She couldn't tell if Zac was blushing beneath his beard, but she wouldn't have been surprised.'

'The Crystal Room it is then.' Stevie didn't even hesitate. 'Come on, let's get on with the celebrating and work out just which outfits are going to work best with crystals… '

Tom scrolled through the messages on his phone, he was in his office in the *Glitz* building where he now seemed to spend most of his time. There were eight texts from Karen. What the hell had he been thinking of? She was desperately searching for a replacement for Graham, someone to build her self-esteem, and Tom needed that kind of complication like a hole in the head. He hadn't done anything, thank God, they'd both been far too drunk.

He looked at the rest of the messages on his phone and sighed, trying to summon up the energy to read them, but it just wasn't happening. There was one from Zac. He was one client who didn't need any help getting on to the front pages of any magazine or newspaper come to that. In fact they were all full of the news that he'd headed off to Vegas, allegedly in hot pursuit of the photographer he'd been seeing since January. Tom couldn't believe that. The papers must have got it wrong, it's not like it was the first time. Much more likely that Zac had gone to explore Calvin Welch's offer, the rest of it was just gutter journalist guesswork. Someone who knew Ashleigh and Zac had obviously put two and two together and made five, and then sold the 'story' to the papers. If his mind had been on business he might have been angry that Zac wasn't involving him in the negotiations with Calvin Welch, but he didn't seem to feel anything much of late – until he opened the email.

From: Zac Starr [mailto:zac@zacstarr.com]
To: Tom Rushworth
Subject: Taking the plunge

Hi Mate

Thought I should let you know before the paps do that I'm finally taking the plunge at The Golden Rock, the day after tomorrow at 6 pm! Calvin's using some of the photos as promo for the hotel, but Glitz can have the rest.

Talk later. Zac

Tom swallowed hard and wondered when he was going to wake up. Zac was getting married to Ashleigh? He shook his head and read the message again, the words swimming in front of his eyes. She'd once said she wanted to get married in Vegas, when they'd been in the chapel for the shoot at Zac's house, but it couldn't be true. No, it would be some eighteen-year-old showgirl, someone he'd known for five minutes and decided to marry whilst he was under the influence. There couldn't be any other explanation. It took him a few seconds to realise that someone was knocking on his office door.

'Tom?' Angus peered round the side of the door, as if he was worried about stepping in.

'Have you heard from Zac too?'

'No, but another story's just broken about him and I don't think you're going to like it, because *Glitz* has missed out on the exclusive for this.' He edged towards Tom's desk and set down a printout of some grainy photos. They might not have been crystal clear, and Zac might have been attempting a half-hearted disguise, but it was obvious who was in the photo. 'A wedding coordinator in Vegas twigged it was Zac and took the photos on her mobile. He was with his fiancée picking a venue apparently.'

'Right.' Tom couldn't manage more than a single word. So it was true.

'You know it's Ashleigh, don't you?' Angus was doing his anxious hopping from side to side, as he always did when stress got to him. 'I was sure the papers had that all wrong, but it seems not…'

'Thanks, I'll sort it.' Tom looked up at his old friend. Angus had been right, he didn't like it one bit, but it had absolutely nothing to do with *Glitz* missing out on an exclusive.

Chapter Thirty-Seven

Ashleigh smoothed the silk dress over her hips and held the bouquet in front of her, as she looked in the mirror. The inside of The Crystal Room changed colours every few seconds, so it had ruined Stevie's attempt to coordinate their outfits. In the end, they'd gone for simple black and white theme. There was just going to be the four of them anyway, Ashleigh in a simple black dress with a bouquet of white stargazer lilies, accompanied by Marcus, who'd happily stepped in for best man duties after meeting Zac and Stevie the day before, and who'd been asked to wear a black suit. Zac and Stevie would be wearing matching white suits – it seemed somehow fitting for Elvis' old stomping ground.

For once her hair had gone right and she smiled at the knock on the door. Marcus could be relied on to be on time, but she wondered whether it was chaos up in the grooms' suite. Zac and Stevie were meeting them in The Crystal Room and she suspected, as she moved to open the door, that she and Marcus would be in for a long wait.

'Ashleigh.' Tom stood in the doorway and her mouth hung just as open as the door for a moment. 'Is it true, you and Zac?'

'I…' She couldn't get the words out. It was like the first time he'd turned up on her doorstep, all those months ago, only this time the stakes were much higher and she didn't know how to be around him anymore. He'd inadvertently broken her heart and she'd been much more settled on the other side of the Atlantic from him. It was easier that way.

'You're making a mistake.' Tom didn't move. Clearly this was a conversation they were going to have in the corridor of one of the busiest hotels in Vegas. 'Look I know it's none of my business, but you don't love him.'

'And you don't believe in love, so what difference does that make?' She gripped her bouquet a little tighter. He was as pragmatic as ever, if she'd expected him to make some decla-ration of undying love, than she was going to be disappointed. 'That's not the point! You do, I know you do, and whatever reason you think you have for marrying Zac, it's not good enough.' Finally he took a step forward. It would have been so easy to tell him that she wasn't the one marrying Zac, but that wasn't her news to impart and why should she do him any favours? It was Zac's business interests he had at heart, so the reality was going to hit him even harder.

'Have you spoken to Zac, then? Warned him off too?' Ashleigh frowned.

'No, I wanted to see you first, but this isn't right for him either. It's not advisable without some legal pre-work and his career…'

'So what you really mean is that I'm not a good business decision?'

'That's not the only thing. I know neither of you are willing to listen to that sort of logic!' Tom was losing control of his argument and she couldn't recall ever seeing him like that. God knows what he was going to do when he found out whom Zac was really marrying; it could kill his career and that was clearly all Tom cared about.

'I've got a wedding to get to, so now really isn't a good time.' She started closing the door, pushing him out into the corridor. 'But if you really want to see what this wedding is about, what real love is, then I suggest you turn up and see it for yourself.' Closing the door, she leant against it. Oh God, had she really told him to go to the wedding? Please don't let him spoil things for Stevie and Zac. She'd never forgive herself or him.

Tom stood in the corridor outside her room and wanted to kick himself. He might even have done it, if it wouldn't have made him look like a mad man. Had he really flown eleven hours for that? To tell her not to marry Zac because she didn't love him? He should have known that Ashleigh would use his own argument against him. Zac was even less likely to listen. He'd told everyone at *Rushworth Associates* and *Glitz* that he was going to make sure that Calvin Welch didn't pull a fast one with Zac's contract, but even as he was driving to the airport he'd known it wasn't that. He hadn't been himself for weeks, trying to fill a hole in his life with all the wrong things, and for once in his life he had no idea how to fix it.

For a moment or two he just stood there, looking at the number on her door, 6752. It wasn't a significant number to him, but he'd never forget it. She'd told him to go to the wedding, see it for himself and the thought was paralysing him. He couldn't just stand in the corridor all night and it took all his energy to turn away and walk towards the elevator.

Pressing the button, he watched the lights change as the lift rose floor by floor towards him. Every second that passed was a second closer to six p.m., the deadline he'd raced across the Atlantic to beat. Now that he was here, he was powerless to do anything about it or offer up any real explanation for why it had seemed so important to come.

A tall dark-haired man got out of the lift and smiled briefly at Tom, before heading down the corridor and stopping outside Ashleigh's room. He knocked and Tom watched, letting the lift doors in front of him close. As she opened the door, the man greeted her warmly, kissing her on both cheeks and offering her his arm. Whoever he was, he was playing the father of the bride role, and as they walked wordlessly past him towards the hotel's Crystal Room, on the same floor, Tom couldn't stop himself following them. The wedding was like rubbernecking a car crash, something that he didn't want to happen, but couldn't stop watching either way.

The Crystal Room was almost over-whelming inside. The changing colours were beautiful but, at the same time, an assault on the senses. Tom sat at the back. It would only have accommodated about twelve guests, although he was the only one. He watched Ashleigh take a seat at the front of the room next to her mystery companion. The registrar, who had a long white beard like Gandalf's, took his place at the front of the room and Tom shivered. Suddenly the strains of *The Way You Look Tonight* began and it was like someone was sitting on Tom's chest. This was all wrong. Was Zac really going to be the one walking down the aisle? If Ashleigh married him, she was always going to be sidelined by his ego. He had to stop it! He jumped to his feet and opened his mouth to speak, just as the doors to The Crystal Room opened. Zac was there, but by his side was Stevie. Tom struggled to process it, for a moment he thought Stevie was taking the best man's role, which made sense, but then he realised Zac was holding on to Stevie's hand as though he never wanted to let it go.

By the time the Gandalf lookalike had finished the ceremony and the grooms had exchanged platinum wedding bands and Rose Quartz crystals, which apparently represented love, Tom had just about got his head around it.

If he'd believed in such things, it might even have looked like they were soulmates. Zac and Stevie didn't take their eyes off each other and the vows they'd written left a lump in Tom's throat. He felt strangely euphoric as the ceremony came to a close, it must have been the atmosphere. Then he saw Ashleigh's companion slip an arm around her waist, as they walked back up the aisle towards him.

'Why didn't you tell me?' He caught hold of her arm, as she walked past, following Stevie and Zac, who'd given him nothing more than a quick wink on the way back up the aisle.

'Sorry, Marcus, can you give me a minute?' Ashleigh turned to the dark-haired man, who raised an eyebrow and nodded. 'It was up to Zac to give you the details. I assume he'd told you he was getting married, but left out the small detail of who to?'

'He did, but you could have put me right.'

'I could have, but I didn't want you rugby tackling the registrar to the ground to stop it. If Zac earns less because of this, then I knew you'd do anything to stop it. It's probably why he did what he did.' She shot him a look that left him with no doubt about what she thought of his priorities. It was like she'd grown a protective shell since that last day on the beach, as if she wasn't even the same person.

'I wouldn't have done that...' He'd been about to say

something, something he'd only just begun to realise for himself, when she'd cut him off.

'Are you sure about that?' Ashleigh narrowed her eyes. 'Zac was determined not to let you, or anyone else, question whether he was serious about Stevie; this was never going to be just another engagement. Either way, for you the damage is done, there's an engagement photo they took days ago and uploaded just before the ceremony, so it will have gone viral by now.'

'Do you really think that's all I care about?' Tom tried to look her in the eyes, but she was already staring past him.

'It's none of my business what you think.' Ashleigh pressed a card into his hand. 'Zac told me to invite you to the wedding breakfast when he spotted you on the way in; this is where it's being held. Come or don't, it's up to you.'

He watched her leave yet again and the card felt cold in his hand. He'd blown it, he knew that now, and the only place he was going was home.

Chapter Thirty-Eight

The *Le Cirque* restaurant in the Bellagio was colourful and fun, the perfect place for Zac and Stevie's wedding breakfast. Marcus had a prior engagement and hadn't been able to make it. Predictably, Tom hadn't shown up either. He'd sent Cristal champagne to the table, with a note saying he'd been called back to London and that the rest of the crate was waiting for Zac and Stevie in their suite. At least he'd done something to congratulate them and not made a scene at the wedding, although Ashleigh suspected he'd really headed back to start on the spin for Zac's revelation or maybe even to arrange some sort of legal safeguarding for his client's finances. Tom wouldn't recognise love if it slapped him in the face and they were all better off without him.

Ashleigh had taken a series of photographs after the wedding and over the course of the evening; the photographer in The Crystal Room had taken a few too. Zac and Stevie had dragged her back to their suite, insisting the honeymoon could wait for a couple of hours. At Zac's say so she'd uploaded some of the photographs to his website, *Instagram* and his

Twitter account when they got there. The engagement shot had already caused a sensation, but as soon as the wedding pictures went up the world had gone slightly mad.

'Thanks babe.' Zac squeezed her thigh as he sat down next to her on the sofa. There was none of the old letchiness and no attempt for his hand to creep any further up her thigh. Those days were well and truly over for good, now that his relationship with Stevie was finally out in the open.

'Are you worried about the damage to your career? I thought that was the reason you were keeping quiet?'

'Not a bit, babe, to be honest I couldn't care less. I've got more money than I can ever spend and I want to be with Stevie instead of spending all my time working anyway. It just seemed like the right time and I wanted the rest of the world to know the truth about my feelings for him and the fact that there's no you and me!'

'I'll try not to be insulted.' They exchanged a smile.

'Don't be, if I was still into women, you'd be right up there.' Zac winked.

'Him and me both!' Stevie walked across from the bar and sat on the other side of her.

'And what about Tom, are you pleased he knows? Isn't under any misapprehension about you and me?' Zac gave her a knowing look. Only he and Stevie really understood how much she'd loved him.

'It doesn't make any difference. He came here to protect your business interests, it was nothing to do with me, and now he's gone back to London to sort them out.' She sighed. 'It's not like he rocked up here to declare his love for me, is it?'

'Okay, babe, you've made your point. Let's stop talking about boring old Tom then shall we?' Zac's eyes lit up as Stevie passed them both another glass of champagne.

'I think you've got the makings of a domestic goddess.' Ashleigh squeezed his leg.

'True enough and I love it. Although I've just seen some of the comments on my phone that have been left on *Twitter* and your role in our household is pivotal too, you know!'

'Nothing horrible I hope?' Ashleigh couldn't stand the thought that the haters might make derogatory comments about her two best friends. If those people knew Zac and Stevie, and saw how they were together, they could never be anything but happy for them.

'Well, there's one or two of those, but most are nice. Although a number of them seem to think we're in some kind of strange polygamous relationship.' Stevie passed his phone to Zac.

'God, yeah, this one says you're the surrogate mother we're using for our honeymoon baby!' Zac started laughing and then his expression changed. 'Actually that's not a bad idea, we could do that! Mix mine and Stevie's sperm together, get ourselves a turkey baster and Bob's your uncle or rather Fanny's your aunt! Well, sort of.'

'Lovely!' She grimaced at the thought. 'Although come back to me if I hit forty and there's still nobody in my life, and we'll talk.'

Back in her own room, Ashleigh had fallen into bed in the early hours when her eyes had started to ache from reading the responses online. Despite the largely positive reaction, she'd woken up with a strange sense of melancholy, less than ready to face the day.

She cleaned her teeth but ignored the state of her hair. She'd

do something about that later, maybe when the Cristal head-
ache started to subside. Grabbing some carbonated water
from the minibar, she positioned herself cross-legged on the
bed and switched on her iPad. Almost instantly a FaceTime
request from Angus came through. He'd be beside himself at
the news and suddenly, more than anything, she wanted to
see a friendly face.

'Angus?' As she accepted the call a big, brown shape filled
the screen and for a few seconds she couldn't make out who
or what it was. 'Bertie!' the *iPad* at the other end was drawn
back slightly by a hand that presumably belonged to Angus
and, at the sound of her voice, Bertie jumped to his feet, his
head on one side. 'I've missed you! I hope Uncle Angus has
been giving you lots of bacon while Tom's been away!' The dog
lurched towards the screen and all she could see was fur and
what looked like some sort of tussle.

'Okay, laddie, maybe not one of my best ideas.' Angus
beamed into the screen, one hand firmly clamped onto Bertie's
collar to calm him down. She could still hear the thud of his
tail on the floor and the imprint of his wet nose had been left
in the middle of the iPad that Angus was holding in his other
hand. 'Do you always have this effect on the men in your life?'

'Not all of them.' Her voice broke. It was no good, this
trying to be like Tom. Putting work first and burying her
emotions so deeply that she couldn't say more than twenty
words to him when he'd arrived at her hotel room. She should
have said something to stop him going back, find out if there'd
been more to why he'd really come all this way.

'I wouldn't be so sure about that.' Angus was still grinning and he hadn't even mentioned the wedding. Something
strange was going on. 'What's that Bertie, you've got a message

from Tom?'

'Angus, please, don't…' She was useless at this, scratch the surface and all the feelings were still there.

'Bertie says Tom is really sorry and he just wants a chance to make it up to you.' He raised his eyebrows and the dog's tail continued its rhythmic thudding on the floor.

'He's got a funny way of showing it.' The words were barely out of her mouth when someone knocked on the door and the iPad slipped out of her hands on to the bed. There wasn't a cat in hell's chance of it being one of the happy couple, but she couldn't let herself believe it might be Tom.

'Can I come in this time?' He looked like he hadn't slept all night.

'Okay.' She moved almost robotically to let him into the room, scared to let herself react.

'Bertie's right. I'm sorry, I've been an idiot.' Tom gave a half-hearted smile. 'In fact I've got a voicemail from Zac to prove it.' He held up his phone. 'He told me last night that if I got on the effing plane back to London, as he put it, without doing what I came here to do, then I was an even bigger idiot than he's been for the past ten years.'

'And what was it you came to do?' She still couldn't look him in the eyes. It was almost as if they'd never been intimate. Her voice sounded monotone, even in her head.

'To tell you not to marry Zac.'

'And you did that, quite efficiently.'

'Yes, but it was the reason why I didn't want you to marry him that I never quite got out.' Tom was pacing the room. 'I wasn't even sure myself when I got on the plane to come over, but I've had a lot of time to think over the last twenty-four hours and it had nothing to do with you not being in love with Zac and everything to do with me being in love with you.' He stopped and for the first time she looked at him. The confident Tom who'd always been there was gone and he was desperately waiting for her to say something.

'But, you don't believe in love.' She sat on the edge of her bed. She'd wanted him to say all this that day on the beach, but now she didn't know how to react. They lived thousands of miles apart and he'd left it all too late.

'You made me believe in it. Since Mum died and you left, I've been doing anything and everything to try and feel okay. I sacked Francine and stop representing Susie-Anne because I couldn't stand being around either of them. I told myself it was a business decision, but it was all about you.' Tom moved to sit next to her on the bed. 'I've been cannoning from one thing to the other, desperately trying to fill the empty space you left behind. I even spent a night listening to Mum's neighbour, Karen, crying about losing her soulmate when Graham left her. All the time not realising I'd let mine walk away. Then she texted me when I was waiting for my plane last night, to tell me that Graham wanted to come home and to ask what she should do.'

'You've been giving marital advice?' She tried to laugh, but it caught in her throat.

'I said she obviously still loved him or she wouldn't even be thinking about it.' Tom had the grace to look slightly embarrassed. 'When I used the word love and meant what I'd said, I realised it was because you'd taught me what it means. When I came here yesterday, I still couldn't admit to myself why I'd done it. I was elated when I realised you weren't marrying Zac, but the way you were after the wedding – I felt like you hated me. I'd deserve that if you did, but I need to know if I've lost my chance'

'I've got a job here. I've done all the things you thought I should do, followed my career and pretended I had no feelings.' Ashleigh was shaking. 'And now you turn up and say you love me and I don't know what to do.'

'Forgive me for being an idiot. I spoke to Angus too last night and he told me Bertie had started to eat for the first time with me not there. I'm worse than useless without you, it was all my fault, even the dog knows that.' He took her face in his hands and very gently kissed her.

At that moment she realised it would never be too late; she could bury her feelings for Tom in concrete and toss them into the bottom of the Grand Canyon, but they'd still be there.

'What about the job, I can't just leave.' She pulled away from him, panic rising in her chest.

'We'll work something out. Bertie and I have been thoroughly miserable without you. We could come here, I don't care where we are and neither does he – as long as we're with you. We've both only ever loved two women and we're not about to let a little thing like the Atlantic or one of Calvin Welch's iron clad contracts stand in our way.' From the way he looked at her, she knew he meant every word. 'But what about you, you still haven't told me how you feel.'

'You want me to tell you that I love you too?' She couldn't help smiling at the irony, those three little words she'd had to hold back for so long, which had come tumbling out in a rush of emotion on the beach. 'You'll do, I suppose.'

'I've created a monster!' Tom laughed, his relief visible

'Okay, the truth? I love you, always have, even when it wasn't allowed, you know that and, despite my best efforts, I know now that I always will.'

A disjointed Scottish accent rose from the iPad on the bed. 'At last! I thought you two would never work out what was blindingly obvious to everyone else.' Angus and Bertie had witnessed it all.

'Thanks for the editorial input. We'll call you both later.' Tom reached across and ended the call. 'Now where were we?'

'You were just begging my forgiveness and explaining how you're going to make things up to me.' Ashleigh smiled as he took her into his arms again.

'I promise to spend the rest of my life making it up to you, because I've finally realised all I need is the one thing everyone's been going on about. Love, wasn't it?' He pulled her closer, until their lips were almost touching. 'Perhaps you could just run me through the concept one more time…'

Acknowledgements

Firstly, I would like to thank the team at So Vain Books for their belief in the novel and for making the process of getting to publication as painless as possible, as well as for sharing their invaluable knowledge of the magazine industry and what stylists really do!

I would also like to thank the readers from the Romantic Novelist Association's New Writers' Scheme for their input and being the first people with industry knowledge to tell me the story was good enough for publication.

I'm sure I would have given up long before I reached this stage, if it hadn't been for my wonderful writing family, The Write Romantics – Sharon Booth, Jackie Ladbury, Deirdre Palmer, Lynne Pardoe, Helen Phifer, Jessica Redland, Helen Rolfe, Rachael Thomas and Alys West – and particularly those who read the early drafts of AATS and encouraged me to keep going.

Thanks too to my beta readers – Jennie Dunn, Toni Hazard and Alex Weston. And most especially, for this version of the story, to my alpha readers Julie Heslington and Paula Stroud, who were the first people I felt brave enough to get feedback from. I can't thank them enough for their honest and supportive critiques.

I also owe a debt to my friends and family for never minding if I was too busy writing to do other things. Especially to my mum for letting me spend hours reading whilst I was growing up, with my back pressed against a warm radiator and a book in my hands – heaven!

Last, but not least, thank you to my husband and children who have taught me all I'll ever need to know about love. From among a thousand stars, I'd always pick you.

Follow Jo Bartlett on her website

Visit www.jobartlettauthor.com and follow her on Twitter and Facebook to stay updated on what's coming up next and to read all the other works by her, including the prologue to *Among a Thousand Stars*!

Sophie Childs
Behind the Scenes

Bethan Brooks works in London for the ultimate boss from Hell, trying to support her wannabe rockstar boyfriend. But are The Vampire Squirrels really ever going to make it big or is she doomed to be a secretary forever? Luckily, Bethan finds the perfect escape when going to the cinema. There she loses herself in another world and forgets all about the dreaded filing and monotonous office work. Imagine her surprise when one day she encounters her favourite actor on the Tube. Suddenly, she finds herself part of the glamorous movie world she only ever dreamed about. With more at stake than she could ever realise, does she really want to know what goes on behind the scenes?

Out now on So Vain Books, Amazon and anywhere else books are sold online!

Jessica Redland

Searching for Steven

When Sarah Peterson accepts her Auntie Kay's unexpected offer to take over her florist's shop, she's prepared for a change of job, home and lifestyle. What she isn't prepared for is the discovery of a scarily accurate clairvoyant reading that's been missing for twelve years. All her predictions have come true, except one: she's about to meet the man of her dreams. Oh, and his name is Steven.

Suddenly Stevens are everywhere. Could it be the window cleaner, the rep, the manager of the coffee shop, or any of the men she's met online?

On top of that, she finds herself quite attracted to a handsome web designer, but his name isn't even Steven...

During this unusual search, will Sarah find her destiny?

Out now on So Vain Books, Amazon and anywhere else books are sold online!

Visit the So Vain Books online store!

Fashion, Beauty and Romance Books

Be part of our glamorous world:

* Buy our books, e-books and unique gadgets, and take advantage of all our special offers
* Read interesting articles on our blog, written by the So Vain Books team and all your favourite authors
* Get exclusive updates and recommendations hand-picked just for you by our team

www.sovainbooks.co.uk
Twitter: @SoVainBooks
Facebook: /SoVainBooks

ND - #0289   020424 - C0 - 198/129/25 - PB - 9780993066085 - Matt Lamination